KINGDOMLESS

THE EVAMORE SERIES BOOK 1

KINGDOMLESS: THE EVAMORE SERIES BOOK 1

This book is a work of fiction. Names, characters, businesses, organizations, places, events and incidents either are the product of the author's imagination or are used fictitiously. Any resemblance to actual persons, living or dead, events, or locales is entirely coincidental.

For contact information visit:
http://www.michellegaryfalakis.com

ISBN: 978-1-7780316-1-2 (eBook)
ISBN: 978-1-7780916-0-5 (Paperback)
ISBN: 978-1-7780916-2-9 (Hardcover)

Author Headshots by Jocelyn Phillips Branding

Book Cover Design by 100Covers.com

Book Edited by Kyla Stocks

First Edition: February 2022

10 9 8 7 6 5 4 3 2 1

MICHELLE GARYFALAKIS

KINGDOMLESS

THE EVAMORE SERIES BOOK 1

SIGN UP FOR MICHELLE'S MONTHLY NEWSLETTER

For upcoming book releases, special offers and bonus content visit:

www.michellegaryfalakis.com

You can also connect with Michelle on her socials:

Twitter: @m_garyfalakis
Facebook: @michellegaryfalakis
Instagram: @michellegaryfalakis
TikTok: @michellegaryfalakis

Cottonmure
Castle Burmstone
Western Kingdom
Western Islands
Border Wall
The Outpo
The Balour Sea
N
Southern Kingdom

Castle Mount
mpest Mountains
Hillsborough
rthern Kingdom
The Northern
Encompmet
Twin Peaks
Haven Mountains
Castle Windshire
Eastern Kingdom
The Continent
le Doplain
Garth

This book is dedicated to
every person struggling to manage their mental health.
Thank you for working on yourself
because the world needs you.
- xo Michelle

PROLOGUE

HOME.

How do you know where it is?

Is it simply where you come from?

Does the location of your birth forever identify you?

If that were true, then I wouldn't know where my home was.

Or is home the place that you cherish the most in the world? A refuge from life. Somewhere that is both tangible and abstract.

Perhaps home is simply a feeling you get around the people who care for you.

Everyone needs a home, to belong somewhere, to belong to someone.

A soul needs to be tethered to safety and love to keep the power of darkness at bay.

This was my home.

CHAPTER ONE

MY HANDS TREMBLED as I quickly wrote out my message.

Would my friends get this in time or was I already too late?

Rolling the paper and securing it with the piece of cloth ripped from my tunic, I shoved it into my sleeve as his footsteps approached the closed door.

I held my breath.

Was he coming back for more?

My lips were still red from earlier. He'd never kissed me like that before. There was a desperation to the way he touched me, as if I was going to disappear and he'd never see me again. Not that long ago, his touch sparked such desire through me, but now I wasn't entirely sure how I felt.

All I knew was that I needed to get this note to them before it was too late. Their lives were in danger, and it was clear that escaping to warn them myself was not going to be an option.

The footsteps retreated. I ran towards the window, still open from earlier.

Where was she?

***

The morning sun had just crested the moors, spilling a warm, orange glow into the training room behind me. Light bounced off the hilts of various weapons lining the walls. I squinted at the blinding appearance of daylight and then closed my eyes as I basked in the warmth of its rays. Each day brought a promise that yesterday was over and something new was waiting.

I leaned forward, placing my hands on the rocky, uneven ledge of the window. The pane was glazed glass. Just murky enough to distort your view, so people looked taller or shorter than they really were as they walked along the courtyard below. My finger picked at a loose rock along the edge as I took in a deep, cleansing breath.

Our castle was small compared to some of the other kingdoms. We had four spires, one in each corner, topped with turrets that offered the best vantage for archers upon an attack – a thick stone wall connected each spire to the next. There was a second wall surrounding our castle; it was much shorter, standing at only twelve feet high. They called the space between the outer wall and the inner wall the "death hole," because if an attacker were to climb the outer wall, which could easily be done (Holden and I had proven that frequently), then archers hiding in the spires would rain arrows down. It would trap attackers between the two walls. However, our castle rarely saw attacks since a secure border wall protected the entire Western Kingdom, monitored day and night by highly skilled soldiers.

The West was known for our wine, our border, and an oddly large number of ginger citizens. Everyone in my family had red hair, except for me and Queen Estra, but I wouldn't exactly consider her a part of my family.

My hair was a stark white and tightly curled against my head. I hated my curls when I first met my brothers; I wanted hair as crimson as theirs. As I grew older, I came to appreciate my own unique beauty. I often had my hair tied back in a tight bun or ponytail, especially when I was training. Average in height, my legs always seemed longer than they should be. With skin the color of warm honey and ice-blue eyes, framed by brown eyebrows and long, dark eyelashes, I didn't look like anyone in the Western Kingdom. My nose was small and pointy, and my lips were large compared to the rest of my face.

Stretching the ache out of my muscles from the long sleepless night I had, I squinted to watch the groundskeeper roll a wagon full of dirt towards the main gate while my breakfast settled in my stomach. I stared out at the rising sun, which had cleared the moors and cast its light upon the rough terrain surrounding the castle. My breath caught for a moment. I'd never tire of this view. The Western Kingdom's terrain was full of rolling glens, forests mixed with moorlands, and a coastline that was speckled with small islands rich with green and rocky cliffs. The ground was fertile and grew everything from potatoes to the grapes that produced the best wine in Garth.

Turning from the window, I leaned against the stone wall with my foot kicked out to give a stretch to my calf muscles. This room used to be a war council chamber, but my brother, Danier, had transformed it into his own private sanctuary for growing muscles. My father, King Wren, didn't mind, since Danier was the fiercest fighter in all four kingdoms. At least that's what I had been told.

This was my favorite room in the castle. Not because of the weaponry that adorned the walls or because it had any remarkable architectural traits. No, this room was my favorite because of the view and the three men who filled it almost every morning with me.

My brothers.

I didn't always have brothers. Well, that's not true. I may have had brothers and sisters. But since my father found me shipwrecked along the coast of the Balour Sea ten years ago, I haven't been able to remember anything from my life before I arrived here. When my father found me, I was lying unconscious, face-first in the wet sand. Scattered around me were the remnants of whatever vessel I was on, broken segments of a ship's hull mixed with barrels, rope and other various debris. He brought me back to the castle, unsure if I would live or die.

Over the next twelve months, I adjusted to my new surroundings and came to peace with my memory loss. My brothers began calling me "Princess Raelle" and shortly after, the King made an official declaration, adopting me as his daughter.

I still remember the look on my brothers' faces as I stood beside our father on the dais of our great hall.

Western banners hung from the ceiling, the smell of roast meats and excellent wine filled the air. The people cheered, and we celebrated through the night until the sun rose the next day. Being named Princess Raelle would have been the happiest day of my life, except for the shadow lurking to my right that day. Queen Estra hated me. I couldn't say why. We barely spoke to each other that first year I lived with my new family, but she sought out opportunities to intimidate me. Once, when my father and brothers were away, she burnt all of my teddy bears and refused me any food except bread and water. Then locked me in my bedchamber for a week.

She was the King's second wife. His first wife, Anna, who was the mother of my brothers, died giving birth to their daughter, Lilith. I'd heard many stories about Anna. She was compassionate and energetic, universally loved by the servants in the castle. My family mourned deeply for her, but just two months after Anna died, Lilith became ill. Verns, our healer, could not make her well, and she passed away one night in her sleep. She had curly hair just like mine, but instead of the white locks I bore, Lilith's hair was as red as fire. This all happened six years before I arrived on the Balour coast.

I startled at the sound of the door bursting open. My gaze broke from the window, and I turned to see Danier enter the room dressed in his usual fighting clothes, carrying two longswords in one hand and a plate spilling over with fresh fruits and cinnamon buns covered in sweet syrup in the other. For someone as fit and strong as he was, Danier ate a lot of sweets. Kolt said that eventually it would catch up to him, and by midlife he'd be soft in the middle, just like father. His red shoulder-length hair fell over half his face, covering one of his green eyes. Unlike our other brothers, Danier preferred a freshly shaven face. He said that the hair on his face made him itchy.

Such a baby.

He was the biggest of my three brothers but only second born. The muscles in his arms were as big as my head, and he earned every single cut and groove on his body. The man never stopped moving. If he wasn't training with us, he was training our army or leading response attacks against Northern soldiers. His voice was deep and rough. He often sounded angry, even when I knew he wasn't.

"Rae, come grab this plate before it spills onto the floor."

I ran over, grabbing the plate and placing it on the water table as I heard the weapons hit the ground.

"I hope you slept well, sister, because it's longswords today. Need to build up that upper arm strength of yours. You can't hold one longer than five minutes before you shake and that's just pathetic."

I scowled at him as I grabbed the biggest cinnamon bun off the plate and licked the sweet syrup off the top.

"Of course she takes the biggest one," he sighed, shaking his head, as he strolled over and grabbed the next biggest bun.

"I can hold a longsword for longer than five minutes." I retorted, my mouth now filled with the sticky bun.

"No, you can't!" I hadn't even heard Holden enter the room.

Holden had a subtle red beard, but his hair was his most noticeable feature. Both sides were shaved as short as his facial hair, with his red hair on top just long enough to form a tightly knotted bun on his head.

Danier was bigger than him, but what Holden lacked in raw muscle mass he compensated for in speed. He was the fastest member of our family in both running and wit. His job was primarily scouting and managing our network of spies throughout Garth. Sometimes he would venture into the other kingdoms himself, and I would hold my breath until he arrived safely back home. He was the youngest of my three brothers and therefore closest to me in age. Only three years separated us. I considered him my most trusted ally and confidant.

Holden strolled over to us and snatched a bun off the plate. He smirked at me, then, taking a big bite, turned to our brother.

"Danier, I thought you had patrol inspections today." Holden licked the evidence of the sweet syrup off his lips.

"I do. Heading out for the border after we're done here. Why? You want to come along?"

"I think I will. There's a dispatch expected today with news from our patrols along the coast. I'd like to meet them upon their arrival."

"What news?" I asked as I walked over to the longswords resting on the ground and picked one up. Damn, it was heavier than I remembered. I was excellent with a short sword, quick and accurate. Even though I wouldn't admit it, Danier was right. I lacked the upper arm strength needed to wield this weapon.

"Raids on some of the smaller islands along the coast. Nothing serious. Just want to make sure we're prepared in case those Northern prats are gearing up for another fight."

We'd been at war with the Northern Kingdom for ten years. It had recently been declared the "Decade War." It was the longest war between two kingdoms since their creation one hundred and fifty years ago, after the United Kingdom of Garth was split into four. The "Decade War" started just one week after I arrived on the shores of the Western Kingdom. I often thought maybe that was why Queen Estra hated me. That she thought I was a bad omen or something.

I must have winced as I twisted the longsword in my hand, because the next voice I heard was full of concern.

"Careful, Rae. We can't have the birthday girl injured already. The sun just rose, and you haven't opened our gift yet."

I turned to see Kolt, my oldest brother, standing at the door in front of me. A neatly trimmed, healthy red beard covered the lower half of his face. His hair was short and curly on top of his head. The world felt safer when Kolt was near. He was fit, to be sure, but carried himself in a very stiff, regal way. As the most educated member of our family, Kolt was our father's advisor and took the role seriously. And although some would mistake his love for books to mean that he neglected his physical training, those people would be very wrong.

I smiled and lowered the sword back onto the ground. I turned just as Kolt joined our brothers at the table. The three of them were grinning at me as Holden pulled a small package from behind his back.

"Happy Birthday Raelle," he said and, for a moment, I stood there, taking in the three of them.

Kolt was my teacher. He helped me learn to read the old languages and understand the basic workings of the four kingdoms, teaching me the history of Garth and the importance of trade, treaties and taking the diplomatic approach in times of conflict. Often, he would be the one to hold my hand during large gatherings when I'd become nervous and scratch my left arm. He was always watchful and never unkind.

Danier was my protector. When I arrived at the castle, I had some natural skill with weapons and sparring. Nearly every day for the past ten years, he has met me in this room to train and expand on my abilities. Even though his exterior appeared tough, he had wiped tears away from my cheeks on more than one occasion.

Holden was my best friend. As children, we ran around the castle and played together for hours. We created secret handshakes and imaginary worlds. His practical jokes and sharp tongue often got him into trouble, but whenever I needed someone to listen or make me laugh, he was always there.

My three red-haired brothers. This was my home, here with them.

"I don't think she wants it," quipped Danier with a challenging look in his eyes.

"Somewhere, some village is missing its idiot," I playfully spouted at him as I strode forward. Placing my hands around the box, I looked up at my brothers. I knew it was selfish, but I wanted things to stay this way forever. Why couldn't the four of us be together all the time, with father too, of course? I wanted to stop growing up and for the outside world to just disappear. I wanted to spend the rest of my life asking Kolt complex questions, finding new ways to annoy Danier during our training, and discover more of the world through Holden's eyes.

But I knew our time was running out. There were already plans of an arranged marriage for Kolt with the southern Princess, and I knew Holden couldn't wait for the war with the Northern Kingdom to be over so he could travel to the continent and explore. At least Danier didn't seem like he was going anywhere anytime soon. I wasn't sure when things would change, but I could feel it in my bones that this wouldn't last forever.

A small tear formed in my eye. I tried to fight it.

With a quick kiss to my cheek, Kolt spoke. "Don't cry, Rae."

"Yeah, save your tears for later when your arms are burning from training," Danier smirked, reaching up to wipe the tear as it escaped down my cheek.

I laughed softly and looked up at Holden.

"Open it," he insisted.

I quickly opened the box to find a necklace inside. It was a silver compass rose with four points. Three of the points were fixed with tiny red stones and the top point was encrusted with a small diamond.

"The smithy made it for us," Holden said as he pointed to the necklace. "The compass is a symbol of finding your way home. We asked him to put the three rubies in there to represent us, but at the top, this diamond belonged to our mother. We placed it there to represent you, Rae."

I had no words. It was the most thoughtful gift anyone had given me.

"Thank you," I finally got the words out. I gently closed the box and wrapped my arms around my brothers, first Holden, then Kolt, and finally Danier.

"Okay. Well, if we're done with all this sap. It's time to get to work," and with that Danier clapped his hands, ushering me towards the middle of the training circle.

CHAPTER TWO

CLANG!

The vibration of Danier's sword as it hit mine moved all the way from my fingers to my toes. My arms were burning from the exertion of the last hour. We had taken a few breaks, but Danier wasn't one to coddle me. With him it was "get stronger, or get hurt," a motto that we'd acted out many times in this room.

Once, about four years ago, I was learning the basics of hand-to-hand combat. Danier refused to ease up on me. I left that training session with a black eye, bruised lip and swollen left hand. Father was furious with Danier, but I was stronger the next time we met in the circle. And so it was with everything he taught me in the training circle.

Not knowing where I'd come from or what brought me to the Western Kingdom had always made me feel a little helpless; because of that, I was determined to gain control over my life. Being strong and ready for a fight made me feel more settled. I think Father knew I needed that, and it was why he allowed me to keep training, despite the occasional injury.

"Your form is still terrible," Danier shouted as he tossed down his sword and reached up to adjust the position of my arms again.

"I'm tired and my arms feel like they are on fire."

"Then get stronger."

I exhaled. That was his usual response.

"Your enemy will not wait for you to get stronger, Rae. Pain is the precursor to strength. If you don't prepare, you will eventually find yourself defeated by an opponent who was more prepared. And then you'll be dead."

"You're cheery this morning."

"You ate my cinnamon bun."

He gathered my sword in his hand and lowered it to the floor.

"Fine, that's it for the swords today. Tomorrow we'll work on stretching and balance, but we're back to the swords the day after that. One day off, that's all I'm giving you. So have a conversation with those biceps of yours and tell 'em to be ready."

I hid my smile and turned to grab some water from the table.

Kolt and Holden were deep in conversation across the room, looking over a map, when the door opened and Queen Estra's manservant Quinton entered. He was short, bald, and always looked like he needed to take a shite. The man couldn't have looked more hubristic if he tried.

"Pardon the interruptions, your Highnesses, but the Queen has requested Raelle–"

"Princess Raelle," Holden sharply corrected him. This was not the first time that Quinton had withheld my title when addressing me, no doubt encouraged to do so by Queen Estra.

"Yes, of course, I apologize." The man was not the least bit sorry.

Queen Estra was from the Eastern Kingdom, traded into an arranged marriage almost 16 years ago to bridge peace between the neighboring kingdoms. Her arrogant manservant traveled with her and had never appeared happy about living here with us.

"The Queen has requested Princess Raelle join her in the private lounge."

My brothers' worried eyes fell upon me. The Queen hated me; everyone knew that. Why would she want to see me today, of all days? Certainly, she didn't have any warm wishes to give. But my brothers said nothing. It was my response that everyone waited for.

I cleared my throat, "Please tell her majesty that I will come to her as soon as I am cleaned up from training."

Without another word, the manservant bowed with distaste on his face and exited the room.

"I hate that man," Danier sneered. "Why father allowed that snake to travel with her and stay here, I'll never understand."

"It was part of the peace treaty," Kolt replied. "They granted Estra a small contingent of servants loyal to her when she arrived."

I filled my water glass and took a big drink.

"Why would she want to see me?" I ask, mostly to myself.

"Do you want me to go with you?"

Holden usually offered to attend any summons by the Queen. His presence always kept my nerves at bay. Over the past ten years, she had summoned me six times. Often it was to chastise me for a minor gaffe that she deemed "unbecoming of a princess." Once, when Holden hadn't attended with me, she struck me across the face for being insolent when I refused to kneel before her. I said nothing to my father or brothers about what happened that day, but I think they knew, since I hid in my bedchamber for three days while the redness went away.

It was always a mystery to me why father allowed her to behave this way, considering there seemed to be no love between the two of them. From my lessons with Kolt, I understood that peace was a fragile thing amongst the four kingdoms of Garth. I imagined it was hard for my father to be caught between what was best for his kingdom and what he wanted.

For the past three years, Queen Estra had stopped summoning me to her private lounge or even speaking to me at all. I would see her at state dinners or occasionally passing in the hallways. We never made eye contact, and that was just fine with me.

"No, you need to get to the border to retrieve the reports from the islands. I'll be fine."

"I can go with you," Kolt offered.

"Honestly, I'm fine."

The look Kolt gave told me that he would respect my answer, but didn't believe me. I refilled my water and wiped the sweat from my forehead. The ache I'd tried to stretch out this morning before training had only grown. Just lifting the water to my mouth was proving very difficult.

"Here," Danier offered me a small tin filled with the smell of a familiar salve and I caught the scent of lavender and eucalyptus. "Rub it on your arms tonight and again in the morning. You did well today. We might make a fighter out of you yet."

I smirked, but it faded as I continued to ponder why Queen Estra had summoned me. It's not that I was afraid of her. I just knew it wouldn't be pleasant.

"Don't let her intimidate you, Rae," Danier spoke firmly as he lifted the box my necklace was in, removed the lid and unclasped it. "And, when we get back from the border, we've got another surprise for you. It may or may not include chocolate cake."

My favorite dessert.

Kolt and Holden smiled as they stood and walked towards us. Danier motioned for me to turn as he placed the compass rose necklace around my neck and secured the clasp.

I took a deep breath, looking down to study the gift for a moment.

Today was my nineteenth birthday. I was nine when my father found me, unaware of where I was born or who my parents were, whether people were looking for me or if anyone missed me. I may not have known where I came from, but in this place, with my family, I was home.

***

Changing out of my training clothes proved to be more difficult than I expected when I refused the help of my chambermaid.

"Are you sure you don't need any help, Princess?"

She always called me Princess, no matter how many times I asked her to just call me Rae. Dalia had been with me for the past five years. Her mother died when she was young, and her father was the groundskeeper for the castle. When he passed away from the pox, leaving Dalia on her own, my father invited her to work and live in the castle. When we were kids, Dalia would play with Holden and I while her father labored on the grounds. She was my only friend. I felt uncomfortable letting her do things for me, and would usually resort to doing them myself after she left the room.

Dalia was beautiful in a way that made people turn and look, with straight, deep mahogany hair and eyes that were so brown they almost looked black. Her skin was fair, with the faintest rose in her cheeks. She had the best laugh and kept all of my secrets. Not that there were many to keep. I'd never really done anything worth keeping a secret, but the small ones that I have, she kept in the strictest of confidence.

Recently, I'd caught Holden looking at her, stricken by her beauty, I'm sure. His fixed stares never went unnoticed by Dalia, and she'd often blush at the attention. I may have daydreamed once or twice of their marriage and little babes running around calling me "Auntie Rae." This thought made me happy because a romance with Dalia would keep Holden from leaving us for the continent.

I undressed and swiftly lowered myself into the bath Dalia had prepared. The warm water wrapped around my aching muscles, the salt and oils revitalizing my skin. This was bliss. Cupping my hands together, I scooped up some of the bath water and splashed it across my face, rubbing my neck and shoulders. Satisfied that every inch of my body had been thoroughly cleaned, I lifted myself out of the tub and stepped onto the cold stone floor. Dalia had left a soft towel on a chair for me, and I quickly wrapped it around my body. I used a second towel to wring the excess water out of my hair. Once I was sufficiently dried off, I reached for the small tin Danier gave me. Dipping my pointer and middle finger into the cream salve, I scooped up a healthy portion and rubbed it into my aching muscles. The massage was both agonizing and relieving.

Moving into the bedchamber, I saw the deep blue dress that had been left out for me to wear. Fitting myself in, I was grateful there were no laces to tie in the back. I straightened the necklace and began brushing out my hair.

The large four-post bed, covered in white blankets and pillows, was the focal point of my room. I had asked my brothers to move it to face the only window in the room. Watching the sunset every night with a cup of tea had become one of my favorite pastimes.

A crackle in the fire drew my attention. The hearth was enormous, definitely oversized for the room. I had littered the mantle with trinkets gifted to me. My tiny jewelry box from Kolt sat almost empty. Although I appreciated fine things, I didn't own many necklaces or rings. Kolt gifted me the box after he returned from his studies at a university in the Southern Kingdom.

Beside it lay a small hand-stitched doll; it was the first present I received from my father. Just two days after I had arrived in the West, he delivered it to my room with a slice of chocolate cake. It was my most prized possession. The last of the space was occupied by a small dagger Danier had gifted me on my twelfth birthday, and rocks and gems from my adventures with Holden over the years.

The room had a sitting area, where I would often read the books that Kolt set aside for me. Beside the door, Danier had arranged for my weapons to be hung and displayed properly. He said it was so that I could be reminded of my strength every day. My dresser and closet were full of brightly colored dresses and tunics that my father had bought me. Every time he left the castle, he came back with some new garment for me to wear.

With my hair brushed out and pinned half back, I opened my door and headed down the hall to the East Wing of the castle.

To Queen Estra.

CHAPTER THREE

ALONG THE CORRIDOR CONNECTING the west and east sides of the castle, I paused frequently, pretending to gaze at the various statues that lined the walls, or look out the stained-glass windows that overlooked the inner courtyard. I was just delaying the inevitable. I lifted my arm to knock on the door as the sleeve of my dress slid down an inch, revealing the evidence from my anxious scratching. Standing still, staring straight ahead, I willed my courage to announce my arrival.

"You may enter," her voice carried through the thick wood easily. The door to her personal lounge was very ornate, with ships carved into the grain. Queen Estra had commissioned it from an Eastern artist after she arrived here. Her quarters were in the East Wing, while my family and I lived in the West Wing. The arrangement seemed to work best for everyone. The two guards positioned outside didn't even look my way as I pushed open the heavy wooden doors into the Queen's private lounge.

The room, which I had now been inside seven times, was brightly lit. They painted the walls in a seafoam green. I had heard that the Eastern Kingdom, whose trade was mostly fish and rice, was full of seafaring people. The land was flat, but they had more ports than any of the other kingdoms, forcing the majority of the trade from the continent to flow through them, and was therefore subject to any tax King Sutton deemed appropriate to charge before allowing passage to the rest of Garth. He sent his eldest daughter to marry my father in order to strengthen the two kingdoms' military and trade interests. Or, at least, that was what Kolt had explained to me.

I usually knew why Queen Estra would summon me to her chambers; often because of a quick remark I had made, or I had embarrassed her in front of someone important. It was hard for us not to hide our hatred for one another. When I was younger, I had hoped that she would be like a mother to me – I used to long for her approval. I would copy the way she did her hair or wear colors she seemed to prefer. The harder I tried to win her love, the more she hated me. Over time, I resigned myself to the reality that this woman and I would never be mother and daughter.

Queen Estra was insufferable. Once, she had her chambermaid flogged in the grand hall for requesting a day off to visit her ailing mother. Father was away, and she only stopped when Kolt stepped in, insisting that the punishment was an overreaction.

I heard that upon her arrival to the West, she somehow convinced my father to evict a farmer from his land to build a private cottage. A cottage she never seemed to visit or use.

She paraded herself around the castle, critiquing the staff on everything from the way they walked to the manner and volume in which they spoke. Whenever dignitaries from other kingdoms came to visit, she'd fall over herself trying to impress them. It was difficult to watch. I believed that it upset her that she never bore a child, although I supposed she would need to share a bed with my father from time to time in order for that to happen.

Queen Estra was not terrible looking. She was very tall, almost taller than Danier, and slight. Although I'd never seen her wield a weapon, her arms always looked toned. She liked to wear her light brown hair pulled back in a long plait down her back. Her eyes were a soft brown, empty and deep set. Her face was tight and drawn out with thin, pursed lips. I sometimes wondered what a child between her and my father would look like.

My father was strong, but his youthful muscles had softened in many areas. His hair was a copper red and more wavy than curly. He sported a thick beard that was now coursed with gray hairs. His eyes were green and soulful.

"Don't just stand there," Queen Estra spoke from her settee. "Come closer and let me see your face, little girl." At nineteen years old, she still called me "little girl." I let it slide because, well, I didn't have the fight in me, and I just wanted to get back to the West Wing of the castle as soon as possible.

I did as she asked and when I met her eyes, my right hand instantly inched over to my left arm and scratched. I wished I had let Kolt come with me. I tried to stop my nervous habit. The last thing I wanted was to give this woman more reason to berate me. I'm sure it would be very unbecoming of a princess to scratch her arm bare just because she was uncomfortable.

It was then that I realized we weren't alone. One of the Queen's chambermaids waited against a bookshelf to be dismissed. I could see the evidence of a healing bruise across her left cheek. The woman who sat in front of me was pure evil. My nose flared. The anger pushed the fear aside.

"Leave." Without turning her head, Queen Estra dismissed the young girl from our presence. As if released from prison, the chambermaid left the room.

"Sit down, girl." I lowered myself into the armchair opposite the Queen and stared at the fire.

Why was I here? What could she possibly want to talk about?

"Do you know why I am Queen of the Western Kingdom?"

Because you were your kingdom's least favorite princess, so vile and evil that they sent you away?

"To establish a peace treaty between our two kingdoms," I said instead of telling her what she actually deserved to hear.

"Hm. That's right," she said with a sardonic smile. "History often records the decisions and movements of powerful men. How they start wars and fight for their people. Their astute decision making and bravery. Although history often forgets to record the power that women wield."

Queen Estra's voice was quite likely the most annoying sound in the world.

"They move us from kingdom to kingdom as peace pawns, forced to leave everything we find comfort in and that is familiar to us, in order for powerful men to become even more powerful."

Her voice reminded me of the cat that liked to visit the back of the kitchen, his sickly cries for food scraps to appease his starving belly.

"Today is your nineteenth birthday, is it not?"

"Yes. It is."

"You're a lady now, Raelle."

"I suppose I am."

"It's time to do your part to keep the peace."

My voice cracked as hands reached around my back, securing my arms to my side, fingers digging into my arm muscles. The ache in my biceps burned through me. The men behind me forced me to my feet as I thrashed out in anger, kicking my legs, knocking over the armchair I just occupied. I ripped in their hold, which only caused their fingers to press in harder. I could feel the bruises forming. Queen Estra rose to meet my eyeline.

"Let me go," I gritted through clenched teeth. One corner of the Queen's lips turned up as the pride of victory danced across her face.

"Tell your men to unhand me now. I'm the King's daughter. You have no right." My face was burning from the strain and anger. I continued to pull, struggling to muster up any strength I had left in me, but their grip was too strong.

"Raelle," the Queen's voice was condescending, yet full of elevation. "Don't be so dramatic."

She opened a small, ornate box that was sitting on the table beside her chair. I watched with wide eyes as she dipped her fingers into a white powdery substance, stirring them around until they were completely dusted. She lifted them to my mouth, but I clamped my jaw shut. A set of heavy hands pried at my lips, forcing them open. Queen Estra shoved her coated fingers into my mouth. The hands gripped my jaw so tightly that tears fell down my face. The powder wasn't sweet like sugar; it had a bitterness to it. I tried to spit it out, but the hands on my jaw covered my mouth. I couldn't breathe. It felt like I was suffocating. The panic was surging in my body and I knew I needed to turn the tables.

This wasn't a fair fight.

Once more I tried to break free of their hold, but a foot kicked the backside of my right knee, forcing me to partially collapse to the side.

Within moments, all the energy left my muscles, forcing me to become lax in my captors' hold. She had drugged me.

"I know this must be confusing, but I assure you, it's for the best. You're to be given over to the Northern Kingdom as a peace offering. The new King there is young and has yet to take a bride. He has agreed to a ceasefire for you. How valuable you've become, Raelle."

The Queen ran her hand down the side of my face, a gesture that, between any other women, would have been considered a motherly touch, but there was nothing motherly or loving about the way she touched me. It was predatory, like a victor, surveying their spoils.

She had won.

"Wh-where is m-my father?"

"Oh, unfortunately, the King had affairs to attend to on the far side of the Kingdom, so he won't be able to see you off today," she motioned to the door with a feral smile on her face. "Shall we?"

The men holding me began walking forward. This could not be happening. Even though my body was subdued, my mind was racing. They dragged me down the hall towards the eastern staircase. My feet laid useless behind me as if they were no longer a part of my body. Their hands dug into my armpits, pulling me further away from where I wanted to be.

"Princess Raelle?" the soft, concerned voice of Dalia appeared from a doorway off of the hall at the bottom of the stairs. She tentatively took a step forward, surveying the situation, glancing from the Queen to the guards to me.

"Where are you going? What's happening?" Her eyes searched mine. Before I could speak, the Queen addressed her.

"No concern of yours, now carry on!"

Queen Estra's voice was threatening as she dismissed Dalia with a wave. The guards continued to carry me closer to the doors at the end of the hall. I forced my head to the side and met Dalia's stare. I barely got the word out.

"Kolt."

In understanding, her eyes widened, and she raced up the staircase.

Would she find my brother in time? Was he still in the castle? Or had he gone with our brothers to the border?

As we came to the end of the hallway, the doors opened and a carriage, surrounded by half a dozen of Queen Estra's personal guards on horseback, waited for us. The sun was around noon and there were no other souls in sight. I could not get in that carriage. I had to stop them, somehow, but it was no use. The drugs had stripped my body of all its strength.

Queen Estra opened the carriage door and turned to me.

"Don't be too upset, Raelle. I've been playing this

game a lot longer than you have." She looked at me with such antipathy. "Now, be a good girl and try to make yourself useful in your new home. The Northern king is expecting his bride, and we shouldn't keep him waiting. I hear he's very handsome. Lucky girl."

With that, they shoved me into the carriage, and the doors locked from the outside. With almost no energy left in my body, I collapsed on to the seat as we jerked forward. Tears slowly flowed down my face as I turned my head to look out the window. We were already moving along the road at an incredible speed.

How was this happening? Where was my father? Where were my brothers?

Damn my restless sleep and Danier's sword training. I couldn't even put up an honest fight. Glancing down at my necklace, I attempted to wrap my fingers around it, but I couldn't move my arm.

"Shit," I whispered as the carriage hit a bump, throwing me against the window, and then everything went dark.

CHAPTER FOUR

TEN YEARS AGO.

"Tell the driver to ride the horses faster. She needs a healer."

The stranger was yelling, his voice filled with alarm. I was soaking wet, my arms aching, and my head was resting on a pillow as I laid on the bench across from a man I did not recognize. Someone had draped a soft cloak over my body, but my teeth were still chattering so fast that I thought they were going to crack.

"It's okay! Everything's alright, my dear. We're going to get you some help. Can you hear me?"

The man's voice was gentle and kind. I did not feel in danger. His eyes were green, watchful, and compassionate.

The hair that peeked out from under his woolen cap was bright red.

I shut my eyes and then everything went dark.

I slowly stirred as I felt myself wrapped in someone's arms, a steadfast hold that promised I would arrive at my destination safely. The chest I was resting my head against was firm, and I heard the echo of a heart beating incredibly fast. Blinking, I took in what was happening around me.

We were now inside. The stone walls, dark and gray, stretched up towards the ceiling. Paintings, filled with vivid colors and characters, spaced out along the corridor. I could hear feet scurrying along the hard floor, soft voices speaking all around us. Then a small voice, a boy's voice, came from behind us.

"Father, what's happening?"

"Holden," the man carrying me did not stop moving while he spoke. "Find Mister Verns and ask him to hurry. I'll meet him in the West Wing. Go! Now!"

The boy ran back from the direction he came, his steps slowly fading into the space I couldn't see.

I was being carried through a faintly lit lobby. The man carrying me was the familiar voice from the carriage. I peered up, lifting my chin to see his face was tense with worry, powerful lines ran out from his clamped lips, eyebrows forced together as sweat beads dripped down his forehead.

Slowing to a stop and turning to speak to someone on our left, I heard him say, "We'll need warm clothes and blankets. Have some chambermaids come and get her out of these damn soaking clothes."

We began moving again as he yelled behind us, "And someone light a godsdamn fire, a big one!"

Nearing the end of the corridor, we passed through an enormous set of wooden doors. This room was enormous. He laid me gently down on a soft bed, on top of the coziest white blankets. My head rested on a mountain of pillows. I was sure that my clothes, filthy and sodden, would ruin them after this. I could feel the sand lodged in every corner of my body. As the kind man left the room, two women entered. They worked to change me out of my soaked clothes and, as they finished, everything went dark once more.

When my eyes opened again, I was warm and tucked into fresh blankets. The room was aglow with a roaring fire lit in the colossal fireplace. My left arm was wrapped up in white bandages and splinted with a wooden board.

"She's broken her wrist and has some bruises that will take time to heal, but other than that, she'll be just fine."

"Thank you Verns. Truly, I appreciate you rushing over here."

"Not at all, your Majesty."

Majesty? I knew that meant something. Reserved for someone important, but I couldn't remember what. Actually, come to think of it, I couldn't remember anything. My name was Raelle, and I was nine years old. I knew I was on a ship, but headed somewhere I couldn't remember. I remembered the storm and then nothing.

Where was I?

"Father, she's waking up."

It was the same young voice as before. A boy. Older than me, but still a boy. I looked to my right to see the friendly man staring down at me. I gazed around the room and saw three more sets of green eyes, all resting underneath mops of red hair, just like the stranger beside me.

"My dear? Can you hear me? How are you feeling?"

"Where am I?"

"You're in the capital of the Western Kingdom. My name is King Wren. This is my home, and these are my sons."

He nodded towards them as I dared another look. They watched me, the oldest offering a sweet smile as he leaned his head forward in a gesture of respect and welcome. The one beside him was brawny and held his arms across his chest. Finally, the smallest boy, the one whose voice I had heard earlier, watched me with a curious, spirited look.

"I promise that you're safe here under our protection," the King assured me.

"What happened?"

"We don't know yet. I found you washed up on the coast, along with the remnants of a shipwreck. We've searched for other survivors, but found none. Were you traveling with your family?"

I shook my head. "I don't know. I don't remember anything."

I tried to sit up. Something was wrong. Why couldn't I remember anything? My chest felt tight as my breath picked up.

"It's okay. It's okay, my dear. Just rest. We'll get it all sorted out."

His gentle words and protective eyes soothed me. I nodded my head. Feeling safe, I slowly drifted off to sleep.

***

At the sound of muffled conversation outside of the carriage, my eyes blinked open. We'd stopped moving and the sun was still up. Or was this a new day? I couldn't sense how much time had passed since my head hit the window. The air was cooler, much cooler, and I rubbed my arms to keep warm. I was still just wearing that deep blue dress from earlier. Nothing else. I looked out the windows of the carriage, which had fogged up, wiping them clear so I could make out my surroundings.

I saw mountains, lots of mountains, in the distance. There was only forest and snow for as far as I could see, occasionally broken up by a large flat mass of white, which were either fields covered for the winter or frozen lakes. There were no signs of homes or people, no roads, except the path we were stopped on. I was literally in the middle of nowhere, but one thing was quite certain – we'd arrived in the Northern Kingdom.

Outside in the snow, the Queen's personal guards spoke quietly and kept glancing around, searching for something or someone. I surveyed the inside of the carriage for anything that I could use as a weapon and, of course, came up empty-handed. The Queen knew of my training and the instruction I had received from Danier. There would be nothing in here to help me fight off my captors.

If my lessons with Danier would not be helpful, then it was time to use what Kolt had taught me; to wield my knowledge as its own power. I closed my eyes and concentrated on what Queen Estra had said to me.

Northern Kingdom. Bride. Peace Treaty.

I was being sent to the Northern Kingdom as a new bride for the King in order to secure peace.

Damnit.

As the adoptive daughter of the Western King, I never believed that my position held much bargaining power in matters of marriage and peace treaties. Why wouldn't my father have mentioned this to me before? Why was it so sudden and violent? Did Dalia find Kolt? Were my brothers on their way to rescue me? No, they couldn't be. If the exchange for me was enough to secure peace from the "Decade War," they couldn't risk intervening.

Concentrate, Raelle. What else did I know?

Kolt had spent hours teaching me the history of Garth. It was once a powerful united nation ruled by the Evamore Dynasty. Our history recorded them as selfish leaders who earned favor with the gods and wielded their magic for their own pleasures. For thousands of years, they ruled the United Kingdom of Garth unopposed, but one hundred and fifty years ago, things changed. The people no longer trusted the Evamore Dynasty. They were tired of the gods' chosen leaders and the use of their magic, so a civil war broke out; the opposition led by three brothers from the continent. Realizing they were defeated and to prevent any more casualties, the Evamores yielded the crown on the condition that a haven be formed for those loyal to the crown. The brothers agreed by dividing Garth into four kingdoms; North, South, East and West. They reserved the Northern Kingdom for those loyal to the Evamore Dynasty, and the brothers each took rule over the other three kingdoms.

They executed the Evamores, along with all of their children. Over time, the alliances between the kingdoms worsened. Consumed by greed, relationships were destroyed, border cities sacked and abandoned. Each kingdom retreated more into itself to protect its own interests and resources. The land was tough to farm and travel on, and their biggest source of trade and revenue was timber and fur. That was all I knew. Oh, and snow. Lots and lots of snow. How could any of this help me now?

I couldn't even remember the Northern King's name. I knew it was his father's death that sparked the Decade War. A small group of spies from the Western Kingdom had infiltrated the Northern mountains. I cannot recall why our spies were in the North, but on their way back, they ran into a caravan of Northern soldiers. They fought their·way across the border, but the Northern King had been traveling with the caravan and died during the skirmish. It wasn't intentional, but the Northern Kingdom retaliated by sacking one of our cities, and ten years later, my life bought peace.

Damn.

Happy Birthday Rae. Surprise, they've kidnapped you and plan to ransom you for peace. Enjoy your new life in this frozen hell hole.

The sound of horses approaching interrupted my brief pity party as I pressed my nose against the window, trying to see who or what was approaching. The Queen's personal guards outside drew their swords and readied their stance, as the approaching horses came to a stop. There was a quiet exchange of words as I heard determined footsteps approaching the carriage.

I had a decision to make. As soon as the doors opened, I'd have to disarm my captors, retrieve a weapon, and fight off the other guards. How many were there? At least half a dozen, plus the drivers of the carriage. And then there were those who just approached by horse to contend with. I can only assume that these new arrivals were Northern soldiers. Also, my head was still aching and the blood was still wet from where I hit it against the window. I could feel the bruises on my arms where the guards had grabbed me, and my muscles were still on fire.

The odds weren't in my favor to win a fight.

If battling my way back home would not be an option, then I'd have to try the diplomatic approach. As I continued to sort through my dilemma, the carriage door was ripped open and a Northern soldier, dressed completely in white, stared at me. His eyes were blue, darker than mine, and I couldn't tell the color of his hair from under his hat. His face was attractive, a few freckles sprinkled over his nose and cheeks, and he had a faint scar across the upper left part of his lip. He was taller than me and carried himself like someone who knew how to fight. He had a sword strapped to his side and at least two daggers, that I could see. Soldiers always had hidden weapons somewhere on their body.

Great.

"Your Highness, if you'd please come with me."

He extended his gloved hand without a smile and waited for me to accept his help. I had decided on the diplomatic approach, but I was still outraged.

"I can get myself out of the carriage, thank you very much."

I brushed past him and stepped out of the carriage as my slipper caught on the door ledge. I fell face first onto the snow-covered ground.

Damnit!

Before I could push myself back up, the soldier crouched down beside me with his gloved hands resting between his thighs.

"Now why would you go and do that? If you had just taken my hand, we could have avoided this embarrassing entrance into your new kingdom."

What a prick.

"Shall we try this again?"

He stood and extended his hand once more. This time, I took it and with his help I pulled myself up out of the wet snow. The soldier looked to be about seven or eight years older than me.

"Thank you." I brushed the snow off of my dress.

"Those are terrible shoes for the North."

Without saying anything else, he dropped my hand and walked away towards the awaiting horses.

Seriously, what a prick.

I then took in the new arrivals. There were five

soldiers. The moody leader who just helped me up from the ground was tall. His broad shoulders pushed back, exposing the evidence of trimmed pecs, likely to match the sculpted thigh muscles I could make out through his fighting clothes. Although the color of his hair was concealed under the hat, the subtle beard across his chiseled jawline and around his mouth was black, lips the faintest pink and those eyes, such a deep blue.

A mountain of a man standing beside a brown horse caught my eye next. I'd only ever seen a man that tall when a group of dignitaries visited from the Southern Kingdom. One of their guards was almost as tall as this soldier. I couldn't see his mouth past the gray-brown scrawly bread hanging from his face, but underneath his right eye, just above his beard line was a marking inked into his skin. His eyes were neither kind nor unkind, but there was something serene to his look, which was in contrast to the brutish presence he emitted.

A thinner, athletic man, around my height with umber skin, stood next to the giant. He was the only one smiling as he brushed the mane of the horse he had just dismounted. He carried two swords sheathed across his back, clearly a warrior, but his fingers were nimble and moved gracefully. I knew that if I needed any help on this journey, he would be the one I asked first.

I was both surprised and relieved to see a woman in the group. She had russet-brown hair, similar to my brothers, poking out from underneath her hat. Green eyes, freckles across her round face. This woman was definitely from the West. Although she was shorter than me, she looked incredibly fit, even underneath her bulky, white uniform. She was busy in quiet conversation with the man next to her, the oldest of the group. He looked to be about the same age as my father, although in areas where my father had gone soft, this man had taken care to keep his body primed for a fight. He had a short gray beard and mustache. The most striking thing about him was that his face had a long, horrendous scar, running down from his left eyebrow to chin, just missing his eye socket.

As the sound of creaking wooden wheels and horses galloping off came from behind me, I spun around to see that the guards who delivered me here were now gone, headed back in the direction we had just come from. So that was it. I was in the middle of the cold ass kingdom with no allies, weapons, or a plan to get home.

Deep breaths.

Don't scratch your arm.

"Don't you have any luggage or belongings?" The blue-eyed leader didn't even turn to look at me while he spoke.

"No, just me."

He stopped at the nearest horse and reached into a bag, pulling out a pair of boots and a long fur cloak. He turned, walked towards me, and pressed the items into my chest. I lifted my hands to hold them in place as he released them.

"You'll want to put these on. It's going to be a bit of a ride before we reach the castle."

"A ride?" My voice sounded surprised, but the smallest hint of fear leaked through. "Like on a horse?"

I thought I saw a flicker of amusement on his face, before being replaced by a dry, unimpressed gaze.

"Have you ever ridden on a horse before, Princess?"

"Yes, I have. Many times. Just not well."

I straightened my neck, lifting my chin up as I

attempted to stare him down. It was an effort to regain any sense of respect these past few moments had stolen from me.

He sighed.

He was annoyed.

He let out a frustrated sigh as he gritted his teeth and shook his head. I should have kept my mouth shut, but it had been a long day and, well, I didn't care. Diplomacy be damned.

"Oh, I'm sorry if this is an inconvenience for you, but as you can see, I wasn't exactly aware I'd be arriving here today. It's been the worst day I've ever experienced and I'm trying very hard to be diplomatic, as that seems preferable to responding violently. Now, if my horse-riding skills aren't up to your standards, then send me back to where I came from. As I'm not all that eager to go any further into the frozen hell hole you call home."

Muffled laughter rose from those waiting by the horses. The old man whistled. I stared at the blue-eyed soldier, trying to keep my composure as I felt my bones shake from the cold. I should have put the cloak on by now, but I wouldn't be the first one to break this stare-down. He sighed and turned towards the waiting horses. I took that moment to pull on the boots and cover myself with the fur cloak.

Over his shoulder he yelled, "Fine, you'll ride with me then, Princess. Let's go."

CHAPTER FIVE

BEFORE I COULD MOVE, the only female among the soldiers approached me.

"Welcome to the North. I'm Sloan. That's Rig, Yuri, and the old man is Bowan." I looked at the men as they stared back at me. "And you've already met Calak, our charming leader."

I glanced over at the blue-eyed soldier who was moving packs from his horse onto the extra horse which they had clearly intended for me to ride.

"What do we call you, Princess?" Sloan asked. There was a genuine tone to her question.

"My name is Raelle. It's nice to meet you, soldiers." I nodded in respect and all five of them broke out in laughter.

"We aren't soldiers, ma'am," Yuri spoke up.

"Speak for yourself. I was a captain in the King's army for over twenty-three years," Bowan's voice had a raspiness that was likely earned from years of smoking and yelling.

"The operative word being 'was,' old man. Now you're just one of us." Sloan smiled and turned to mount her horse.

"Well, someone has to watch your backs. Without me, you kids would be long dead." Bowan smirked at the group.

"Well, if you aren't soldiers, then what are you?"

"Trackers...and murderers," Rig confessed.

Murderers? Great, that made me feel very unsettled. The look on my face must have been obvious because Rig let out a deep chuckle as Yuri smacked him in the arm and they both got ready to ride again. So was that a joke? And if so, what kind of sick ass joke was that. I wasn't completely convinced that I trusted this group, but my options were limited.

"If we're done with the small talk, we need to get moving," Calak spoke up. "We'll ride to Greystone Ridge before stopping to make camp."

He turned and nodded to Bowan. My empty horse was tied to the old man's, ladened with extra packs.

"Will you need a boost to get up on the horse or can you manage yourself?" Calak asked me.

"I can manage."

I walked over to his horse and placed my left foot in the stirrup. Using the last of my strength, I pushed myself up and nothing happened. This was embarrassing. There was no energy left in my body.

"Everything alright?"

I jumped as Calak spoke quietly into my ear. His voice sounded anything but concerned.

"I may need a bit of help," I admitted, begrudgingly.

Without another word, his hands were on my ass and he hoisted me into the air. I swung my right leg over the horse. Within a moment, I felt Calak settle into the saddle behind me.

We were close, uncomfortably close.

He was much taller than I was, with the back of my head hitting just below his jaw. He reached his arms around me to grab the reins. I startled at the touch as he squeezed against my sides. Other than training with my brothers, this was the closest I'd ever been to a man. Without another word, Calak silently motioned for the other riders to follow us as we moved forward.

There were few words exchanged between the group as we made our way down the snow-covered path. Just the sound of hooves crunching their way through the trail, and the howling of the winter wind. It relieved me when we reached a line of trees. Even though the branches blocked out the warmth of the sun, they provided a reprieve from the onslaught of the wind against my skin. Every single part of me felt frozen solid, except for my backside, thanks to Calak. The warmth was a relief, but we both sat completely rigid, only allowing our bodies to touch when it was completely unavoidable.

The horses slowed, and as we came to a halt, I could hear the rippling of a stream nearby.

"We only stop long enough to water the animals and take care of our personal business." And with that, Calak dismounted. He turned, raising his arms for me. Without making eye contact, I sighed and lowered myself towards him. When I made it safely to the ground, Yuri was standing right in front of me.

"With your permission, Princess, I'd like to have a look at that cut on your forehead. How did it happen?"

"I hit my head on the carriage ride over." I still wasn't sure how much information to share with these trackers and alleged murderers, if Rig was to be believed. Yuri led me to a rock, where I sat down. He dug out some bandages and an ointment from his pack. Dabbing the cream onto the white material, he cleaned the cut. I sucked in air at the sting, but immediately regretted it when Yuri smirked.

"It's not too deep, Princess."

"Please, just call me Raelle."

"Right. Sorry. It doesn't need to be stitched closed, but we should monitor it as we move. You'll need to tell me if it hurts anymore."

"I will. Thank you."

Yuri nodded, put his supplies back in his bag, and returned to his horse. Sloan and Rig had disappeared into the trees, no doubt to take care of their personal business. Bowan had led the horses down to the stream, which ran about ten feet from where we had stopped. I took the moment to take in my surroundings, something that Holden had often talked about.

The trees were tall here, and covered in pine needles. The ground had less snow; I assumed because of the covering the trees provided. There were no obvious landmarks or signs of inhabitants. So far, the North seemed silent and empty.

And cold.

It was freezing here. Without the sun's strong rays, it was hard to get myself warm. I blew air into my hands as I rubbed them together. I had never been this cold in my life.

"Here."

I hadn't seen Calak approach me as he held out a pair of woolen mittens. Glancing up at him, I took the offering.

"Thank you." I made quick work of putting them on.

"It's best if you move around. You need to get your blood moving down to your limbs. We have another couple of hours of riding before we can make camp for the night."

"Okay."

"Are you hungry?"

"Always."

Calak looked slightly amused, probably not expecting that response. Then he dug into his pack and pulled out a cloth. Unwrapping it, he handed me a brown, flaky stick. I, honest to the gods, couldn't identify if this was food or not.

"Um, what is this?"

"Dried deer meat."

"Oh."

"Have you never had dried meat before, Princess?"

"It's Raelle. And no, I don't think I have."

"Well, it's the best we're going to get until we reach the castle."

With that, he walked away to join Bowan at the stream. The two of them fell into simple conversation. I couldn't make out what they were saying, but the way they interacted reminded me of Kolt and my father. Bowan grinned at something Calak said as they both shook their heads and laughed.

Lifting the dried deer meat to my lips, I tried very hard not to smell it. I contemplated just going hungry, but I didn't know exactly when I'd eaten last. If I was going to regain my strength, I would need nourishment. It seemed clear that this was the only food I'd be offered until we reached our destination, however far away that might be. I nibbled the edge of the brown stick. It didn't taste great, but I took a bigger bite. Father had once suggested that plugging your nose helped remove the taste of foods. So, I pinched my nose closed and made quick work of finishing the dried deer meat.

Rig and Sloan reappeared from the treeline and everyone started getting ready to ride again. I made my way toward Calak and our horse.

It was odd how quiet we rode. This group seemed to have a good rapport with one another, but as we moved, there was no banter. Each of them surveyed the trees and path, not breaking their concentration for anything. I could only assume they were using those tracking skills, but what could they possibly be tracking right now? The thought created a few questions in my mind, and I was about to ask one when, suddenly, my stomach turned sour.

"Oh..."

I tensed and leaned forward towards the mane of the horse.

"What's wro-" Before Calak could finish the question, I vomited down the side of the horse. He sighed heavily, but we didn't stop moving.

"Looks like the Princess can't handle her deer meat," Bowan laughed from further back on the path.

I was mortified. Sloan rode up next to us and handed me her waterskin. I washed my mouth and spit the water out. After I took a long drink, I passed the waterskin back to Sloan, thanking her, wiping my wind-chapped lips with the cloak that hung around me.

My first day in the Northern Kingdom was nothing short of disastrous. My clumsiness and weak stomach were both intent on embarrassing me, and worse than that, I was traveling with self-proclaimed murderers. I wrapped the cloak around my shivering body and wished to be at home, defrosting in front of a blazing fire with my brothers.

We continued to ride in silence. Calak's front was now pressed against my back, his shoulders leaning forward, arms still around me, resting now on top of my thighs. I didn't dare move, save the occasional wiggle of my toes and fingers, just to make sure I still could.

Gods, I was so cold.

I let my mind imagine how warm I would be if I turned in the saddle and wrapped my arms around Calak, folding the cloak over us so our shared body heat could burn away the chill. I had just met the man, but I assumed that having the intended bride of his King using him for body heat in such an intimate way was probably off the table, but it didn't need to be anything more than that. I just wanted to stop shivering.

"Yuri and Rig, scout ahead and make sure the clearing is secure."

As soon as Calak spoke, the two riders took off ahead of us.

"Are they checking for wild animals?" I hadn't spoken in hours, and my voice was groggy. I sounded like Rig.

"Not animals."

Calak pushed the horse forward as we reached a clearing in the trees. The sun had set and the only light to guide us came from the moon and stars, with a faint glow of auroras. Streaks of purples, blues, and greens danced across the night sky. I took it all in. This clearing provided a magnificent view. I'd never seen the auroras before, but my father had told me about them. They were beautiful.

Calak dismounted and waited on the ground for

me. Ignoring his outstretched arms, I balanced my weight back onto my left foot, shifting my hips off the saddle, and swung my right leg down to the ground. Calak quietly stayed beside the horse until I was safely on the ground.

"You good?" He nodded at me with the hint of a smirk.

"Just cold."

"Bowan will start the fire. We don't travel with tents or coverings. We sleep on mats, in the open air. Probably not what you are used to, but it'll have to do until..."

"Until we reach our destination. I'll be fine."

The five of them made quick work of gathering wood, tying up our horses and laying out mats. Bowan made an impressive fire, and I planted myself directly in front of it, allowing my limbs to thaw from the long day. Sloan settled in beside me and offered the waterskin again. I took a healthy drink and handed it back to her.

"So, Raelle. Have you ever been to the Northern Kingdom before?"

"Never."

"And is it all you dreamed it would be?"

"You're assuming I've dreamt of coming here."

Sloan smirked. "I used to dream of the North, running through the snow and watching the auroras until the sun rose." She was staring up into the sky. "Tonight, you'll sleep between Yuri and I. Rig kicks in his sleep, hard. Calak will probably stay awake and pace all night, keeping watch. And Bowan snores."

"Sounds fine to me."

We sat silently for a few more minutes, staring at the flames. Calak indeed walked around the small encampment, scanning the forest as he circled around us.

"What is he watching for?"

"Raiders."

I turned to Yuri.

"Raiders?"

"That's what we track, when we aren't babysitting the King's new bride, that is." He smiled, not meaning to insult me. Yuri was being playful. I didn't smile back though, instead waited for more information. "Thirty years ago, the Northern King made a deal with the other three kingdoms. Our timber trade was failing, and we needed the revenue, so they sent us their prisoners to work in the sawmills. We basically became prison guards and oversaw their efforts. For a while it helped boost our trade and sales, but some prisoners escaped and formed a group of bandits called the Raiders. When the King died and his son took the throne, he immediately disbanded the sawmills, sending the remaining prisoners back to their respective kingdoms. He didn't believe the risk of exposing his people to the prisoners was worth the boost in timber sales. But for well over a decade now, the Raiders that are left in the North have festered, pillaging our towns and murdering our people."

"That's awful."

"The King charged Calak with tracking the Raiders and keeping them in check. Calak found each of us and asked us to join his Unit. Rig was from a wrestling pit somewhere in the East. Sloan was a farmer's daughter from your neck of the woods, the West. And I was indebted to a merchant in the South. Calak bought my indenture and gave me my freedom. I've been following him ever since."

"And Bowan?"

"Bowan was an advisor to the former King, and like a father to Calak. After the love of his life went missing, things got bad." Yuri ran his finger up and down his face, mimicking the pattern of the scar Bowan carried. "Bowan left the army and disappeared. Calak found him two years later, pissing his life away at a tavern every night. Somehow he convinced Bowan to gear up again and join us."

"It must be dangerous, tracking Raiders."

"Wouldn't be worth it if it wasn't."

I thought that was a strange answer, but I said nothing else. My eyes were burning and getting heavy. Every muscle in my body was still aching from everything that had happened these past few days. I needed to rest. I turned myself away from Yuri, so I was facing a sleeping Sloan and laid down on my mat. Pulling the fur blanket over myself, I allowed the heat from the fire to lull me into a deep sleep.

In my dreams, I was back in the West, running through the tall grass outside of the castle with Holden and Dalia, with the warm afternoon sun shining down on me. We were laughing and pretending we were pirates. I could hear Father calling my name from the stables.

"Raelle."

I turned to look in his direction. He was waving at me, calling us in for dinner, most likely.

"Raelle!"

I smiled at him as his eyes grew wide in fear...

"RAELLE!"

That wasn't my father's voice. It was Sloan's.

"RAELLE! GET UP!"

CHAPTER SIX

"RAELLE, GET UP. NOW!"

A body slammed to the ground beside me, loose snow and stones flew up to my face, as I looked and saw two empty eyes staring back at me. The blood from a deadly head wound dripped down his front, staining the ground crimson. His face was dirty and a front tooth was missing. Blood from the gash across his neck was thick as it spilled out. His death was fast but not painless. Swords clanged around me, as I willed myself to sit up.

Chaos.

Bodies colliding, weapons wet with the proof of their effects, I struggled to make sense of what was happening.

We were being attacked.

On the far side of the fire, Calak swiped his sword through the air, slicing one of his attackers across the chest. A painful wail erupted from his lips as his companion twisted his sword in hand and lunged for Calak. Without looking, Calak sidestepped out of the way of the blow, swinging his sword down on the backside of his second attacker. Before he could catch his breath, another ran from the trees towards him carrying a battle axe.

Raiders.

To the left of the fire, Rig had taken down three Raiders by the body count on the ground. The sounds of men groaning in agony and pleading for mercy as Rig used his bare hands to crush their eye sockets and their break bones would haunt me forever. I couldn't even see a weapon in Rig's hands. He was the weapon. Good gods.

Bowan, Yuri, and Sloan were surrounding me, fighting off Raiders that came from the treeline as if they were trying to get past them to reach me. Yuri wielded the two swords that had been sheathed on his back. The blades were an extension of his arms. As a Raider came at him with a sword in one hand and a dagger in the other, Yuri spun around with great force. There was a slice, then a thud as the Raider's head fell to the ground and rolled away. His body slumped to its knees as Yuri heaved it aside with his foot.

Sloan sidestepped the fallen Raider as she grabbed the arm of her attacker, flipping him forward onto his back. With such intensity, she barreled her sword into his throat. I heard him call her a bitch through the gurgle of the blood pooling in his mouth. She was unrelenting and seemed to gain intensity from one opponent to another. I noticed her sword was short, like the ones I preferred, as she ran it through the abdomen of an approaching Raider, cutting him open across his navel, his intestines spilling out through his clothing. A desperate attempt to swing back at Sloan followed his ear-piercing scream, but she easily dodged the blow and brought her sword down, severing the man's right arm from his body.

Bowan, to my right, moved like a man trained for traditional warfare. I recognized the movements from how Danier trained the soldiers back home. Despite his age, Bowan moved just as quickly as the rest, taking down anyone who dared to approach. I watched as he speared his sword into the gut of a Raider, but it must have caught on the ribcage, which pulled the sword from Bowan's grip. Without hesitation, Bowan unsheathed a dagger from his belt. With a hand in the man's hair, he pulled back his head and ran the knife across the throat. Blood spit from the Raider's neck as he cursed us, then collapsed onto the ground. Using his foot as leverage, Bowan pushed down on the man's chest as he heaved his sword from the body and turned towards me.

"Good sleep there, Princess?"

His skill with a blade showcased years of experience. I really wanted to know how he got that scar, but now didn't seem like the right time to ask.

How deep of a sleep must I have been in?

There were half a dozen Raiders still standing. And from what I could see from the low light of the fire, at least three times as many were already on the ground.

Feeling useless and slightly embarrassed that I slept so deeply, I looked around for a weapon I could wield. On the ground, near Sloan's sleeping mat, I spotted a bow and a quiver full of arrows. Out of all the weapons Danier had trained me to use, this was the one I had the most natural talent for.

That would work. I flung off my cloak and slid the quiver across my back. Nocking the first arrow, ignoring the burn from my arm muscles as they groaned in protest, I glanced around, looking for my first target.

Two Raiders were attacking Rig. They had been disarmed of their weapons, but their punches were landing their blows against Rig's abdomen and sides. I sucked in my breath, exhaling slowly as I released the arrow right into the chest of a Raider. Before he could fall to the ground, I nocked another arrow, turned, and let it fly into the eye socket of a man running towards Sloan.

My feet were standing on soil that was soaked in blood; I tried to focus as I took in the mangled bodies covering the ground where we were just sleeping.

This was my first battle.

I nocked a third arrow, but the fight was over. Calak had a Raider on his knees, still alive. Bowan and Rig made quick work checking the fallen, dropping their swords through the necks of those on the ground to make sure they weren't getting back up. There were cries of pain and death filling my ears, but no one begged for mercy.

"The Princess can shoot. Good to know."

Sloan sheathed her blade and walked towards me. I kept my arrow nocked, glancing around the treeline once more.

"You were out cold. I thought you were going to sleep through the whole thing."

I kept monitoring the treeline. My adrenaline was pumping so hard that I couldn't lower my guard, not yet. I saw a shadow move in the trees behind Calak as he secured bindings around the hands of his prisoner. I released the arrow, and it landed in the attacker's heart as he lifted his sword to strike down Calak. Satisfied that the threat was over, I lowered the bow and took off the quiver, putting them both back down by Sloan's sleeping mat. I picked up my cloak and brushed it off, placing it over my shoulders as I glanced up to see five sets of eyes staring at me.

I wasn't ready to process what had just happened, so I plopped myself back down on the mat by the fire and started rubbing my hands together. A slight tremor ran through my limbs, proof that I was not okay.

Rig huffed out what I can only assume was a low laugh as they all began to drag the dead Raiders into a pile. They would light the bodies on fire. I knew this from conversations with Danier. Burying the dead wasn't an option because the ground was frozen.

Seeing all of the lives that had ended, I needed to help. There was something inside of me that wanted to honor the fallen, regardless of what side they had fought. So I got up from my spot by the fire and walked towards Bowan, lifting the legs of a man he was carrying. We threw him onto the growing pile of dead Raiders. When I turned, I bumped face first into Calak's chest. His hands instinctively grabbed my biceps to keep me from falling backwards onto a corpse, but I let out a gasp of pain as his hold pressed down on my existing bruises. His eyes flickered with confusion, then concern, and he immediately released me.

"Were you injured during the fight?" he asked as his eyes glanced over my body.

"No," I said, shaking my head and averting my eyes

from him. I felt his stare on my face as he waited for me to say more. I said nothing else.

"If you're hurt, let Yuri have a look at you."

"I'm fine."

I brushed past him towards Sloan, who was working to carry the last Raider. I felt Calak's eyes on the back of me as I walked away.

***

"You're all dead," the captured Raider spit.

His lip was cut and swollen from a punch that Bowan had delivered to his face. The Raider was being questioned by Calak while the rest of us packed up camp. The sun had just risen, but the smell of charred flesh was heavy in the air. I counted twenty-six bodies. Twenty-six Raiders — well, twenty-seven if I counted the prisoner — had attacked us in the night, with not a single injury to anyone in Calak's Unit.

"Here, Raelle," Yuri passed me some dry crackers and a small lump of cheese wrapped in cloth. "This should fare better in your gut than that dried deer meat. You'll always find a small stash of edible food in my pack."

I nodded in gratitude and made quick work of eating. I was starving.

"I'll ask again, just once. Why did Leon order this attack?" Calak asked firmly.

The Raider said nothing, but he looked directly at me.

No one else saw him do it.

Did I know this man?

Shifting his eyes back to Calak, he spewed, "I'm

gunna watch while Leon cuts you down and kills you like he did to your bitch of a mother."

The threat was cut short as Bowan thrust his dagger, piercing the side of the Raider's throat. With a menacing smile still on his lips, the Raider fell to the ground.

"He didn't deserve another breath. None of them do. Not after what they did to your mother." Bowan reached down and wiped his blade on the pants of the fallen Raider. I watched as Calak dragged the prisoner's body, tossing him onto the top of the smoldering pile of bone and ash. Staring at the side of Calak's face, I could see the hint of grief as he turned to walk away.

Sloan was securing her bags, and we were almost ready to continue on our way.

Bowan mounted his horse. "I'll ride on ahead and scout the path. We should be able to reach Castle Mount before noon with the early start to the day."

Calak nodded. "Take Rig with you."

The two members of our Unit rode up the trail in silence.

"Raelle, let me have a look at your head before we leave." Yuri approached me, carrying another small bandage and the same ointment as before. He dabbed gently at my forehead, the cut stinging much less than it had the last time he did this; with Yuri tending to my wounds, healing was coming along much quicker than I expected. "Looks good. Any additional pain?" I shook my head and Yuri smiled as he walked back to his horse, placed the ointment inside of his pack and lifting himself up.

"What happened on your way here, before you met us?" Calak was behind me now. "Were you attacked?"

I looked at him. He was eyeing the cut on my forehead. I tried to decide how much information to give away. I still didn't know my position with the new King or how to play the diplomatic game. All I knew was that I needed to get home, and I still didn't know the best way to accomplish that.

"The cut on your head," Calak gently pointed to my forehead, "and your arms. When I grabbed you earlier, you winced. How bad is it?"

I instinctively raised my right hand to scratch at my left arm and shook my head. "Just some bruising. It'll heal. I'm fine."

"Was it the Raiders?"

"What? No, I've never even heard of the Raiders before last night. Why did they attack us?"

I was thinking of the look that Raider gave me before Bowan killed him.

"Because they want what's not theirs and they don't care who they hurt to get it."

"And it's your job to stop them."

"It's my job to do whatever the King commands."

He walked away.

"Who's Leon?"

Calak turned, "He leads the Raiders."

"Did he kill your mother?"

"Yes."

"I'm sorry."

"You didn't know her and you didn't kill her. So don't apologize. We need to get moving."

"Rig said you were murderers." I tried to pull myself up onto the horse, but again could not find the strength. I supposed I used it all up in the fight. Those hands were becoming a little too familiar with my body, as I was pushed up towards the saddle. Calak lifted himself next, settling in close behind me. Our bodies pressed together as he adjusted himself into the saddle.

He reached forward for the reins, squeezing his arms around me as he leaned over and whispered into my ear.

"We are."

CHAPTER SEVEN

MY EYES WIDENED AT HIS ADMISSION. After what I just witnessed, this Unit was clearly battle-experienced and had taken many lives, but murderers? Murder insinuated malice or revenge. Although, what was war except for an endless cycle of revenge? Maybe they were murderers.

Then I suppose, after today, I was also a murderer.

That was a thought that I had to push deep down as I took in a breath, and then another. Refusing to come apart, I looked around, trying to distract myself.

The tree limbs were heavy with the weight of freshly fallen snow. I heard the soft thud as some snow broke free from its branch, landing on the ground.

We were leaving the covering of the forest and the air lashed across my face, filled with the scent of pine.

The snow was so bright and the landscape appeared untouched, like this winter world was just waking up for the first time, and we were the first ones to see it. Nothing would ever compare to the views back home, but this place held its own kind of beauty. Even if this was the coldest I had ever been in my entire life.

Bowan and Rig rejoined us on the path and, once again, no one spoke.

My body was exhausted from the events of the day. Slowly I caved to my instinctual desire to lean back into the man sitting behind me. I tried not to think about it as my back made contact with his chest, but I couldn't help but over-examine every shift in his positioning or exhale out of his mouth. There was no way that I would be able to rest properly riding with Calak, but at least my spine wasn't aching anymore from standing so straight.

Getting bored, I busied myself studying the path and looking for any landmarks that may be useful on a journey back to the West. I was about to ask how much further our destination was when I heard a strange bird call. Calak answered with a whistle. Then two soldiers, also wearing all white, appeared from the treeline about fifty feet ahead of us. One of them smiled as we approached.

"Welcome back. You pricks look like you could use a good night's sleep and a proper dinner. Oh, my apologies." he bowed his head slightly as he caught my eye. "Your Highness, welcome to the Northern Kingdom. I hope your journey here was enjoyable."

"It wasn't."

"Well, that's too bad. I'm sorry for it, but they've prepared the castle for your arrival. Heard there's going to be a big feast tomorrow in your honor. Isn't that right, Calak?"

"That's what I hear."

"Well, we won't keep you any longer. All the best, my lady, and I truly hope things improve for you."

"Well, it can't get any worse."

Why was I being so unkind? I didn't know this man, and he had done nothing to me personally. A diplomatic approach would require me to make friends, not enemies. So with that thought in mind, I offered a half-smile, it was the best I could muster, to the man as we rode past him. He returned the gesture, and we moved on. Clearing the hill ahead, my eyes blinked twice, trying to focus, as I took in our destination.

This castle was truly unique. I'd seen nothing like it in the West or anything similar depicted in drawings. Sitting in front of the tremendous mountain was a partial castle with exterior corridors, turrets, and lines of windows and balconies, but it was as if the mountain had swallowed the back half of the castle. Along the mountain face, above the fortress, was another series of balconies and entrances carved into the stone. It was a marvel.

As we followed the well-traveled road that would lead us to the castle, we passed tents with soldiers gathered around them. This appeared to be a military encampment mixed with tradespeople. Those along the path greeted us with nods and grunts. Although, not everyone looked happy to see me. Some of the soldiers glared at me as we passed by. I thought I even saw a man spit on the ground. This was to be expected, of course. I was the daughter of the man they'd been at war with for the past ten years. A few older children came running past, chased closely by dogs that looked like wolves I had seen in picture books back home, and it drew my attention back to the castle in front of us.

Upon our approach, a heavy, metallic groan purred from the castle gates as they opened for us. Looking up, I saw more soldiers lining the castle walls, armed and standing guard. The inner courtyard that we entered was long and narrow, stretching the length of the outer wall of the castle. Stairs to the palace's entrance went up before us, but once Calak's Unit was inside, the gates shut again and we rode to the left, entering a corridor burrowed into the mountain. By the smell alone I knew this was where we'd be leaving the animals that brought us safely here. I didn't mind the smell of horses. Even though I was a terrible rider, I loved them. I'd often find my way into the stables back home to brush them and talk freely, the horses my only audience to listen. I had tried to master riding many times. Holden and I once rode out towards the coast. I lost control of my mare along a rocky ridge and fell. The horse took off and left me on the ground with a twisted ankle. Father sent a dozen guards out looking for us when we didn't return by nightfall. A dull ache spread across my chest as I thought about my father.

Calak dismounted and turned to help me off the horse. After being held up against him for the better part of the last twenty-four hours, I didn't shy away from his touch. I leaned forward into his arms, my hands resting on his shoulders as he placed his hands up under me, easily carrying my weight. He lowered me to the ground, our bodies slowly brushing against each other. I looked up into his eyes, clearing my throat before I offered a "thank you." Calak quickly released me and I stepped backwards, tucking a curl behind my ear.

Was I flustered? My gods, I needed a cold bath and a nap.

Leading down to an open stall, Calak left me standing alone without a word. This man was moody, but I followed him because I didn't actually know where to go next.

Bowan, Rig, Yuri and Sloan were behind us, caught up in conversation about comfortable beds and hot food. Other than their voices, this space was quiet and empty. I suppose I had assumed there would be more of a welcoming party for the King's new bride. Not that I was disappointed. Crowds made me nervous, and my diplomatic skills needed to be tested before I attempted to win over an entire castle full of people.

Calak untied a satchel and walked towards me.

"I believe they've prepared a chamber for you. Follow me."

As I turned, I saw the rest of our traveling party heading in the opposite direction. I started to yell out a "goodbye," but thought better of it. It's not like we were friends. I wasn't even sure if I'd ever see them again. Returning my eyes to the back of Calak's head, I followed him up a stairwell.

"Does the King know I've arrived?"

"No idea."

"How many people live in the castle?"

"A lot."

"Do you live in the castle?"

"Sometimes."

"Are you always this helpful?"

No response.

"You know, I'm going to be your Queen. The least you could do is answer my questions." I was tired, sore, annoyed, and still trying to figure out what it was about Calak that made me both want to be near him and throw things at his head. He didn't really need to answer any of my questions, and I didn't even care that much.

Immediately, I regretted pulling the "queen" card. It reminded me of something Queen Estra might say, and that thought made me shudder.

"Sorry. I'm just exhausted. I haven't really had any time to wrap my head around all of this, you know?"

Calak said nothing. He was so cantankerous, although I suppose I was no better.

As we reached the top of the stairs and entered an open hall, beams of light streaked in from the windows, high above my reach. Dust particles danced throughout the room. The ceiling was a masterpiece. There were intricate details carved into the curved beams. In the center of the hall was a grand staircase that led to corridors that split off in different directions. Running my hand along the stone walls, I continued to follow Calak's steps. I committed to memory the number of doors we passed. We carried on in silence, and I noted the tapestries that hung around the hall. Whoever created them wove each one to tell a story. The colors were vivid, and the workmanship impressive.

Distracted by the art on the wall, I turned a corner and I bumped into a woman, smacking my nose on her chin.

"Damn," I felt up to see if there was any blood.

There was none.

"Well, that's one way to make an introduction," the woman smiled as she rubbed her chin. She stuck out her hand for a handshake. "Bree."

I instinctively grabbed her hand. "Raelle."

"I know. I've been waiting for you. The adopted Princess from the Western Kingdom, sent as a peace treaty to end the Decade War."

"The one and only."

Calak shifted beside me. "Where's the King?"

"Just finished a meeting, but Calak, you shouldn't be here." Bree looked concerned. The look reminded me of what a mother might look like if she was worried about her child, but Bree was too young to be Calak's mother, who I knew to be dead, anyway. They looked similar. A sister, maybe?

"What's going on?" Calak studied her face.

"He brought in Leon."

"What? Why?"

"To continue peace talks, why else? He's committed to finding a peaceful resolution."

"Well, tell that to the two dozen Raiders who attacked us last night."

Bree exhaled a curse and shook her head.

"Leon will never agree to peace."

"I know."

"He's wasting his time." Calak was agitated, his voice rising.

Bree lifted her eyebrows and nudged her head in my direction. I watched them silently speak to one another and then I saw it. Twins. Calak and Bree were definitely twins. They had the same straight nose and round eyes – that blue iris, like the part of the ocean that's deepest. Bree's hair was jet black, a trait I'm sure her brother shared, although I've never seen him without his hat. She only lacked the slight beard and scar that ran down Calak's lip.

Before I could confirm, footsteps down the hall's main staircase caught my attention. I turned to see a man with six Northern guards flanking him. From

Calak's change in posture and quickened breathing, I assumed this man was Leon.

Calak took one step forward, "I'm going to kill him."

CHAPTER EIGHT

WE LEFT CALAK STANDING in the grand hall. Clearly, his admission of attempted murder didn't mean much to his twin. I, for one, was fine with getting as far away from him as possible.

"Come on," Bree said, placing her arm inside of mine. "Let's get you to your room and into some more...Northern-appropriate clothing. You must've been freezing out there."

Leading me up the stairs to another corridor, Bree pushed open the third door on our right, and I was pleasantly surprised at what I saw. There was a fire going in the hearth against the far wall and the floor was lined with various furs and rugs. Two large wing-backed chairs were placed by the fireplace, a table set between them, and shelves lined with books and trinkets. The bed was smaller than my own bed back home, but they filled it with more pillows and blankets than I could count. I suppose I didn't expect a castle carved into a mountain to feel so warm and inviting.

Bree walked past me, sitting on the bed and leaning back on her forearms.

"So, an arranged marriage?"

"That's the plan." I was still thinking about Calak back where we left him. "Is he really going to kill Leon?"

"Not today."

"And Calak is your twin?"

"He is. You're quick."

"You look identical and you carry the same air of confidence."

"Ha!" Bree jumped off the bed and opened a chest of drawers, pulling out some clothes for me. "There's a bathing chamber through that door there if you'd like to wash up. I'll go let the King know you've arrived and come back for you in an hour. Will you be okay?"

"I think so."

With a smile and a nod, Bree quickly left the room.

I fell backwards on the bed and against all odds, despite being in a strange place with no one I knew, I drifted off to sleep.

***

Nine years ago.

"Holden, wait! I can't run that fast." I chased after my friend, stumbling through the tall grass that surrounded the castle.

"Come on, Princess. You've got to pick up your feet if you're going to catch me."

I'd lived in the West for about a year, still unable to remember life before I arrived. King Wren had called healers from all over the kingdom, and some from other kingdoms, to help restore my memory. But nothing they tried worked.

I wasn't sad that I couldn't remember.

It sometimes felt like I should be sad, but I loved living here.

Kolt had taught me different languages and the history of the kingdoms. Danier had announced that he'd like to train me in combat one night at dinner after he saw me shoot a bow in the fields with Holden. King Wren had spoiled me with beautiful dresses and trinkets from his travels.

I felt like I belonged here with them. Well, with all of them, except the Queen.

At first, I thought I was just imagining that she hated me, but over the months it became clear that she resented my presence in the castle. Last night, I heard the King and Queen arguing as I passed by the Queen's private lounge.

"She needs to go. I don't want her here."

"Estra, it's not for you to decide."

"My father will certainly not approve."

"I don't care. I'm the King in the West."

"The boys have called her Princess, did you know that?"

"Yes, I know. The people love her. She is our princess. Sent to us as a miracle."

"Oh gods, you are insufferable."

"I am King of the Western Kingdom. Adding to this family is my decision and although I would have liked for you to have been supportive, your approval is not something that I require. Raelle will be the next Princess of the Western Kingdom. I will announce it in a fortnight, so I suggest you come to peace with it before then."

Princess?

Before anyone could see me, I rushed down the hall back towards the West Wing where my chamber was. The King's words filled me with a rush of joy and fear. I reached my door and slammed it shut behind me. A moment later, there was a knock. I was leaning against the door, still panting from my sprint. As I turned the handle and peaked around to see who was there, I saw King Wren's kind eyes staring back at me.

"Hello my dear. May I come in?"

"Of course." I open the door fully to allow him into my chamber.

He walked into the room and sat on the chair closest to the fire. I sat on the edge of my bed, waiting for him to speak first.

"How much did you hear?"

Of course, he knew I was listening. Somehow, King Wren knew everything. I could tell by his tone that I was not in trouble.

"Some of it. I heard you mean to make me your princess and that the Queen is not happy about it."

King Wren sighed, rubbed his neck and looked towards me.

"Have I ever told you about my daughter, Lilith?"

My eyes widened. "No."

"She would have been a few years younger than you. She passed away shortly after she was born. That's how we lost my first wife, the boys' mother. Anna was the love of my life, but she had a fragile constitution. The births took their toll, and the healers said there was nothing we could have done differently. The boys and I mourned the loss of their mother and sister for a long time."

I didn't know what to say. King Wren looked down at the fire.

"When Anna and Lilith died, I felt such incredible

sadness. My heart was full of so much love for them that I'd never be able to express. But that day we found you on the coast, seeing you with your curly hair, you reminded me of our Lilith. I knew the gods had given us a fresh start. An opportunity to make our family whole again. You were everything we didn't know we needed to heal our broken hearts. You have been the joy of our lives, Raelle, and we never want to lose you."

My eyes filled with tears. This past year, all I have wanted was to be their actual sister. To be his actual daughter. I felt like I belonged here.

"I'd like for you to be our Princess, officially."

He looked up then to watch my face. His eyes were just as wet as mine.

"I'd really like that." I burst out, no longer able to hold back my tears. In a moment, King Wren was up from his seat and held me in his arms. I leaned into his chest as I sobbed.

He chuckled softly, "There, there, my Princess. It's alright. I'm so thankful for you and the joy you've brought into our lives."

I lifted my chin. "What about the Queen?"

"Don't you worry for one minute about anything you heard in that room tonight."

I sniffled once more, wiping my eyes with the sleeve of my gown.

"If I'm going to be your princess, could I call you Father?"

"Always," he choked out as a fresh tear fell from his eye.

I hugged him again. Resting in the safety of his arms.

Resting in the safety of my father's arms.

***

I woke up, confused about where I was. The room didn't look familiar, and it took me a few moments to realize everything that had happened wasn't a dream. I was in the Northern Kingdom. The Queen's personal guard had seized me from my home and I never got to say goodbye to my brothers or my father. Shortly, I would meet the King, who would expect me to be his new bride. There was a loud knock at the door. Not waiting for an answer, it swung open. Bree smiled as she stepped in.

"Oh good, you're up! I came back earlier, but you were sound asleep. I figured you needed it after the last couple of days. And...you still haven't changed. No worries. We've got time. The King was just heading out to inspect a new arrival of goods from the Eastern Kingdom. So get dressed and I'll take you down to the kitchens to grab some food. I would have them send some food up, but if we go straight to the kitchen, Clara, the cook, always gives us the fresh stuff. It's worth the trek down for it, trust me."

I sat up and adjusted myself on the bed as I tried to find the right thing to say next. Attempting to maintain my course of being diplomatic, I asked, "What sort of goods from the Eastern Kingdom?"

Of all the things to ask, that's what I picked. Gods, I was so boring.

"Oh, um, I'm not completely sure. Usually rice and anything shipped from the continent."

Bree walked over to where the clothes were still laid on the bed and passed them to me as I stood to walk towards the bathing chamber.

"Do you have questions, besides wondering about shipments of rice? Calak said you had lots of questions for him. Knowing how chatty my brother can be, I'm sure you didn't get many answers."

"Yes, he's an open book," I laughed. I started to

undress in the next room. "But, I do have a question. Where exactly are we?"

"We call this Castle Mount. The capital of the Northern Kingdom and residence of King Veras."

King Veras. That was his name. And I remembered seeing Castle Mount on the maps that Kolt had me study. It rested on the eastern side of the mountain range that spanned the length of the Northern Kingdom.

"So, what's your role in all of this? Are you the official babysitter of new guests?" I asked as I returned to the bedchamber in my new clothes.

"Ha! No, not at all. I'm actually the general commander of the King's army."

My jaw must have dislodged itself as I stared at her in disbelief. I would never have assumed this slender, but actually quite muscular (now that I look more closely) woman, who clearly had no trouble striking up conversation, would have such a position in the army.

"Excuse me if this is out of turn, but why is a general in the King's army getting me clothes and helping me find food?"

"Beats me. I'm just following orders. The King was insistent that you were to stay well protected and in good spirits. So, until further notice, you're stuck with me."

She smiled, and I returned it. Being around Bree was easy. She reminded me a lot of Holden, which made me sad, but grateful. If I had to be stuck with someone, I'd much rather it be someone like Bree.

"Alright Princess, are you ready? I'm starving and if we get down to Clara soon, she'll likely have some fresh pastries for us to sample."

I nodded, and we left the bedchamber.

Fresh pastries sounded amazing right now, but over the sound of my stomach growling, I could feel my heart break as I remembered the last time I saw my brothers sharing cinnamon buns with sweet syrup. I lifted my hand to clasp the necklace. A compass rose to help find my way home. That will not be the last time I see my brothers. I will find a way home, no matter what it takes.

CHAPTER NINE

"SOMEONE GRAB THIS BLASTED POT and go fill it with water before I swat one of your useless twigs and find myself some real kitchen help who don'ts need as much hand holding."

Clara was a round woman who sounded like her bark and bite would be equally painful. A young kitchen maid ran out carrying the empty pot, while the others busied themselves chopping and peeling vegetables. Not one dared to look up.

"Good morning, Clara," Bree practically sung the greeting as she graced over and planted a kiss on the cook's red face.

"Bree. What's do ye want?"

"Clara, I'm hurt. Can't the most decorated general

of the King's army come down to visit the best cook in the Kingdom and not need anything?"

From the look on Clara's face, this was a regular sparing these two shared. Clara raised her eyebrows and tilted her head down, keeping her eyes fixed on Bree.

"Who's the new girl?"

"Ah, yes! Clara, I would like for you to meet Princess Raelle of the Western Kingdom, adoptive daughter of King Wren and soon to be married to our King Veras." Bree wrapped her arm around my shoulder and leaned into me.

I lifted my hand into a shortwave and replied with a simple, "Hi."

"That sounds like a long way to say that she's someone who's got no business in my kitchen while I'm prepping for a big feast tomorrow. Princess or no. Get yerselves out of my way, before I move ye meself."

I liked Clara.

"Of course. Happy to get out of your way. Just as soon as you point us towards some freshly baked goods that maybe require sampling..."

With a loud sigh, Clara pointed her finger to the left of the kitchen. "Over there, but stay out of me way."

"Yes, ma'am!"

Bree ushered me to the left side of the kitchen and plopped herself up on the counter while lifting a cloth revealing a tray of baked goods. With a squeal of delight, she reached down and grabbed a round one covered in drizzled chocolate.

"Oh, my gods. These are my favorite," Bree said through a mouthful. "Raelle, try one. Do you have anything like this in the Western Kingdom?"

"We have lots of baked goods, but I've never seen this one before." Reaching down and grabbing a matching one to the one Bree had almost finished, I took a bite and groaned in pure satisfaction. I loved food, especially good food.

"See? I told you it was worth coming down here."

"Oh. You were right. This is amazing."

"Of course, I knew I'd find you down here."

The voice belonged to Calak. He had entered the kitchen behind me and strutted towards his sister. With his hat now off his head, I could confirm that his hair matched his sister's jet black. It was short and sat straight on top of his head. Calak reached down to steal the next baked good Bree had picked up to devour.

"Hey! Get your own."

"I just did," he replied as he bit into it.

"Someone seems less cranky now that they've had a nap," Bree wiped her fingers on the cloth beside her as she looked to replace the treat her brother had stolen.

"Just a quick nap. That's all I needed." He then turned in my direction, "Princess, glad to see you found some more suitable clothes for our northern temperatures. I don't know what you were thinking wearing that dress and not even bringing a cloak with you. You seemed very unprepared for your travels. You know what Northern means, right?"

"I didn't know I was coming here."

Calak stared at me for a moment with a slightly puzzled look, licking his lips, then turned his attention to his sister, who looked equally confused. Something about what I said sparked a wordless conversation between the twins. Clara interrupted their silence, shouting, "Calak! Is that you, dear? Come, give me a kiss."

"Ah! Clara, my love. These pastries are amazing, as always."

Calak sauntered over and planted a kiss on the cheek of the cook as she beamed at him. Now I was the puzzled one. Calak was nice and playful? And Clara, who from the short time I've met her moments ago didn't seem to like anyone else, was gushing over Calak in her kitchen.

"Is there anything else you want, dear?" Clara had all of her attention on Calak now.

"Could I trouble you for some cider?"

"There's some in that pot there on the stove."

"What would we do without you?" Calak gave the cook another kiss on her other cheek. Clara smiled as she mixed whatever was in the bowl in front of her, pushing him away with her free hand. Calak grabbed three glasses from the shelf and filled them each with cider. He walked back to where Bree and I stood, offering us some drink.

"Thank you," I said as I took a sip. It was so flavorful, warming me to my toes and tasting like baked apples. "This is delicious."

"Clara makes the best cider," Bree said between sips of her own.

I took another drink as I looked up to see Calak staring at me, like he was trying to read something that wasn't there. The reprieve of a nap, food, and a hot drink was enough to lift my spirits, but not to forget my focus. I needed to get back home, by whatever means possible.

***

We finished our snack and left the kitchen loaded with a plate of fresh fruit and cold cuts of meat and cheese, thanks to Calak's charm with Clara the cook. The three of us made our way back up to the level of the castle where my bedchamber was located and found an empty alcove with chairs and a table to settle into. Before I sat down at the table, I took in the tapestries that hung on the walls. The first one was the landmass of Garth before they divided it into kingdoms. Some cities marked on the map were familiar, and others I did not recognize. I traced my hand along the portion of the map that now belonged to the Western Kingdom. I imagined the moors and cliffs. The coast and the sound of the waves crashing against the rocks.

The next tapestry was a portrait of a king and queen I'd never seen before. Their features were nothing remarkable, except for a shimmer of silver across their forehead that resembled crowns. The thread the artist used to depict their hair was a cobalt blue. An interesting choice. I looked down to see the words "Evamore Dynasty" sewn into the tapestry.

"The last king and queen of the United Kingdom of Garth," Calak said from behind me. "The end of the Evamore Dynasty."

"Why did the artist use the blue thread for their hair?"

"Do they not teach the history of Garth in the Western Kingdom?"

"No, they do. My brother Kolt taught me all about the histories of the kingdoms, and the war that created them and the United Kingdom of Garth."

"Well, he left out one pretty remarkable detail. The gods gave the ruling members of the Evamore Dynasty blue hair and a mark of the gods across their forehead as a symbol of their favor. It was also how they charted the succession line. Only the chosen heirs of an Evamore family and their lovetie had the blue hair and the mark, when it was their time to rule."

"Lovetie? I've never heard that term before."

"It's not used anymore. It describes the connection between two people. The connection is strong. Stronger than anything else in the world. Writers would use words like soulmates, but that doesn't really capture what a lovetie is, or was, I guess. Our mother told us that once a lovetied Evamore died, then the other could no longer rule. The severed connection was like a fracture to their soul and the dynasty would pass to the next Evamore heir in line for the throne, and their lovetie."

"But why blue hair?"

"Why does the sun rise in the east? Why is snow white? Some questions don't need to be asked or answered. They just are."

I studied the tapestry again and wondered why our histories left out this strangely insignificant, yet very interesting detail.

"I don't understand why the gods would grant their favor to such terrible leaders."

"Of course a princess from the West would think that."

"What's that supposed to mean?"

"History is written and recorded from the perspective of whoever holds the quill. I wouldn't trust everything you've been taught in the West to be the truth."

I twisted my nose at Calak. He was insinuating that what Kolt had taught me may have been an altered version of the truth. Choosing to ignore him for the moment, I turned to sit down at the table beside Bree, who had already made a healthy start on the plates we brought up from the kitchen. I grabbed some grapes and a few slices of cheese.

"The King will be back shortly. He's eager to speak with you."

I turned to look at Bree. "Is he kind?"

She nodded her head and shoved a piece of cheese into her mouth. "Very. The King is kind and just. It's an honor to serve him."

This confused me. I had assumed that the King of the Northern Kingdom, who would have been privy to Queen Estra's plan to kidnap me from my home and force me into an unwanted marriage, could not have been a kind or just man. Maybe Bree didn't know him well. Even a general couldn't be sure of the motivations behind a King's choices.

Regardless of Bree's opinion of King Veras, I would need to put all of my diplomatic cards on the table if I planned to return home, but how far was I willing to go? Would I really marry King Veras? Would he expect me to lie with him? I'd never even kissed a man before. And what would happen if I tried to leave Castle Mount? Would he stop me? Would he have Calak and his Unit track me down and kill me?

I felt less confident in my ability to use diplomacy to find my way home, but in the kingdom's capital, with no allies, weapons, or knowledge of the terrain, fighting my way out would be impossible. I forced out a deep sigh as I ate another grape. Just then, Yuri approached the alcove. He smiled at me and motioned for Calak, who joined him where he stood as they whispered back and forth. With a nod, Yuri smiled again and continued down the corridor as Calak turned to face me.

"The King will see you now."

CHAPTER TEN

I WAS COMPLETELY ON EDGE as I stood outside of the King's chamber door. Reaching over, scratching my left arm, I wasn't sure I wanted to go inside, not that I had a choice. Damn Queen Estra. Damn the North. Damn Calak standing behind me, flanking my left with Bree on my right.

"What is she waiting for?" Calak whispered loudly to his sister, knowing I could hear him.

"Give her a minute," Bree retorted.

"It's been a few minutes already. I just want to know if I should grab a chair, or if we'll be moving forward soon."

I exhaled, turning my head, eyes like daggers, and took in Calak's face that was full with a vexatious grin.

I lifted my arm up to knock and...

"Are you sure you're ready?" Calak joked from behind me, interrupting me. Bree elbowed him, hard I guessed from the sound of his grunt.

"Oh, just open the door already."

His voice carried through the wood as Bree reached around me and pushed the handle down. The door swung open, revealing the largest bed chamber I'd ever seen. Besides the walls, which were adorned with more tapestries and the heads of various animals, his room was just like my bedchamber, with rugs and fur skins strewed on the ground. There was a set of open double doors to our right, revealing a massive four-post bed covered in what appeared to be a plain white blanket with perfectly lined pillows. A dining room table, with seating for a dozen people, sat inside of the main bedchamber. Who needs a dining table in their bedchamber?

King Veras stood, leaning against the table with his arms folded across his chest. He was tall and very handsome. He had blond hair that waved down around his ears and neck and the faintest stubble that could either have been intentional, or just a result of a rushed morning. Everything about this man was sensual, from the way his lips parted ever so slightly exposing the tip of his tongue resting on his bottom teeth, to the chocolate eyes, so warm that you could get lost in them and never bother to find your way out.

Gods. I really needed that cold bath.

"Finally. I was wondering if you'd ever make it inside." I walked towards the King as he gently lifted my hand to his lips. "Princess." He smiled and released my hand. "Come, come, let's sit and have a proper chat. Bree and Cal, you two stay as well. What we're going to discuss affects all of us."

I was so confused. What did we need to discuss? Our marriage? And how did that involve Bree or Calak? With no questions, my entourage made their way to the dining room table and sat down beside each other. I sat across from Bree and King Veras sat at the head of the table to my left.

"First, I want to apologize to you Raelle for not greeting you upon your arrival at Castle Mount. It was a scheduling oversight, but a grave mistake. I hope Calak and Bree have helped you get settled and made you feel at home."

"Yes, Bree has been wonderful." The slight did not go unnoticed as all three of them smirked, but I maintained a straight face. "I also met Clara, your cook."

"Did you really? Well, that must have gone well since you are still here to tell the tale."

"Yes, she was kind enough to offer us food and drink. Although I'm not sure if her kitchen maids have fared well after what I overheard."

"They'll be fine. Clara loves those girls like her own daughters."

Since Queen Estra was the only mother I'd ever really known, the love of a mother didn't stir up warm feelings for me.

"Do you know why you're here, Raelle?"

Wow, straight to the point. I could respect that.

"I'm to be your wife, I suppose, in exchange for an end to the Decade War between our two kingdoms."

"Yes, that is true. I offered a peace treaty to Queen Estra in exchange for you being delivered here, to me, in the Northern Kingdom. However, I will not be marrying you."

I stared at the King as I processed his words to make sure I'd heard him correctly. It seemed I wasn't the only surprised one, as Bree and Calak were both now staring at their King, waiting for an explanation that I assumed was coming.

"This surprises you?"

"Well, yeah. Actually, it does. Why? Why won't you marry me?"

"Do you want to marry me?"

"No."

Damnit, I wasn't good at this diplomatic thing.

King Veras just smiled.

"I appreciate your candor, Princess, but you don't need to worry. I've no desire to marry you either. Arranged marriages aren't really my thing."

"Then.. then why am I here?" My frustration was rising to the surface. "Why was I taken from my home, away from everyone I knew and loved, if you would've extended peace without the contract of a marriage?"

"I agreed to have you brought to the Northern Kingdom to save your life."

"I'm just going to grab us something to drink," Bree pushed back from the table and walked over to a beverage cart on the side wall. She returned with a pitcher of ale and a stack of glasses.

"What do you mean, 'save my life?'"

The statement seemed a tad dramatic and unlikely. If my life were in danger, then my brothers, or my father, would have had some clue. They held extensive spy networks. It was unlikely this held any truth.

"As you're aware, our two kingdoms have been at war for some time. Part of war is the accumulation of information and secrets. We've had spies inside of the Western Kingdom for years, as I'm sure your father has within our kingdom. It is an assumed risk in war." King Veras poured himself a glass and took a sip. "One of our most trusted informants brought us word that Queen Estra had planned to have you assassinated on your nineteenth birthday."

"Oh gods," Bree was next to fill her glass and take a big drink. Although I was skeptical of King Veras' assertion, Queen Estra was definitely capable of such a thing.

I realized then that Calak's eyes were locked on my face, reading my every emotion as the King spoke. I glanced at him, holding his stare, until the King spoke again.

"I persuaded Queen Estra that a lifetime in our 'frozen hell,' I believe you called it, would be a fitting alternative to murder, especially with the bonus of a peace treaty. We made her an offer she couldn't refuse, and she jumped at the opportunity."

"Raelle has said twice to me now that she didn't know she was coming to the Northern Kingdom," Calak spoke out. "Are you saying that they indeed took her from her home, without her father's consent and brought her into our Kingdom against her will?"

"And drugged me," I added, lifting my empty glass.

"Damn," Bree refilled her glass and then filled mine.

Calak's eyes met mine again as I continued, "the Queen called me into her private lounge on my nineteenth birthday. My brothers had offered to come with me, but I insisted I would be fine to go on my own. After a brief conversation, she had her personal guards apprehend me and forced a white powdery substance into my mouth, which limited my ability to fight off my abductors. The wretch knew I wouldn't make it easy for her henchmen, so she needed to even the odds."

"I didn't know about the drugs and I apologize for the violent manner in which you came into our kingdom. I assure you, it was all to preserve your life." King Veras seemed genuine. I wanted to believe he meant that.

"What do you mean, 'even the odds'?" Bree stared at me curiously.

"My brother Danier has trained me nearly every day for the past ten years in all forms of combat and weaponry."

"It's true. She took out Raiders during the attack using Sloan's bow." Calak reported. "Danier is renowned, even here in the Northern Kingdom, for his skill."

"Yea well, his aim with a bow is laughable." King Veras chuckled under his breath as Calak lifted a corner of his lip. Almost a smile, but not quite.

"Oh, I am absolutely taking you into the training circle as soon as possible," Bree could not have sounded more excited.

"So, just to make sure I'm following this correctly, you claim your spies told you that Queen Estra was going to kill me. You intervened by pretending you wanted me as your bride, so she would send me to you in exchange for a peace treaty. And this whole time my father did not know."

Liars were often hard to spot, but Holden had tried to teach me some signs that people were trying to mislead you. The way that Veras held his body and spoke made me want to believe him, but I didn't know this man or his people.

"I don't believe your father, nor your brothers,

were aware of the Queen's intentions, both to have you murdered and then to give you to me."

I let out a deep sigh, both of relief and also exhaustion. If what King Veras said was true, then my father hadn't given me away in an arranged marriage without consulting me. I desperately wanted to believe that, but it broke my heart to think of the pain he'd now be experiencing. I was far away from him, unsure if I'd ever see him again. Unsure if, or when, I'd return home.

"Wait, why offer a peace treaty if you get nothing in return?" I pointed my question towards the King, but Bree was the one to answer.

"We've been actively looking to end the war with the Western Kingdom for a while now. Our people have no desire to continue to pour resources and soldiers into a war with no end in sight."

"But what about avenging your father's death?" I turned to ask King Veras.

"Well, that's the reason Bree and Calak are here. We've just received confirmed reports that my father's death was not the cause of a scrummage between Western spies and the Northern convoy. The Western spies were sent by a tip received through Queen Estra's contacts. The Queen herself falsified the tip. When the Western spies did not recover the information they went out to seek, and turned towards home, that's when they ran into the Northern convoy."

"Yes, we knew this, Veras." The fact that Calak had just used the King's first name without his title did not go unnoticed by me.

"What we didn't know is that while the scrummage took place, an assassin from the Eastern Kingdom snuck into the chaos and murdered my father. They staged the entire thing to look as if it was a Western spy. Thus leading to the Decade War which bled both our kingdom and Western Kingdom of its valuable resources, including the lives of our soldiers, while the East has profited from outrageous import taxes over the past decade. It made King Sutton the richest and arguably most powerful leader in Garth."

"How accurate is this information?" Bree asked.

"Three different sources have verified it. The Eastern Kingdom sent Princess Estra to marry King Wren and plant false information into their spy network. Then they sent their best assassin to intercept the scrummage between our two kingdoms and murder my father. King Sutton may be old, but the bastard plans. And we've all been paying for it ever since."

I emptied my glass and refilled it.

"Damn!"

CHAPTER ELEVEN

BACK IN MY BEDCHAMBER, I replayed the rest of the conversation with King Veras in my head.

"I believe that the best way to ensure your safety, Raelle, is for us to continue with the ruse of our engagement. You'll have the benefit of my household guard, as well as the eyes of the entire kingdom on you. Until we know the extent of the Eastern Kingdom's reach, we need to take every precaution. Calak, I want a member of your Unit with Raelle at all times. If we require your Unit outside of the castle, then Bree will step in."

"Veras, a group of Raiders attacked us last night. It was completely unprovoked. I'm not sure what lies Leon is feeding you, but he has no interest in peace." Calak was

getting worked up. This seemed like a conversation they'd had before.

"We'll deal with Leon and the Raiders in time. I know the threat, Cal, but for the sake of the people, I need to attempt at a peaceful resolution." Calak did not look convinced, but the King continued anyway. "In the meantime, we need to prepare for the feast tomorrow, where I will introduce Princess Raelle to the Kingdom as my betrothed. Then we can work through the logistics of what the next few months will look like while we gather intelligence and come up with a plan."

I just sat there, staring down at the table, scratching my left arm, while the sound of their three voices drowned out. What the King suggested was a lot for my mind to process. Queen Estra was a spy in our home. She may have made plans to have me killed. Were my father or brothers in danger? King Veras planned to announce me as his future bride in a few days. We had just arrived. I wasn't ready for this yet. And then there was the Raider attack, which was the first time I had...oh gods, I still hadn't processed that yet.

Was it getting hot in here? I needed some air. My Father would be home by now. I already missed Dalia and Holden. All I wanted was for Danier to burst through those doors with Kolt, who'd grab my hand and take me home. I shouldn't be here. This is not where I should be. I could feel myself unraveling. I needed to get out of this room before I became unhinged.

I stood abruptly from my seat. King Veras and Calak also stood as Bree eyed me warily.

"I would like..." I paused, trying to let my jumbled thoughts settle into a course of action for my next move. "I mean, I think I need some air."

I walked towards the doors and pushed my way through. The guards standing watch didn't even glance my way as I looked down the hallway, trying to remember which way my bedchamber was. Left. I'm pretty sure it was left. I turned quickly and started walking. At some point my feet picked up and before I knew it, I was jogging down the corridor, then up the staircase before I passed the familiar alcove. With just a few more steps, I was in front of my door. I pushed it open and went straight for the window.

And here I was. Staring out into a strange world that I didn't belong in. I was panting, and I felt my hands shaking. I darted my eyes around, trying to focus on something, anything. My heart was racing, and I felt dizzy. Suddenly there was a knock at my door and before I could say anything, Calak pushed his way in. He took a few steps in my direction and then paused as I turned to him. I knew he was standing there, but I couldn't focus on him. I couldn't focus on anything.

"Are you okay?"

"No. I don't know. It's just a lot and I really, I need... I need you to punch me."

Calak's eyes shot open. "What?"

"No, just try to punch me. I need to fight. I need to do something. Just, please, fight me."

I thought Calak was about to protest as his lips thinned and eyes narrowed, but he took a step towards me and I lifted my shaking hands in a defensive position. "Just do it."

Calak hesitated.

"Raelle, if you need to talk, we can just-" I landed a right hook across his jaw as his neck recoiled from the impact. It was a risk. I hadn't really thought it through, but I needed him to engage me. He cursed and readied himself for a fight. Good.

"Fine. No talking. Whatever you want, Princess."

He jabbed with his left. I easily blocked it as we

paced in a circle. Kicking out, I clipped the side of his kneecap. Calak stumbled for a second, but regained his footing. Was he smiling? My head was buzzing as I tried to shake the feelings out of me.

I lunged towards him, attempting to catch him off guard and failed. Calak expected my move and countered it with a blow to my abdomen. It wasn't very hard. He was pulling his punch. This would normally annoy me, but I just needed to move my body. He blocked my next punch, gripping my fist in his hand. Struggling to break free, I spun around, using his own body weight to flip him over my back and onto the ground.

"Seriously?"

Calak sounded more pissed off than hurt. He jumped back to his feet. Before he could make another move, I kicked out and swiped his leg out from under him. He stumbled backwards but caught his balance, taking a stride forward and throwing his left fist towards me. I turned, but not before his punch grazed my rib. It didn't hurt, but it launched me into a feral release of emotions.

We fought. Occasionally landing a blow, nothing that would leave a mark. Just enough to release the panic that had been building inside of me. Calak reached out and grabbed my wrist, twisting me around so my back was pressed against his stomach. Just as close as we had been on the horse. He used his other hand to restrain my arms as we both stilled, catching our breath.

I blew out loudly. His hold was firm, but silent. He waited for me to gather myself. Letting my head fall back and rest on his firm, heaving chest, the emotions of the last few days melted away and somehow his hold went from restraining me to embracing me.

I kept my eyes closed though, as I breathed in the comfort his touch brought.

"That was the first time I'd ever killed anyone." My eyes still closed, Calak just listened. "Today. The Raiders. Practicing shooting an arrow and fighting with my brothers is one thing, but I've never actually been in a proper fight before. I thought it would be harder, you know, to shoot at a real person, but it just happened. I didn't even really think about it."

Calak held me silently, as my tired voice continued with the confession.

"What a damn mess. You know, it was my birthday and she, the Queen, just ripped everything away from me; my family, my friend and my home. And what can I do? Nothing. I thought about fighting back when you opened that carriage door, but I knew I wouldn't make it that far with my muscles spent and still recovering from the drug. And now, I'm pretending to be engaged to a stranger, about to be presented to a kingdom, and I hate crowds. I just..."

Calak let me go and I stepped forward towards my bed. I turned and sat down on the edge, taking in another deep breath.

"I'm not weak."

"I know."

"It's just, a lot."

"Yes, it is."

"Thank you for that. It helps me refocus."

Calak was silent as he leaned against one of the sitting chairs by the fireplace. I looked up at him then and he was staring at the floor. With his arms crossed against his chest, the corded muscles popped in his forearms, defined and covered in tattoos. I couldn't make out the mix of pictures and words from here.

"Veras is a good man. You're safe here and once the threat is over, he won't keep you against your will."

"I know you believe that, but you're all strangers to me."

Calak looked up at me then. Was I safe here? I didn't know these people at all. So far, everyone seemed nice enough, and no one had tried to hurt me. There was that issue with Calak admitting to being a murderer, but my gut told me there was more to that statement. Besides, I just fought him hand to hand, alone in a room, and he didn't kill me or take advantage of me. Although I suppose King Veras wouldn't like it very much if he did either of those things. What kind of man are you, Calak? The question rolled through my head as we held each other's gaze for a few more moments before the door opened and Bree walked in.

"So, is everything all good here? You looked like you were going to puke when you ran out of the room."

"I'm okay now. I just needed some air."

I looked back up at Calak, and he was still staring at me. He nodded and turned to his sister.

"I'll send someone up to take the first shift tonight. Then we'll sort out some kind of schedule later. If you've got her, I'll head down to the barracks and let the Unit know the plan."

Bree nodded as Calak headed towards the door and left. Bree watched him leave and then turned on a heel to face me, "Yeah, I'm pretty sure I'm missing something here, but whatever. You look like you could use a bath. I'll have someone come up and draw you one. Do you wish to change before you have your dinner?"

"I didn't bring any clothes."

"Oh right! We'll get you fitted for some new clothes in the morning. Listen, Raelle," she reached out and grabbed my hands from my lap and gave them a squeeze, then gently pulled me to my feet. "It's going to be okay. I can't imagine what's going through your mind, but I'm sorry, truly. Calak mentioned that you might have some bruises from before you got here? Is that something that happened a lot? Were you mistreated?"

"No, it's not like that. It happened when the Queen's guards grabbed my arms. I tried to fight, but their grip was tight. I honestly haven't even looked at it myself yet. And this," I touched my forehead, "happened in the carriage. I fell when it jerked forward, then I blacked out."

"Well, I've got something we can rub on the muscles and bruises that will help. Raelle, no one will ever hurt you here. You have my word."

I smiled at her, and a bit of calm rushed through my body. Bree released my hands and went to the door. She called out to someone in the hall about a bath and then came back inside. Two women entered after her and made quick work in the bathing chamber, filling the bathtub and pouring oils into the water.

A few moments later, another knock at the door revealed Bowan, looking well rested and dressed in a plain black tunic and brown pants. He had a sword strapped to his side and a dagger on his right leg.

"Nice room, Princess."

He was being kind, so I smirked as the women left the bathing chamber announcing that it was ready for me. I walked towards the sound of water and the smell of lavender, then shut the door behind me. Bree and Bowan had a muffled conversation, and I heard my bedroom chamber door close.

I undressed and slowly lowered my body into the steaming water. I winced as the water reached my sensitive areas, but the aching muscles screamed in delight. With my entire body submerged, I pushed my neck back to rest along the edge.

I tried to relax my mind, but all I kept imagining was the feel of Calak's arms wrapped around me as he held me tightly against his body. Hoping the water could help wash away the images, I let my entire head fall under the surface, but it didn't work.

Calak was still there.

CHAPTER TWELVE

"HAVE YOU HEARD they sent us a veritable warrior to be our Queen?"

I was out of the bath, dressed in a casual tunic and pair of pants that Bree had acquired for me. I turned my head to see Sloan entering the room. She was out of her uniform, but still armed to the teeth.

"She saved Calak's ass," she continued.

"Tell me more." Bree was lounging in one of my armchairs, but she leaned forward now. I still stood in the middle of the room, not sure where I belonged.

"We all thought the fight was over, but the Princess Warrior here wouldn't put down the bow. A Raider came running out of the tree line, sword ready to slice Cal in half, and she put an arrow right through the bastard's heart."

"I think we should take her to the training circle and see what skills they teach princesses in the West."

"That's a great idea." Sloan pointed her finger at Bree, then walked over to take a seat in the opposite chair. These women held such confidence. I was almost jealous of it. What would it be like to be so sure of yourself?

"Calak sent you up first? I thought Bowan was going to be with me tonight." I asked.

"No. I offered. Figured you'd rather have me sitting watch on your first night than any of the rest of them."

It was a thoughtful gesture, so I smiled and nodded in appreciation.

"Have you seen your friend since you arrived?"

The tone in which Bree asked Sloan this question insinuated that the term friend meant more than just an acquaintance. Likely a sexual partner.

"No, not yet. I find that patience makes for greater pleasure."

"I don't."

The two women laughed as if they shared some knowledge that I wasn't privy to.

"Well, if you're here, then I'm going to leave. I'm supposed to be at dinner tonight with the King and the Eastern delegation that brought the shipment today."

Bree stood up in front of me.

"Are you going to be alright? We didn't think that it was fair to shove you into a dignitary role on your first night. So, I've had the kitchen prepare some food to send up for your dinner."

"Thank you."

"I'll come by in the morning with the castle seamstress and see about getting you some clothes." She was almost at the door now. It still surprised me that the King's general would be involved in such trivial matters. "Oh, and don't let that one drink too much." She pointed at Sloan. "She's a sloppy drunk."

The women laughed again as Bree left. The room grew quiet, and I wasn't sure where to sit or stand, what to do or say. It must've been obvious to Sloan.

"I bet it's a shock, being in the North."

"It is."

"You know, I remember the day they crowned you as Princess."

"Really?" The casual mention of the West instantly made me feel more relaxed. I walked over and took Bree's empty seat.

"Yeah. We didn't live close to the castle, so I wasn't at the ceremony. But the village had a celebration. Any reason to break out the good wine."

I smiled, but it faded as my thoughts went to my family. I should be at home, having dinner with my brothers, listening to them argue over who should get the last scoop of potatoes.

"Kiss, marry, or kill?" Sloan had placed her feet up on the table between us.

"Pardon?"

"It's a game. Kiss, marry, or kill?"

"I don't know what that means."

"Let's use the Unit. Out of the four of them, if you had to, who would you kiss? Who would you marry? And who would you kill?"

I was dumbfounded.

"And for fun, let's add the King into it."

"I couldn't pick one of them to kill."

"Fine. Make it punch, if killing is too severe for you."

Kiss, marry, or punch? I didn't know Sloan well. This could be a trap to get me to admit to something, or she may just be playing a harmless game with me. Being exhausted from such an emotional day, a game actually seemed like fun at the moment. So, I played along.

"Marry the King."

"Boring." Sloan bellowed out. "You have to say that."

She was right. I couldn't very well put someone else in a hypothetical marriage with me, but it was just a game. And technically, my marriage, or future marriage, to Veras was only a ruse. I wasn't sure if Sloan knew that part yet, so I thought it best to keep it to myself for the night.

"Who would you kiss, then?"

This seemed like a dangerous game to play. What if she told people what I said and a rumor went out. Although Sloan didn't seem like the type to worry about petty gossip. Unsure what to do, I just said the first thing that came to my mind.

"Kiss Yuri."

"Mmm. Good choice. Great kisser."

My eyes bulged, and she grinned.

"And now, who'd you punch?"

I stalled. Honestly, I wouldn't punch any of them. Except maybe Calak, but I'd already punched him today.

"I don't know. Rig? But only because I know I couldn't hurt him." I blurted out.

Sloan roared, laughing. Something about the pure joy of the sound coming from her made me happy, so I joined her.

There was a knock at the door, and Sloan went to answer. A kitchenmaid I recognized from earlier curtsied as she entered and placed a tray overflowing with food on the table in front of me.

"Thank you." I made certain to make eye contact with her before she turned and quickly left the room.

After the food was mostly eaten by Sloan, I got myself ready for bed.

"I'll be out in the hall. Someone will come relieve me, so I won't be here in the morning."

"Thank you, Sloan, for tonight. It helped."

"Anytime, Raelle."

Sloan left my room, and I crawled into the unfamiliar bed. Getting comfortable was difficult. I was accustomed to my mattress at home.

The fire was still glowing slowly on the other side of the room. I laid on my back, watching the shadows move across the ceiling. My mind was flooded with thoughts and worries. Sleep was not going to come easily.

Trying every technique I could think of to calm my mind, I resorted to just tossing and turning. Listening to the sounds of the new castle. There were faint animal calls from outside my window. The occasional scuffle of someone walking past my door, which was no doubt guarded by Sloan or another member of the Unit.

What a terrible job for these warriors. I felt guilty. Did they resent me? Sloan didn't seem upset when she was here with me earlier, but that didn't mean she enjoyed what the King had asked of them. I decided I would do my best to thank them as often as I could and try to make their jobs easy.

I'm not sure how many hours passed by, but my stomach, likely angry that I didn't indulge in the feast they had sent me for dinner, grumbled in protest. Trying to ignore it, I turned to count the stars I could see in the sky through my window, but it was no use. The grumble turned to acute pains of hunger. I wondered if Sloan was still standing watch. Maybe it'd be possible to get something to eat this late in the night, or early in the morning. I honestly couldn't tell what time it was.

I threw off the blankets and wrapped one around myself. The fire had almost completely died out, and the room was chilly. Heading to the door, I dragged it open and saw Calak sitting on the ground across the corridor.

His eyes squinted when he saw me.

"What's wrong?"

He was standing now.

"Nothing. I thought maybe Sloan would still be here."

"Do you need something?"

"I was just hungry. It's fine. I can wait."

I started to close the door, but Calak's hand was already there, blocking it from closing.

"We can't have the King's future bride starving in her bedchambers," he jested, the faint evidence of a smile forming on his lips.

"It's fine. I don't want to trouble anyone."

"Well, I'm already troubled. Put some clothes on and we can raid Clara's pantry. There's bound to be something hiding in there we can scrounge up."

Wanting to refuse the offer, I started to say no, but my stomach again groaned in protest at that thought. So I simply nodded my head and closed the door, this time without Calak's hand blocking it.

After I'd thrown my tunic and pants back on, I grabbed a small blanket to cover my shoulders. The castle was quite cool, and I'd had enough shivering this week to last a lifetime.

"Ready?" Calak asked when I joined him in the hallway.

"Lead the way."

We walked side by side through the empty, dark corridors.

***

"You said that you'd punch Rig?" Calak barked out a sound that I assumed was a laugh. We were sitting on the counters of the kitchens. My mood was cheery after finding quite the stash of delectables. We'd been engorging on a rare midnight buffet, and it surprised me how easily the conversation was flowing between us.

"I'd like to see that."

"I had little choice. I figured he could handle a punch, so maybe it wouldn't matter."

"You don't think I could handle your punch?"

"I think you seemed a little surprised by my right hook today."

Calak's eyes were fixed on me and I couldn't place the emotion behind them. He said nothing, just bit his bottom lip and picked up another grape.

"Who was your kiss?"

I swallowed. Did I trust Calak enough to keep feeding him this information? But then again, it was just a stupid game. Anyone could see that. I just needed to relax.

"Yuri."

"I knew I saw something in your eyes when he was cleaning your wound."

Instantly regretting my decision to tell him, I became defensive.

"There was no look in my eyes."

"Oh, come on, girls love it when a man takes care of them."

I scoffed.

"Not all girls. And it would take more than just a few dabs of ointment on my head for me to kiss someone."

"What would it take?"

Oh gods. Dangerous question to answer. I was alone, in a poorly lit room with a strange man I'd only known for a handful of days. I'd already imagined myself wrapped up in his body, albeit it was to stop from freezing to death, but still. And I'd admitted that I found him handsome. It was time to shut this conversation down.

"I, uh, wanted to thank you for getting me to the castle safely." What a ridiculous thing to say. I'd officially killed the fun mood.

"Sure." He slid off the counter and started cleaning up our mess.

"Here, let me help." I lifted a bowl filled with some kind of pudding, but as I shifted myself to the floor, the bowl slipped from my hands and landed down the front of Calak's tunic. My eyes wide, I threw my hand over my mouth to stop the laughter building. He was a mess.

Unsure if Calak was frustrated or not, he looked down at the pudding for a long minute, then slowly lifted his head to me.

"You think this is funny?"

I shook my head from side to side, but my giggles proved otherwise.

"Hm, is it funny now?" Calak grabbed a handful

of the pudding and pushed it across my cheek. The laughing stopped as I stood there, shocked. Not really thinking it through, I grabbed whatever food was left on the counter and threw it at him. He ducked, but I could hear him laughing now. I was laughing too. We were engaged in a legitimate food fight. If Clara had walked in, I'm not entirely sure what she would say, but I had a feeling that Calak could charm his way even out of this.

When we were out of ammunition, we sat on the floor of the kitchen, backs resting against the counter. Calak turned his head to look at me.

"You wear it well. Vanilla pudding is definitely your color." I chuckled, wiping a line of the pudding off my face with my finger. Holding it in front of me, I had every intention of licking it clean, but then Calak grabbed my hand. He pulled it towards his mouth and slid his lips over my finger, sucking every morsel of food off of it.

I froze.

Once he was finished, Calak released my hand and flashed me a dangerously attractive grin as he hoisted himself up from the ground.

What just happened?

CHAPTER THIRTEEN

WITH THE MEMORIES OF MY FOOD FIGHT with Calak last night fresh on my mind, I desperately tried to focus as the castle seamstress worked to take my measurements. She spoke quickly to her assistant, a small boy whose job, it seemed, was to remember everything this woman said.

Bree was standing by my window, looking down at something that was clearly more interesting than me being turned around in circles, raising my arms, and then lowering my arms. I was expecting a member of the Unit to be with me, as the King had suggested that Bree would only intervene if they were otherwise engaged. I was grateful that she was here; something about her put me at ease.

There was a knock at my bedchamber door and it slowly opened. King Veras walked in, followed by Calak. My breath caught as we made eye contact. There was a hint of amusement in his eyes as he bore witness to my ridiculous positioning. The seamstress was measuring my inseam. My legs were spread apart, and she was straddled on a stool in between them.

"Your Majesty." The woman stood and curtsied, as the small boy bowed. Was I meant to do that? No one had told me how to properly greet King Veras when he entered a room.

"We just came by to see how Princess Raelle was this morning." Veras was talking about me, but seemed to address the entire room.

"She will be fitted with the most beautiful dresses in all the North, perhaps all of Garth, when I'm finished." The seamstress flashed a ridiculously full smile to the King and fluttered her eyelashes. I knew that my engagement to him was a ruse, but she didn't know that. I was impressed and annoyed at the nerve she had to flirt with him in front of me.

"Are we all finished here?" I asked. Drawing her attention back to me.

"Yes, Princess. I'll have some things for you to try on in a day or two."

"Thank you."

She made quick work of gathering her supplies and shuffled out of the room, her little assistant in tow.

Once the door was shut, Calak spoke up. "If Raelle doesn't want to marry you, Veras, I think that woman would."

The King laughed as Bree left my window and plopped herself down on the edge of my bed. She patted the spot next to her, an invitation for me to join her, and I quickly complied. King Veras and Calak took the two seats by the fire, turning them to face us.

"Fresh reports from our network of spies arrived this morning," Veras announced. Calak looked in my direction.

"We're going to do this now? Here?" I assumed he was referring to the fact that I was in the room with them. This appeared to be an informal meeting of the King and his two advisors, about to discuss kingdom secrets. Should I be here for this conversation? But they were in my bedchamber.

"Raelle is part of our court now." That was the King's only response before he continued. No one argued with him. "There have been more riots in the East. Mostly contained to the larger cities. Reports of shipments from the continent being burned and destroyed. King Sutton has increased the number of public executions to deter the rebels."

All of this was brand new information to me. I'd never heard of such things happening in the East. I worked very hard to conceal my shock as the King continued.

"The West continues to struggle with the fertility of their crops. The soil has turned to clay, causing a record number of farmers to burn their yields this season."

"Wait, what did you say?" I asked.

"The crops in the West are failing," Veras repeated himself. My confusion must have been clear on my face, as all three of them were looking at me now.

"Since when?"

"Raelle, the West has struggled to grow things for decades now. The worst being in the last few years. Slowly, all the land is becoming unusable to the local farmers. You really didn't know?" Bree asked me.

I shook my head. It was possible this was another lie. An attempt for them to fill my mind with false stories and fears.

"I've lived in the West for ten years and not once have I heard tell of this."

"Have you been to many farms?" Calak's question held a smidgen of condescension.

"No, I haven't. But our cooks can get the produce they need for meals. If there were supply issues, I believe I would have noticed."

"Not likely," Calak continued. "King Wren famously stocks his pantries well." I didn't like the way he spoke about my father.

"Let's table this topic and move on. There's been a disturbing report from the Southern Kingdom." Veras was looking directly at Bree now. "Someone made an assassination attempt on King Adock."

Calak, who had been staring at the ground, also looked at Bree.

"Was it successful?" Bree's tone was cool, lacking her usual warmth.

"No. He survived. According to our scouts." No one spoke for a moment.

"Too bad." That was all Bree said, and it piqued my curiosity. What had the Southern King done or said to make the general commander of the Northern army want him dead? I supposed in the game of war and peace that the kingdoms played, it likely didn't need to be a major grievance.

"So basically the world's still falling apart, as it has been for decades now." Calak surmised the reports Veras had shared fairly accurately.

"That's the gist of it." King Veras sat further into the chair he was sitting on, looking anything but relaxed. I didn't know there was so much unrest and instability across Garth. When Kolt taught me the histories and the workings of the kingdoms, he mentioned none of this. Of course, there was no way for me to confirm that anything the King had just shared was true. I'd have to wait and decide for myself.

"Who's coming to dinner tonight?" Calak asked.

"The usual dignitaries and a few guests that are visiting from outlying villages," Veras responded.

"And it's mandatory?" It didn't sound like Calak enjoyed this type of dinner, either.

"Yes. It's mandatory." The King didn't sound sorry at all about making his tracker attend which caused an exaggerated huff to come from Calak.

"Speaking of the dinner, you men need to bug off. We've got lots to do before tonight, and I don't need you gawking around while we do it." The two of them stood as Bree practically pushed them out the door. Once it was closed, she turned around and sighed. "We don't actually have that much to do, but I could hear Calak getting moody and I don't have the energy for that today."

I smiled.

I liked Bree.

***

Yuri came to stand watch over me that afternoon. I had nothing to do until later that night, when Bree said she'd return with dresses for me to try on for the dinner, so Yuri took me for a walk around the castle.

He took his time explaining the meaning behind different portraits and tapestries that hung around the corridors. Mostly, everyone I passed on our walk greeted me with a curtsey or bow, sometimes a smile or a short "Welcome to the North, Princess." A few of those we passed just glared at me, hurrying past us without saying a word, but I could hear them whisper softly behind our backs.

"Ignore them," Yuri tried to encourage me.

"I am."

"People are quick to judge what they don't know or understand. In time, the people in the North will come to love you if you allow them to see who you really are."

It was a nice thing for him to say, but I doubted it would happen. I wasn't very good at winning people over. That was something that Kolt, or likely King Veras, would be great at. I was more inclined to say something sarcastic or challenging. That's why I avoided crowds; too many people to impress and charm.

After a few hours of walking, I asked Yuri to bring me back to my room so I could properly bathe and get myself ready for whatever I was to face at dinner that night. Bowan and Bree were waiting inside of my chamber when we arrived.

"About time. Where'd you take her for a walk? Back to the West?" Bowan barked out at Yuri, who just grinned at the old man and nodded his head towards me before taking his leave. I didn't even have time to thank him for the pleasant afternoon. I'd be sure to do that the next time I saw him.

"Well, I'm on babysitting duty tonight, Princess."

"I don't need a babysitter."

"Well, the King feels otherwise." Bowan was right. The King had specifically asked the Unit to watch over me while they determined if there was any immediate threat to my life. I should be more grateful for their service.

"I think I'll take a bath before dinner." I moved

towards the bathing chamber, then stopped, realizing I didn't know who to ask to help me with that.

"Um." Turning back towards Bree, she just smiled at me.

"I'll let the chambermaids know." She popped out of the door, leaving me alone with Bowan. He looked about as uncomfortable about the situation as I did. Neither one of us looked directly at the other. After a few moments, Bree returned. Thank the gods.

"They'll be in momentarily."

"Thank you."

"I found some dresses you could borrow for tonight. I'll fetch them while you bathe, as well as that salve for your arms."

"What's wrong with her arms?" Bowan asked. He looked concerned.

"Just some bruises," I explained.

"Bruises? From who?" Bowan's voice was austere, and his attention was fully on me.

"Some guards that brought me to the North."

"If anyone here, and I don't care if it's the fucking King himself, lays a hand on you, you come directly to me. Understand?" The protectiveness in his voice took me aback. If I hadn't been so shocked, I think the display of fatherly concern would've stirred me. The way he said that reminded me of Danier. I nodded in agreement.

A chambermaid knocked on the door. Once inside, she quickly got to work, and I escorted myself into the bathing chamber suddenly feeling exhausted.

CHAPTER FOURTEEN

FIVE YEARS AGO.

"So, what does a spymaster do, anyway?"

I passed Holden the bow as I hoisted myself up onto the ruins where he already stood. We were on the south side of the castle. These outbuildings had been abandoned for centuries, which made them the perfect spot for target practice.

"I don't know exactly and it's not called a spymaster. I'm just going to learn how the intelligence network works, so eventually I can take it over. Lord Trenton will explain more tomorrow when I meet with him and father, but it sounds pretty bad ass."

"It sounds dangerous."

"Awe, come on Rae, what's life without a little danger?"

At that, Holden jumped up onto the top ledge of the ruin, which was only half a foot wide. He wobbled slightly at first as he caught his balance, then grabbed an arrow from the quiver on his back and nocked it.

"Ten pence says I can hit the old elm tree from here."

"Nice try. I've seen you hit that elm tree a dozen times."

"Fine." Holden glanced around the clearing between the ruins and the castle walls. "Twenty pence says I can knock that jar off the ledge in the kitchen window."

"Holden. That's at least two hundred feet away and the jar is tiny. There's no way."

"So, take the bet."

"Fine. Twenty pence says you can't knock that jar off the window ledge."

Holden grinned as he pulled back the arrow, took a few breaths, and then released it. We watched it fly quickly through the air towards the castle, heading right for the kitchen window. Damn, he was going to make it.

I spoke too soon; the arrow flew right through the kitchen window, just left of the jar. The faint sound of pots clanging against the stone floor rang all the way out to the ruins. Surprised, I turned to Holden.

"Damn," he said, his eyes, just as wide as mine, flicked over to me and then we burst out laughing.

Leaving all bets aside, we continued with target practice, using the elm and other landmarks around the castle grounds. When the sun got low, we gathered up the rest of our arrows and made our way back. While we approached the lower east entrance of the castle, deep in conversation about which dessert was better, chocolate cake or apple pie, Kolt appeared in the doorway.

He was holding an arrow. The arrow – the one that Holden shot through the window. Oh gods, we were in trouble.

"The new cook, Marjorie, was preparing dinner when

her, um, rear was grazed by this arrow. Lucky for you two, Mister Verns said that it was just a scratch, however she won't be able to sit down comfortably for at least a week."

"Oh."

I looked at Kolt, trying desperately to stifle the giggle I could feel forming inside of me. I felt terrible, but Holden had literally shot her in the ass.

"Should, uh, we apologize for being such a pain in her ass?"

Holden didn't get the words out before breaking into a boyish giggle. That was it. I couldn't hold it in. We were both shaking from laughter. I glanced up at Kolt, who was doing his best not to join us, but the tension at the corner of his mouth gave him away. He knew this was hilarious.

"Well, as an apology, Father has offered both of you to serve as dishwashers after dinner tonight."

With that, he pushed the arrow towards Holden's chest and turned to walk away. With a sigh and a roguish smile, Holden looked at me as we walked into the castle.

***

"Raelle, are you finished?"

The sound of Bree knocking on the bathing chamber door woke me up. My fingers had not yet pruned, so I didn't sleep for that long.

"Almost." I quickly washed myself off then got out of the water, dripping onto the stone floor as I reached for a towel to dry myself.

"Is Bowan still out there?"

"No, he jumped out as soon as he saw me arriving down the hallway with these dresses."

Knowing that the coast was clear, I wrapped the towel around my body and opened the bathing chamber door, water still dripping from me as I shuffled across the room to where Bree stood.

"Now, we've got just a few options." She held up a dress that was long and simple. The sleeves were tight along the biceps, but flared out slightly as they opened up. It was a deep crimson. "This one is plain, but classic." Then she picked up a dress that was made of a satin, it gathered along the shoulders, giving them a puffed look. The sleeves ran tight all the way down the arm. The bottom of the dress was bunched up in places, adding lots of volume. It clinched at the waist and the fabric crisscrossed across the chest. It was a deep green and definitely not what I was wearing tonight. "I can tell by the scrunch of your nose that this is a no." She threw the green dress on top of the first one and picked up the third dress she brought. "Now this one gets my vote." The last dress was ivory and fit tightly around the waist. There was a silver belt that wrapped around the hips and hung delicately down the front of the dress to the floor. It had a scooped neckline and sleeves that were loose fitting, opening up very wide at the ends. It was perfect. The dress had the slightest train pooling on the floor behind it and a hood fixed on the back. The sleeves, hood and train were all trimmed out in white fur. I reached out to touch the fabric. It was sturdy but smooth. "Before you try it on, let me have a look at those bruises."

Bree placed the dress on the bed and pulled a tin from her bag. Unscrewing the lid, I immediately recognized the smell. It was just like the treatment that Danier always had me use. She turned to me and inspected the marks along my arms.

"Bastards," she muttered as she slowly rubbed the salve onto my skin.

I took a moment to glance down at the marks.

Multiple purple dots covered the upper half of my arm, all from the fingers of the men who'd grabbed me. They really were bastards. I dropped the towel and stepped into the dress. It slid up my torso perfectly. Bree started tying the laces on the back.

"Did you grow up in the North?"

"Yes. Calak and I were born right here, in Castle Mount."

"Did your parents work in the castle?"

"Our mother was the chief storyteller and advisor to the previous King."

"And your father?"

"We never met our father. Our mother never spoke of him. I suppose Bowan would be the closest thing we had to a father. He was also an advisor to the King and loved my mother very much, so he stepped in to help her raise us, even though my mother couldn't love him the way he loved her."

"That's beautiful. And sad."

"I know."

"Wait, Yuri told me that Bowan got his scar after the woman he loved disappeared. Was that your mother?"

"She was last seen entering the Raiders encampment, escorted by Leon. No one ever saw her again. Bowan went looking for her, but she was already gone. He never told us the details, but he didn't need to. He lost a piece of himself that day. We all did, I suppose."

"I'm sorry. Do you remember much about her?"

"We were about seventeen when she left, so I remember everything about her. I remember the way Calak made her laugh, the smell of her hair when I hugged her, every story she ever told us."

Bree pulled tight on the laces as I sucked in air.

"What's a storyteller?"

"A storyteller keeps our history. They pass down

stories and wisdom to the next generation. It's a very revered position here. Veras always wanted to be a storyteller. I think he would have, had he not become King."

"Why do you call the King by his first name?"

Bree laughed softly, "We all grew up in the castle together like family. Behind closed doors, he's Veras, but in front of anyone besides each other and Bowan – and I suppose you too now – he's King Veras. We'd never dishonor him that way."

I nodded. Bree was loyal. I admired it. She finished up with the laces on my back and I took a step towards the mirror in the corner of my room to inspect myself. I ran my hands down the front of the dress to straighten it out. I glanced up at my reflection and my breath caught for a moment. It was stunning.

"This dress is amazing. Where did you get it?"

"It belonged to my mother. I rarely have occasion to wear such things, so I'm glad it's getting some air tonight."

"Thank you."

I spent the next half hour brushing out my curls and squeezing my feet into the slippers Bree found for me to wear. I straightened the necklace my brothers had bought me, taking one more look at myself in the mirror.

"I haven't seen that dress in a very long time."

Turning to see Bowan standing at the door, I hadn't even noticed that Bree had left. She had likely taken the extra dresses and her bag back to her room.

"If you're ready, I'm to escort you to the formal dining room." He extended his arm for me to hold, and I reached up for it. I nodded as he led me away.

"Thank you," Bowan turned his head towards me, a bit confused. "For protecting me on the way here and

I know that looking after a princess probably isn't the best use of your time, but I appreciate it."

"When the King asks you to guard something that he considers priceless and irreplaceable, it is an honor."

I smiled at him. My hand was still resting on his arm.

"And where'd the hell you learn to shoot a bow like that?" He asked.

I laughed at the return of the rough old man I'd let in the forest.

"My brothers."

"Ah. Makes sense."

We headed through the corridor, past the alcove, and down a set of stairs. At the bottom, we stopped and Bowan motioned towards a closed door.

"The King would like to speak to you privately before dinner."

"Oh." I wasn't expecting that. "Okay."

Bowan pushed open the door and the King's silhouette was stark against the large window in what I assumed was a private office of some sort. There was a dull fire going in the fireplace, and multiple candles lit around the room. Bowan shut the door behind me, leaving me alone with the King for the first time. My heart raced again. I was nervous and a little excited. Why was I excited? Sometimes nervousness and excitement felt the same in my body. I'm sure I was just tired and misreading my emotions.

The King turned, and I took in the view. He was wearing a tight, white tunic which showcased his incredibly well-maintained physique. Layered over the top of the tunic was a dark green jacket lined with fur, similar to what I was wearing. The jacket sleeves puffed out slightly and had gold threading and buttons along them. His brown pants were tight, hugging his muscular thighs and tucked neatly into knee-high boots. His blond hair combed and pushed to the side. He was smiling. A warm, inviting smile. I couldn't help but reciprocate. He was a very attractive man, but could I trust him?

"You look beautiful, Raelle."

His voice was like velvet and I felt my heart skip for a moment. It was as if his words left his mouth and landed all over my body, caressing each curve. I imagined him filling the space between us with two quick strides, wrapping his arms around my waist and pulling me up to his mouth, then pressing his lips into mine with a fiery passion.

I shook my head.

What was happening to me?

CHAPTER FIFTEEN

"YOUR MAJESTY," I curtsied and lowered my head. Glancing up at him, I didn't let silence fill the room before I raced to speak first. "Bree lent me one of her mother's dresses. It was very generous of her."

"Well, it suits you."

His eyes studied me for a moment. Even though he was still on the other side of the room, I felt like he was standing right in front of me. His lips daring me to touch them.

"Thank you for joining me. I thought it best for us to speak privately before we entered the dining room."

"Oh?"

"Our conversation earlier was sudden and filled

with lots of revelations. I'm sorry you've been through so much these past few days. You must have lots of questions."

"Not really. Mostly I'm exhausted and I miss my family."

"Of course. Would you like to write to them?"

"Yes, I would love that."

"We'd have to be careful with what you share. Either the Queen or someone who has ill intentions could intercept any correspondence."

"Of course."

"We can have a letter sent first thing in the morning, if you wish."

His offer went a long way to helping me trust him.

"Raelle, I think it would be good for us to have an understanding. This is a very unconventional situation we find ourselves in and I wouldn't feel comfortable moving forward without first making sure we were both on the same page."

"Okay."

"To everyone besides Calak and Bree, we're engaged to be married. Now, people may expect a wedding immediately..."

I choked on my spit. Oh gods.

"But I believe we can put them off by announcing that you'd like to wait until your family can be present for a wedding. With the complexities of our peace treaty, it would surprise no one if having your family come to visit took months to arrange. This will buy us time."

"Okay."

"In the meantime, even with an arranged marriage, people may expect to see a measure of intimacy between us."

I wasn't breathing. I was sure that I had stopped breathing.

"I would do nothing you were uncomfortable with."

Oh, my gods. Was he going to kiss me? No, Raelle. Calm yourself.

"I'm referring to things as natural as hand holding, or placing my hand on your back to escort you somewhere. They may expect us to dance from time to time. Things of that nature. Are you comfortable with that?"

"Uh huh."

Uh, huh? That's not even a word. You made a noise. A King asked to touch you and you just made a noise. Well done, Raelle. If Dalia or Holden had been here I'd never have heard the end of it.

"Okay. I also want to give you permission to speak with me whenever you need to. You're my guest and if you need anything, you just need to ask."

"Thank you."

"Do you have questions for me?"

Did I have any questions? Probably only a thousand of them, but none of them would be asked tonight. I chose one thread to pull at.

"Do Bowan and the rest of the Unit know about our ruse?"

"I was not clear with Calak about what he would share with the Unit. Obviously, as I have charged them with your protection, he may have shared some of this with them. I will confer with Calak and advise you once I know."

"Okay."

"Tonight's dinner is a gathering of advisors, senior members of our army, and leaders from our outlying settlements. You need not answer questions you're not comfortable with. You'll sit to my left. Calak and

Bree will both be present, so you'll at least have a few familiar faces. Once we've managed this dinner and you've had the proper time to rest, then we can talk further about what these next few months will look like."

"Okay, your Majesty."

Veras smiled, "You can call me Veras in private. I know you must be in shock, and I'm asking a lot of you right now. But I hope in time you'll feel comfortable to be yourself around me. I wish to be your friend, and I hope that in time, I can prove that to you."

"I appreciate that...Veras."

With a wide grin, Veras nodded his head towards me.

"Are you ready to meet the Northern Kingdom, Raelle?"

"No, but I'm hungry."

"Well then," Veras chuckled, "let's not delay."

Veras placed a hand on my lower back. My skin broke out in goose pimples with awareness of his touch. His hand rested gently across the fabric of my dress, but he led me towards the doors with authority. Bowan was waiting in the hall for us.

"Good to see you got back in one piece, old man," Veras greeted him.

"And not a moment too soon, I hear. What's this about trying to make peace with the Raiders?"

"Now's not the time, but we'll talk soon, I promise."

"King Veras." Bowan gripped Veras' arm so that he couldn't move past him. "Leon's nothing but a bastard. A bastard who killed Sylvette and hundreds of our own people. We should wipe them out, not sign peace treaties."

Veras, his hand still resting on my back, looked

straight at Bowan. It was clear that the King respected this man.

"I haven't forgotten who they are or what they're capable of. I assure you. Now, release my arm so I can take my betrothed to dinner."

Bowan let go of Veras, bowed his head in respect and followed us down the hall towards a massive set of double doors. We paused briefly, and I realized Veras was giving me a moment to collect myself before we walked into the dining room.

"I probably should have mentioned this before, but I don't really like crowds."

"Just pretend they're all naked," Veras whispered into my ear.

I was not expecting that, but the lightness of what he just said sent an honest smile to my lips. Veras knocked twice on the double doors and within a moment, they both opened, the wood creaking, as the sound of chairs pushing back filled the room.

All the guests around the table had risen to their feet as a man to my right announced, "His Majesty King Veras of the Northern Kingdom and his betrothed, Her Highness Princess Raelle of the Western Kingdom."

The guests erupted in cheers and clapping as Veras led me forward towards the only two empty seats in the room. Bowan walked to the left, and I recognized Rig, Yuri and Sloan standing guard against the wall. I smiled at them and Sloan winked at me. I turned my attention forward as we kept walking. There were close to fifty people at the table. I tried not to look to my left or right, as Veras pulled out my chair and I sat down. The King sat down beside me as the rest of the room also took their seats.

Instantly, conversations began, and the sounds of glasses clinking and laughter filled the room. I was grateful that the silence was over and everyone seemed to have moved on from our entrance. A servant reached over my shoulder and poured a healthy amount of wine into my glass. I immediately lifted it to my lips and took a drink.

Veras had struck up a conversation with a middle-aged man sitting on the other side of him. I felt calm listening to the many voices in the room, because as long as they were all talking to each other, then no one would focus on me, or worse, be waiting to hear me say something. The table was full of candles and the middle lined with boughs made from evergreen branches. The smell of pine and cedar wafted in the air. I took a deep breath and closed my eyes, imagining I was out in a forest clearing. Trees towering over my head, their branches stretching out towards each other, creating a canopy of shade from the sun. Faint rustles from above, proof that a breeze was blowing. Small creatures scurried about, collecting morsels of food. The ground, padded in moss, grass and fallen needles, felt soft beneath my feet. Looking up, a winter owl sat perched on the nearest tree.

A tap against my leg interrupted my visualization. I opened my eyes and saw Calak staring at me. Did he just kick me under the table?

"Wake up," he mouthed.

I scowled at him, and he smirked. Bree was sitting to his right and shamelessly flirting with a handsome man beside her. The way she talked to people was effortless. Bree laughed, insinuating that the man had said something funny, lifting her glass to her mouth and taking a drink, as the man closely monitored the movement of her lips.

"So as General of the King's army, I'm assuming

you'd be very good at telling people what to do." The man's voice was full of heat.

"I know how to get what I want." Bree leaned even closer to the handsome stranger.

I smirked and looked over at Calak. He tightened his lips as they turned up into a tiny smile, then shrugged his shoulders, lifted his glass towards me and took a drink.

"Princess Raelle," I shifted my attention to Veras as he spoke to me. "I'd like for you to meet Judd Trews." This was the name of the man sitting on the other side of the King. "Trews is a good friend to the court. He manages our timber trade with the other kingdoms."

"It's a pleasure to meet you, your Highness." Trews had the voice of someone who was always trying to sell you something, but there was a hint of slickness to him that I didn't like.

"Likewise, Mister Trews."

"As I was saying, your Majesty. Not only has the production from the sawmills consistently decreased over the past eight years, but we've had three attacks by the Raiders in the past five months. Each time, they destroy the product and machinery. I'm concerned that with production so low, we may lose business to the continent."

"I can assure you, Trews, I'm doing all I can to remove the obstacles to our timber trade."

"Perhaps we can negotiate with the Raiders. Find a solution that would benefit both sides." Trews clearly had a motive to this conversation, and I was ready to watch it all play out when Calak huffed from across the table.

"There's no negotiating with the Raiders."

Veras sat up, pushing his shoulders back. He was actively trying to negotiate peace with Leon and I was curious how he felt about this admission from Calak. They were friends, but they clearly had different perspectives on how best to deal with the threat.

"You've had over eight years to deal with this problem, Calak, and we're still losing the profits hand over fist. Maybe you aren't the best advisor to our King in this situation." Trews had no respect for the tracker across the table.

"Trews," Veras interrupted, before Calak could retort. "We'll supply the sawmills with more workforce and a contingent of soldiers to keep the peace. In the meantime, we are in talks with Leon to organize the extradition of the Raiders back to their respective kingdoms."

"Well, Leon did not sound receptive to your last offer, your Majesty."

Calak slammed his glass down on the table, and some of the conversation died down.

"And when the hell did you become so cozy with Leon, Trews?"

"Mind your business, and I'll mind mine. The point is, your tactics aren't working. It's time to try something new."

"We don't need to take advice-"

The King raised his hand and interrupted Calak.

"Trews, as always, we appreciate your insight into these matters. Let's continue this conversation tomorrow when we meet with the Treasury."

Veras motioned to the nearest servant, requesting that they bring out the first course. Trews only nodded, and Calak brooded silently across the table. Before I could let my thoughts go anywhere else, the elderly woman sitting to my left squealed with delight.

"Oh, your Highness, what a pleasure to sit by your side tonight. You know, I've met your father. King

Wren visited the Northern Kingdom some time ago and our family hosted him for dinner one evening. Isn't that right, dear?" She nudged her husband, who turned, looked at me and without saying a word, turned again. Another example that not everyone was happy I was here. "Ignore him," she whispered. "Your father was a very kind gentleman as I remember."

"Yes, he is," I smiled. It was nice to have someone who knew my family at the table.

"Your dress, it's simply stunning. Where was it made?"

"Actually, this dress belonged to my friend's mother, and she granted me the honor of wearing it tonight."

I looked up at Bree, who broke her conversation with the handsome man beside her just long enough to wink my way. She definitely heard everything that was being said around her.

"Well, what a lovely thing that is."

The arrival of our first course cut the woman's conversation short. I picked up my fork to dig into the fresh greens placed in front of me, but I could feel the burn of his stare. I raised my eyes to find Calak's eyes on me and his mother's dress. Was he upset that Bree loaned it to me?

"If I may offer a toast before we start our meal together," Veras stood up beside me and his chair groaned on its way back. "To my future bride. Princess Raelle, I look forward to earning your trust and love. My kingdom and my heart are yours. Cheers."

The table erupted in "awes," "cheers," and the clinking of glasses.

Veras took a sip from his drink, sat back down beside me and pressed a soft kiss to my cheek as he whispered in my ear, "You're doing great."

The intimacy of his lips against my skin made me flush. Gathering myself I nodded, taking a drink, still feeling the weight of Calak's stare on me, but refusing to look his way again.

CHAPTER SIXTEEN

DINNER WAS DELICIOUS. Each course better than the one before it. Clara and her kitchen maids had done an excellent job, and I planned to head down to the kitchens tomorrow to show my gratitude. Thankfully, Trews refrained from discussing Raiders and the timber trade as per the King's request, and busied himself debating farming practices with the gentleman on his other side while I listened to Veras, Calak, and Bree tell stories of their childhood.

"Calak and I were out riding together. We were about thirteen."

"Twelve," Calak corrected with a grin.

"Okay, we were twelve, and we raced each other

across a clearing. It was close, but at the last second Calak's horse picked up and took off in front of me."

"I was the better rider."

"Well, Calak's horse takes off, and he turns back to gloat on his win. I saw the tree coming, but he was so wrapped up in celebrating. When he turned to face forward, a low branch caught him in the chest and threw him off of the back of the horse. Knocked the wind right out of him."

The friends laughed, even though it sounded like they'd told this story many times. I could appreciate the value of nostalgia. Remembering the best parts of the past gave the mind a break from dealing with the stresses of the day. Looking at the three of them, they seemed harmless. Perhaps Veras was telling the truth about why I was here. I wished I could speak freely with my brothers to learn more. They'd be able to use their sources to confirm what the King had said. I'd have to communicate my concerns to them by writing nothing incriminating, just in case the letter was intercepted.

I continued to listen while the friends regaled stories from their childhood, and I marveled at how effortless their friendship was.

"Have you ever been tobogganing, Raelle?" Bree asked.

We'd had her full attention since they served the main course, and the handsome man beside her had excused himself from the table.

"I don't think so."

"What do you mean, you don't think so? I feel you'd know if you'd gone tobogganing or not." Calak took a sip of his drink with a hint of a challenge in his eyes.

"I may have when I was younger, but I don't remember."

"Where did you grow up, before the West?" Veras casually draped his arm across the back of my chair. A gesture that seemed natural for two people planning to wed.

"I don't actually have any memories before the West. When my father found me, I had no recollection of my life before washing up on that shore. He called in healers from all the kingdoms, but nothing helped to restore my memory. No one came looking for me, so I don't know where I came from before the West."

"How curious," Veras studied the side of my face.

"Well, then I'll have to take you out tobogganing sometime," Bree offered.

"I think I'd like that," I smiled and took another bite of my dessert.

Yuri approached the table and whispered something into Calak's ear. His eyebrows pressed together, his jaw clenched, as he looked over at Bree and then Veras. He nodded back to Yuri, who retreated from the table and out the double doors with Rig and Sloan by his side. Only Bowan remained behind because he was my guard for tonight. Veras removed his arm from the back of my chair and leaned forward, waiting for Calak. In a hushed voice, low enough for only the four of us to hear, Calak shared Yuri's report.

"A Raider has approached the Western gate. He says he has a message from Leon." They sat still for a moment and looked at each other until Veras nodded.

Turning to me he asked, "Are you ready to retire for the evening, Raelle?"

"I am."

Veras stood and addressed our guests, "Thank you all for joining us tonight to celebrate Princess Raelle and her arrival to our kingdom. Please stay and enjoy yourselves, but we must bid you goodnight."

He reached down for my hand and gently balanced me as I stood up, turning towards the double doors. When we reached the hall, and only once the doors were closed tightly behind us, did the group speak out again.

"Do we know the rider?" Veras asked.

"Yuri didn't recognize him," Calak responded. "It appears he has arrived alone, but they've sent out a scouting party to make sure. There's more, Veras. Raiders have sacked Hillsborough. They killed everyone. Burnt everything to the ground. One hundred and forty-three people live in Hillsborough, and the bastards killed them all, including the children."

Oh gods. One hundred and forty-three people murdered while we ate and drank, laughing about carefree days in the past. Calak looked like he was shaking. This news had unhinged him in a way. I studied the anger rolling off of each of those standing around me, but Bowan was the first to speak.

"I say we ride out and butcher them all."

"I feel your anger, Bowan. Maybe I don't show it in the same way, but trust me, I want justice too. For now, we bring the Raider to the cells for questioning. I want to speak with him. Raelle," Veras turned towards me, lowering my hand from his arm. "Thank you for this evening. Bowan will escort you back to your chamber and ensure your safety."

At that, Veras and Bree started walking down the hallway, already engaged in conversation about security details.

"He needs to make a move," Bowan said to Calak.

"I know. I hate Trews, but maybe he's right. We need to find a way to rid ourselves of this filth. Take her back to her room and make sure she stays there."

Calak talked about me like I wasn't standing right here.

"Um, she is right here and where do you get off telling me I can't leave my room?"

"Since the King has put your safety under my charge. So yes, Princess, you will stay in your room tonight because the enemy is at our doorstep and we don't exactly know why or if he came alone."

"I can protect myself if it comes to that."

"That doesn't change the fact that you're staying in your room tonight."

I crossed my arms in silent protest.

"How about I go to my room when I'm ready and you can kiss my ass."

I'm not even sure why I was fighting him on this. I was so exhausted that I would probably end up sleeping until lunchtime tomorrow. There was just something about Calak thinking he could tell me what to do that got under my skin. He stepped in closer.

"Don't test me, Raelle. Not tonight."

"Or what? It's not like you can do anything about it. I'm engaged to the King."

Calak grabbed my hand and yanked me towards a hidden alcove, pushing me against the wall.

"Let's get something clear, Princess. I don't know how they do things back in the West, but here we follow orders or people get killed. You're naïve, self-entitled, and I won't allow you to put yourself or anyone else in danger just because you don't like being told what to do. So you can either go with Bowan right now, or I'll drag you to your room and lock the door myself."

I was angry, but he was right. I didn't want to put anyone else in danger and, with an unknown threat; it was safest for me to be in my room tonight.

"Fine."

"I'll send Rig to take over at midnight." Calak was speaking to Bowan as he turned to follow Veras and Bree and walked away. I stared at the back of his head.

***

Dear Father,

I'm writing to you from the safety of Castle Mount in the Northern Kingdom. My departure from home was abrupt and I can only imagine the difficulty it has caused. The details around how and why I left are complicated, and I hope you've been able to find answers. I wanted to assure you I'm well. King Veras has been incredibly kind to me. Although I miss you all so desperately, I'm confident that we'll see each other soon. Please give my love to my brothers.

Your princess forever,

Raelle.

I folded the letter in thirds and sealed it shut. It wasn't much, but at the very least, it would assure my family that I was safe. The shock of discovering my absence would have been hard for all of them, but especially my father. I wondered what the fallout with Queen Estra would be; I hoped he would investigate her motives. My heart was sick, thinking that any of their lives could be in danger. How would Queen Estra explain herself? Or had father banished her for acting without his consent? How would that affect their diplomatic relationships with the East? Did that even matter now?

A soft flutter and tap at the pane glass caught my attention. Slowly walking towards the window, I saw a snow owl resting on the ledge as the morning sun poured in. It was magnificent. She looked around, surveying the ground below and beyond. Wanting to get a closer look, I opened the window. To my surprise, the owl didn't fly away. Her eyes scanned around, possibly searching for her next meal. I slowed my breathing, trying not to scare it away. I reached my hand up and, with two gentle finger strokes, I pet the top of her head. Her feathers were soft and her eyes were a deep shade of yellow. She turned her head towards me. I froze, returning her gaze as she cocked her head to the right and studied me.

"Beautiful," I said to her softly.

Then she shifted, flapping her wings and, in one giant leap, launched herself off the ledge. Her wings, which spanned around four or five feet, spread out, gliding her through the air towards the nearest trees. Staring out the window, I had a thought and I hurried towards my door. Flinging it open, I saw Rig standing guard against the opposite wall, resting his hand on the hilt of his sword.

"Help me with something, Rig?" I turned to go back inside of my chamber, assuming he'd follow me.

He didn't.

"Rig? You can come into my room. I just need your help with something."

He reluctantly pushed off of the wall and walked inside. I noticed he didn't shut the door behind him.

"Back home, my bed faced the windows, but here it faces the fireplace. I want to turn the bed so I can look out the window. Can you help me with that?"

He looked confused, but nodded. We each went to opposite sides of the bed. After lots of swearing, and Rig doing most of the heavy lifting, we had turned my bed so it faced the window.

"What did you two do?" Calak entered through the ajar door.

"Thank you for your help, Rig."

"Anytime, Princess."

"I told you, it's Raelle."

Rig let out a sigh and lifted his eyebrows towards Calak as he walked towards the door.

"You've got her, Cal?" Calak nodded and with that, Rig disappeared down the hall.

"I'm on watch this morning." I didn't even look at Calak. "Still upset with me from last night? I'd say that I'm sorry, but I'm not." He walked around towards the fireplace, resting his arm on the mantle. I stayed silent. "Okay, I'm sorry about the self-entitled and naïve part, but not for making you come back to your room. The threats we're facing are very real Raelle." He turned and looked at me. "Fine, don't talk, but I know you have to be hungry. Hungry enough perhaps to follow me down to the kitchens and see what Clara has this morning."

I was hungry, and Clara's food was delicious. Rolling my eyes, I sighed out, "Lead the way." Calak smirked and motioned for the door. He closed it behind us and we started walking.

I took in his appearance. Calak was rough. His hands bore calluses from years of wielding weapons and living outside the walls of a castle. His arms were covered in tattoos, which I could now see had intricate details of landscapes and people. Words weaved through the images. It reminded me of a storybook. His tunic was black and hugged the tops of his shoulders and pecs, but was looser around the midsection, where it was tucked into his pants. He had a sword hanging from his belt and a dagger strapped to his thigh.

"Get a good look?" Calak asked, and I instantly blushed. He'd obviously noticed I'd been staring at his body. "If you need a closer look I'm sure we could sneak into one of these alcoves unnoticed."

"You're an ass," I sneered as he chuckled and we continued towards the stairs. "What happened last night, with the Raider?"

"We questioned him. I wanted answers about what they did in Hillsborough."

"And did you get any? Any answers, I mean."

"Some."

We followed the smell of freshly baked bread and rosemary coming from the staircase. It led us down the cobbled stone hallway, straight towards the bustling kitchens. I paused before we opened the door.

"Why does Clara like you?"

"Why wouldn't she like me?"

"You're arrogant, insufferable, stubborn and moody, and Clara isn't someone who gives her approval away freely. And yet, somehow, you have her wrapped around your little finger."

"First, none of my fingers are 'little.' Second, I'm a delight."

I shook my head and allowed myself the briefest glance at his hands, which were, in fact, not little.

"Clara knew our mother. We spent a lot of time down in the kitchens growing up. I used to help her, and she'd teach me how to make things."

"You're serious?"

"Dead serious. I'm very good in the kitchen. So, I guess I won her over with my impressive cooking skills and charm."

We pushed through the door into the kitchens. My mouth instantly watered as the smell of cooked bacon wafted through the air. The scene was frantic. Kitchen maids shuffled past one another, running from counter to counter. A pile of apple skins, already turning brown, sat on the edge of a sink, while two maids made quick work of slicing the fruit into a bowl. Clara was standing guard over the grill, which was covered in a variety of breakfast meats. The sizzle of grease popped as she flipped each piece over.

"Good morning, Clara." The charming and playful Calak of yesterday reappeared. He planted a kiss on her cheek and grabbed a slice of bacon from the pan in front of her. "Dinner was delicious, as usual."

"Thank you, my dear."

"Mind if we grab some food, then we'll get out of your hair?"

"Of course. There's fresh fruit on the platter over there and muffins in the oven."

Calak worked his way around the kitchen, filling up two plates with various foods. A kitchen maid, who was probably around my age, eyed him from the counter where she was peeling carrots. She picked up a bowl and moved closer to where he stood. Placing the bowl on the counter, she touched his bicep. Her eyes looked him over, and she bit her bottom lip.

"Can I help you find anything?"

Her voice was soft but sultry. She was flirting with him. He smirked, still looking through a shelf in front of him.

"I've got it, but thanks, Odetta."

She lowered her hand and trudged back to her carrots. The kitchen maid was blatant; she wanted Calak.

Shaking my head to refocus, I slowly stepped towards Clara. Nervous about the strong cook, I started scratching at my left arm.

"Excuse me Clara, but I wanted to thank you and your girls for last night. It was the most delicious meal I've ever had."

Clara stopped what she was doing and turned her attention to me, wiping her brow with the back of her hand and puffing the hair out of her face that had slipped out of her tight bun.

"You're welcome, your Highness."

I grinned, not really sure what else to say to the woman. She absolutely intimidated me. Thankfully, Calak had returned to my side with plates full of delicious breakfast foods and nodded his head for me to follow him. I turned to see Odetta watching us leave with a defeated look on her face. I even saw her scowl at me.

Ignoring that, I shouted back to Clara, "Thank you again!"

Then Calak led me into the hallway.

We were halfway up the staircase when I blurted out, "Is that kitchen maid your lover?"

Calak stopped dead in his tracks and stared at me. "Why in the gods name would you think that?"

"She looked like she could be your lover?"

"Odetta?"

"Yes, the one just now in the kitchen." I pointed over my shoulder towards the doors we had just exited.

"Ha. No, I'm not sleeping with Odetta," Calak stared at me, his eyes squinting and then returning to normal.

"But you're sleeping with someone."

Damn, I was crossing a serious line if I misread our relationship. This friend-foe dance we've been doing the past couple of days had me confused.

Calak smiled, "I've slept with women. If that's what you are asking."

"Oh, gods," I shook my head, trying to erase the last few seconds. "No, that's not - never mind. Let's just keep walking." I went to take a step up, but Calak blocked me with his body.

"No. No. Let's keep talking. Why did you think she was my lover?"

"It was the way she touched you."

"She touched me?" His eyebrows popped up. "When?"

I sighed loudly, "When you were looking on the shelf, she reached up and touched your arm and asked if you needed help to find anything."

"And because of that, you thought I was sleeping with her? You asked Rig to help you move your bed this morning. Did you two sleep together?"

"What? No. I've never even...are you serious?"

"Are you?" He smiled. "Wait, you sound jealous."

"Jealous?" I pushed off the wall past him as I started climbing the stairs again. "Jealous of what, that she got to touch your arm?"

Calak started walking behind me and I could hear the grin in his words, "Oh, definitely jealous. Interesting."

"You're an ass," I muttered as I moved even further ahead of him on the stairs.

"Oh, come on, Princess." He took the steps two at a time to catch up to me. "I was only joking."

"Whatever. I shouldn't even have asked. It's not my business."

"Did you have a lover back in the West?"

I turned to him, almost causing us to collide. "What? No!"

"Why not? You're attractive. I'm sure there were lots of young men back in the West lined up to be your suitors."

"Actually, no. There weren't a lot of young men

around the castle, except my brothers. I hardly left the castle grounds."

"Your father kept you locked up pretty good, huh?"

"You know nothing about my father."

I shoved him in the shoulder. He stumbled back a step as a few grapes rolled off the plate and onto the floor. Walking past him, I found our alcove. Calak was not far behind me, setting the plates down on the table as he approached. I had walked to the far side away from him, and crossed my arms over my chest as I stared into the Evamore Dynasty tapestry.

"Have you ever had a lover, Raelle?" He was directly behind me and spoke so softly, but I didn't reply. This was not a conversation I was having with Calak. "There's nothing to be ashamed of, but if you were interested in a suitor, there are lots of young men here at Castle Mount. I could put a list together for you. Make it easier." He was still teasing me, so I turned to face him. He was close, close enough that if I reached out to grab him, it wouldn't be hard to flatten him on his ass.

"I'm engaged to the King."

"No...you aren't."

Calak stepped in closer, challenging me with his words, pushing me. I sucked in a breath. If anyone walked past us right now, it would be most inappropriate.

"You know what I meant. I couldn't very well go around with anyone else when I..." I swallowed hard. "When I'm meant to only be with the King."

Calak watched me closely, studying my face with his eyes. I knew I shouldn't, but I slowly shifted myself closer to him, like I was being pulled by an invisible force that connected us. What was I doing? He slowly lifted his left hand and tucked a white curl behind my ear. Instinctively, my face turned into his touch, and I shut my eyes. His hand lingered against my cheek as I opened my eyes and lifted my gaze to his. Clearing his throat, he dropped his hand and took a step back.

"Hungry?"

"Always," I nodded as the flush slowly drained from my cheeks, confused about the way this man made me feel. Did I like him or want to hurt him?

Either way, this wasn't good.

CHAPTER SEVENTEEN

"THAT'S A BEAUTIFUL NECKLACE."

Bree had brought me to the training circle, which was somewhere on the east side of the castle. After my invasive questioning of Calak on the stairs, followed by the awkward moment in the alcove and a quiet breakfast, it relieved me when she found us and asked if I'd like to go train with her. Calak didn't seem upset about the change of plans. He mentioned heading to the barracks to check in with the Unit.

"My brothers gave it to me for my birthday. It was the same day I left," I replied as I stretched my arms over my head. "It's a compass rose, and they said it symbolizes finding your way home. Ironic, now that I think of it. They put the three rubies on the east, west, and south points to represent them – red because of their hair. Then the diamond at the top belonged to their mother, and they placed it there to represent me."

"Hm."

"What?"

"Well, it's just that the diamond represents you, right?" Bree pointed to the top of the compass rose, "you're North."

"I suppose I am."

I unclasped the necklace and placed it on the water table, then finished stretching. My muscles were feeling better and there was only a dull ache remaining.

This training room was different from the one I was used to. The only natural light coming into the chamber was from a few windows several feet in the air. The ceiling was high, almost creating an echo. Nothing hung on the walls, but there were racks of weapons, ropes, sandbags and anything else you'd need. Being in this space instantly made me feel more relaxed.

"So, where do you want to start?" Bree had already stretched and was waiting for me.

"When I left the West, Danier was training me with a longsword. He said I needed to build up my strength so I could handle the weight of it."

"Well, in my experience," Bree walked over to the racks and picked up two longswords. "Wielding this weapon has less to do with strength and more to do with technique. Most men hold their long swords like this." Bree handed me the extra sword and backed up while she held hers with two hands. "But I find if you adjust your grip and raise your hands up the hilt, you get a more precise strike. Stand placing your right foot forward." I took a few steps back and copied the position of her body.

"Now, with your arms in front of you, slightly bend your elbows, but keep your arms at the height of your sternum. Yes, like that. Now, moving only your wrist and your forearm, swing the sword back over your left shoulder, up over your head and down, slicing your opponent from their neck to their hip."

I followed her instructions as she moved closer and corrected my position. "Yes, just like that. And you can even make your circles bigger." She showed me using her own sword, and then we stood there practicing.

"That's a front edge technique. Now let's practice slicing with your back edge. You'll swing the sword down again and up over your shoulder, but as you come towards your opponent, twist your blade so the back edge catches them in their chest."

We continued practicing the basic movements over and over, but my muscles barely felt a thing. During one of our water breaks, Sloan sauntered into the room.

"Reporting for babysitting duty," she smiled at me as I leaned against the water table. I didn't love the term 'babysitting.' I made a point of bringing that up with Calak the next time I saw him.

"So, Bree," Sloan jumped up to sit on the water table on my left side, swinging her feet in the air, "what happened to your handsome man after dinner last night?"

"Well," Bree leaned against the water table on my other side, "after dealing with the Raider, I was crossing the main lobby and he found me."

"And..." Sloan was ready for dirty details and from the smirk on Bree's face, there was more to the story.

"He led me towards an alcove where he had wine waiting for us. He poured us both a glass and we just talked. I don't even remember what we talked about because he was tracing small circles on the back of my neck with his pointer finger and didn't take his eyes off my lips as I spoke. It was all I could do not to jump on him."

"Ha! You're such a horndog." Sloan teased her friend.

"I was honest to the gods trying to behave, but then his fingers trailed down to my back. I just leaned into him. We sat there silently, just breathing each other in. His eyes were liquid fire, daring me to dive in. I was completely lost in them until our noses brushed against one another and it was like lightning shot through my body. I sucked in and then his lips were on mine."

"Damn," Sloan sounded impressed. I sat there listening to Bree's tale; she was excellent at telling stories.

"What happened next?" I asked, trying not to sound too naïve. I'd never even kissed a man before.

"Just some kissing. Some really, really delicious kissing, but that's all."

"Where is he now? I didn't recognize him." Sloan asked. I suppose she would be familiar with most of the people that passed through Castle Mount.

"He was a travel companion of that priggish Judd Trews, here to discuss some business with the Treasury regarding the sawmills. I believe they're meeting with the King right now."

"Does he have a name?" I asked.

"Zane."

"It's actually, Zane Xavier Cumberland the third."

The three of us looked up towards the deep,

commanding voice. Zane entered the training room followed by six men – I assumed were Raiders by their appearance – and Judd Trews. They sauntered in, swords drawn, locking the door behind them. I stole a glance at Bree, her facial expressions only allowing herself a moment of shock, before she assessed the threat these men were posing. Sloan stood to her feet, drawing her sword. Bree slowly picked up the two long swords we were practicing with and handed one to me. I darted my eyes around the room, taking in each of the opponents as they spread out in front of us.

"Thank you for last night. I don't normally mix business with pleasure." Zane was handsome, but there was something sinister in his look this morning. The Raiders started closing in on us. Their eyes were haunted; they were ready for a fight.

"It was a great kiss." Bree was calm and coy. If our situation rattled her, I couldn't hear it in her voice at all. "Trews," she shifted her head towards the man standing at the back of the group. "It seems like you've made some new friends."

"I'm here in the best interest of our kingdom." Last night he sounded like a man who could sell you anything, but standing in this room, surrounded by deadly weapons and those who knew how to use them, his voice was shaky. Trews had aligned himself with the other side and was helping to stage an attack inside of Castle Mount. I thought that Trews and Estra would have made a splendid match for their impaired judgment.

"The best interest of our kingdom, huh? And what would that be?" Bree drifted forward as she positioned herself in front of me.

"Her."

Zane pointed directly at me.

"Me?"

Sloan turned her face towards me as I stared directly at Zane. Bree didn't shift. I couldn't have heard him correctly. Did he just say that I was in the best interest of the kingdom?

"You're a popular woman, Princess. The Raiders have agreed to leave the North in exchange for you." I shifted my gaze to Trews until Bree spoke up.

"Sounds like a good deal."

Wait. That wasn't good. What was Bree saying? I immediately started questioning my new friend's intentions. Was she seriously considering trading me to the Raiders? Although, I couldn't say I would blame her. I was insignificant compared to the safety of an entire kingdom. And after what the Raiders did in Hillsborough last night, the children that they murdered, maybe it would be best for me to surrender myself to them. I could always attempt to escape after they got me out of the castle and make my way back to the West, back home. Either way, if I could save innocent people, I had to at least try. Right? Damnit. My heart raced as I stopped contemplating what I was about to say and just blurted it out.

"If I go with you, will you give me your word that all the Raiders leave the North?"

"That's the deal," said Zane.

I paused for a moment. This wasn't a great idea, but I couldn't live with myself if I knew I could've helped and didn't even try. I was brave enough to at least try. This wouldn't break me.

"Okay."

Trews' eyebrows lifted in surprise. I think he was expecting more of a fight. I lowered my sword and took a step forward when Bree spoke up, placing her sword across my path, blocking my way across the room.

"The problem is, I like my new friend. And the King, well, he wouldn't be happy about losing his future bride. Also, we had plans to go tobogganing, so I'm afraid you won't be taking Raelle today. Oh, and if any of you take another step forward, let's just say you won't be leaving this room with all of your favorite parts. Isn't that right, Sloan?"

"You shit-shovelers are dead." Sloan twisted her sword in her hand and spit on the ground.

"We figured it would take a fight, so we came prepared for one."

Zane nodded his head and two of the Raiders raced towards us. Sloan used her free hand to push me hard against the water table as she and Bree took defensive positions in front of me. The men approaching let out a war cry as they threw their weight into the downswing of their heavy swords. My friends didn't hesitate to engage. Soon, the entire room echoed with the sound of a battle. I couldn't decide who to keep my eyes on. I already knew Sloan could fight. I observed the brutality of her movements, as she ducked under her attacker's blade, spun around, slicing her sword across his back as a splatter of blood arched up. It made me appreciate how she held her own in this world of men. The Raider's eyes widened in pain and he turned towards her, jutting his sword towards her midsection. With another spin, she met his side with her blade, slicing open his abdomen and releasing body fluids all over the stone floor. He dropped to the ground as another Raider charged towards her.

I turned to watch Bree. Sloan was as savage as a beast, her movements ruthless and deafening. Bree was her polar opposite; the way she fought was a performance. Her sword moved with ease and grace, like an extension of herself. Her trim, muscular body was poised, her movements like those of a dancer, swift and soundless. Her first attacker was down, shrieking in pain as he looked down at his missing hand in horror. Bree's face remained calm and lethal. Her refined movements gave the illusion that she could float across the floor, that even gravity itself would bend to her will. She effortlessly dodged a second attacker and blocked it with her long sword. Knocking the attacker back, she fell to her knees in a spin, unsheathing a hidden blade from her boot. She lunged upwards, twisting the knife into his neck and grinning as blood oozed from his slackened jaw.

I looked around the room for a weapon that I could use. I'd be no use in a fight with a long sword. Lying next to the water table was a longbow and a quiver with seven arrows. I dropped my sword and threw the quiver over my back, grabbing an arrow and nocking it in one motion. I steadied my breathing as I took in the room. Bree and Sloan were both engaged by the last two Raiders, leaving me to kill either Zane or Trews. Trews looked like he was about to shite himself, but Zane was smiling like a smug bastard as he watched the two women unleash on his companions.

I took aim at Zane, trying to decide whether to send the arrow through an eye socket or his heart, as he flicked his eyes to me. Before I could react, he launched a throwing knife towards my head and I dropped to the ground as it clanged against the stone wall behind me. In a blur of speed, he charged, grabbing my left arm, twisting it behind my back, and using his right hand to hold a dagger against my throat so tight I felt a bead of blood trickle down my neck towards my tunic.

"Stop!" he yelled.

In unison, Bree and Sloan took a fatal swipe of their blades, dropping the Raiders to their knees before turning to face us.

"You won't kill her," Bree sounded quite confident. I couldn't say I felt the same way. The knife dug further into my skin.

"You're right, Leon wants her, preferably alive, but accidents can happen." Zane's grip on my left arm tightened. The skin where his finger dug burnt from the pressure. I wriggled my arm and hips, trying to loosen his grip, but he just pressed the dagger even tighter.

"Careful there, love." He leaned into me so his lips were caressing my ear. "You're about to cause a different issue."

His tongue flicked my earlobe, then he bit down on it. I widened my eyes and stared at Bree. I may be inexperienced, but I knew what kind of issue he was talking about and the hardness growing behind my back confirmed it.

Crack!

Wood splinters shot away from the fastened doors as the end of an axe poked through. A second later the axe hit again, and this time the doors shuddered in response. I could hear Calak's voice before the doors opened, pushed to either side by Rig's enormous arms.

Calak rushed into the room, sword in hand, scanning the bodies on the floor, noting Trews, who was weaponless. Then he looked to Bree, Sloan, and when his eyes met mine, I saw a flicker of alarm across his face, as his gaze focused on the dagger at my throat. He narrowed his stare at Zane.

"Let her go."

CHAPTER EIGHTEEN

"I DON'T THINK I WILL. I rather enjoy having her pressed against me."

Zane ran his nose against my cheek, sliding his tongue along my jawline. The stench of ale and smoke in his breath turned my stomach. Calak's nose flared as he tightened the grip on his sword, turning his knuckles white. Veras stormed through the broken door, followed by a dozen Northern soldiers. He looked straight at me and flexed his jaw.

"Trews, tell your man to stand down." He spoke to Trews, but his eyes didn't leave mine.

"I'm not his man," Zane retorted, nodding his head towards me. "Leon sent me to get her."

Calak and Veras exchanged a look, while Bree and

Sloan took up defensive positions on either side of them. My eyes moved between the two men before me: a king and a tracker. I cursed myself as my heart fluttered seeing them there, ready to fight for me. But this was not time for my heart to skip a beat. I narrowed my senses and continued to search for a way out of this situation.

"Why does Leon want the Princess?" Veras asked.

"He has his reasons, but as I told the women, the Princess comes with me and the Raiders leave the North. That's the deal."

Calak's gaze hit the floor. Veras' eyebrows bunched together as he processed the offer on the table. I couldn't fault him for considering it. Would turning me over to the Raiders jeopardize the peace treaty with the West? Probably. Although they could forge letters from me, claiming I was too ill to see my family for a while. But, in the short time I've known Veras, that didn't seem like something he would agree to. These people wouldn't offer my life for anyone else's. However, one-hundred and forty-three people were murdered last night. Not just soldiers. Innocent families who were peacefully resting in their homes. The Raiders were ruthless and so I attempted one more time to be the solution.

"I think you should let him take me."

"Not happening," Veras snapped, staring straight at Zane. Calak was positioned beside his King, looking lost in thought. My captor tightened his grip on me and I involuntarily let out a stifle of pain.

Zane watched the group in front of us. All of them standing, ready to fight to save my life. Calak and Veras had inched closer, weapons at the ready.

"Hm, you are a very popular princess." Zane took his free hand, lifting it to my neck. He slowly ran his calloused fingers across my naked collarbone, then trailed the hemline of my tunic. "Maybe I should have sat next to you at dinner."

He rested his hand along the side of my rib cage, his finger reaching as he groped my breasts, pushing himself against me. Pulling down the top of my dress, Zane exposed my chest, twisting my nipple, and I stifled a yelp from the pain. Veras' chest was heaving from the rapid breaths he was taking. Calak looked like he would murder this man as soon as the opportunity presented itself.

A depraved smirk stretched across Zane's face. He got off on getting a rise out of them; it aroused him, as evidenced by the tiny prick I felt against my back. He held me tighter, and his maniacal lips met the soft curve of my neck. His porcelain white teeth tugged at the delicate skin before sucking it into his mouth. His hands continued to violate me. He stopped between kisses to taunt the men before us, getting pleasure from their irate expressions. Every touch was nauseating. Everything about this man repulsed me. Blood from the cut where the dagger sat ran down my chest into the top of my tunic as I pushed away from his hold.

"That's enough!" Veras' voice boomed through the room and echoed off of every wall.

Zane pulled his lips off my neck, a carnal smile on his face. I bit my bottom lip to keep it from shaking. Filled with anger, adrenaline, and shame, I found Calak's eyes. He looked conflicted.

I took a deep breath, searching my memories for anything that could help me. I had no weapon. My life hung in the balance with the cold steel inches from an artery that would bleed me dry. I knew my new friends were also calculating the risks involved in trying to get me free from Zane's hold. I shut my eyes to focus.

One year ago.

Kolt stood behind me, holding a wooden stick to my throat.

"Now, what would you do?"

Danier was standing in front of me giving his instructions. I grunted as I pushed against Kolt's arm.

"No. You just pushed the dagger further into your throat, nicked the artery, and are now bleeding to death on the ground."

I sighed, trying to think of another solution. I reached up to grab the stick.

"Getting closer, but don't grab the blade. You'll just slice open your hands. You need to grab his right hand with your right hand, like this." Danier placed my hands over top of Kolt's. "Don't use your left, okay? Get a good grip and pull his hand down away from your body. Don't grab the blade. And don't grab his forearm too close to the elbow. You'll lose all of your leverage. So, control his arm by pushing his hand down."

I grabbed Kolt's hand and forcibly shoved it down.

"Not bad," Kolt laughed.

"Now when you do it," Darian moved Kolt's hand and stick back against my throat, "as soon as you have enough room, slip your head out of his hold and use your left hand to twist his arm around and in towards his back."

"Like this," I showed what Danier just explained, now holding Kolt's arm behind him.

"And use your right hand to keep pressure on his elbow. Now, twist his hand and the dagger away from him."

Kolt yelped as I manipulated his hold on the stick, and he released it.

"Ha! I did it."

Danier smiled while Kolt flexed his right hand.

I knew that I would have to be quick. I caught Calak's eyes and dipped my head ever so slightly. He nodded in acknowledgement. I reached up and grabbed Zane's hand. Using all of my strength, I pushed it down, away from my body and slipped my head out from his hold, but before I could finish the move, Calak charged towards us, pushing me to the side and he tackled Zane to the ground. The dagger clanged against the stone and Bree rushed to my side, pulling up my tunic as she ushered me away. I turned in her embrace to watch.

Zane stumbled to his feet, drawing the sword from his side as Calak swung a preemptive strike. With a swift movement of his arm, Zane blocked the blow and spun to his left, trying to get his footing as a rage-filled Calak pushed forward. Unaware of how close the water table was, Zane's legs bumped into the sides, leaving him trapped before a feral Calak who pummeled at his opponent, finally disarming him of his blade.

"What are you waiting for?" Zane asked. "Cut me down. Do it!"

But Calak took a step backwards, throwing his sword to the ground. The challenge of hand-to-hand combat was assumed. A bloodlust Zane charged forward, attempting to use the moment to deliver a right hook to Calak's face. The fist met its mark as Calak swore. Regaining his position, he swung and landed a flying kick to Zane's chest, knocking the air out of him. Using the moment to his advantage, Calak hammered in two gut-punches, then kneed Zane in the nose. Blood rushed out. Zane wheezed, leaning over as he collapsed on the ground.

Resting against Bree, I was having trouble staying focused and my head felt light. My heart was racing, the room was spinning. I leaned back into her and felt my feet leave the floor. The last thing I remember is Bree saying, "I've got you."

***

I opened my eyes and I was in my bed, facing the afternoon sun pouring in through my window. Laying on top of the blankets and still in my boots, I reached up to touch my neck, which was still wet from the blood. This meant that I hadn't passed out for very long.

I patted my neck again. My necklace. I had left it on the water table before Zane's attack. Damnit.

Hearing water being poured out in the bathing chamber, I turned my head as Yuri appeared.

"How do you feel?" He asked as he approached. I saw Bree stand from one of the sitting chairs that rested in front of my fireplace.

"Embarrassed. Did I really faint?"

"Out cold," Bree smiled as she sat on the bed next to me.

"Thanks to Bree you didn't hit your head, but I would like to have a look at that cut on your neck."

I nodded and sat up further against the pillows. Yuri had a few bandages in his hands and the same ointment he had used on my head. The first touch of the bandage against the cut stung.

"Where's Zane now?"

"In the cells, with Trews. Veras and Calak will question them. There'll be a trial for Trews here in Castle Mount, but I don't know what Veras' plans for Zane are yet."

Bree watched as Yuri cleaned the cut.

"Is it deep?" I asked Yuri.

"It could use some sutures. Could you handle that?"

"Is there wine?"

Yuri smiled, and Bree jumped to her feet, heading for the door and raising her hand.

"On it!"

As the door closed behind Bree, Yuri gathered his bag from the table between the chairs. He pulled out a needle and some thread.

"I've only ever had to be stitched once before. I fell out of a tree when I was twelve and split open my elbow. My brother, Holden, carried me all the way back to the castle, even though I insisted I could walk. It was my elbow, not my leg."

Yuri smiled. "He sounds like a good brother."

"He is."

Blinking away the tears that threatened to slip out, my heart ached for my brothers. I missed my home. The trauma of the past few days had been slowly settling in. Unsure if I'd ever come to terms with it all, I had tried my best to only worry about what was right in front of me. Forcing myself to be present was exhausting, when every fiber of my being wanted to revisit the pain. I knew eventually I'd have to face it all, but not today.

Bree returned with a bottle of wine.

"I didn't bother with glasses, and look what I found," she turned the bottle towards me so I could read the markings on it, "Western wine!"

"We do make the best wine!" I confessed.

Bree popped the cork and handed me the bottle. I immediately chugged down a healthy amount, then nodded at Yuri to start.

After half of the bottle, Yuri finished his work,

cleaned up the mess, and left Bree and I alone. He explained that the stitches would need to come out in a week and I'd likely carry a scar down my neck. I slowly stood up to make my way to the bathroom chamber, but stumbled sideways.

Contagious laughter escaped my mouth. "I'm drunk."

"I think you are," Bree laughed, reaching me before I fell completely over. She helped me to the bathing chamber where I took care of my personal needs. Walking back to the bed, I tripped over one of the animal furs lining the floor.

"Damn bear," I shouted at the ground as I stomped my foot on top of the fur. I looked up at Bree, who was still holding my arm, and we both burst out in hysterics.

I was crying, my side aching from the giggles as I sat back down on the bed. Bree adjusted my pillows and then looked me over.

"How are you doing?"

"I don't know. My life was pretty boring back at home. I used to joke that I had no secrets to keep because nothing ever happened to me. I loved it that way, but these past couple of days…it's a lot."

"What Zane did to you…" Bree looked down at her hands resting in her lap, laughter gone, she spoke with a somber tone, "I'm sorry Raelle, I'm just, gods I'm sorry."

"I know, but it's not your fault. I just don't understand why they wanted me?"

"We don't either. That's what Veras and Calak are trying to find out."

With an exaggerated gasp, I threw my eyes open and clasped my hands.

"That's why we were attacked in the forest on the

way here!" It was too much enthusiasm. I behaved as if I had just solved the world's one and only problem.

Bree just chuckled, "It's possible."

I hiccupped, and the fits of giggles resumed. How much of that wine did I drink?

A knock at the door interrupted us.

"That was fast. I think he's come to talk to you."

Bree stood, walking around the bed, to answer the door. I had a lot of questions for Calak, but mostly I just wanted to see that he was okay. He was the only person I realized I wanted to talk to, and that surprised me.

Turning to greet him, I smiled and saw Veras walking into the room.

CHAPTER NINETEEN

"GOOD AFTERNOON, YOU'RE HANDSOME," I let out a silent gaff and slapped my hand over my mouth. Damn Western wine. But the truth was plain. The man was handsome. "I mean, your Majesty."

Veras side-eyed Bree, as if to ask what was going on. Bree nodded at the bottle resting on the table beside my bed and Veras smiled in understanding.

"Got myself all stitched up, thanks to Yuri." I lifted my chin, and tilted my head to the side to expose my neck injury to Veras. "See?"

"I see, and other than that, is everything okay?"

Veras was asking me, but glancing between where I sat on the bed and Bree.

"Peachy," and I hiccupped again.

"Raelle seems to really like her Western wine." Bree clicked her tongue and winked at me. "I'll leave you two to talk. Good luck, Veras. She's in a giggly mood."

Veras smiled, "I think we'll manage. Could you have Clara send up some food? I think I'll stay with her, at least until the wine wears off."

"Of course. I'm just going to take this with me."

Bree grabbed the half empty bottle and sent me a look that said I was cut off for the rest of the day, which was fine. I already knew my headache tomorrow was going to be awful. Bree left my room and shut the door tightly behind her. I was alone with the King for the second time in less than a day. And he was very handsome.

"Are you sure you're okay, Raelle?" Veras stood by my bedside, his face full of concern. I hated seeing him look so sad. He was too handsome to be sad.

"Honestly, I think the wine is helping right now. Maybe ask me tomorrow."

"Oh, here." Reaching into his pocket, Veras pulled out the necklace my brothers' had gifted me. My face lit up.

"You found it."

The King smiled as he walked closer to where I was sitting on my bed.

"After all the commotion, I saw it sitting on the ground. We had it cleaned, so it should be just as good as new. May I?"

He was offering to clasp it around my neck. Nodding, I leaned my head forward as his fingers lightly grazed the skin just below my hairline.

"Thank you."

Veras nodded and took in a deep breath, looking back towards the chest of drawers.

"Do you like playing games?"

"Um, sometimes."

"When Calak and I were younger, we would play Nine Men's Morris for hours." Veras walked over to the chest of drawers on the far side of the room. Bending down, he opened the bottom drawer and pulled out a box. Veras was oddly familiar with where things were in this room. He brought the box to the small table that sat between the two chairs by the fireplace.

He looked up at me. "Shall we?"

"I don't know how to play."

"I'll teach you." Veras held out his hand as an invitation to join him. I rolled my legs off the side of the bed and grabbed the white, furry blanket that I was just laying on. I wrapped it around myself, shuffling towards the chairs. Veras had already taken his seat, opening the box to reveal a board with wooden circles in two different colors. He got to work preparing the game. I plopped down on the chair across from him, pulling my legs so they were tucked under my rear. I watched as Veras finished setting things up, then he clapped his hands.

"Ready?"

I smiled. He was so easy to like. Gentle. Considerate. For the moment I had decided that his intentions were good, and he was trustworthy; however, I reserved a small part of my heart for skepticism. Everyone had secrets, or at least that's what Holden always said. I considered the fact that Veras could be anywhere right now, but he was standing watch, getting ready to teach me a child's board game. My mind wondered why he would choose to be here. Surely there were more important things that required his attention.

"The aim of the game is to capture your opponent's pieces by forming lines of three. It's like Crosses, if you've ever played that." I shook my head, not having played many board games. I was usually outside with Holden or Dalia instead. "Why don't I start and you can just ask questions if you get stuck."

After the first round of play, I was starting to understand the concept of the game. My mind was clearing from the wine and I had so many questions for the King.

"Bree told me that their mother was a storyteller and advisor to your father. Is that common? Having someone as a designated storyteller?"

"Here it is. Our history is tragic and runs deep. It was always the intention that each generation was aware of what happened before them. Storytellers were prominent members of society during the Evamore Dynasty. We were the only kingdom to continue the tradition."

"Does the castle have a storyteller now?"

"We do. Her name is Nichelle. I could arrange for you to meet her if you'd like?"

"I'd love that."

Conversation was easy as we shared stories of our childhoods and laughed together. When Veras smiled, he had the faintest dimple in his right cheek. I listened as he told me about his family and how they celebrated different holidays. My stories centered on my brothers and father.

"What's your father like, as a man, I mean?" Veras asked.

It was then that I realized we had been discussing his enemies, men he had fought against for the past decade.

"Do you really want to know what the man you've been at war against for the past decade is like?"

Veras nodded. "The war against your kingdom was never my first choice. I was only seventeen when my father was killed. Two days after I learned of his death, I wore the crown and was seated amongst my father's advisors, who were all pushing for war. I suppose the pressure of that and the inexperience of leading is why I caved. My preference has always been to find peace, to negotiate. Those who decide to go to war are never the ones who have to pay its price. So, your father has never really been my enemy, and even if he was, I can appreciate that he may be one man at war and another at home with you."

If I could have kissed this man, I would have.

"My father is wonderful. Since the moment he found me, he has always protected me. I know I must have another father somewhere in the world, if he's even still alive, but I've never felt sad about that. I often worried that I should feel bad for being happy when someone could mourn me, but I was just grateful to be safe and cherished so dearly."

"I think, whoever or wherever your family may be, they'd be happy to know you have been loved and cared for."

By the end of our fourth game, the effects of the wine had almost completely worn off. Veras had once again beaten me.

"You win again. What happened to beginner's luck?"

"You almost had me that last round."

"You're a terrible liar, your Majesty."

Veras exhaled as he smiled, brushing the hair away from his face as I leaned back in my seat. There was a knock at the door and he jumped up to answer it. Two kitchen maids entered carrying trays piled high with delicious foods: cold meats, cheese, bread, dried apricots, and pickles. My stomach growled. After placing the trays on top of the chest of drawers, they promptly left the room.

"I'm going to assume that you're hungry."

"Always."

I smiled, standing up and walking towards where Veras was already sampling some of the dried apricots. He popped another one into his mouth, the slightest moan of satisfaction leaving his lips. The King really liked dried apricots, and I bet Clara knew that by the number of them on the trays. I spread some jam onto a slice of bread and took a huge bite.

Veras smiled, "You've got something, just right here." Lifting his thumb, he gently wiped the mess away from the corners of my mouth. The touch was intimate, but innocent.

"Thank you."

We both finished filling a plate with food and sat back down by the fire.

"I have to admit, Raelle, I find you more fascinating than I expected."

"Is that a good thing?"

"I think so. When I agreed to bring you here, I didn't know your temperament or what your personality was like."

"And what do you think now?"

I looked down to find a piece of cheese on my plate, but also feeling vulnerable as I waited for his answer.

"I think you are goodness." I lifted my eyes to him, waiting for an elaboration. "You approach the world with curiosity, wit and bravery, willing to sacrifice yourself for others, thanking Clara for dinner last night..."

How did he know about that?

"Embracing the art of learning and exposing your

heart to those around you." We looked at each other for a quiet moment. That was the most romantic thing anyone had ever said to me. I wish my words were as elegant so I could reciprocate, but Veras spoke again. "I'm sorry that -"

"I need everyone to stop apologizing," I interrupted him.

"Oh, I didn't mean to offend."

"No, I'm not offended. I'm just tired of convincing people I'm fine or that things are okay. Today was terrible, but I don't blame anyone for it. The short time that I've been outside of the Western Kingdom has been thrilling, scary and adventurous, but I feel safe here, with you, and I didn't expect that."

Veras looked pleased, but there was another knock at the door. He wandered over to answer it and a Northern soldier, dressed in their usual white uniforms, stood outside the frame. Their conversation was quick and quiet. I took a moment to take in the sight of the King inside of my bedchamber. He was tall, well groomed, and muscular. The sleeves of his tunic were rolled up, exposing the cords of muscles along his forearms. The back of his tunic was tucked into his pants, exposing the perfect roundness of his -

"Sorry about that interruption," Veras turned to rejoin me. "That was an update from the castle guard." He watched me stare at him. "What would you like to know?"

I had so many questions, I just had to decide which one to ask first.

"How did the Raiders get into the castle?"

"Last night, Zane went missing from the dinner party. We suspect he used the distraction of the dinner and the Raider messenger at our gates to keep us busy while he ushered in his small contingent of intruders."

"Where's Zane now?"

"Calak, Bowan and Rig have left to bring Zane to a secure meeting place. They'll trade him for some of our own people that the Raiders are holding prisoner."

"They've left already?" It disappointed me that Calak had left the castle. I hoped my question didn't give too much away. Although there wasn't much to give away, Calak was maddening, but for some reason I found myself wanting to be around him more.

"Just heading out. They'll be back in a few days. Zane is valuable to Leon, so the trade is favorable for him."

"Did you find out why they wanted me?"

"Unfortunately, Zane didn't share that information with us. We couldn't be sure if it was because of his ignorance or if they trained him to withstand our interrogation tactics. We're very persuasive in our questioning. I believe that if he knew something, we would've caught on. Leon isn't a trusting man. If he has a reason for wanting you, it's possible he's the only Raider who knows why."

"But I've never met Leon or even heard of Raiders before coming here."

"I know. We have to explore the possibility that Queen Estra could be involved."

"You mean she hired the Raiders to come after me?"

"At this moment, we keep all options on the table while we gather more information."

I stood up to refill my plate with cheese and bread. As I sat back down a thought occurred to me. "Why wouldn't you just let me give myself over to them? I know what the Raiders have done to your people. As the King, it would have been wise for you to sacrifice one life to save others."

"For a moment I considered it."

"I thought you may have."

"The chief reason is that I don't trust Leon or Zane's promise to leave the North. If we had given you over to them, we'd still face the threat they pose and you'd be in danger. The other reason proves that I'm more selfish than a king ought to be, because if you had gone with them, then I wouldn't be sitting here with you right now, and I'm thrilled that I'm sitting here with you right now."

His eyes swallowed me up, and I was speechless. Before I could find words to respond to him, there was a flutter and faint tap on my window. We both turned our heads to see the snow owl on my ledge.

"She's back!"

Jumping to my feet, leaving the blanket behind, I could feel Veras' curious gaze on me as he slowly stood to follow. I opened the window and my friend turned her head towards me.

"Hello lovely."

Without hesitating this time, I lifted my finger to stroke the feathers on top of her head. Veras was standing directly behind me now. I could feel the heat of his body radiating off of him.

"Amazing," He breathed out. "I've never been this close to one before. And she'll just let you touch her like that?"

"Yes, this is the second time she's visited me today, actually. Would you like to try?"

"I'm afraid you'll think less of me for it, but I'm nervous around birds."

Smiling at how adorable that statement was, I reached over and lifted Veras' hand. His skin was soft and warm. Placing both of our hands over the owl's backside, I coaxed his fingers down to stoke the bird.

"See? Nothing to be afraid of." We stood together, slowly caressing the feathers.

"You're stunning." I assumed Veras was speaking to the bird, but I angled my neck to see him looking down at me.

The owl turned her body back out towards the castle grounds, and we dropped our hands. Staring out, she surveyed the tree line. It was then that I noticed four mounted horses walking away from the castle.

Calak.

The owl jumped off the ledge, spreading her wings, gliding down towards our friends. She swooped just above their heads and veered around them as she banked towards the trees.

Calak shifted, looking for the owl, but then our eyes met. We stared at each other from across the distance. He nodded, and I slowly lifted my hand in a still wave. Then he faced back towards his path, turning away from me and the King, in my bedchamber window.

CHAPTER TWENTY

IT HAD BEEN TWO DAYS since Calak left. Two days since Zane assaulted me. Two days since I realized I may have feelings for both the King and the tracker. I spent the first twenty-four hours in my bedchamber, sleeping and resting. Mostly nursing a wicked headache from all the wine. Sloan and Bree took turns keeping me company. Yuri came by once to check on my sutures, but Veras stayed away, although he had flowers sent up to me. The hyssops and catnip sat in a vase on my chest of drawers.

By the second day, I was ready to leave my room. Sloan suggested some fresh air, and we found our way down to the stables. Leaving me alone for a moment, she spoke with some men I didn't recognize a few stalls down. I picked up a brush and stroked the mare in front of me.

"Can you keep a secret?" Whispering to the horse as she devoured the fresh hay in front of her, I continued. "I don't know what I'm doing. I should work to find a way back home, but something inside of me wants to stay in the North. Is that insane? It's these people. I'm not ready to walk away from them yet. And it has nothing to do with Calak and Veras. Well, it has a little to do with them. Oh gods. Maybe I should go home before my heart gets entangled. Is this what happens when you keep a girl locked up for years? She falls for the first handsome men she comes across?" The mare shook her mane, letting out a snort. "But these aren't just any men. Veras said that I am goodness, but he is. I feel safe and comforted when I'm around him. I believe now that the man would never do a thing to cause me a moment of harm or unhappiness. And Calak is exhausting and exhilarating. The harder I try to push him out of my mind, the more space he occupies. His touch and stare burnt into my memories. I can't trust my heart here with them and there's still the threat of Leon. My gut tells me that he won't stop coming after me. Going back home is for the best. I could speak with Veras and try convincing him to allow me to go back to my father."

I let out a deep sigh, thankful that only the beast in front of me had heard my confessional.

At the sound of footsteps approaching I placed the brush back down. It wasn't Sloan, but a man I didn't recognize. By the look on his face, I knew he wasn't happy about my being here. Whether that opinion was limited to just the stables, or his displeasure was to my presence in the North remained to be seen.

"Western bitch."

It was the latter.

"My brother and father died fighting in the Decade War against your asshole brothers."

I removed all emotion from my face and met his stare full on. He would not intimidate me. The still-healing wound on my neck was proof that I'd already survived worse than a few mean words here in Castle Mount. And although I held sympathy for his losses, it was not my fault.

His eyes were full of threats, but he said no more words. I adjusted my stance, readying myself for a fight. Quickly glancing around to see what could be used as a weapon, I made a mental note to demand a sword or dagger that I could wear when I left my chamber.

"Do you have anything else to say to me?"

My voice was strong. I saw a tick in his clenched jaw.

"Boyce, shouldn't you be somewhere else right now."

Sloan had returned from her conversation, and by the way she was eyeing the stranger in front of me, I knew she could sense the potential threat. Boyce couldn't be stupid enough to try something with Sloan so close now. I'm sure her skills were well known here. My abilities were yet to be demonstrated, and that part of me wished that he had tried something.

The man sneered, walking away without saying another word to either of us. Taking a breath, I turned my attention back to the horse as my pulse slowed down.

"She's one of my favorites. Great nature and easy to ride. Reminds me of a mare I had back home in the West. Trained her myself. I tried to bring her with me when I left, but my father wouldn't allow it." Sloan had joined me in the stall and patted the horse's neck. "The King has requested your presence."

I nodded and followed her out of the stables back into the castle. I would make my case to Veras, requesting to be sent home. He'd protest because of the danger from Estra, but my family would protect me, especially if they realized the threat. Even though part of my heart wanted to remain in the North, it wasn't worth the risks.

On our way to the King's chamber, I rehearsed in my head what I was going to say. Sloan followed me through the corridors, allowing me the silence I needed. Before long, we were standing in front of his room and without a second thought; I reached up, knocking on the door, remembering my hesitation the first time I came here. The doors opened and Veras smiled, his perfection on full display. My heart skipped as the sun poured in behind him.

"Thank you, Sloan."

Sloan bowed, "Your Majesty."

And then she retreated. Still standing in the doorway, I opened my mouth, but Veras interrupted me. "We'll need to hurry if we're to make it on time."

Confused, I asked, "Where are we going?"

"To meet our storyteller."

He closed the door behind him and joined me in the hallway. Slowly, he slid his hand down my palm, intertwining our fingers. He searched my face for any protest, but I gave none. We'd agreed to this type of physical touch my first night at Castle Mount to maintain the ruse of our engagement. I didn't know how tight to hold on to him and I was sure my hand was sweating. This type of physical touch was new to me.

Everything was new to me.

Four of the King's personal guards surrounded us as we made our way through the castle, our hands still interlaced.

Approaching a partial open door I'd never seen before, I heard a voice floating into the hallway. Veras led us into the dimly-lit room. Surprised, I saw rows of children, all sitting crossed-legged on the floor facing the woman who spoke.

I knew this was Nichelle. Her hair was gray, soft waves of it floating down her shoulders. She wore a colorful robe, intricately woven with many shades and hues. Sitting on a stool, the entire room was willingly held captive by her story.

Veras led us to two chairs along the back of the wall, keeping our presence hidden from the group, but our hands still together, resting now on his thigh. I leaned forward to hear the storyteller.

"For his greed and selfishness, the gods banished Kellar from their realm and confined him to an island, the Island of Garth. There he would wander, searching for humans to influence with his wickedness and dark magic, but he found none. For centuries he wallowed, alone, until one day a man and woman appeared on the island shores, Edric and Alys Evamore. Unaware of Kellar's presence, they explored the island and made it their home. Kellar tried to lure them towards greed with his dark magic, but their souls were too pure and their love for one another too strong. Edric and Alys were lovetied, and the gods favored them, deciding to give them the island of Garth to live on, free from Kellar's influence. They banished Kellar into the depths of the Earth, trapped under the soil, never to see the light of day or the glow of the stars, but with one condition. As long as two lovetied Evamores sat on the throne of the United Kingdom of Garth, then the power of Kellar and his dark magic would not invade this land. Edric and Alys' descendants ruled for thousands of years peacefully. But one hundred and fifty years ago, the people of Garth revolted against their King and Queen, murdering the last lovetied Evamores and dividing the United Kingdom of Garth into four separate kingdoms: north, south, east and west. They set aside the Northern Kingdom for those loyal to the Evamore Dynasty. So we continue to tell their stories, to remember. We work hard to keep our hearts pure, as the influence of Kellar is roaming, turning men's hearts towards greed and hatred."

A small boy in the front asked, "Who were the last Evamores?"

"The last Evamores to exist were King Asher and Queen Yolanda."

"Did they have any children?" another child asked.

"Yes, but sadly, all were executed with their parents."

"So there's nothing left to protect us from Kellar?" The first boy asked again.

"All we can do is to live well, in kindness and peace, praying that the old gods take pleasure in us and one day banish Kellar again."

Nichelle looked up at the King and I. With a respectful nod she announced to the room, "Storytime is over. Now all of you out and back to your chores."

The children all rose to their feet and shuffled out of the room. A few of them glanced our way, a mixed reaction of excitement and wonder at the sight of the King in their presence. Veras returned a few waves from some boys who seemed excited to see him. Once the room was cleared, except for ourselves, the guards, and Nichelle, we rose and made our way towards the storyteller.

"I could listen to you tell our stories all day, Nichelle." The King beamed as he embraced the older woman.

"As I remember, you always asked our Sylvette the most questions. A curious prince you were." Her attention shifted to me. "You must be Princess Raelle. It's an honor to meet you." Nichelle bowed her head.

"That story was captivating. Is it a true story? I've never heard of Kellar, the fallen god, before."

"It is true. The history of our kingdoms is not told as freely in the other parts of Garth. Some do not value the gift of storytelling like the North does."

"Kellar? What kind of influence would he have over the people who live in Garth?"

"An evil, vile influence. He tempts broken souls to do the most heinous crimes. Innocents slaughtered. The Earth refuses to produce what we need. Kellar's agents will soon destroy everything if they are not stopped." Nichelle's face was solemn, as was Veras'.

"Nichelle, I was hoping to ask a favor of you. Princess Raelle has shared with me that as a child, she suffered severe memory loss. I know you've had some experience in the past with restoring memories, and with Princess' permission, maybe you could help restore hers as well."

"What?"

I looked at Veras, confused and astonished. That was not what I was expecting to hear. Not even sure how I felt about the request the King had just made on my behalf, I gave myself a moment to consider the possibility that I could remember who I was or where I really came from.

Were my parents looking for me? Did I have a bedchamber left vacant these past ten years, waiting for my return? I was discovered along the shoreline;

did I belong to a merchant family, trading goods? What adventures had I forgotten or missed because of my amnesia?

As a tentative excitement built, I remembered something.

"Actually, my father went to great lengths to seek anyone in Garth who could help restore my memories, but there was nothing to be done about it," I informed them.

Nichelle shifted. Her posture assured me that there was something she wished to say. Veras noticed the change too.

"What is it, Nichelle?"

"It's just that I'm not entirely sure it's my place to say anything."

Veras looked at me. It was clear that whatever Nichelle was or was not saying had everything to do with me. He waited for my input.

"Please, if you have anything to say about my family or what happened to me, I'd like to hear it."

She took a moment, then met my eyes. "Princess, what you just said, about your father seeking aid throughout the kingdom, that's not entirely true."

I stared at Nichelle.

"What do you mean?" I asked.

She continued, "My sister works in the West. In your castle, in fact. She's a chambermaid and when you arrived there, she reached out to me to see if I could help. I have, as the King mentioned, successfully restored many memories over the years. Being new to my position as the storyteller, I wasn't sure if they'd receive my letter offering to help, but weeks later a response came from King Wren himself. He wrote he wouldn't need my services. I know of other healers across Garth whose help was also turned down by your father."

"That cannot be. Someone else must have written those letters. My father did everything he could to help me regain my memory."

Nichelle was suggesting that my father knowingly refused the aid of people who believed they could help restore my memories. This couldn't be true. Father had reached out to every kingdom. He told me so himself. Healers saw me. Unless they weren't truly healers? I shook my head at the insinuation. My father wouldn't lie to me. He wouldn't knowingly deceive me. Her claim was simply untrue.

Nichelle gently reached for my hands, cupping them in her own.

"My child, I'm sorry for the pain this revelation is clearly causing you, but I swear to you, on the old gods and my sister's life, I offered King Wren my help and I was turned away."

Taking a step back, I shook my head, my gaze on the stone floor.

"No, no. He wouldn't do that. He loves me. I'm his daughter. Why would he keep that from me?"

"Perhaps, my dear, it's because of how much he loved you, he didn't want to lose you. If you learned of who you were or where you came from, then he could risk losing you to your actual family."

"He's my actual family." My voice was louder. "My brothers; Kolt, Danier and Holden, they're my family."

Retreating from Veras and Nichelle, I backed up towards the door.

"Princess Raelle."

Veras took a small step towards me.

My hands were shaking and I could feel the heat in my face. Why would this woman lie to me? It could be a ruse to try and taint my view of my father. These people had been his enemies, our enemies, for the past decade. Even though my experiences here had been pleasant, that could still be working against me to undermine my relationship with my father. The look in Veras' eyes challenged that thought. Nothing but care radiated off of him. Reaching up, he softly touched my fingers. I pulled my hand away.

"I need some air."

Turning to run through the doors, I heard Veras call out after me again.

CHAPTER TWENTY-ONE

I WANDERED THROUGH THE CASTLE corridors, shadowed by two of the King's personal guards, no doubt sent to protect me by Veras. The possibility that my father had been lying to me for a decade was a lot to process. Did my brothers know? Were they all lying to me? Either subconsciously led by the low grumble in my stomach or by the alluring scent of freshly baked bread in the air, I found myself at the entrance of the kitchens. I pushed the doors open and found Clara sitting at the counter alone. The quietness of the kitchens was a surprise. Clara looked up from the list she was preparing, pushing her eyeglasses to rest on her head.

"Can I help ye, Princess?"

"I don't really know how I ended up here. I was just walking, and here I am."

"Well, since yer here, we may as well put some food in yer belly. Come, grab a stool and pull up. I got just the thing for ye."

Leaving the guards standing watch at the door, I moved into the kitchen and sat down. Where were the kitchen maids? This must be one of the few breaks they get throughout the day. Clara returned to the counter with a small plate filled with fresh bread, cheese, and some fruit.

"Thank you," I said as Clara took her seat next to me. I nibbled at the bread and cheese while I continued to process the repercussions of Nichelle's admission.

"Okay, out with it." I looked at Clara. "Your thoughts are as loud as yer chewin'. I'm not gettin' a thing done sitting here. So, out with it. What's on yer mind?"

"I just discovered something that changes everything."

"Oh my, sounds dramatic."

"The problem is that I don't know if it's true or not."

"I see. What does yer gut tell ya?"

"I'm not sure I trust my gut anymore."

"Not trusting yerself is a dangerous place to be, Princess."

"That's true, but how can you trust your gut when you don't have all the information?"

"Hm, that's a good point. I think ye try to find the information ye can and then use faith to fill in the details."

Taking another bite of cheese, I continued, "I just want to know where I'm from and who I am. I stopped caring years ago because I found somewhere safe and people who loved me, but now being here,

I can't help but wonder if there's somewhere else in the world where I belong or where I could be loved."

"I reckon there're many places ye could find those things."

"But I don't want just any place. I want a home. This morning I decided I would attempt to convince the King to send me back to the West, and now I'm not sure if that's home anymore. If that's true, then I don't have a home."

"Sometimes yer given a home, and sometimes ye have to make one."

A slow, single tear escaped the corner of my eye. I quickly wiped it away.

"I desperately wanted to go back. I miss them so badly. I'm just confused and angry. If they lied to me, I don't know what that means, or if I'll ever be able to forgive them."

Reaching up, I clasped on to the necklace my brothers had gifted me.

"Whatever was done to ye, confront it. Get yer answer. Don't run or hide." I nodded in agreement. "And be prepared for what ye learn and for gods' sake, girl, trust yerself. There's a strength inside ye that will need to come out if yer gunna face the truths."

I cleared my throat and stood up, "Thank you, Clara. I appreciate your kind words."

I lifted my plate, intent on cleaning up after myself, but Clara stopped me.

"No need, my girls will be back shortly and they'll be doing the cleaning."

I smiled and headed for the door. The two guards followed behind me. I knew what I wanted to do. It was time to send my father another letter, but I didn't think I could wait a week for the reply. There had to be a faster way. In the West, we used ravens to send urgent messages that couldn't wait to be delivered by hand. Perhaps Veras had such ravens. I headed straight for my chamber; with the guards standing post outside, I sat down to pen my questions.

***

Veras sent his fastest bird to deliver my message to the West, but not before reading it himself. I would've expected nothing less from a King. As much as they were strangers to me, I was still a stranger to them, but there was nothing incriminating in my letter.

That night we dined with some prominent tradespeople visiting from outlying villages. I was wearing one of the dresses the seamstress had made for me. It was bright red with black satin trim around the bodice and sleeves. Leaving my curls down, I'm sure they looked a little untamed for the occasion, but I didn't care. Throughout the meal I was distracted by thoughts of Nichelle's confession and what my father's response would be. Playing the role of the betrothed princess, I reminded myself to offer smiles and nods when conversation was directed towards me. Veras knew how I was feeling and kept offering me reassuring glances.

I was shocked when music came from the corner of the dining room. Not even noticing the arrival of musicians, the quartet played a well-rehearsed tune.

Standing to his feet, the King extended his hand for me to join him. Were we going to dance? Alone? In front of everyone? The desire to itch overtook me. I wanted to leave and hide in my bedchamber, but instead, remembering the agreement we'd made about maintaining the appearance of our engagement, I took Veras' offer and slowly stood.

He escorted me to the center of the room, lifting his hand to hold mine and placing his other on my waist.

"I'm not sure I know this dance," I admitted to him quietly.

"Don't worry. I've got you." Veras moved us across the floor, gently guiding my steps. My heart was racing as I caught glimpses of the guests staring at us. What were they looking at? Oh. For a moment I'd forgotten about the gash across my neck, stitched closed. It was probably hideous. I lifted my hand to cover it, but Veras softly moved it out of the way.

"Raelle." I looked up at Veras. "Just look at me. They stare because they think you're beautiful. That dress is..." He shook his head as he stole another look at what I was wearing. "Worth every penny." His smile eased my discomfort. "I'm going to spin you now."

"What?"

Before I could get the question out, he twirled me in front of him, catching my body as I came back to him. The room echoed with light clapping and shouts of approval. The thrill of the small movement broke through the tension on my face as the corner of my lips turned up.

When the music picked up into a faster song, others came to join us. Soon I forgot where we were and who was watching. My entire focus was just on the man that was holding me, moving me safely from step to step. He felt strong and assured. I muffled a giggle when he whispered a little joke into my ear. The King was very good at making people feel comfortable.

After a while, we made our excuses and left the dinner. My feet were aching from all of the dancing, but my heart felt lighter. I was so grateful for the distraction.

Walking up the stairwell, I paused.

"Is something the matter?" Veras observed me. Our entourage of guards waited patiently.

"It's just, my feet are incredibly sore." I let out a little laugh. "Just a moment and I'll be fine."

Without seeking my permission, Veras scooped me up into his arms. The movement forced a sound out of me that expressed both surprise and mild delight. He held me as if I weighed nothing.

"Allow me, Princess."

Veras carried me up the rest of the stairs and to the door of my room. Placing me gently back on the ground, I turned towards him. Lifting myself up onto my toes, without really thinking, I planted a quick kiss on his cheek.

"Thank you."

Without waiting for his response, I made my way inside and shut the door behind me. What did I just do? If I was being honest, I wanted to kiss him on more than just his cheek, but did he feel the same way? This was supposed to be just a ruse, but the way he touched me and smiled at me, was it all fake?

I floated over to my bed and collapsed on it.

What an unexpected evening.

***

The next afternoon I waited inside of the King's chamber with Veras and Bree. The response from my father was due anytime.

"I think it's going to snow tonight, which means the hills will be fresh for some tobogganing."

Bree had mentioned taking me tobogganing every day since that first dinner.

"Will it be safe? To leave the castle grounds?"

I asked because I'd overheard the two of them discuss the continued Raider threat this morning over breakfast.

"There are places we can go that are safe and well-guarded," Bree replied, taking another drink from her wine glass.

"Any word from Calak or the others?" I hadn't seen Calak since he left the castle to return Zane to the Raiders.

"Nothing yet, but that's not unusual. I would expect them to arrive back in the next day or so."

Veras was sitting next to me at the table.

"We haven't talked about Nichelle's offer yet, Raelle. It's not my intention to pressure you into a decision, but have you considered trying to get your memories back?"

I had considered it.

When I was younger and believed that regaining my memories was impossible, I came to accept that I would never know where I came from or what brought me to the Balour seashore that day. Now that I knew it was a possibility, I'd spent the last day imagining the past I had forgotten.

"I'd like to speak with Nichelle more about it," I answered.

There was a knock at the door, then Sloan and Yuri entered, the latter carrying a small scroll. A letter from my father. My heart raced, my palms suddenly slick as I rubbed them against my thighs. Yuri handed the scroll to the King, who paused before handing it to me.

"Raelle, this is your decision to make. Would you like us to stay while you read this letter, or would you prefer privacy?"

"Stay, please."

I didn't want to be alone, no matter what the letter said. When I had written to my father, I was very direct. I told him I knew healers had offered to help restore my memories and that he refused their services, demanding an explanation for his betrayal. Even if Nichelle's confession was false, I thought this would be the best way to force any truth out of him.

Veras passed me the note. I broke the Western seal and unrolled it. My eyebrows shot up in surprise.

"What is it?" Bree asked.

This was not my father's handwriting. I recognized the curve of the letters that came from Kolt's hand. My elder brother had written the response to my letter. This both annoyed and relieved me as I read.

Dearest Rae,

Our hearts are full knowing that you are safe and well cared for in the North. We have mourned the sudden loss of you and look forward to the day we can be together again. Regarding your previous letter, I have no acceptable excuses to offer you. We discovered months ago that Father had not done all he could to restore your memories. At his bequest, we kept this information from you. A decision all three of us regret deeply. You trusted us to care for you, and we betrayed that trust. Father isn't himself. After Queen Estra had you kidnapped, he banished her back to the Eastern Kingdom. Things are unstable here and we ask that you remain in the North for your own protection. We will see you again.

Your loving brothers.

The letter crumpled in my hand as I processed the information. They all knew, and they never told me, denying me the right to know who I truly was.

"Raelle?"

Veras put his hand on mine as I fought back a tear.

"They knew."

I barely got the words out, the whisper so soft, I wasn't sure my friends could hear me.

"The letter, it's not from my father. Kolt wrote it. He said that they all knew. He didn't attempt to find my other family, or restore my memories. They lied to me."

A long exhale blew from my lips. No one spoke for a moment, then Veras addressed our friends, "Could you please give us the room?"

Bree stood, walked around the table, and planted a kiss on the top of my head.

"When you're ready, we're here for you."

They left the room, leaving me alone with the King. With his hand still on mine, Veras turned, resting his other arm on the back of my chair.

"What can I do? Tell me what I can do to help you, Raelle."

The tenor of his voice broke through me. My tears flowed now as I faced him.

"They lied."

The crack in my voice left me more exposed than I wanted.

"I'm sorry. They didn't think you were strong enough to know, but you are. This won't break you. I've seen your strength, and it matches your goodness."

He pressed his forehead against mine. We'd never been this close before, but just being with him eased some of the pain. He was a comfort to me.

"What do you need?"

He asked again. I felt his words against my lips. We were so close. I had a thousand feelings running through my body; anger towards my family, hopelessness at not knowing who I was, grateful for my new friends and a desire to close the space between us and feel his mouth on mine. I bit my bottom lip as Veras moved his mouth closer. Our breaths mingled together, and I felt the soft touch of his lips against mine. Not quite a kiss, but a gentle offer for a different comfort.

This was my first kiss.

I did not know what to do, so I allowed instinct to take over. Pushing my mouth tighter against his, with the lingering taste of salty tears still on my lips, I kissed him back. It was quick, but firm. His hand moved from the back of my chair to the side of my face. He cradled it as he pulled away first, searching my face again for any sign of regret, when a knock sounded at the door.

Ignoring it, we just stared back at each other.

I couldn't believe I'd just had my first kiss... with a King. Whoever was at the door banged again with more urgency.

Letting go of my face, straightening himself in the chair, Veras called out, "Come in."

Bree rushed into the room, breathless from running so hard. Her eyes were wild with fear.

"What is it?" Veras stood quickly.

"It's Bowan. They're back, but there was...he's hurt. Bad. We've sent for Yuri, but...it's not good."

Bowan was like a father to my friends. That's what I should've been thinking about, but all my ridiculous, betraying heart heard was that Calak was back.

CHAPTER TWENTY-TWO

THREE YEARS AGO.

"What happened?"

I was running out the castle door as Kolt's horse came to a quick stop, with Danier's body draped over in front of him, the mane stained with blood. My breath caught in my throat, as my eyes widened. Holden came rushing out behind me with two guards. All the men carefully lowered Danier off of the horse.

"He's been cut."

Kolt, breathless, explained.

"There was a group of Northern raiders who breached the wall. Danier intercepted them before our unit arrived. He took down six of them before one bastard got him."

"Find Mister Verns," Holden shouted to a servant standing by. "NOW!"

They were carrying my brother up the steps, a trail of crimson blood following them. Danier's eyes were closed. I raced up ahead, shouting for clean sheets and hot water, as I swiped my arm across the table in the middle of the grand hallway, pushing the clutter to the ground. Dropping Danier's weakened body down onto the now clear tabletop, we all just stood there, helpless.

Father and Queen Estra were on a diplomatic trip to the Eastern Kingdom to attend a wedding of someone's niece to a Southern lord. I didn't really pay attention when the details were explained. Danier couldn't die. He had to live. Verns raced in from a back corridor, his medical bag in hand as servants appeared carrying the supplies I had ordered. Dropping his bag, the healer made quick work, telling each of us what to do.

"We need to undress him. I can't see the wound clearly."

My brothers cut away Danier's blood-soaked tunic using their daggers, revealing a near fatal injury spanning from his left pectoral to his right hipbone. The skin was sliced away, exposing layers of muscle.

"Gods."

The word choked out of me through my sobs. There was so much blood. Our brother was dying.

"I'll need to clean and close it before an infection can set in," Verns explained. "Then we pray that his body can come back from this."

That didn't sound promising. I took a step back as the servants handed Verns jars of vinegar and hot water. He poured them over the wound and I begged the gods to allow Danier to live. His eyes were still closed as I moved closer to Kolt. He wrapped his arm around me, pulling me tight against him as my tears discolored his shirt. Holden stood on his other side, his eyes also red from crying. The three of us watched as the healer worked to save our brother's life.

After a long while, Verns completed the endless line of sutures down Danier's abdominal wall. Recovering from this injury would take time, but if anyone could do it, it was him.

We eased Danier to a guest bedchamber on the main level of the castle and waited. Through the course of the night, my brothers and I sat in that room, being sure to check for a fever. Verns came by twice to look for any discharge on the dressings. Thankfully, there was none. At some point I fell asleep on the settee, exhausted from weeping. When I awoke, the morning sun was just starting to pour into the room. Wiping my eyes, I blinked, adjusting to the unexpected brightness and then I gasped.

The bed was empty. Danier's body was gone. He must have died in the night. The wound was extensive and Verns didn't sound confident when he last left us.

I'd never get to talk to my brother again, listen to him correct my form during training or watch him stuff his face with pastries. My throat felt like it was closing. My hands were shaking. Panicked breaths were coming too quickly as I collapsed on the floor. I cried out, screaming from the pain of the loss. A hand pressed to my back.

"Rae, what happened? Are you okay?"

It was Holden.

"He's gone."

"No, no. Rae, look at me. Danier isn't dead. Oh, gods..."

He sat on the ground and pulled me into a hug. My chest was shuttering as the tears slowed down.

"But, I thought, when the bed was empty..."

"We should've woken you up, but you were so exhausted. He's alive. The mullish dunkerhead woke up and insisted on resting in his own room. We just finished bringing him up there when I came down to check on you."

Slowly coming down from the emotional stress, I took a few deep breaths. Yes, they should have woken me up and I would berate them for that later, but the most important thing right now was that Danier was alive.

Standing up, I adjusted my dress and wiped my nose with the back of my hand.

"Can I see him?"

Holden nodded and led me out of the room.

***

Running from Veras' chambers to the infirmary at the lowest level of the castle, I tried to shake the memory of that day. That was the closest I ever came to losing someone I loved. Even though it only lasted a few moments, the pain was overwhelming. I prayed my friends would be spared that agony.

The deafening howl of a man suffering alerted me that we were close. Turning the corner, I saw Rig and Sloan sitting against the wall, facing a closed door. Rig's head hung between his arms that were resting on his towering knees. Sloan was paler than usual, shifting her attention to us as our pace slowed.

Another scream came from behind the door.

"Yuri's with them now."

Sloan spoke up, her dread palpable. I came forward, taking a seat next to Sloan on the stone floor, clasping her forearm in an attempt to provide comfort. I had no words, so my presence was all I could offer.

"You two should go in there," Rig said to Bree and Veras.

They didn't hesitate opening the door across from me. I saw Bowan's legs stretched out on a worktable. So much blood covered the ground, and there was Calak. The front of his white uniform was now stained scarlet. He looked bewildered. I wanted to help, but there was nothing to be done. My heart cracked as the door slowly swung shut.

For two hours we sat in the corridor listening to Bowan's screams, watching servants carry in basins of water and leave with armfuls of soiled linens. Each time the door opened, I was given a glimpse of Calak. Sometimes he was standing over the table assessing Yuri's work, other times he was leaning against the wall, head back and eyes closed. Was he saying a prayer?

Sloan was a nervous talker, something I didn't expect. She would alternate from sitting next to me to pacing in front of the door, using the time to tell me about her childhood and life on a Western farm.

Rig had not moved. His head was still resting on his arms. At one point, I thought he had fallen asleep, but then I saw his eyes shift, staring at different spots on the cobbled ground.

Finally, Veras emerged from the infirmary as we all stood for an update.

"He's alive."

Exhales of relief echoed from the hall.

"Yuri said that Bowan dislocated his right elbow and suffered a nearly catastrophic wound to his chest. There was a collapsed lung as well. We believe he's out of the woods, for now."

Calak and Bree joined us. Suddenly Rig was there, hand around Calak's throat, shoving him against the wall.

"You bastard!"

"Rig, what are you doing?" Veras demanded, but Rig's intense hold on Calak only tightened.

"Release him," Bree's voice was calm, holding a blade to the side of Rig's neck.

No one moved. I held my breath, denying my instinct to push through and defend Calak from this attack.

"He did this," Rig seethed through his clenched teeth.

Calak just stared at Rig with unforgiving eyes. I was so confused and it seemed I wasn't the only one.

"Will someone tell me what's going on?"

Veras asked, one arm straight out in front of me, an attempt to shield me from any harm. I saw Calak's gaze flick over to us. He observed the King's defensive positioning and then his eyes, filled with an unexplained fury, landed on mine.

"He's a traitor. Calak sold us out to the Raiders. I should've taken him down right then, but we needed to get Bowan back here and I couldn't do it alone."

Bree's sword still rested against Rig's throat.

"My brother's not a traitor."

"Tell that to the dead Northerners they sent us to ransom."

His face inches from Calak's, Rig sounded like he was ready to rip him apart. My nose flared at the threatening posture, Rig needed to back up, right now.

"You walked us right into a trap. I should snap your neck."

"Step back, Rig," Veras ordered.

The King's guard had inched closer, weapons drawn. Releasing Calak's neck, Rig stepped back and Bree lowered her weapon as the sound of metal sliding out of a sheath drew my eyes back.

Calak had drawn his sword. Immediately, the guards were surrounding us. I noticed that Sloan, Veras, and Bree also had their weapons drawn.

Why had Calak drawn his sword? He held it, ready

for a fight. What was happening? I just wanted him to look at me. He was glancing at everyone around us, but me. More guards arrived in the corridor. It was obvious that if Calak persisted in this fight, he wouldn't walk away cleanly. He was outnumbered and his back was literally against a wall.

"Cal, lower your sword," The King commanded.

Calak huffed. "You could never make the hard choices, Veras."

I couldn't believe that he just addressed the King so informally in front of others. Shaking my head, I tried again to get Calak to look at me. Maybe I could get through to him before he made another mistake. He was probably just exhausted from everything that had happened.

"After all we've lived through, you're willing to put your own desires ahead of the entire Kingdom."

Calak's eyes narrowed on me as he spoke. My eyes softened, pleading with him. We hadn't known each other that long, but I felt connected to him. I was searching for something I could say that might be able to help diffuse the situation.

"Was she worth it?" Calak looked at the King. "I hope you at least got to bed her because she won't be here for long."

My mouth dropped open. Had he really just said that? His eyes were so cold and uncaring. Desperately, I searched for any hint or sign that the man that held me after my nervous episode or that had a food fight with me in the middle of the night was still in there.

What was he even saying? It sounded like he just threatened to kill me. He pointed his weapon right at me, then dropped it on the ground. Arms raised.

"Seize him."

At Veras' word, the guards took hold of Calak. He

didn't fight them. Seeing him in their hold, bound and forced forward, was awful. Unnatural. Calak was the King's advisor and best friend, not a lawless traitor. My breathing quickened. Watching him being dragged away, I worried that I'd never see him or talk to him again.

"Take him down to the cells."

The King was angry. The guards were almost out of the corridor now. Everything inside me wanted to run after them. I don't know what I'd do once I caught up to them, but those couldn't be the last words that Calak ever said to me.

I turned to Bree. She looked distressed and confused, just staring at the wall where her brother had just stood.

We had to be missing something. I couldn't believe that Calak would ever betray his friends, his family. Maybe Rig misunderstood, but then why would Calak say those things to Veras? What had changed from the time he left the castle three days ago to now?

Weapons sheathed, the group stood quietly. I'm sure each of them was still trying to understand the repercussions of what just took place. My hands were shaking ever so slightly. The adrenaline was still pumping through my body.

"Bree, I want a tactical plan of attack against the Raiders' camp by the end of the week. Lay out all scenarios. I'll need a report on our troop numbers and a weapons manifold."

Veras slid his hand down to hold mine. His hand was clammy. As much as the King was putting up a strong front, I knew he was shaken.

"I'll question Calak tomorrow. No one is to speak of what just transpired. Do not make assumptions or take any course of action."

That was directed at Rig.

"Calak has been a member of this court for as long as I've been King. We will sort this out, you have my word."

Not waiting for a reply, Veras led me away from them.

And I heard Sloan quietly ask Rig, "What the hell happened out there?"

CHAPTER TWENTY-THREE

FLOATING ACROSS THE DANCE FLOOR, my feet moved in unison with my partner's. The room had emptied. Everyone was gone for the night, but we stayed. The world had disappeared and it was just the two of us here, in each other's arms. Lowering my head to rest on his chest, I took a deep breath. He smelled like the fresh air. I nuzzled my nose into him, then lifted my chin.

Calak stared down at me. His facial expression pulled between desire and questions. Our movements slowed as he lifted his hand to my hair. Pulling gently on a curl he examined me.

"What do you want, Raelle?"

I had no answer. Did I want to go home or stay in the North? Did I want him or did I want Veras? The more questions that popped into my mind the more certain I was that I didn't want to make the choices.

"What do you want?"

Calak leaned into me, his deep blue eyes begging me to get closer. There was a swell of tingling sensations racing through my lower abdomen. I swallowed.

He let go of the curl, as he slowly ran the pad of his fingertip across my jaw line and then brushed my lips with his thumb. I stood still and silent. Waiting. My mouth parted, ready for him. My pulse was racing. Gently lifting my chin closer to his mouth, I held my breath.

Calak was going to kiss me. And I was ready to let him.

Dropping his hold on my chin, he grabbed hold of my wrist, tightly. I winced at the pain. Twisting me around so my back was against him, I felt the steel of a blade against my throat.

"Too late," he whispered into my ear.

"Raelle, did you hear me?" Sloan asked, snapping me out of my memories of my dream from the night before. Dream or nightmare. It could've been both.

We'd volunteered to muck out the horse stalls while the servants assisted Bree with a weapons inventory. I hadn't built up the nerve to ask anyone about Calak yet.

Last night, Veras escorted me to my bedchamber. He offered for me to dine privately with him, but I declined, choosing instead to have my dinner sent up. The truth of it was that I didn't know what to say to him, or any of them.

Two of the King's guards stood watch outside of my room, as the Unit was otherwise engaged. It was a long, quiet night that I spent either staring out my window or cuddled by the fire. Just me, alone with my thoughts. I didn't feel qualified for what was facing me.

How could anyone be at just nineteen years old? No one had ever taught me what to do when your entire family conceals something from you, or how to act while pretending to be engaged to a man who you are developing feelings for, or how to feel when people are actively trying to take your life. I had been assaulted, betrayed, kidnapped, and kissed all in the past week.

Gods, had it only been a week?

I needed to reconcile the losses I was feeling. With Kolt's revelation yesterday, I felt the loss of my home. In time, I may have been able to forgive them, but the West no longer felt like my safe harbor. I deeply loved my family and I would see them again one day. For now, I needed time. The opportunity that Nichelle had offered me to regain the memory of who I was and where I came from was alluring. But that information could prove to be revolutionary or destructive, depending on what the past held for me.

The shame of what Zane had done in the training room did not hold weight, like I thought it would. I had accepted that it was not my fault, and there was nothing I could have done differently. That day resulted from madness and greed, likely the growing influence of Kellar. Although, did I really believe that the gods had banished one of their own, only to let him be released because two people died?

After a calming bath, I wrapped myself in the fur-lined blankets on my bed and waited for sleep to take me. Laying there, I kept seeing Calak's eyes looking at me. My feelings towards him were complicated, but I knew I had missed him while he was gone those two days. Now I was more confused than ever. Had he hated me this entire time? Was he working with Leon? That was the most unbelievable scenario.

The way he looked at me though. I felt my soul tear. Whatever drew me to Calak was still there. The idea that he'd never smile at me or tease me again was agonizing.

At some point I must have drifted off because I awoke to a knock on my door, the sun already up and that dream still replaying in my head.

"No, sorry, I didn't hear you. What did you say?" I shook my head and continued mucking the stall.

"Is this the first time you've cleaned out a stable?" Sloan repeated her question.

"Yes, actually it is." I smiled and shoveled up some straw, turning to dump it into the barrel. "Did you see Bowan this morning?"

"Yes, I brought him some breakfast. He's in his own room now in the barracks. The old man is as crusty as ever, but no signs of infection yet."

I smiled. Sloan tried to hide it, but she cared deeply for Bowan. He was important to all of them, but the weight of Calak's betrayal was all over her face. He was their leader, their friend.

Bree had been correct when she predicted the heavy snowfall. On our way to the stalls this morning, Sloan led me across the outer courtyard. The heavy flakes fell, landing on everything in sight. Some attached to my eyelashes and melted instantly. I even stuck my tongue out to catch a few.

We finished the last stall, my clothes covered in dirt and smudges of manure, the evidence of my physical labor. Many of my curls, which were held back in a tight bun, had broken free and rested around my face. My cheeks flushed from the work, but I was as content as I could expect to be. Something about moving my body made the weight of everything else feel less heavy. I desperately wanted to head straight for the kitchens to see if Clara had anything to spare, but I was certain I'd be turned away in my state, and she reminded me too much of Calak. So, I'd head back to my room to wash up first. Sloan knew of some back corridors and staircases, which allowed me to feel less guilty about the mess we were trekking through the castle.

As we approached my bedchamber, the four royal guards posted in the corridor gave away what was waiting for me inside, or rather, who was waiting for me. Sloan said her farewells, satisfied that I was well protected, and disappeared.

My room was toasty from a raging fire. The wood crackled and snapped, and Veras was sitting on a chair, eyes fixed on the flames. He had a glass of ale in his hands, his posture was slumped. He looked defeated.

"Veras?"

I was still standing by the closed door, worried about tracking the mess through the room. He adjusted himself in the seat, turning to look at me. It was then that I saw the redness around his eyes, either from tears or lack of sleep, or perhaps both.

"I'm not really sure why I'm here," he stood, walking towards me.

This was a broken man.

"He won't speak with me or Bree. We were with him most of the morning, pleading for him to explain himself."

He lifted his eyes to mine and I couldn't take his pain anymore. I placed both of my hands on his cheeks, holding his face.

"You are an excellent king, Veras, but you are also a good man. I'm sorry. I wish I could help. Maybe if I had insisted on going with Zane, we could have avoided all of this."

Veras raised his hands to rest against mine. His touch was tender.

"No, Raelle. As I've told you before, the Raiders and Leon wouldn't have followed through on their end of the agreement. We would have lost you and still been at war against them." His thumb brushed against the back of my palms. Then he lifted my hands, looking at them.

"What were you two doing?"

A hint of a smile in his voice.

"Mucking out the stalls. The servants were off helping Bree, so we offered. Seemed like a good way to blow off some steam, but I'm afraid the job was messier than I planned."

I lifted my arms, letting them drop to my sides.

"You really are..." Veras leaned in towards me. "Goodness."

He pressed a gentle kiss on the tip of my nose, likely the only part of me that wasn't filthy.

"Wait here."

The King disappeared into my bathing chamber and I heard water being poured out. Was he preparing a bath for me? I looked around and stripped my clothes off before he came back. Kicking my boots off, then shrugging off my pants, I wondered if we'd be better off burning them. It would take a lot to get that smell out. Lifting my tunic up over my head, I dropped it to the ground as I reached for a blanket draped over my bed. I covered myself just as Veras reappeared. His eyes widened. I'm sure he wasn't expecting me to be naked, wrapped in a fur lined throw.

"I figured it was better to leave the mess here and not track it through the room."

"Very thoughtful." He averted his eyes, looking everywhere except at me. "I started the bath for you."

"Veras, you can look at me. All my indecent parts are covered, I promise."

"I wasn't sure what you wanted. Would you like me to leave, or -"

"You can stay, if you'd like." He popped his gaze at me. What kind of invitation did I just extend? "Out here that is, by the fire." I clarified and Veras smiled.

"I'll wait here then, unless you decide you need my help in there." He was flirting with me and I didn't mind it at all.

Following the smell of lavender, I headed towards my bath. Once the door was shut, I quickly lowered myself into the water, letting the dirt lift from my skin. Knowing that Veras was waiting in the next room, I didn't linger. After I was satisfied that I had washed everything off, I stood, dried off and dressed in some clothes left from earlier. Still running the brush through my hair, I went out to sit by the fire.

"All clean?"

"Yes."

We sat across from each other quietly, and I continued to work through my knots. The room was silent, but it wasn't uncomfortable. I assumed the King had come here to talk, so I just waited until he was ready.

"When my father died, I had very little experience in politics. My father's advisors each had their own greedy agendas. After a few months, I dismissed them all and appointed Bree and Calak as my only advisors. I lost the support of a lot of the Northern lords, but with Bree's experience in the army, I had the respect of the military. Those two have always been beside me. I don't know how to be a king without them. Calak is stubborn and often acts rashly, but I've always trusted him. There are things he knows about me that no one else does, but if he doesn't explain himself and give me a chance to understand what is happening, then I'll have to charge him with treason. He all but threatened your life. The guards heard it. It can't be left unpunished."

I took a deep breath.

"How's Bree?"

"She's confused. We all are."

I wanted to help. The threats the Northern Kingdom faced started long before I arrived, but with the Raiders' interest in my capture, I was now involved. Ever since my birthday, they have made me to play the victim; first Queen Estra, then the Raiders, Zane, my family, and now Calak. I may not have known who I was or where I came from, but it was time to decide what I was not, and I would not be the victim. I wouldn't sit back. There was a fight growing inside of me. Maybe it was always there, but I was ready to show my teeth. Of all the obstacles that faced us, there was one thing I needed to prioritize for myself.

"Will you take me to Nichelle?"

"Now? Are you sure?"

"Yes. I need to know who I am."

CHAPTER TWENTY-FOUR

VERAS ESCORTED ME back to the room where I'd first heard Nichelle's storytelling – where she'd exposed my father's lies. Filled with conflicting emotions, I sat in the space, waiting. Nichelle was on her way to meet with us. When Veras sent the request, I assumed I'd have to wait days to see the storyteller, not one hour. It was probably best that things were moving so quickly. If given too much time to overthink this decision, I may have backed out.

Reaching over to squeeze my hand, Veras offered me one of his reassuring smiles.

"As a boy, I spent many hours in this room listening to Sylvette. The gods blessed her with the gift of storytelling. Every detail was captivating."

"She sounds lovely."

"She was."

Nichelle entered the room carrying a satchel over her shoulder.

"Forgive my lateness, your Majesty, your Highness."

"There's nothing to forgive." Veras stood to greet her, and I did the same. "Thank you for coming so quickly. Princess Raelle has considered your request."

The King turned towards me, offering me the chance to speak.

"I'd like to know who I am."

Nodding her head, the storyteller slowly lowered her bag onto the table nearby.

"I can only restore your memories, child. I cannot tell you who you are. That is something that only you can determine."

"I understand. What I mean to say is that I'd like to know where I come from, who my people are, and why I ended up in the West."

"Information can be powerful, but it can also destroy. Are you certain that you're prepared to confront whatever memories arise?"

I'd given this a lot of thought. There could be a reason that no one had come looking for me these last ten years. My past might be riddled with pain or abandonment. Perhaps my family was unkind to me. It's possible that my memory loss was shielding me from years of trauma. In a moment, all of those feelings could come flooding back.

However, the possibility that I had people waiting for me, that there was a family that had mourned their loss and prayed for my return, was enough to take the risk. Even if the beginning of my life wasn't all I hoped it would be, I wanted to know. I needed to know. The choice was taken from me years ago by my father, but in this room I had the power to decide for myself.

"I am."

My answer was sure, and Nichelle respected it.

"Okay. Then we shall proceed."

Opening her bag, the storyteller took various items out and placed them on the table.

"How does it work?" I asked, coming closer to the table with Veras standing right beside me.

"Magic."

My eyes almost shot out of my head.

"Magic?"

Nichelle laughed. "Yes, child."

I looked at Veras, who seemed unfazed by the word. Other than in the histories of Garth and children's storybooks, I'd never heard tell of magic in the West.

"You mean that magic is real?" I asked, immediately regretting how young I sounded.

"It's very real, Princess. However, only the gods can give someone their magic and no human alive can wield it without using a relic. This is one of the last magical elements left in the North that I know of. We have passed it down from storyteller to storyteller, always keeping it well protected."

She picked up a stone that had gleams of colors running through it. They pulsed, reminding me of the auroras. It was the most beautiful thing I'd ever seen. As I leaned in for a closer look, the streaks of light within the relic flashed brighter. Captivated, I reached out to press the tips of my fingers to it. As soon as my skin made contact, a jolt of energy burst through my arm, causing me to jump back in surprise.

"What was that?" I asked.

"Magic," Nichelle smiled.

She made herself busy preparing for whatever was

about to happen. I had paced the room, mostly to hold off the worrisome curiosity that was settling in my chest. Veras walked over and stood in front of me. Slowly, he wrapped his arms around, pulling me into his chest. I didn't resist, allowing the comfort of his body to relax my nerves.

"Only if you want to, Raelle. We can leave at any point."

"I know."

Despite how I felt, I wanted this.

"I can't believe that magic really exists."

Veras chuckled.

"Don't laugh."

"Sorry." He didn't sound all that sorry.

"Is there magic everywhere? Or only in the North?"

"The magic of the gods can exist anywhere there is a relic. I know for certain that each kingdom has them, although the other courts do not officially recognize their power."

"Why?"

"Magic is from another time. When the Evamores ruled, they readily used magic throughout the kingdom. I suppose the people associated magic with their former rulers, and they slowly eradicated it from the other three kingdoms."

I don't know why, but that made me sad.

"Why did Nichelle say that 'no human alive' can wield magic without a relic?"

"The ruling Evamores were gifted, not just with the look of the gods, but the use of their magic as well."

"The Evamores had magic?" My eyebrows raised.

"Yes." Veras smiled while he said it. "According to our stories, they didn't require a relic to call on the gods' magic. They used it to protect their people and keep the land fruitful."

If the Evamores had magic, then how were they defeated? That was one of many questions racing through my mind when Nichelle called out to us from the table.

"It's ready."

Taking a deep breath, I slowly laid myself down on top of the table she'd prepared. The stone was cold, even through the blanket she had put out for me. Veras came and stood by my other side. I grabbed ahold of his hand. He held on tightly and gave me a squeeze.

"Now what?" I asked, a bit impatiently.

Nichelle looked down at me. Her face had seen many years, but there was a youthfulness to her. Maybe it was the magic. I scoffed at myself. I didn't think I'd be able to stop imagining what one could do with a magical relic.

"The process is quite simple, but in order to start, we must calm your mind."

"How do we do that?" I asked.

"You must clear away all thoughts."

I closed my eyes, but as soon as I did, my mind instantly flooded with images of what one could do with a magical relic. Could it conjure up your favorite foods? Chocolate cake? Would one be able to use it to exact revenge on an enemy? I wondered if you'd be able to control someone's decisions and words with magic.

"It's not working," I announced in defeat.

Nichelle just smiled at me. "You cannot clear thoughts away with more thoughts. Imagine them as waves. When one thought comes, you let it drift away.

Do not visit it or hold on to it. As you practice that, watch my finger carefully."

She moved her pointer finger slowly in front of my eyes. I tracked it, trying to do as she had instructed. When a thought came, I let it keep rolling away. Then another. And another. Eventually, the words and images in my head slowed, and I felt a heavy relaxation rest on my entire body.

"Excellent."

Nichelle praised my efforts. I noticed in the corner of my eye that she had picked up the magical stone and was holding it in her other hand as she continued to move her finger in front of my eyes. I didn't break my concentration. Back and forth. Back and forth.

The storyteller repeated a prayer or a limerick I'd never heard before, but as she spoke, a tingling sensation grew in my feet. I widened my eyes as it moved up my legs and into my torso. Nichelle continued to speak until the feeling wrapped itself around my head, releasing a bit of pressure, and then everything went dark.

The ship was rocking harder than it had the past few days. I held my arm up to block the wind that ripped against my face. Sprays of seawater crashed over the side of the ship. Sailors were everywhere, pulling and holding rope lines. I was supposed to stay below deck, but I had to see the storm for myself. My curiosity was always my father's favorite quality about me...and my mother's biggest worry. Thinking of them shot a twinge of grief through my chest. A hand grabbed my small wrist. "Raelle, you must come down below. It's not safe up here for you." I turned to see my chaperone; the person charged with my safe travels. She was gentle and wise. Her jet-black hair was half-pinned up, revealing her deep blue eyes and freckled nose. We hadn't known each other very long, but she cared deeply for my family. At night, when I had trouble sleeping, she would tell me stories of the past. Her art of storytelling was so well crafted that I struggled to separate the fact from the fiction. I looked into her eyes, which were now pleading with worry.

"I'm sorry, Sylvette," I shouted over the sound of the waves. "I just wanted to see the storm for myself."

There was a loud crack as the mast snapped under the pressure of the raging tempest. The ship heaved to the port side, and I lost my balance. My little body slid down the deck towards the railings. The last thing I remembered was the sound of my head striking against something, and then everything went black.

I opened my eyes and stared at Nichelle. Her look was one of understanding. Did she see what I saw? Is that how this worked?

Veras still held onto my hand, squeezing it to remind me he was there. How long had I been unconscious for? I looked at him and then back at the storyteller.

"I think it worked. I remembered something."

The intense rise and fall of my chest was from the adrenaline of the memory, or the weight of what it revealed.

I knew Sylvette.

CHAPTER TWENTY-FIVE

"How's that possible?"

Bree sat across from me in our regular alcove.

"The memory was as clear as the events of yesterday, but I can only recall that moment. I still don't know where I'm from or anything else about my real family."

"But my mother? Why would she have been on that ship with you and in charge of your care? I was seventeen when she died. If she knew your family, then I would have met you or at least been aware of you."

"I don't know what to say. I hoped Bowan might help me piece it together. Perhaps he knew my family, but never connected them to me. Regardless, it seems likely that I was from the North or staying in the North prior to the shipwreck."

"I'll have the castle recordkeepers look for notices of missing children from around that time. Perhaps there will be some answers there."

Veras had joined us, but stopped first in the kitchens to request our dinner be sent here. We were in the middle of feasting on a roasted duck, something that seemed so natural and in stark comparison to what I experienced that afternoon.

Nichelle had used the magic of the gods to restore my memories. I couldn't decide which was more outrageous: that magic actually existed, or that fate had brought me face-to-face with the children of the mysterious woman charged with my care ten years ago. On the outside I was maintaining a cool front, but on the inside, I was freaking out. Everything I knew about the world was being torn down day by day. But instead of being terrified, I found myself embracing it.

But there were still more truths to discover. Were the Evamores evil or good? Was the influence of Kellar responsible for the increased violence throughout the kingdoms? What about the decaying crops in the West? If magic existed, could we not use that to balance things?

These were questions that no one could give me today. There was one person who'd be able to help me solve some of the mystery surrounding my new memory.

"I'd like to speak with Bowan."

"I'm sure that can be arranged, but Raelle, losing Sylvette nearly destroyed him, and his body is frail right now. I must insist that if recalling thoughts of her proves to be too much for him, that you try another time."

Veras was next to me, our thighs pressed against each other. His arm rested on the back of my chair, as his hand idly traced circles down my back. This was an example of the physical touch we agreed was necessary to maintain the pretense of our engagement, but every moment with Veras had me wondering where the ruse stopped and genuine feelings grew.

Perhaps it was all in my head. Maybe the affection he had shown me behind closed doors was only an effort to solidify the connection between us, to further convince people we would wed.

Whatever the reason, I liked his attention. It was exciting and new. At worst, it was a distraction from the onslaught of troubles we've had to face this week.

"What else did you remember?" Bree wiped her hands on the cloth napkin and leaned back in her chair.

"Just the storm and the ship. I knew that my family had entrusted me to your mother. When I thought about my parents, I was sad, but that was the extent of it. They could be dead, or still alive, and I was just missing them. I remember that your mother told stories to me at bedtime to help calm me. The last thing I saw was falling and hitting my head. I'm assuming that's what caused my memory loss."

"Will you keep getting your memories back?" Bree lifted her glass to her mouth.

"Nichelle said that the process is different for each person. I could wake up tomorrow and know everything about my past, or it may come back in pieces."

Somehow, the knowledge that I had a family that cared enough about me to trust my safety to someone like Sylvette, who was regarded as a respectable woman by many here in the castle, was a comfort. It meant that whoever my parents were, they loved me.

Were they still in the North mourning me? Did I have an extended family here? The thought that some of them could even be in the castle, working and serving under Veras, was intriguing.

I truly hoped that my revelation wouldn't cause any pain for my new friends, but I didn't see how that would be. This news meant that Sylvette dedicated herself to care for a child, to the extent of traveling on a ship, even if it never reached its destination.

Oh gods. How did I just now make this connection?

If she was with me on the ship, and the shipwrecked...

Father said that they searched for survivors and they found none.

That means that Bree and Calak's mother wasn't murdered by the Raiders, but died in the sea because of me. They had committed their lives to tracking and fighting Raiders, in hopes of avenging their mother's death. How would they feel knowing that I was the reason she was dead?

I must have gone ghostly white because Veras leaned towards me.

"Are you unwell?"

I wasn't sure if they had reached the same conclusions I had; I didn't have the nerve to ask it out loud. Would Bree hate me if she realized that her mother's death was my fault? Perhaps that was what had turned Calak against me, but how would he know if I only just discovered it myself? It seemed like every time a question got answered around here, three more sprouted up in its place. It was exhausting.

"I think I'd like to retire."

I smiled at Veras and then Bree.

"Of course," Veras stood, helping me to my feet.

We walked out of the alcove, greeted by the King's guards that had been standing watch. Once we reached my bedchamber, I found some of my nerves.

"Will you stay with me for a little while?"

I saw Veras' throat bob as he swallowed. His lips parted, but nothing came out. He just nodded his head slightly in agreement. We left our guards in the corridor and went inside.

The room was dark, save for the fire the servants must have lit over an hour ago, by the look of the logs that had already burned up. Veras immediately went over to stoke the flames and add more fuel. I slowly paced the room, trying to muster all of my courage. I may not be ready to speak with Bree about this, but I had to talk to someone.

"Why does everyone believe the Raiders murdered Sylvette?"

Veras stood.

"Our scouts saw her entering their encampment alone. That was the last anyone saw her."

"But if she was on the ship with me, as far as I know, no one else survived the storm. Do you think it's possible that all of that occurred after the scouts saw her? Meaning that she wasn't in fact murdered by Raiders, but that she died taking care of me." My eyes searched his. "Veras, I think I'm the reason Sylvette is dead."

We were standing together now. Veras' hands slowly stroked my arms.

"It's possible."

"They're going to hate me."

"Bree has mourned the loss of her mother and with her tactical thinking, she won't hold this against you. You were a child. Sylvette and your family made those decisions. No one can blame you for them."

"But Calak will?"

"Calak is not himself right now."

"And what about Bowan? He loved Sylvette, and he was injured trying to avenge her death."

"Bowan would never harm an innocent; however, I'd like to be present when you speak with him."

It wasn't a request. Veras was the King and could be anywhere he wanted. I had just enough courage for my next question.

"Do you have feelings for me?"

"Yes."

This man was confident and straight to the point. If my question shocked him, then it didn't show.

"Okay."

Veras chuckled. "That's it?"

"Honestly, I barely had the courage to ask that question in the first place, let alone come up with a second one."

"Okay, then I'll ask you a question. Do you have feelings for Calak?"

I took a step back. I was not expecting that.

"It's okay if you do. You've done nothing wrong."

My mind raced to make sense of both my feelings and thoughts before I replied. "I thought I might, but..."

"You don't have to explain it to me, Raelle."

I had feelings for both of them. The attraction I felt to Calak was raw and undisciplined, but every bone in my body knew that nothing good could come of it. He was sitting in a cell because he threatened my life and betrayed his Unit. I wouldn't even allow myself to continue entertaining any feelings I may or may not have towards him.

The King that stood before me was gentle and loving. I felt safe when I talked with him, certain I could spend an eternity in his presence, never tiring of it. He was handsome, but it was his soul that was most attractive. There was something so pure about him. Holden's warning echoed through my mind: everyone has secrets. Veras may have secrets worthy of a king, but I didn't care. I retraced my steps so I was in front of him again.

"You were my first kiss." Veras said nothing as I placed my hands on his chest. "I don't have a lot of experience, but I know I enjoy being with you. I thought maybe this thing between us was just part of the ruse, to convince people we would have wed, but when your lips touched mine, it washed away all the pain, like a magical relic," I smiled. "There are so many things going wrong right now. And the only time anything feels right is when I'm with you. I'm not sure I'm worthy of your feelings, but I'm also not sure I care. And if that makes me a terrible person-"

Veras' hands clasped the back of my neck, lowering his head as his lips pushed against mine. I moved my hands up his chest to rest around his face. This kiss was more passionate than our first kiss. He pulled his head away, and we just looked at each other.

"What do you want, Raelle?"

"Right now, I want to kiss you, and then later, I want chocolate cake."

Veras threw his head back and laughed. I moved my hands up and pulled his face back down towards me. This time when we kissed, he used his tongue to part my curved lips and explored every inch of my mouth.

***

"I'm definitely going down to the kitchens tomorrow to thank Clara for this."

My mouth was still full from my last bite of the most decadent chocolate cake. Veras and I sat on the floor, our backs against the end of my bed, with a fur blanket underneath us and another laying overtop of us. I was leaning against him, a plate of the dessert on my lap. From this spot in my room we could see out the window a display of auroras dancing in the night sky. I would've been happy to stay there forever, forgetting everything that was waiting out in the world. For just one night we could steal ourselves away, but once the morning came, we'd need to face it all.

"How do you know what to do, as the King?"

"What do you mean?"

"The Raiders? Calak? Queen Estra? Me? It's just so much. How can you possibly know what to do next?"

"I don't know."

"Huh. Ever the confident King." I looked up at him and smirked.

"I'm not sure that anyone really knows what to do. For me, I collect as much information as possible and try to make a wise decision. There is no perfect path. My goal has always been to make peace, but the longer I serve as King, the more difficult that seems. Being the one in charge is very lonely. I have had no one close to me in many years, besides Calak and Bree. Which makes me very thankful to have you here, now." He lifted one of my curls and twisted it around his finger. "I didn't expect this when you first arrived. As soon as I saw you, I was taken by how beautiful you were, but when I heard the strength in your voice and saw the goodness of your actions, I became transfixed by you, Raelle. The gods must favor me, to send me such a gift."

Damn. He was so eloquent.

"So what do we do next?"

"Well, Bree will continue to prepare for an attack against the Raiders. In the morning we will speak with Bowan and, gods willing, Calak will explain himself."

"And tonight?" I left the invitation hanging in the air, for what exactly I wasn't sure.

"Tonight, I'd just like to sit here and hold you, if that's alright?"

Settling deeper into his hold, I turned so my head now rested on his chest, looking back out at the sky, "I'd like that."

CHAPTER TWENTY-SIX

BOWAN'S ROOM WAS SMALL. It reminded me of the barracks by the western wall I'd visited once with my brothers. There was nothing unique about this space: a bed, a small desk, a chest of drawers, and one window facing the eastern forest beside Castle Mount. Veras had explained that they offered Bowan his former quarters when he returned with Calak years ago to join the Unit, but he declined.

Sitting in bed, propped up by some pillows, he was making quick work of the broth we had brought him.

This morning I woke up still on the floor in Veras' arms. He was snoring ever so slightly. I laid there quietly, listening to him and watching the sun's rays break over the window ledge. After about ten minutes,

I realized I needed to take care of some personal issues and tried to slip out of his hold without waking him.

As soon as I shifted, his arm tightened around me and I was greeted with a groggy, "Good morning."

I turned to look at him. "Good morning, your Majesty."

I jumped to my feet and hurried to the bathing chamber. After a few moments, I washed myself off and returned to the room. Veras was already up, folding the blankets we had used and returning them to their rightful place. I took note that he was a tidy person.

"Breakfast?" he asked me.

"I'm too nervous to eat. I could use some tea though."

We switched places, and I gave the King privacy while he attended to his personal needs. Minutes later, we were walking down the corridor, hand in hand, with a host of royal guards. They were different men than the night before. For a moment I wondered what the guards must have thought about Veras spending the night in my bedchamber until I realized I didn't care what they thought. That level of confidence surprised me.

Clara and her kitchen maids were already in a frenzy when we arrived, and we caught them off guard. They fell all over themselves making sure that the King had everything he requested, including the hot broth for Bowan. Now we sat in his room, me in a chair at his bedside and Veras leaning against the desk.

"Are you sure it was Sylvette?" Bowan asked as he slurped another spoon full.

I hadn't seen him since, oh gods, when was the last

time I saw him? The night of the dinner, when the Raiders attacked Hillsborough. Regardless, he looked better than I expected. He was shirtless, with bandages wrapped around his chest. His left arm was held in a sling, leaving him to eat with his right hand. The bowl rested on a tray which sat across his lap. I had offered to help him eat, but he rejected that with a scowl.

"As sure as I can be. I have no other recollection of her, yet." It mildly disappointed me when I woke up that morning with no fresh memories.

"Veras, in my top drawer, pull out the blue box."

Veras did as requested, handing Bowan the rectangular box, painted a sapphire blue. I quickly removed the tray, setting it on the chest of drawers, while he opened it up. Pulling out a small frame, he paused, looking at it for a moment.

"This was Sylvette."

He slowly turned the portrait over to me. She was gorgeous, just as I had remembered her, with that jet black hair, deep blue eyes and freckles. The spitting image of her children.

"That was her. The woman in my memory was Sylvette."

I handed the image back to Bowan, and he tucked it back away safely inside of the box.

"We were hoping you could help us make sense of this," Veras spoke from behind me. "Are you sure you never met Raelle before she arrived at the Northern border that day?"

"As sure as I can be. You have a unique look and I'm sure I would have remembered seeing anyone who looks like you up here in the North. I'm sorry I can't say that I ever met you or anyone who may resemble family."

"The day that Sylvette left Castle Mount, did she say anything to you?"

I kept reminding myself of Veras' warning last night. He'd asked me to be mindful of how difficult this could be for Bowan. So far, he seemed comfortable with my question, except for the look of physical pain from his injuries.

"She had mentioned asking an old friend for a favor, but that was it. We were busy that day with a tournament being held in honor of your father's birth date. I barely saw her before she left. When she didn't come back, we sent trackers out looking. Calak joined them. They returned with a report from the scouts saying they saw her walking into the Raiders' encampment. Your father tried to talk me out of it, but I was set on rescuing her. Calak and Bree begged to join me, but I forbade it. I placed them under guard to ensure they wouldn't follow me. When I got to the camp, she was nowhere to be found. Her death was certain, or so I thought. Gods, I should have looked harder for her. I gave up too easily."

Bowan was reliving the grief of losing Sylvette.

"You loved her."

I wasn't asking him a question. It was clear.

"Love isn't strong enough a word for what I felt for that woman."

"I'm sorry, Bowan. If she hadn't been on that ship with me, then maybe she'd still be here with you. I'm so terribly sorry for your loss."

"Sylvette had her own mind. If she was on that ship with you, there was a damn good reason. No one would have been able to talk her out of it."

Bowan offered me a half smile as I admired his strength.

"It's hard to believe that the scouts wouldn't have

noticed Sylvette leaving the encampment. That's the piece that makes little sense. How did she go from being in the Raiders' camp to being on the sea with a mysterious child that none of us knew?" Veras was mulling it over from his spot at the desk.

"More questions," I muttered.

"If we still had the scouts' reports, you could look through them to see if there was anything that helped, but Calak burnt them."

"Why the hell would he do that?" Veras clearly was unaware of this bit of information, and he was not happy about it.

"I never asked. He told me, when he came to find me all those years ago, that he studied them for weeks, looking for any inconsistencies, then burned them. I assumed it was out of his grief and frustration. I couldn't very well blame the boy."

I knew what I wanted to ask next, but I was certain that Veras would be opposed to it.

"I should go talk to Calak."

"Raelle, he won't speak with you."

I turned to Veras. "We don't know that for sure. You said so yourself, he's refusing to talk with you or Bree. Bowan clearly can't go see him. I have to find a way to at least try to get some answers. Maybe he'll talk to me, maybe he won't, but he can't hurt me from his cell."

I could see Veras thinking about it, so I tried to strengthen my argument. "Something is going on with him. Perhaps there's a way for me to get him to open up. I'm clearly a trigger for him. We saw how he reacted to me in the hall the other day. He could get himself all worked up and say something that will help us get him back."

The room was quiet.

"There is something that could help, but the gods and Sylvette forgive me if I'm wrong." We were both staring at Bowan now. He looked torn, as if he wasn't sure he should continue speaking. "I helped Sylvette raise those two kids. You know that, Veras. So what I'm about to tell you could be the gravest act of betrayal against Calak's trust in me, but the bastard's not thinking right. I think he's got himself all confused and I can't think of any other way to snap him out of it."

Veras and I waited for Bowan to speak again. I watched his face go from confused to resolute.

"Calak has a son."

Veras moved closer to Bowan's beside.

"When?"

"The boy is seven. He lives with a good Northern family in a nearby village. No one knows, not even Bree. His mother was a tavern wench and dropped the child off at the barracks entrance after he was born with a note. I found him and helped Calak secure a safe place for the child to live."

"Wait? Are you suggesting that we threaten the child's life?" Veras would not agree to this plan. I knew that before I even heard the tone of his voice.

"He knows that you'll never hurt the child, but he doesn't know Raelle well. She's a mystery to us still. If she's convincing enough, perhaps he'll believe the boy's life is in danger and will reveal what he knows. Both about the scouts' report and what happened the other day in the forest with Zane."

"Calak will suspect that it was you who told us about the boy," Veras said.

"He'll get over it."

I took a deep breath. Could I do this? As a child, I would pretend many scenarios in my playtime with

Holden and Dalia; an evil queen, pirates searching for treasure, or a maiden lost in the forest. But this was real life. I'd have to stand in front of Calak and convince him that I would be willing to hurt his only son.

"Raelle, you don't have to do this." Veras' concern was also his permission. If I wanted to, I could.

"He's lost to all of you right now. And he alone holds any chance of understanding how Sylvette came to be on that ship with me, which could lead us to my family. I can do this. I will do this, but you have to trust me. I have an idea, but I don't think you'll like it."

Veras and Bowan exchanged a look as I stood, taking another deep breath. I could do this. The child would never actually be injured, but I would make Calak believe otherwise. It was the only way.

"What's your idea?" Veras reluctantly asked.

***

The grinding sound of metal on metal bounced off the damp stone walls as the door to Calak's cell swung open. My first idea, I had to convince Veras to agree to, was allowing me to speak with Calak in his cell, alone. Walking down here was a bit unnerving. Sloan had escorted me, then stayed back in the warden's room with the rest of the guards while I walked the long corridor alone. There were muffled coughs coming from the other cells. I wondered if one of them belonged to Trews. Some of the prisoners greeted me with vulgar slurs, reaching their arms through the gates. My chin held high, I ignored them all.

Once I was inside of Calak's cell I looked around; the room was only lit by a lantern sitting on a small table against the wall and the glow of torches coming from the hallway. Before me was Calak, still wearing his blood-stained uniform, chained to the wall. That was Veras' compromise.

"So they sent you? Really? I'm disappointed. I thought Veras and Bree would be more creative in their interrogations."

"They don't know I'm here."

My second idea, lie about getting Veras' permission.

"That's unlikely. How did you get into the cells without their permission? The place is crawling with guards."

I then took off my cloak, revealing a tightly fitted dress that pushed my bosom into my throat. I'd taken my necklace off. Somehow it didn't feel right to wear it while I was in this outfit. It was by far the most ridiculous thing I'd ever worn, but definitely something that would allure most men, even if my neck was covered in stitches.

This, however, was an idea that I left out when convincing Veras. I didn't think he'd agree to dressing myself up as a whore to throw Calak off.

"So the Princess isn't all she seems, then?"

"You know nothing about me."

Calak's eyes narrowed as he tried to take a step forward, but was held back by his chains. I huffed out a laugh. Taunting him.

"I brought something for you."

"I want nothing from you."

"We both know that's not true." I bit my lip and placed the basket I brought on the table. "Clara misses you. Odetta too."

I smiled at him, remembering our conversation on the stairs that day. He accused me of being jealous.

Still no reaction from Calak.

I lifted the cloth covering the basket to reveal a selection of fresh pastries, similar to the ones we had sampled on my first day at the castle.

"Hungry?" Calak said nothing. "Oh, come on. Eating something reveals nothing. Besides, how good can the food be down here anyway. Don't be an ass. Just eat one."

Calak pulled on the chains, reminding me he could not move his arms to eat anything. I smiled, as my third idea was about to play out; feeding Calak food. Veras didn't understand why this was necessary, but I was working off some techniques Kolt and Holden had discussed around the dinner table many times.

I picked up the top sweet and slowly walked over to Calak. Our eyes never broke contact. The spark of raw attraction was still there, for me at least. Which was completely messed up, but I shoved that thought aside and focused on my task.

"Hungry?"

I asked again. Now just a foot away from him. My breasts were heaving from how fast I was breathing, the adrenaline was working against me. I tried to slow my breaths down, so as not to give too much away.

"Always." Calak finally spoke, his eyes full of challenge.

I lifted the bun to his lips, and he took a bite. It was messy, as I had hoped. I put my thumb in my mouth and sucked it so it was damp. Then I lifted it to his mouth, wiping the syrup mess from his lips. Taking an extra long time as I dragged it across the bottom one. To my surprise, he didn't shift away from my touch.

This might actually work.

CHAPTER TWENTY-SEVEN

"WHY ARE YOU HERE, RAELLE?"

"I missed you."

That lie was easy, because it was, in fact, true. I had missed Calak, but not this version of him.

"Veras isn't fulfilling you?" He was intentionally being an ass to get a reaction out of me. I was glad that the King wasn't here to witness how callously Calak spoke of his friend.

"I'm not here to talk about Veras."

"So, I'll ask again, why are you here?"

"The castle is boring without you."

"You shouldn't be here."

"Here? As in your cell?"

"No, you shouldn't be in the North. If I were the

King, Zane would have left with you and that would be the end of things."

"But you aren't King, are you? And if you wanted Zane to take me so badly, then why did you beat the piss out of him that day?"

"Passions got the best of me, I suppose."

"You want to know what I think?"

"No."

"Too bad. I think you wanted to be the one touching me, and that's why you got so angry. I think that the idea of someone else's hands on my body made you sick."

"And whose hands have been on your body exactly besides Zane…the King's, I suppose?"

"It's part of the arrangement. You knew that."

"You don't seem to mind that part of the arrangement."

"He's a handsome man." I tried to sound dismissive as I ran the palm of my hand down his chest.

"Why are you here, Raelle?"

Calak practically screamed the words at me. He was tired of the wordplay, but I wasn't.

"You have information that I want."

"I won't tell you what happened that day in the forest."

"Fine. Then tell me what was in the scouts' report you burned after your mother died."

Calak looked shocked. He didn't expect me to ask about that. "And why would I tell you that? What's it for you?"

"Because I got some of my memories back. I went to see Nichelle, and I remembered something about my past. It was the day of the shipwreck on the Balour Sea ten years ago. The storm was raging, and I went above deck to see it for myself. A woman was traveling with me. She tried to get me to go back down below. Her hair was jet black."

I lifted my hand to tuck some of Calak's hair behind his ear.

"Her eyes were a deep blue."

I ran my finger across his eyebrow.

"And she had these freckles across her nose."

My finger stopped at the tip of Calak's nose. He was searching my eyes for any sign of deceit. This was the truth, so it wasn't hard for me to convince him of it.

"Your mother was with me on that ship. My family had entrusted her to bring me somewhere. When the ship crashed, I believe she died in the sea."

"You're lying. My mother was murdered by the Raiders."

"Why would I lie?"

He didn't trust me, and I couldn't blame him. His entire adult life had been focused on punishing the Raiders for what they had done to his mother. Although, from what I could see, the Raiders had many reasons to be hated. By the way his gaze moved from my eyes to my lips, I knew Calak was thinking about more than just the words that had come out of my mouth. I leaned into him, pushing my chest against his, and lifted my chin to meet his stare.

"I'm not lying to you. She was there. I remember her stories, the feel of her touch on my wrist as she pleaded with me to listen to her. Her voice was deep and yet soft. Bowan showed me a portrait of Sylvette and it was her."

"Step back," Calak practically growled at me.

It was unclear if his anger was solely directed towards my line of questioning, or the news I'd just broken to him. I complied, but only because I was playing a game that I didn't know the rules for and any minor mishap could upset the entire plan. I needed to keep all of his emotions on high, from desire to hatred.

"Why would she be on that ship with you?"

"I don't know. I've gotten no other memories back. But everyone here believes that she died after entering the Raiders camp with Leon that day. Clearly that's not true. So, perhaps the scouts' reports hold a clue as to where she may have gone after. But someone had a tantrum and burnt them."

Calak scowled at me. "It was a long time ago. Besides, there was nothing significant in those reports."

"Maybe you overlooked a detail."

"Not likely. I'm a tracker. Details are my specialty." The smug bastard was annoying, but right. He would have an eye for detail, but I couldn't rule out the possibility that he was lying to me.

I decided to shift my questioning.

"Why do you want to send me to the Raiders?"

"It's the only way to avoid a war and save us."

"I didn't count you as a coward."

I could see the anger burning in Calak's eyes as his lips thinned and he pulled on the chains. "I'm not a coward, but your freedom is a small price to pay for the security that our Kingdom needs."

"Your King and sister would disagree."

"The King is thinking with his cock and my sister, well, she's given me reason in the past to doubt her decision-making skills."

I was avoiding using the knowledge of Calak's son. I hoped I could use other emotions to push him into speaking. There were still some ideas I had yet to use, but I prayed no one was watching from the shadows in the corridor.

"He's not the only one who thinks with his cock, is he?"

I walked towards Calak, no hint of jest in my eyes, only sultry desire. I placed my hand lightly on his chest and ran it across his body as I walked around him, stepping over and ducking under the chains where they connected to the wall. Calak was frozen still, but he allowed this touch.

When I came back to his face, I ran my hands up his chest, to his neck and then through his hair. I lightly pulled his face down towards mine, so our lips were close, but not touching.

"I never slept with him."

Calak's eyes snapped to mine.

"I wanted it to be you. That day that Zane attacked me, I was waiting for you to come, but you just left."

The seeds of truth to what I was saying helped.

"So, I waited."

Twisting his head to the side so our lips were perfectly aligned, but still not touching, I was in complete control right now and he still wasn't speaking. He just watched me. I licked my lips.

"I wanted you."

And there it was. The truth that I hadn't spoken out loud yet. I wanted Calak. Damn. I should've turned around and left the cell at that moment, but I stayed.

"Raelle." His voice was quiet, like a lover, or at least what I thought a lover would sound like.

I swallowed. "Yes?"

"Stop playing the whore, it doesn't suit you."

My eyes popped open, and I let him go. Stepping back, I watched as he flashed a wicked grin. He wouldn't fall for my tricks. My heart cracked, because I knew what I had to do next. I turned my back to him, taking a deep breath and getting ready for the performance I was about to play.

"You know, Calak, your problem is that you think you're smarter than the rest of us. Which is dangerous. It leaves you exposed. It leaves those you love exposed."

I turned back towards him, staying further away this time.

"Lucky for me, I don't love anyone." He had to be lying. I had seen him with his Unit, Bree and Veras. This man loved those closest to him, but that wasn't the truth I needed to expose right now. I took another deep breath and told myself to focus.

"Is that so? You never fell in love while you were out in the world being a tracker, moving from village to village?"

Calak lifted the corner of his mouth, "No."

"Hm. Never fell in love with a tavern wench? Never got so caught up in a moment's passion that you forgot to protect yourself?"

Calak wasn't breaking my stare. I took one more step towards him and let the faintest smile show. I tried to remember every time I saw Estra's evil smile before she said or did something awful. I hoped I was portraying her convincingly.

"Oh, poor Calak. It's hard when your secrets get out. It makes you vulnerable." He was seething, and I hadn't even made my threat yet. I prayed the gods would forgive me. "When's the last time you saw your son?"

"Don't be foolish, Raelle."

"Ha. Calak, come on. You don't know me. I came out of nowhere. Why do you think everyone keeps coming after me? I'm dangerous and I always get what I want no matter the cost."

"You're lying."

"You're really willing to risk his life on that guess? Now you're the one being foolish. How old is he now? Seven? Hm, I wonder what it'll sound like when I shoot an arrow through his eye socket. I've been practicing on a smaller target these past few days. It should be a painless death. That's a comfort at least, right?"

The sound of Calak's chains rattled as he urged himself forward.

"I will kill you if you touch him, you know that?"

"I know that you're here, chained to a wall, so I'm not sure exactly how you'll accomplish that." My acting was too good. Calak let out a roar. He was angry, no, he was furious, but I wasn't done.

"Calak, it's simple. Tell me what happened in the forest. Why did you betray the Unit? And then tell me what you remember from the scouts' reports. If you do as I say, then no harm needs to come to the child. I give you my word."

His nostrils were flaring. If those chains gave out, then I knew he would choke the life out of me. Had I gone too far? Was this a fool's errand? I took a deep breath and Calak still hadn't spoken. What else could I do to convince him to speak with me? After this day, we would no longer be friends. We would no longer flirt and tease one another. I had just killed any chance of him looking at me with any sense of desire, but I did it for our friends. I did it for Veras.

The sound of feet running down the darkened hallway broke the tension. Sloan appeared, surrounded by four royal guards. She paused in front of the cell, first taking in the sight of Calak in chains. I thought she might say something to her leader. I wondered if she had been down here to visit him yet? She looked at me and it was then that I remembered what I was wearing. Oh gods. I reached over for the cloak and covered myself up.

"Raelle, come with us now."

"What's going on?" The tone of her voice was strained with fear, not something I would expect to hear from Sloan.

"We're under attack."

Instinctively, I turned to look at Calak, who was staring at Sloan.

"By who?"

"The Eastern Kingdom."

CHAPTER TWENTY-EIGHT

THE EASTERN ARMY had breached the border closest to Castle Mount. They were still a half a day's ride from us, but the scouts had just arrived with the news. I followed Sloan to Veras' chambers, but instead of being brought to the main entrance, she led me through a side passage into his bathing chamber. My curiosity peaked. It wasn't until we entered the room where his bed sat that I heard muffled voices coming from the closed door I knew led to the space I was accustomed to.

Veras was definitely a tidy man, as I had expected. On the chest of drawers, he had perfectly lined up several small bottles and jars, all evenly spaced apart. A tidy stack of papers sat on a desk, paired with a quill and ink. There was not a speck of dust anywhere to be seen. The walls were bare except for a portrait of a man I didn't recognize. I assumed it was his father, the former King.

"He wants you to wait. I'm leaving to update Bowan and rendezvous with the Unit. There are guards posted outside the passage we just went through. You are safe here, but for the gods' sake Raelle, don't wander off."

Then Sloan was gone, back the way we'd come from.

Don't wander off? I was insulted that she was insinuating I was some young child who had the tendency to get lost and not follow directions. I plopped myself down on the edge of Veras' bed, which was covered by a large, wrinkle-free blanket, and waited.

The voices coming from the other room were strong and commanding. I could make out the sounds of Veras and Bree's voices, among many others. My assumption was that this was a gathering of the military leadership, making plans for the impending arrival of the East.

Kolt had said in his letter that Father sent Queen Estra back home to her own Kingdom. Surely King Sutton wouldn't rally his entire army and march to the North just to get back at me, but nothing would surprise me. The world was much more greedy and violent than I had expected. Maybe we all had some level of darkness inside of us. Fighting for space against the pureness of our souls.

I stood and walked towards the closed door and the voices that carried through it. I pressed my ear to the wood, closing my eyes and tried to make out the conversations.

"What did King Sutton's letter say?" An unknown voice asked.

"He wants an audience with me tomorrow. His army marches to Castle Mount. They have assured me none of our citizens will be harmed or property damaged," Veras explained.

"He marched his entire army all the way from the Eastern Kingdom just to have a conversation with you?"

Someone in the room was not convinced of King Sutton's intentions, and neither was I. If he was anything like his daughter, then Veras should slit his throat the moment he stepped foot in the castle, but then we'd be left with the retribution of the Eastern army.

"We've sent riders to call in our forces from across the North. Many of them will arrive by nightfall and stay hidden in the mountain passes." Bree's voice fit amongst the mens'.

"And you don't know what he wants to discuss with you?" The first voice asked.

"I have my suspicions, but I'll make no assumptions until his intentions are made clear. He has our backs against the wall, but we'll defend the North if we have to. It would be wise not to provoke the Easterners, for the sake of our people who aren't protected behind the walls of Castle Mount."

"And what of the Raiders? Surely they'll use this distraction as an opportunity to cause more trouble?" The question came from another unknown voice.

"I don't think that'll be an issue. According to King Sutton's letter, the Raiders ride with him."

Damnit.

***

"Leon," Sylvette was speaking quietly so no one outside of the tent could hear. I knew we weren't safe this far inside of the Raiders camp. "We must leave at once. The ship will not wait."

"The way is not yet clear. You asked me for help, so we'll be doing this my way."

Leon had a gray mustache that hung down both sides of his mouth and no hair on top of his head, which was instead covered in swirls of tattoos. From what I could see, he still had all of his teeth, which wasn't common in the Raiders camp, or so I'd been told. The tent they'd kept us in was large, with fur blankets laid out to create a false floor. A table with six chairs sat in the center, covered in various paperwork stained with spilt ale and two straw beds in the corner, where Sylvette and I had slept last night. The sounds of the men laughing and drinking kept me up, so she told me stories and rubbed my back until I fell asleep. I missed my family, but something about this woman reminded me of my mother.

I sat up abruptly, unaware that I had dozed off waiting for Veras' meeting to end. The room was still bright from the afternoon sun. No voices carried from the other room. Before I went to see if Veras or Bree were out there, I needed to digest what I just remembered. These memories felt like dreams. Could I trust they were real? I already knew that my remembrance of Sylvette was accurate and I had seen Leon coming down the stairs when I first arrived at the castle. Although it was far away and he was wearing a hat, that long gray mustache was the same.

So there it was. I had met Leon when I was a child. My heart was racing. Why was I in the Raiders camp?

Were my parents allies of the Raiders? I couldn't believe that. Why would Sylvette agree to help anyone aligned with such brutes? But the way she spoke with Leon, they knew each other? He was helping secure us passage to the ship.

It was a dangerous time to be a friend of the Raiders in Castle Mount, so I kept this recent memory to myself. What if Veras or Bree locked me up in the cells next to Calak until they knew I wasn't a threat? They wouldn't want to do it, but would they have a choice? I couldn't risk it, not when I didn't have enough information to tell them.

Standing to my feet, I allowed myself a few deep breaths before I walked towards the door. Just as I was about to open it, I heard an unfamiliar man's voice.

"Your Majesty," he greeted Veras.

"What have you heard? And be quick about it."

"The instruction is to wait."

"Wait? For what?"

"It wasn't clear, but she must be protected."

"I've already taken measures."

"The message also asked if it was complete."

Veras sighed. He didn't answer. Was what complete?

"I have my next target." This strange soldier was piquing my curiosity.

"Then take your leave."

I heard the door to the main corridor open and then close again. What a strange conversation. Nothing that was said made any sense to me. I supposed that I was the "she" that was being protected, but even that could be wrong. I'd only known Veras for a short time, and as King there were many things he would be responsible for. Waiting another few moments so as not to draw suspicion that I'd been eavesdropping, I slowly opened the bedchamber door.

Veras was leaning against the table, his arms supporting him as he poured over maps and, what I assumed, were scout reports. His shoulders were broad and I could almost see all the weight they were carrying at the moment. I came up behind him, slipping my arms around his waist, and pressed my head against his back. He sighed.

Straightening himself, he turned to embrace me.

"Enjoy your nap?"

"I did. How long have I been asleep?"

"Less than one hour." Veras hugged me tighter. "How'd it go with Calak?" I realized then that I was still wearing the cloak which was hiding the revealing dress.

"It didn't work. He may have eventually told me something, but Sloan came to retrieve me. Regardless, he hates me. I'm afraid I was too convincing." I took another deep breath.

"Once we get this mess figured out, I'll explain it all to him. He'll forgive you, in time. You never would've hurt that child. I know that and he'll understand that too."

I wasn't convinced. Veras didn't see the way Calak looked at me or the sound he made when he tried to reach for me. If given the chance, I think he would take my life.

"I heard that King Sutton is joining us."

"Yes, he is."

"Is this my fault?"

"No. There's more at work here than just your arrival to the North. But to be safe, you won't be joining me at the meeting tomorrow. The Unit will stay with you and if anything goes awry, they have their instructions."

"What do you mean 'if anything goes awry'?"

"I just want to be prepared." He ran his hand through my blond curls. "You're very important to me, Raelle, and I won't let any harm come to you." I lifted on my toes, planting a kiss on his lips this time. His hands ran over my shoulders, pushing the cloak back. The dress caught his eye, and he leaned back to survey it.

"What's this?"

I stepped away from him, pulling the cloak closed.

"I...it was part of the ruse."

"Is that so?"

"I had to convince Calak that the guards let me into the cells without your knowledge and I thought it would be more believable if I looked likc someone a man couldn't say no to."

Veras smiled, then his face turned serious. "Actually, I didn't really get that good of a look at it. As the King, I should probably know what kind of dress would make my guards forget their duties."

The smile returned. There was a rush of something down in my stomach...no, lower, a burning between my legs, and a flutter in my chest. His eyes were daring me to remove the cloak. I bit my lip and unfastened the clasp holding it together at the base of my neck. Lifting the cloak off my shoulders, I let it fall to the ground behind me. Veras' chest stopped moving. With his smile gone, he looked me up and down until his gaze finally rested on mine.

"You said I was a good man," Veras took a step towards me. "But if you knew the thoughts that were in my head right now, I don't think you'd call me that again." He took two more steps towards me.

What was about to happen?

"There's an army marching to my front gate. The only father I've left in this world is laying in his bed, unable to get up. I locked my best friend in the cells. And yet, all I want to do is get you out of that dress and carry you to my bed."

"And then what would happen?"

I truly didn't know. I'd heard stories from some of the younger female servants back in the West, and my brothers would often tease each other in front of me about their experiences with women. None of those things prepared me for whatever Veras may want to do with me. I needed to decide. Did I want to stay and find out, or did I want to leave? Almost as if my body had decided for me, I took a step towards the King.

"Then I'd kiss every inch of your skin. Memorize the way you tasted and felt under my touch. Make love to you until the gods themselves had to stop me. I would make you forget every man you've ever laid eyes on until it was just you and I alone in the world."

"Oh."

"Is that what you want, Raelle?"

I swallowed.

"I would like you to kiss me and touch me, but I'd like to keep my dress on."

There were some experiences I didn't feel ready for. Again, I was surprised by my confidence. I knew what I wanted right now, but I also knew what I wasn't ready for.

Veras smirked and leaned down. This man would respect my wishes. His lips landed with force against my own as his hands folded around my back and pulled me up towards him. Lifting me with ease, I wrapped my legs around his waist, still deeply kissing him. Our tongues were now intertwined as a soft moan left my lips. He walked us towards his bed and shut the door.

CHAPTER TWENTY-NINE

BREE JOINED US FOR DINNER in Veras' chamber that evening. My lips felt swollen from the afternoon of kissing and touching with the King. It was glorious. I'd never felt such desire for something or someone as I did when we were wrapped up together in his bed. My dress stayed on, but I had a better understanding of what could've happened if I let him take it off. Thankfully I had enough sense to send someone to retrieve another dress from my bedchamber before dinner.

"You two look...satisfied." Bree took a sip of her wine as I choked on mine.

"It was a productive afternoon." Veras took another bite of his dinner. I was certain that my face was as red as Sloan's hair, while he continued the conversation like nothing had happened. "What's the progress on the troops' arrival?"

"The mountain passes are almost full. We're still waiting for some regiments from the Western coast to arrive. It's extremely unlikely that the Raiders or the Eastern scouts are aware of their presence. We'll have the element of surprise on our side if a fight breaks out."

"Excellent. You'll join me for the meeting tomorrow, along with Hughs and Reaves. I've already explained to Raelle that she'll stay with the Unit."

I turned my nose ever so slightly at the idea of not being able to be in the meeting with them. I wanted to stare at King Sutton's face and hear what lies he'd try to weave, but I knew the Raiders were with him, which meant that Leon could be at this meeting. And I couldn't risk him exposing me to my friends.

"What of Calak? If there's a fight, if the Raiders make it down to the cells, they'll execute him." Bree was worried about her brother, and for good reason. Even though he wanted to trade me to the Raiders for peace, that didn't make him their ally.

"The Unit has their orders." Veras' reply was ominous, but I didn't probe for more information.

"Well, Rae," Bree used my nickname. It was the first time anyone in the North had used it, and it felt nice. "Let's hope tomorrow is uneventful because the snow is still here and I promised you we'd go tobogganing."

"Yes, you did."

"Now, tell me what happened with my brother today and why Sloan said you were dressed like a streetwalker."

I choked on my wine again. Veras chuckled into his glass and Bree just smiled, waiting for an answer.

***

From Veras' window, I could see the glow of fire from the Eastern army's encampment. They had kept their word. No Northern citizens were molested, and no property damaged as they made their way to Castle Mount. Those in the castle unable to fight, including the children who lived here, were taken to safe shelters built into the mountain passes. I made a note to ask someone to give me a tour of these tunnels after all of this was over. Bowan would be among those taken to the shelters, and I was certain he'd be furious about that.

The moon was bright this evening, and the snow was lightly blowing across the courtyard below. "Did you always want to be King?" I was still looking out the window, but I felt Veras' body against mine when he joined me.

"No. I actually wasn't born to be a King."

"What does that mean?"

"I had an older brother."

"Really?" I turned to face him.

"Edward. He was four years older than me."

"Did he die?"

"When I was ten, he took me ice skating. We didn't check the thickness. Edward fell into the cold water, broke right through the ice. I couldn't reach him. He was swept under and taken by the current." Veras' head was bowed. He still carried the guilt over his brother's death.

I placed my hand on his cheek. "I'm so sorry, Veras."

"It was difficult. My father blamed me for Edward's death. We were never close after that. I think that's why I became so attached to Bowan. He didn't hold me responsible."

I wasn't sure what to say, so I just stood there with him in silence. He pulled me into his chest, which I realized was bare. Whoa. His skin was so smooth and perfect. I placed my hand on his abdominals and traced their indentations. Veras' body was a work of art. My finger ran up to his pectorales, then his collar bone. I was trying to commit every line of his body to my memory.

"Have you had any fresh memories from your past?"

"No." I lied.

"Nichelle said it could take time. You shouldn't be discouraged."

"I'm not. Besides, the present isn't all that bad."

I twisted in his hold, bringing my hands up around his neck. I felt the evidence of his attraction to me growing against my stomach. A chambermaid had brought me a nightshirt to wear. I'd chosen to spend the night in Veras' chamber. Since tomorrow held so many unknowns, I wanted to be with him as long as possible.

"Raelle, no matter what happens tomorrow, promise me you'll stay with the Unit."

"I promise."

"No matter what?"

"Why are you so worried?"

"I'm just trying to be prepared. Please, Raelle." He pressed his lips to mine. "Stay with the Unit."

"I will."

With a kiss to my nose, he took my hand and led me towards the bed. Still respecting my wishes from the afternoon, Veras had agreed that we would limit all activities to kisses and holding one another.

Gods, I could love this man.

***

After a quick breakfast, I said goodbye to Bree and Veras. The latter kissed me in front of the entire Unit — well, what was left of it. I would've been embarrassed if I hadn't been so satiated by the taste of his lips. Bree gave me a wink as she followed the King down the corridor. Within the hour, they would meet with King Sutton and his envoy from the Eastern Kingdom.

I turned to my friends. They were dressed in the same uniforms I'd seen them in when they picked me up at the border.

"So? What do we do now?"

"We sit tight and see how this meeting turns out," Sloan answered.

"Okay. Where do we sit tight exactly?"

"Anywhere on this side of the castle works. There's an access point to the tunnels this way, in case we need to use it."

Along with the double swords across his back, Yuri had an additional pack, which I assumed was full of medical supplies, in case we needed to leave at a moment's notice.

I had dressed in Northern-appropriate clothes and outerwear, which were getting a little too warm for the inside of the castle. Each of us had bags that Clara and her kitchen maids filled with supplies before being ordered to join the others in the tunnels. The halls of Castle Mount were eerily quiet, but I knew where I'd like to sit tight. So I suggested we head towards my alcove.

***

"How exactly does the game work?" Sloan asked.

"You tell us two things about yourself that are true and one thing that is false. We'll try to guess which is the lie." It was my turn to teach Sloan a new game.

"Okay. Give me a minute to think." Sloan looked at the ceiling then smiled. "My father made me kill my first chicken when I was three years old, I've never been on a boat, and I've kissed one of Raelle's brothers."

I nearly choked. Rig and Yuri burst out laughing at my response.

"There's no way you've kissed one of my brothers."

Sloan grinned.

"Which one and when?"

"Danier. I was twelve and he'd come to our village with your father on some business. We were playing in a barn with some other children and we kissed."

"I can't believe you didn't tell me this before."

"I guess I was waiting for the right moment."

I chuckled.

"So, which one was the lie?" Yuri asked.

"I was five when my father made me kill my first chicken."

We sat and played games for the better part of an hour until I realized I required a bathing chamber to take care of my personal needs. My room was close to the alcove, so Rig escorted me, staying outside in the corridor, of course. After I was finished and washed up, I recognized a faint tap at my window.

The snow owl was back.

"Have you been waiting for me?" I asked her, running my fingers down her back. She cocked her head, and I looked down to see their arrival through the castle gates.

As I suspected, Leon was there, beside a man I assumed to be King Sutton. He was old and moved slower than the rest. There was a host of personal guards with them, and a woman. She walked beside the King. I focused on her, finding something familiar in the way she moved. Her hands reached up, pulling back her hood.

Queen Estra was in the North.

The group walked up towards the entrance of our castle, out of my line of sight. Why had she come to the North? It had to have something to do with me. I don't know why, but I wanted to see her. I needed to see her. Knowing the Unit wouldn't allow it, I darted out into the hall, catching Rig off guard. I ran down the corridor towards the main stairwell. From there, I could see the grand hall. I crouched down, laying flat on my stomach. Peering over the edge of the landing, I saw Bree and Veras, along with many other Northern military leaders and soldiers, waiting for the Eastern party to enter.

Rig had caught up to me.

"Princess, you must come back to the alcove. It's the King's orders."

"Just give me one minute. I want to see her."

Much to my surprise, Rig allowed it. He backed up against the wall to remain unseen, but I glanced over to see his hand resting on the hilt of his sword. Not that he needed weapons to take down an opponent. Looking back down, I could see her now, standing in front of Bree, her eyes fixed on Veras. The look was predatory, like she owned part of him. If I hadn't already hated her, that would have done it.

I focused on hearing what they were saying.

"King Sutton, if you're looking for an alliance with us, then I must ask why you've brought Leon into my court. His men recently tried to kidnap my betrothed and murdered my soldiers during a peaceful prisoner exchange."

Veras always sounded so diplomatic.

"Leon was misguided in his actions. I've outbid his previous employer and the Raiders now belong to me. But be careful how you talk to me, boy. My army is more decorated than yours and I've seen more battles. It would be wise for you to hold your tongue and not question my choices."

"Your army is soft. Money doesn't buy courage."

Bree's remark earned a sneer from a guard standing behind King Sutton.

"Veras, you should have your women trained when to speak."

Leon's voice was identical to my dream.

This meeting had barely started, but I didn't have high hopes for its outcome. The conversation grew louder.

I pushed forward so I could see more clearly.

Lots of voices were carrying back and forth. I couldn't make sense of anything. A man standing behind Veras spit on the ground, as two more guards stepped forward from behind King Sutton. Someone was shouting. I thought it sounded like Bree.

Then I heard the familiar sound of a weapon being drawn.

"No!"

Veras shouted as I watched a sword puncture through Bree's chest. Right at her heart. Before she collapsed, Bree swung a dagger, slicing at her attacker, Queen Estra.

My friend fell to the floor and Veras let out a war

cry as the two parties began fighting across the stone floor.

I was frozen, staring at Bree's fallen body laying on the ground, a pool of blood spreading out from her. Soldiers stepped over her as they fought one another. I lost sight of Veras in the middle of it all. Then Rig's hands grabbed me, pulling me to my feet. I couldn't move. He was shouting at me, but I couldn't hear him. Suddenly, I was hoisted in the air and flipped over his shoulder as he hurried back towards the alcove.

Still in Rig's hold, my mind spinning from what just occurred.

Bree was dead.

Veras might be too.

I couldn't take a deep breath. My body went limp. Yuri and Sloan had heard the commotion and met us on our way back. They spoke to each other, and I remembered seeing Yuri run off in a different direction. Sloan trailed behind Rig as we entered the hidden tunnel access point they'd mentioned earlier. Sloan was trying to speak with me, but I was unresponsive.

Once deep inside of the tunnels, Rig pulled me off his shoulder and I collapsed, leaning against the dirt wall and sliding down to the ground. Sloan was cursing. Rig was silent. They'd just lost a friend and maybe more. I looked around the passage for any sign of the Northern army. There was none. Where were we? And where did Yuri go? Maybe he went to help Bree, to see if there was anything that could be done, but I knew that injury was fatal. Tears rolled down my face. I lowered my head into my hands. This couldn't be happening. Was Veras dead too? I prayed to the gods that he was still alive.

The sound of rushed footsteps echoed in the

chamber. As they drew near, I saw Yuri, but he wasn't alone. The darkness concealed his face, but as he got closer, I saw Calak walking towards me.

CHAPTER THIRTY

MY BREATH CAUGHT IN MY THROAT as Calak's eyes settled on me with a deadly glare. I was certain he wanted to kill me, but I saw they bound his hands and he carried no weapons.

"What the hell is he doing here?" I demanded.

"This was Veras' idea. If a fight broke out, he ordered us to escape with you and Calak," Yuri explained.

"What happened?" Calak asked. He looked at all of them, except me. He didn't care what I had to say. Not since I'd threatened to kill his son, who no one else knew existed. When no one in the Unit answered I realized that Yuri hadn't told him about Bree yet. A fresh tear fell down my cheek as Sloan stood in front of him.

"They killed Bree." Her voice was firm, but a tinge of grief made it wave ever so slightly.

Calak's eyes widened as he shook his head. He took a step backwards and then another.

"No. That's not possible. She - no, no, no."

He fell to his knees and Sloan kneeled in front of him, her hands on his shoulders. He burst into sobs of pure pain. The agony was raw. I had little experience with mourning, but this sounded like someone had ripped away a part of him. Which I suppose they had.

My heart broke for him. Despite everything we had said to one another, I never would have wished this upon him.

Calak kept saying her name over and over. "Bree. Oh gods. Bree."

Yuri wiped tears away from his eyes and even Rig looked close to crying. We all waited there. An occasional moan coming from Calak. She may not have been an official member of the Unit, but Bree was a part of them.

"I'm sorry, but we can't stay here." Rig was the first to speak. Sloan helped Calak to his feet, and we all headed deeper into the mountain pass.

***

We carried on for hours. I forgot the Unit traveled in silence. Completely at their mercy, because I didn't know where we were, and with only the light of our torches to guide us, I kept my head down, keeping in step with Rig in front of me and Yuri at my back. Thankfully, they'd brought me a bow and quiver full of arrows, which were both hung across my back which made me feel more useful.

"We'll stop here for the night," Rig announced.

I settled against the edge of a wall, opening my bag to see what food Clara had packed us. Sitting at the top of my pack was a package wrapped in brown paper, tied with twine and a flower stuck in the knot. Was this a gift from Veras? When would he have had the time to get this together? Perhaps it was a request he made through Clara. I made quick work of opening it, finding a slice of chocolate cake waiting for me. Letting out a happy sigh, another tear slipped out as my heart ached for my King. I decided to eat the dessert immediately so it didn't spoil on the journey. The journey to where, though, I didn't know.

The first bite was delicious and messy. With no utensils, I was left to eat with my fingers. I must've moaned because it caught Sloan's attention.

"What did Clara pack you that made you moan like that?"

I jumped to my feet, walked over to where she sat, and offered her some of the cake.

"Clara is a goddess," Sloan moaned, her mouth filled with cake.

I laughed as the sound matched my own. Offering some to Yuri and then Rig, they both expressed their gratitude and praised the gods for the Northern cook's talent. I turned to see Calak sitting with his legs stretched out in front of him, staring at his hands. His eyes were still red from the grief. I paced over to him, stopping in front of his feet. He looked up at me.

"I don't want any of your fucking cake, Raelle."

This man absolutely hated me. Looking to see if anyone was listening to us, I used this moment to explain myself. Who knew how long we'd be traveling together. I thought it was best to get this out of the way, even though I was doubtful he'd ever forgive me.

"I never would've done it." He looked away from

me. "It was a foolish idea, like you said. Everyone was desperate to understand why you did what you did, so Bowan told us about your..." I checked again to make sure no one was watching us, then whispered, "son. He thought I could use it to coerce you into talking. It made me sick to do it, but Calak, you have to know, I would never, ever hurt him or tell anyone that he exists."

My voice was low. The emotions of this day had drained me. Calak still didn't speak to me, so I turned to walk away, but had one more thing to say.

"I'm sorry about Bree. She was my friend, but I know how much you loved her."

Once I was settled on my sleeping mat, I closed my eyes and prayed that sleep would find me quickly. My capacity to handle emotions was gone. I needed an escape from it all.

"Karissa, you must wait your turn. It's a tea party and you'll be served after our guests."

I was in a garden with my younger sister, Karissa.

She was born two years after me and followed me around everywhere. When we had tea parties, we'd fill the table with our dolls and Cook would bring us small sandwiches on little plates to snack on.

They only filled the teapot with water. One time we used proper tea, and I burnt my hand. After that, Mother forbid us from using anything but water.

"My doll wants two sandwiches," Karissa announced.

She had white hair like me, but hers was straight and always tied half back out of her face.

"Then your doll shall have two sandwiches," I smiled.

I awoke to Yuri gently shaking my shoulders.

"Raelle, it's time to move on now." I shook my head in understanding and sat up to repack my bag.

The reality of why I was waking up in a dark, empty tunnel hit me. Veras was lost to me and we'd never see Bree again. I secretly had hoped that she would be like a sister to me if I ended up staying in the North. Someone I could confide in and laugh with.

But I had a little sister, somewhere. The memory was still foggy, but she was real. She'd be seventeen now, wherever she was. I felt a flood of hope rush through me. There was a family waiting for me somewhere. I knew in my heart there had to be. Even though I still couldn't remember my mother or father, or where I was from, I remembered Karissa.

Without the sun to mark the day, I didn't know what time it was.

"How long will we be in the tunnels?" I asked, to no one in particular.

"If we keep moving, we should reach the northwestern pass before tonight," Rig answered me.

We made quick work of eating a small breakfast from the rations in our packs. I noticed then that someone had brought Calak his own supplies. Why wouldn't Veras have shared this plan with me? The night before he had asked me to go with the Unit "no matter what." Maybe this was the "what."

Traveling with Calak wouldn't be easy. I wasn't sure how Rig could do it. Last time they were together, he tried to strangle Calak, calling him a traitor and a bastard.

Calak had wanted to give me over to the Raiders, which meant that he didn't care if I lived or died. Thank the gods he was still bound, or else he might have killed me in my sleep last night.

After a few hours of walking silently, my feet ached,

but I refused to complain. I stopped to adjust my boot when I heard a noise from a connecting tunnel ahead of us. I looked around and the rest of the Unit was also on alert. We slowly lowered our bags to the ground and readied our weapons. The voices were getting louder. There were perhaps five or six of them. This far away from the castle, I supposed they could be anyone. Maybe they were some soldiers coming from the western coast that Bree had mentioned, or perhaps they were Raiders.

"Sloan, untie me and give me a sword," Calak commanded, but it was no use.

None of his friends offered to do what he requested. It was clear they still didn't trust their former leader. He cursed, kicking at the dirt wall. I shouldn't have, but I smirked, turning my head so no one could see. We moved towards the approaching threat.

"If they're friendly, we stand down. If they're Raiders or Easterners, no one lives."

Rig was ruthless and angry. I took one more deep breath, as nine Raiders turned the corner carrying torches of their own and weapons.

"RAIDERS!" Rig yelled, and they charged forward.

I readied my arrow and took aim at the nearest one. My shot was true, and it caught him in the chest, right where his heart sat. Rig had discarded the torch he carried into the dirt and took a swipe with his bare hands at a man running towards him with an axe. The massive weight of Rig's fist contacted the man's face, and I saw teeth spit out onto the ground. Grabbing the handle to the axe, Rig turned it, burying it into the neck of his attacker. Blood sprayed across them both.

Sloan pushed past them, engaged in a sword battle with two of the Raiders. Her body twisted as she sidestepped a deadly swing of one of their swords. Reaching down, she unsheathed her dagger into her free hand, now wielding two weapons. Faster than both of her attackers, she blocked one of their blows with her sword and ran the dagger across both of their midsections, slicing them open and spilling their innards out. Their cries echoed down the tunnels in all directions.

I glanced at Yuri as he lifted his two swords above his head, bringing them down across the chest of a Raider who was already on his knees. The man fell forward, blood ran down towards my feet.

I nocked another arrow and searched the tunnel for a target. It was harder to see in the darkness as many of our torches had gone out. I squinted. A man fell to the ground. I thought maybe it was Rig who took him out. I moved forward, trying to get a clearer view. It was almost pitch black down here and I didn't want to accidently hit one of my friends. I was stepping over fallen bodies as I forced my eyes to focus.

A loud grunt came from behind me and I turned to see a Raider face-to-face with me, my arrow pointed directly at his mouth. His arm was swung upwards, readied with a bloodied sword, his eyes fixed on me, but he wasn't looking at me. He was looking through me. Falling to his knees, I backed up so he wouldn't hit me, as he collapsed to the ground.

Then I saw Calak standing in the space where the Raider had just been with a red soaked dagger in his bound hands.

CHAPTER THIRTY-ONE

WE REACHED THE NORTHWESTERN PASS just as the sun was setting. Leaving the dampness of the tunnels, the air was milder than I was expecting. Birds were chirping as we climbed up the ridge ahead of us. I only stumbled on the rocks once, but at the top, the view astounded me. Everywhere I could see was a stretch of mountains speckled with trees and patches of snow. To the West, the setting sun glistened off of the sea — the Balour Sea.

"Raelle, sit down here. I need to remove those stitches." Yuri motioned me towards a boulder.

"Here? Can't we wait until we arrive wherever it is we're going?" I asked.

"We could. But Rig's gone to take a shite and that'll

take a while. We have time." I smiled, taking a seat and moving my head so the injury was exposed to him. Yuri pulled out a pair of scissors and started cutting. Looking straight, I saw Calak standing off to the side of us, staring at Yuri's work. His face was full of disgust. He went to turn away.

"No, no. Don't look away, Calak. This is what you wanted."

He whipped his head towards me.

"I'm sure Zane would've done much worse than this if you'd actually gone through with your plans." I was pissed off. At him. At the Raiders. At Estra. At the whole damn world. Calak said nothing. He just turned and walked further into the forest.

"Feel better?" Yuri asked. He wasn't talking about my neck, he was talking about how I'd just spoken to Calak.

"No."

"We're close to the outpost," Rig said after he reappeared from the tree line.

In the absence of Bowan and with Calak tied up, Rig was the appointed leader of the Unit, which surprised me. I'd always seen him as the quiet, raw strength member of the group, but since we'd left the castle, he'd been in charge.

Trekking down the other side of the ridge we just climbed, I was careful to watch my footing as we walked in single file, and of course, didn't speak. I had planned to talk with Calak after he saved my life during the fight with the Raiders, but then seeing him stare at me when Yuri worked on my neck, like he was sorry for me, I just snapped. He'd been avoiding my eye contact all day. Anytime we stopped for water breaks or personal needs, he made himself scarce. Which, at this point, was fine with me.

The long, silent journey we'd been on these past twenty-four hours left me with nothing to do but pray that Veras had survived the battle. I couldn't bear the thought of never holding him or feeling his touch ever again. I completely drained my tear ducts from crying over the losses we'd suffered and all the unknowns. Had they overtaken the castle? Were those in the shelters able to escape? Did our army prevail?

Our army? But I wasn't a Northerner. And clearly I wasn't born in the West, either. The more I discovered about myself, the more I realized that I don't belong to any of the kingdoms. I was kingdomless. A princess without a place to call home.

A weathered building appeared through the trees. There were three simple steps leading up to a veranda which had several chairs and round tables spread across it. It was a single level dwelling made mostly of timber, with a bit of stone around the chimney and foundation. I looked around for any sign of other inhabitants and saw none. No smoke came from the chimney. This must be the outpost we were on route to.

"What is this place?" I asked.

"One of the army outposts. We use them when traveling across the Kingdom. It's a break from sleeping on the ground, although I prefer the view of the stars above me then the bottom of a bunk."

Sloan was standing beside me as I took in the view. The idea of sleeping in a bed and eating a hot meal seemed right for my soul. Nothing could erase the pain, but these little things would help piece us back together.

Entering the main door, my nose got a whiff of stale air and a bit of mildew, a common smell from old, stagnant buildings. The furnishings were simple.

A few settees framed the fireplace. Behind them a long table, able to host at least a dozen people, sat empty. There was a doorway that I believed led to the kitchen, and a corridor to the right.

"This way and I'll show you where you'll be sleeping." I followed Sloan down the corridor and into a chamber. There was a bunk bed lacking any linens or blankets, a small table with a chair, and a tall wardrobe. "You and I will stay here. The others will be across the hall." I placed my bag on the table and took another look around the room. How long would we be here for? I didn't ask out loud because I assumed no one really knew the answer. We'd need to gather more information first.

I had offered to make us dinner, not really sure what I was doing, but wanting to be helpful. Rig and Sloan had left to chop wood for the fire and Yuri was digging out blankets for us to sleep on from a storage shed outside. Which left Calak and me alone in the house. His hands were still bound, and he stayed in the main living space while I worked away in the kitchen.

I had shot a rabbit and was attempting to skin it, which was something I'd seen my brothers do a few times, but never attempted myself. The knife I was holding caught on a muscle. I yanked at it. It broke through, but slipped out of the carcass and into my left thumb.

"Damnit!"

There was blood. Grabbing a cloth, I wrapped up my left hand and then slammed the knife down on the countertop.

Calak walked into the kitchen. Instinctively, I grabbed the knife, took a step back, and pointed it towards him. This was ridiculous. Even with his hands bound, he could easily disarm me and use my measly weapon against me. He knew it too, so I placed the knife back down.

"Good choice," He mocked me.

"What do you want?"

"You're bleeding."

"Barely."

"Raelle, the cloth is almost completely red."

Damn, it was. I put it down and grabbed a fresh one.

"You can't make dinner with your hand like that."

Was he offering to cook for me? I remembered all the time he spent in the kitchens with Clara growing up. Maybe he was more qualified to make our meal than I was.

"Are you offering to take over?" He held his bound hands up at me. "You murdered a man today tied up like that. I think you can handle a little rabbit."

He scoffed and walked towards my workstation. I was still uneasy around him, unsure of his motivations or if he would retaliate with my threats against his son. Even though I had apologized, he definitely hadn't forgiven me.

"You're using the wrong knife to skin small game like this."

Opening a drawer and pulling out a different knife, I realized that he'd likely stayed in this outpost many times over the years. He tried to hold the rabbit and the knife at the same time, but it was not possible. I was going to have to help him.

Taking a deep breath, I stood beside him. "Tell me what to do."

I followed his instructions as we worked together to skin and clean the rabbit. Weaving it onto a spit, we lit a fire in the kitchen and laid the meat over it, then started washing and chopping some potatoes we'd found in the pantry. Other than his directives, we didn't speak, but unsure of how much time we'd have alone, I wanted to take advantage of the moment.

"I don't understand why you did it."

"Did what?" He didn't bother to look at me as he finished putting our potatoes into a pot of water.

"Betray me. Betray them."

With his back to me, Calak said nothing. Of course, he wouldn't explain himself to me. I sighed deeply out of frustration and headed to the door.

"My son lives two towns away from Hillsborough."

That was the village that the Raiders ransacked on my second night at Castle Mount. They killed everyone, including the children.

Oh, my gods.

"You were trying to protect your son."

"It was only a matter of time before they attacked his town. I've spent his entire life trying to protect him from the Raiders. And not just him, but all the children in the North. When Zane said that they would leave in exchange for you...I knew I'd hate myself for it, but how could I not? You were nothing to me."

Ouch.

"So you just let the Raiders attack Rig and Bowan? That doesn't make sense to me."

"I pulled Zane aside just before the transfer to arrange the details. I would kidnap you from the castle and bring you to them."

I kicked one of the lower cupboards with my foot. What a prick. Calak watched as Zane mauled me in front of all of them, and he was okay with me being handed over to him. To do gods knows what with. And yet, I was more frustrated with myself, because I understood. My father and brothers would stop at nothing to protect me. Or at least that's what I used to think.

"Back at the castle, before Bree...I heard King Sutton say that he outbid the Raiders' last employer," I said, once I had cooled down.

"Apparently they had a wealthy buyer who was very interested in you."

"So you were going to allow me to be sold. Just like that."

"Yes, I was. I couldn't see any other way to save him. You wouldn't understand." Calak was raising his voice at me now. I blew a deep breath out of my nose and gritted my teeth.

"Why does Rig think you're a traitor?"

"He saw me leave with Zane, and then the Raiders attacked. Likely he thinks that I coordinated it. By the time I got back to them, Bowan was injured, and they killed our prisoners. We raced back to the castle, to Yuri. When I saw you in the hallway, Veras using his own body to shield you, I snapped. He'd never give you up to save them. To save him. I lost all hope of saving my son's life."

And there it was. The explanation that everyone was looking for. Calak loved his kingdom, loved his son so much, and they branded him a traitor for it. Thrown into the cells. Why didn't he just tell them all the truth? I already knew the answer to that. It wouldn't have mattered. I don't believe Veras would've given me over to the Raiders, even if he knew of Calak's son. Maybe he could've brought his son into the castle, protected him behind our walls, but it was too late for all of that now.

Yuri walked into the kitchen and stopped at the sight of the two of us together. Calak, still bound, walked past him and back into the living space.

"You're cut?" Yuri rushed over to me, removing the cloth I held around my left hand.

"Just a small one."

"Did he do this?" Yuri motioned towards where Calak just exited.

"No, it was from the knife."

"Okay. It will need a few sutures. Let's get it cleaned up before an infection sets in." I nodded and followed him out the door. Calak was nowhere to be seen. I looked out the window and saw him walking away from the outpost with no cloak on. Where was he going? It couldn't be far. Maybe he just needed to clear his head.

Sitting at the table, as Yuri cleaned and stitched up my cut, I thought through everything Calak had confessed. If he just came clean to the Unit, especially to Rig, then I think they'd understand his motivations. That had to be better than being an assumed traitor. I was positive that it was Rig's idea to keep him still bound. Even if it was pointless, at least it reminded everyone, including Calak, that he wasn't to be trusted.

Without knowing how long we'd be stuck out here together, trust was going to be an important asset if we were going to survive. Knowing what I'd have to do, I decided to just add it to the list of things I'd need his forgiveness for.

I was going to tell the Unit about Calak's son.

CHAPTER THIRTY-TWO

"YOU HAD NO RIGHT TO TELL THEM!" Calak was screaming at me as we all sat around the fireplace. Before he had come back from his walk, I broke the news to the Unit. Calak had a son, and it was his fear of losing him that drove Calak to take the Raiders up on their offer of exchanging me for their promise to depart the North.

"You're right, Calak. She shouldn't have told us. You should've." Sloan was just as angry as Calak. "We could've protected him with you."

"No, you couldn't have."

"And why not?"

"Because he doesn't know that I'm his father."

The room was quiet.

"I know what it's like to grow up without a father, and I didn't want that for him. Our lives are dangerous and we aren't often in the same place for too long. So Bowan helped me find a family that would raise him, with a father that would see him every day."

I understood what it was like to grow up without a mother, for at least part of my life. So many nights I would lie in bed and dream of her sitting with me, or brushing my hair. I'd have given anything to see my mother every day.

"The whole situation was a mess. Hillsborough had me worried that my son's town could be next, and I just acted on instinct. When I pulled Zane aside to make a plan, the Raiders attacked and Bowan was injured. I should have known that Leon wouldn't stick to a peaceful prisoner exchange. It's my fault that all of this happened."

Rig stood up from his seat and walked towards Calak, his dagger in his hand. I held my breath. If a fight broke out between these two, we wouldn't be able to break it up. Lifting the dagger, Rig cut off the bounds around Calak's hands. They fell to the floor and Rig returned to his seat without saying a word.

"And you're just okay with this?" Sloan was looking at me.

"Okay with what?"

"That he was willing to hand you over to the Raiders to be sold off to the highest bidder?"

"No, but considering I threatened to shoot an arrow through his son's eye socket, I was hoping we could call it even."

"You did what?" Yuri twisted in his seat to look at me, and it was clear we had a lot to talk about tonight.

***

Calak didn't speak to me for the rest of the evening. Something I was getting used to. After cleaning up from the meal, Sloan and I retired to our shared room.

"I don't know if you're the best secret keeper or the worst." She hoisted herself up to the top bunk, laying out the blankets that Yuri had found for us.

"He's never going to forgive me."

"Well, I'm not sure you should forgive him either." I sighed, wishing I was back in Veras' room, wrapped in his arms, tracing his muscles with my fingers. A heaviness pressed down on my chest as I thought about him.

"You miss him?"

"Yes."

"He's valuable. If we lost, Sutton wouldn't have him killed. They'd want him alive."

I wasn't sure if that was comforting or not. I crawled into bed, staring at the bottom of Sloan's bunk. Veras could be alive, but not necessarily safe. Although I'd take alive over dead.

"Bree." I whispered her name. I wasn't sure why, but I felt like I needed to give her something more than just my thoughts. My eyes widened, and I had an idea. "Sloan, we need to mourn Bree, send her off into the afterlife properly. I don't really have any experience with those sorts of things, but I think we should have a memorial for Bree tomorrow."

The room was silent.

"Yes, we should."

The day the three of us were together in the training room, I could see how close Sloan and Bree were. They were two strong women in a world full of men. I could only imagine the bond they'd formed over the years.

"How long did you know Bree?"

"When Calak found me in the Western Kingdom, I'd gained a bit of a reputation for fighting and petty thievery."

"Seriously? You were a thief?"

"Nothing big. I was young and bored, but thankfully Calak found me before I got myself into too much trouble. Bree was the first person I met in the North. She joined us at the border. That was around six years ago."

"I wish I had more time to get to know her." If I had any more tears left to cry, I'm sure one would have slipped out then. Needing to change the subject I moved on to a question that had been looming in my mind for the past two days.

"So, what do we do now?"

"First, we need to find out what happened at Castle Mount after we left. There are channels for that, but with all the troops called in to the passes, it may take time. For now, the plan is to stay here where it's safe. We now know why the Raiders wanted you, but we don't know who originally hired them. Although I'm not sure that matters now that they've aligned themselves with the bitch Queen and her father."

Estra.

For what she did to Bree, I would kill her, slowly. I'm sure Sloan would help me. She deserved everything that was coming to her.

***

I had a hard time falling asleep that night. Not wanting to wake Sloan with my tossing and turning, I wrapped a blanket around myself and quietly opened the door. I made my way to the living space, thankful that the fire was still burning slowly. I sat down in front of the flames.

"Couldn't sleep?" Calak was reclined on a settee. I didn't even notice him when I came into the room. Damn, I was not very alert.

"No." I looked back at the fire.

"Me neither." We didn't speak again for several minutes.

"What's his name?" I asked. Calak didn't answer. Did I even have a right to ask this? After what I had said about the boy.

"Nial."

"Nial. I like it." The room went quiet again. The only sound was a few crackles as the logs burned apart. "I have a sister."

"What?"

"My memories, they're coming back slowly, but I remembered my little sister, Karissa. She'd be seventeen now."

"Do you know where your family's from?"

"Not yet." I paused. Did I want to tell Calak about my memories of his mother? Our friendship was on thin ice, or completely sunk at this point. Adding another dramatic secret to the mix couldn't make it any worse, I supposed. I spun around, so I was facing him, and took a deep breath.

"I remembered something else about your mother." Calak sat up and leaned his elbows on his knees. It was an invitation for me to continue sharing.

"We were with Leon in the Raiders camp."

"What?" Calak looked betrayed and confused. "Are you a Raider?"

"No. Of course not. I was only nine. Are there many nine-year-old girl Raiders running around?"

"No."

"I think Leon was helping us get to the ship. Your mother was eager to leave, but he said it wasn't safe yet." Calak shook his head. Of course he wouldn't believe me, but I didn't care. I knew what I saw.

"I mean, we knew that my mother went into the Raider camp with Leon. So this would make sense. All these years I never understood why my mother would be there willingly. So, do you think your parents were Raiders?"

"I don't think so. The memory I had with my sister was in a garden and we had a cook who made us sandwiches. That doesn't sound like the life of a girl being raised by Raiders."

"No, it doesn't."

"I didn't tell Veras or Bree about that memory." Calak looked at me, his eyebrows bunched together.

"Why?"

"Honestly, I was afraid they'd put me in the cells next to you while they figured out the truth of it."

Calak huffed out a laugh. "Veras would never put you in the cells, even if you stabbed him in the chest."

"That's not true."

"Please, I've been his friend our entire lives. That man is in love with you." I looked down, hoping my cheeks were warm from the closeness of the fire. Could Veras actually love me? We barely knew each other. "That's not a bad thing, you're engaged after all."

"Yes, I suppose we are."

Calak and I stared at each other for a moment. The light of the fire was dancing across his face. His deep blue eyes looked much darker from the shadows and I could barely make out the scar down his lip.

Those lips. I could still feel them under my thumb. Still feel how his hand felt against my face that morning in the alcove. Still feel his tongue wrap around my finger, licking the pudding off.

For a moment, the room felt like it was growing smaller until the sound of a door opening grabbed my attention. I turned to see Rig walking down the hall towards me, completely naked.

"Oh, my gods. Rig!"

I covered my face with the blanket.

"Gotta piss."

I heard the front door open and close behind him and then Calak burst out laughing. I peeked my eyes out of the blanket, checking that the coast was clear. Calak was laughing so hard he had rolled to his side on the settee. I grabbed a nearby pillow and threw it at him.

"I'll never be able to get that image out of my head. It's burned in there forever, now." That just made Calak laugh harder. I felt my lips turning upwards. It was funny. No matter how scared my brain felt. Eventually I started laughing too as another log popped, sending sparks floating up the chimney.

***

"Mistress, hurry!" A woman was running beside me. I held part of my dress in my hand so I wouldn't trip on it. There were shouts coming from all over. My tiny heart was pounding harder than it ever had in my entire life. A soldier that I recognized came around the corner in front of us.

"Get her out of here. Now!" He ordered the woman. "Quick, before they find her."

We turned down a stairwell that led to the back courtyard. Where was Karissa? I didn't want to leave without my sister. I searched as we ran down another corridor. The clanging of swords echoed down from the level we just left. They had breached the walls. I knew we were out of time.

I woke up covered in sweat. This memory was vivid. Searching through what I just saw, I tried to look for details that would give away where I was or what was happening. All I knew was that my family was in trouble.

CHAPTER THIRTY-THREE

"BUT, WHY DID YOU have to flee your home?"

Calak and I were building a pyre to light for Bree's memorial this evening.

"I can't remember."

We'd been gathering sticks all morning and were almost finished. Sloan had left at first light to see if she could retrieve any news from Castle Mount. I still didn't understand how their information network worked. Yuri and Rig were hunting for food. I'd been removed from hunting and cooking duties, which was fine by me. Apparently, a single rabbit wasn't enough food for this group.

"I knew we were rushing and something dangerous was happening, but I can't remember any of the details.

My sister wasn't with me. I knew I was searching, not wanting to leave without her."

Calak lifted the last branch to the top of our pile.

"Looks like we'll need a few more branches. We should check the east side of the outpost. I thought I saw some fallen trees yesterday."

I nodded for Calak to lead the way. Rig had given him back his weapons, a long sword and two daggers, and he'd found a fresh uniform in the outpost to wear. I was still wearing the clothes I had on when we fled the castle. I left the warm cloak inside since the weather was mild. My tunic was white, with thick long sleeves and a pale blue cape over top. The blue almost matched my eyes, I thought. The pants were dark gray and tucked into my brown boots. I had a leather belt wrapped around my midsection with a small, sheathed dagger hanging from it. My bow and quiver of arrows were around my back. It felt good to be armed. I had pulled my hair up into a tight bun to keep the curls out of my face while we worked.

I followed Calak through the trees, away from the outpost. The wind was rustling as the branches swayed towards each other, high above our heads. A faint rush of water somewhere to our right indicated that a stream or river was nearby. In the distance, I could see the mountains we had passed through. Castle Mount felt worlds away from here. As I took another step, Calak held out his hand to stop me. He lifted his finger to his mouth, commanding me to be silent, and pointed toward a line of evergreen trees. Something or someone was out there.

I nocked an arrow as Calak silently drew his sword. We crept forward, alert. Leaning to the side, the sound of an arrow whistled past my head and lodged into the tree behind me. Someone had just shot at us.

We fell to the ground, taking cover behind some trees and a small ridge.

"Did you see anything?" Calak asked.

"No."

We waited.

"Who's there?" A woman's voice I didn't recognize yelled out from the tree line.

"We mean you no harm." Calak yelled back. "We're just looking for fallen branches. We're building a pyre for my sister. I'm a Northern soldier."

"There aren't any soldiers left out here. They all went to the castle."

"I know. We came from there." Calak was speaking calmly to the woman. "We're going to come out now. I'm asking that you don't shoot at us again." He lifted his hands, and I did the same. Slowly, we rose to our feet and out of the safety of our cover.

A woman in her mid-forties came through the tree line, bow still drawn and pointed at us. Why did Calak have us come out? She could've easily taken us both down before we could get to her if she wanted to.

"What's your name?" Calak asked her.

"Raina." The woman was getting closer now.

"Hello Raina. I'm a tracker with the King's army and this is -"

"Mistress Raelle?"

The woman lowered her bow as her face turned pale. She was wearing a simple robe; it was a forest green, almost invisible amongst the trees. I could see shades of gray peeking through the hood covering her head.

"You know this woman?"

Calak stood defensively in front of me and my stupid heart fluttered.

"Of course I know her, and she knows me. Mistress, tell this man."

"I'm sorry, but I don't know who you are," I admitted.

The woman looked puzzled. She studied me for a long moment, then Calak.

"What has happened to you, Princess?"

Princess? Did this woman know me from the West? I searched my memories, but I only interacted with a few people outside of the castle when I was growing up. I would have remembered this woman.

"How do you know me?"

"I'm part of the sisterhood, charged to care for you, as was my mother before me."

"Sisterhood?"

I'd never heard that term before.

"Mistress, do you truly not remember me?"

I looked at Calak. His eyes were weary of this woman, but I was curious enough to want to see what Raina thought she knew about me. It was possible this was a trap, so I proceeded with caution.

"I have no memories, save for the last ten years."

"But how is that possible?"

"There was a shipwreck. I awoke on the coast of the Balour Sea and was rescued by the Western King, King Wren."

"You never made it to the continent?"

I didn't answer. Why would I be on my way to the continent?

"What of Sylvette?"

My breath caught.

This woman knew Calak's mother. I looked over at him. He hadn't stopped staring at Raina since we'd come out from behind the ridge.

"How do you know my mother?" He asked.

"Your mother?" Raina's eyes widened. "Calak?"

Sweet gods, she knew his name too. Either she was a witch, or we had a lot of catching up to do, but I was getting bored with the back and forth.

"Listen Raina, it's been a long couple of weeks and I'd normally try to be more diplomatic." Calak scoffed. I ignored him. "Can you just tell us how you know me, Sylvette, Calak, and what the hell a sisterhood is?"

Raina smiled.

"Still that same spirit, even all these years later. Come to the Twin Peaks cavern in two days. We'll explain it all. My mother will be so pleased to see you again."

"You expect us to trust you? This could very well be a trap."

Calak was right. We'd be fools to just take her word for it.

"Your mother was the most renowned storyteller the North had seen in many years and she was a friend of mine. From the pain in your eyes, I can see that she is gone, and if I'm correct, that pyre you are building is for Bree. I'm very sorry for your losses. I met you once, when you were a child. Please take whatever precautions you feel necessary before you arrive, but I do hope you will join us." She looked at me. "It's been a very long time, mistress."

With that, Raina bowed and turned back to the tree line.

We waited until she was completely out of sight before we spoke to each other.

I went first.

"What in the gods names just happened?"

"I don't even know what to say."

"She knew me, your mother, Bree...do you think it's safe to meet with her?"

"We'll discuss it with the Unit tonight. If we plan it correctly, then we should be fine. I'll do some scouting. We've been near the Twin Hills cavern before. It's close to here."

"Okay."

The idea that more details of my past were about to be revealed made me equally excited and nauseous.

On our way back to the outpost, we gathered as many sticks and branches as we could carry. Then finished building Bree's pyre.

***

"Bree was better than me in every way." Calak stood in front of the pyre, holding a torch. "When we were kids, everything was a competition. She made me faster and stronger, just by being herself. I've never known a day on this Earth without her." His voice caught, and he cleared his throat. "I'm mad as hell that she's not here right now, but I know that wherever she is, she's watching us. We will avenge your death, Bree, and we will restore the North in your honor. Peace before death!"

"Peace before death!" The Unit repeated in unison.

Calak held out the torch, and the pyre ignited. The flames grew higher and higher, licking the sky and dancing in the wind. Without really thinking, I lifted my hand and placed it on Calak's back. He didn't move or acknowledge the touch. We just stood there. Bree was no longer here in her own body, but she lived inside each of us. I was forever changed because I knew her.

I stayed beside Calak until the fire reduced itself to ashes. The Unit had gone inside to prepare our meal.

"Bree asked me why I looked like a streetwalker the day I came to see you in the cells."

"What did you say?"

"I told her I tried to seduce you and you called me a whore."

That got a small chuckle from Calak.

"And what did she say to that?"

"She said, 'well, takes one to know one'."

I smiled and looked at Calak. Tears were streaming silently down his face. He didn't look at me. His eyes were fixed on the fire. So much had happened between us. At one point, I may have considered him a friend, but I didn't know what I was to him anymore. Regardless, I wanted to comfort him. His family was all gone. I reached over and threw my arms around him.

He hesitated for a moment, his arms straight down his side, but I squeezed him harder. I felt his body push against mine and his hands gripped together behind my back. He was shaking. I felt his tears damping the shoulder of my cape as he rested his head there. I held him tighter, crying along with him. There were no more words to say. We were saying goodbye to Bree, and it was awful. I slowly lifted my hand to the back of his head, calmly stroking his hair, similar to how his mother used to comfort me all those years ago. I don't know exactly how long we stayed there. We both let out a cathartic deep breath and released each other from the hold. I lifted my hands to wipe the tears away from my face.

Calak looked down at me, his face still wet from his grief.

"Thank you."

CHAPTER THIRTY-FOUR

RIG AND YURI WERE ACTUALLY decent cooks.

"Where the hell did you two learn to make food like this?" Sloan asked before I could.

"We all have our secrets." Yuri smiled, taking a sip of the wine we'd found in one of the pantry cupboards. And not just any wine, Western wine. And three bottles of it, at that. Yuri, likely remembering the day he sutured my neck, suggested that I take it easy with the alcohol. I, of course, had no intention of listening to him.

I lifted my glass.

"To secrets."

The group paused for a moment, then followed my gesture. We all drank. It was a dumb thing to toast, but I could feel a buzz settling in as I was already on my third refill.

Rig stood up and lifted his glass.

Everyone stared at him.

"Come, drink about the weary souls,
Derrie-don-lee-mindly,
Caution tales of long patrols,
Derrie-don-lee-mindly,
Fast approach the long, cold night,
Derrie-don-lee-mindly,
He lost his cock to the frostbite,
Derrie-don-lee-mindly."

Damn. Rig could sing.

The group exploded with laughter and they each took a turn singing a verse from what I could only assume was a Northern soldiers' drinking tune.

After that song was over, another one began. I'd just downed my fourth glass of wine when Rig grabbed my wrist and pulled me towards the space in front of the fire. We twirled and danced, while the rest of the Unit sang, banging their hands against the table to keep the beat.

Rig lifted me up and rotated us around. I squealed with delight, beaming with joy. Yuri was next. Pulling me towards him as we swung to the melody of a new drinking song. Out of the corner of my eye, I saw Calak escort Sloan beside us. They moved in unison with us and Rig supervised, leaning against the mighty hearth of the fireplace.

Lifting my hand above our heads, Yuri spun me and then I was in Calak's arms. We'd traded partners. Before I could register it, we were moving even faster than before. My left hand rested up on top of Calak's broad shoulder. I could feel the tension of his muscles under the pads of my fingers. His left hand securely held my right hand as he led me around the small space, keeping in step with the song. The touch of his other hand on my lower back sparked me full of awareness. It rested so low; it was skimming the top of my ass. Did he mean to have it so low or was it just shifting from the movement? I tried to focus on the lyrics of the song, anything other than the feeling of his pinky, slowly inching lower and lower. Finally daring to meet his gaze, I lifted my eyelashes to see Calak's chin dipped down towards me.

Earlier I was holding him. An act of comfort. Now he was holding me and I felt anything but comfort. The burn of his touch against my body was distracting in the best way possible, and I hated myself for that. I fixed my eyes on him. Desperately, I tried to push any sign of lust or need out of them. He was looking at me so intently and I couldn't tell if he was repulsed by the closeness of our bodies or turned on. Unable to hold his stare any longer, I looked away. No one else in the room was aware of what was happening between us.

When the song ended, we all collapsed. Exhausted from the impromptu celebration and the emotional weight of the day. It was easy for me to fall asleep that night.

***

"It's training time, Princess."

Sloan had woken me up at an ungodly hour that morning. My head was still pounding from the excessive drinking I'd done the night before. How was she so mobile and cheery this early in the day? I trudged myself down the stairs that led to the grassy area in front of the outpost where she already had some weapons waiting for us.

I stretched out my tight muscles. It'd been too long since I'd last done this. We had agreed that considering our potentially dangerous venture tomorrow to meet with Raina and see what the Sisterhood was, it would be best for me to freshen up on fighting skills.

We started off with light sparring. Sloan led me through some of her favorite hand-to-hand exercises and I welcomed the alternative approach. Being trained by Danier, my entire knowledge of fighting was only from his perspective. It was stimulating to see another take on things I'd been doing for years.

Sweat was already beading down my forehead, despite the chill in the morning air. I welcomed the burn in my muscles as they came back to life.

We'd gained an audience, as our three male counterparts took to the veranda to have their breakfast. Determined that their attention wouldn't distract me, I dug in. Sloan noticed my increased intensity and just smiled. I matched each of her moves and threw in a few of my own. Her eyes lit up when I surprised her with a maneuver that Danier had taught me, landing her flat on her back.

"My turn." Yuri sauntered down the steps. He already had his swords in tow. He drew a circle in the grass with the edge of his weapon, establishing the training space. With one of his swords now in my hand, I positioned myself as my brothers had taught me to do. The first swing came harder and faster than I expected. Taking a step back, my eyes widened. The Unit would not go easy on me this morning and, honestly, I loved it

The clanging of our swords sounded like a melody

of its own kind of song. Occasionally Yuri would outmatch me, thankfully with enough skill to stop the blade from actually doing any damage to my body. The few sutures he'd done on my finger were loosening from all the aggressive movements. I twirled around on my knee, blocking his final swipe.

"Excellent," he praised me. I straightened myself up and handed the sword back to Yuri. The hilt was now covered in my blood, but he didn't seem to mind. Pausing for a moment, I wondered whether Rig or Calak would claim the next spot in the circle with me. Looking up at the veranda, they both seemed lost in a conversation with Sloan, so I took that as a sign that my training session was over.

"Help!"

The scream came from somewhere in the forest. I looked around, but no one else in the Unit was responding. Did they not hear that?

"Raelle!" A woman's voice. She was screaming in pain. My heart rate picked up as I tried to determine the direction the sound was coming from. Still confused why the rest of my friends weren't able to hear her, I grabbed the bow and quiver laying in the grass and sprinted away from the outpost.

I heard them call after me, but I didn't stop. I had to find whoever was hurt. She knew my name. As improbable as it seemed, someone out there needed my help.

The ground was uneven, and I faltered in my strides a few times. Trying to still my heavy breathing so I could hear where she was.

"Help me!" Her voice sounded closer. I was almost there.

The Unit was not far behind me. I could hear Rig swear as they likely stumbled in the same spots I did.

Sensing I was near to where I was needed, I slowed my pace and nocked an arrow in the bow. Moving as stealthily as I could through the thickets. There was a shift in the trees forty feet from me. A figure moved, and I aimed, still walking forward. Not wanting to injure the woman who had called for my help.

"Raelle." Her voice was weak now. Barely any strength behind it. Was I too late? Who was she? Could it be Raina from yesterday? Other than her, I couldn't think of anyone else this far out in the North who'd known me. Although she implied that there were others who were a part of this Sisterhood. Perhaps it was one of them.

Taking shelter behind a large tree, I peeked around to see what I could make out. A massive brown bear was hovering over something on the ground. I could see blood spilled out over the moss that clung to the fallen trees. The grunts of the bear weren't feral, but satisfied. Was I too late? Had this bear attacked the woman I was trying to save?

I crept around the tree, an arrow pointed directly at the beast. He was majestic, but a threat. Lifting his head, he turned towards me as my foot stepped on a small twig; the snap echoing through the forest. Holden would've chastised me for my lack of awareness. It was a juvenile mistake to give away my position like that.

Moving away from his prey, I saw the broken carcass of a deer laying on the ground. I shifted my eyes around, looking for the woman who had called me. Did I head in the wrong direction? Damnit. She could still be in trouble. Leaving would not be easy anymore, as the brown bear's attention had completely landed on me.

I swallowed.

Where was the best place to shoot this creature? If I stood a chance at escaping with my life, then the shot would need to be fatal. He slowly walked towards me. A fresh growl erupted from his mouth. A mouth that was already stained with the blood of his last catch.

I cleared my mind and aimed the arrow at his eye. Not that I had a thing for eye sockets, it just seemed like the quickest and cleanest way to end a life. Releasing the arrow as it flew straight for the bear. At the last second, a sound from my right startled the beast, and he adjusted his stance. My arrow landed on the flesh of his shoulder.

Not a kill shot. Just enough to piss him off more, though. He burst into a run, heading straight for me. Then my tracker was there. The slash of his sword ripped through the bear's exposed neck as I stumped back into Rig's hold. Calak moved out of the swing of the giant paw. It's claws ready to maul. Yuri appeared next, using his dual weapons to slice at the other side of the animal. A thud on the ground told me the fight was over. Blood poured out of his injuries. This beast would not be getting back up.

Slowly tracking its breathing and movements, Calak walked over, allowing his blade to penetrate the bear's head. Mercifully ending its slow, painful death.

We took a moment to catch our breaths, but I moved out of Rig's hold as I searched the area. Where was she? I couldn't hear her calling out to me anymore. Was she already dead? There were no sounds coming from the forest now, except for a faint howl of the wind.

I turned back towards my friends and the two bloodied animals on the ground. The brown bear and the deer.

CHAPTER THIRTY-FIVE

STANDING IN FRONT OF THE OPENING to Twin Peaks cavern, I could see how it got its namesake. Nestled in between two voluminous hills, covered in rocky trails and evergreens, they looked like-

"Breasts." Rig barked out behind me. "Those hills look like the bosom of that girl who works at the tavern in Cottonmure. You remember, Calak? The brunette you had a thing for."

"Lousie?" Calak responded.

"Yes. That vixen was trouble. Didn't Yuri end up going back to his room with her?"

"Yes, I did." Yuri surprised me with his confidence and clear experience with women. "She stayed until the morning, if I recall."

I rolled my eyes.

"Ha. That she did!" Rig laughed.

"If you men are finished, I believe the sisterhood is expecting us."

Sloan was no nonsense this morning. After Calak had done some scouting last night, she raided the armory storage in the outpost, fitting us with both seen and unseen weapons.

I took a deep breath. There could be answers waiting for me inside of this cavern. Aware that not everything about my past may be pleasant, I was ready.

The Unit waited for my move. I took one more deep breath and moved forward, but Calak put his hand out and stepped in front of me. It was clear that I wouldn't be allowed to enter the cavern first, so I went along with it, following Calak as he led us towards the sisterhood.

The first thirty steps inside of the cavern led us through a narrow passageway that ended with a sealed door. Calak lifted his hand and knocked. Moments later, the hinges creaked as Raina appeared.

"Welcome."

She ushered us through the entrance into a large circular space. There were no tables or chairs here. No decorations or markings of any kind. Raina circled around us, standing at the base of a set of stairs that led to another doorway. No one spoke. Glancing over at the Unit, we all expressed the same thing — caution and curiosity.

The doorway at the top of the stairs opened and a frail woman, assisted by a young man, entered, making her way down towards us. This woman wore a robe similar to Raina. She was elderly, based on her posture and movements. I could see her entire head of gray, thinned-out hair. Silently, we waited until she safely reached the bottom. She thanked the young man, who turned and disappeared through another door to our left. I was marking all the escape routes in my mind.

Slowly lifting her head, the old woman's eyes landed on mine.

"Mistress. Is it truly you?"

"It is. Although I don't know who you are, or where I am. Is this my home?"

"No, my dear. This is not your home."

"Then where are we?"

"This place is a sacred holdfast, once protected by the gods themselves. We are the Sisterhood, tasked with caring for what the gods treasure most in the world."

"And what would that be?"

"You."

Out of my peripheral vision, I saw Calak's head turn towards me, as I kept staring into this woman's eyes.

"My name is Thedra. You've met my daughter, Raina. But you've also met my grandmother, Gilda."

I laughed. "I came here for answers. If you don't have any, I'm not interested in riddles."

"They're not riddles, mistress. Who do you think you are?"

"That's why I'm here. I don't know who I am or where I'm from. I keep getting these random memories that make little sense to me."

"What memories?"

"One time I was with Sylvette on the ship that was carrying us. I remember the storm and falling, hitting my head. Then we were in the Raiders encampment with Leon."

It was at this moment that I remembered I hadn't shared that detail with the rest of the Unit. I'm sure we'd be discussing that later tonight.

"And I remembered having tea parties with Karissa, my little sister."

"You remember Princess Karissa?"

"Yes. I also remember fleeing my home because of danger."

"Was this woman helping you?"

Thedra reached into her satchel and pulled out a portrait, handing it to me. I studied it for a moment. It was old and worn down, but the image was clear enough for me to see. This was the woman who was leading me out of my home that day.

"Who's this woman?" I asked Thedra.

"This was my grandmother, Gilda. She was a part of the Sisterhood, appointed to serve in the capital of Garth."

"The capital of Garth?" Calak spoke up. "There hasn't been a capital of Garth in over one hundred and fifty years."

"I know." Thedra stared at me.

My head was feeling light as I passed the portrait back to her. Was Thedra suggesting what I thought? That somehow I was in the capital of Garth over one-hundred and fifty years ago.

"How is that possible?" Yuri spoke up. "Raelle is only nineteen years old. She couldn't possibly have been alive that long ago."

"Unless she just looks damn good for her age." Rig was not being helpful and Thedra's side eye glance proved that she was not amused.

"She is nineteen years old," Raina now spoke. I threw my hands in the air as Thedra placed the portrait back in her bag.

"Riddles!" I shouted.

I turned to walk away, frustrated that these women were wasting our time and playing with my mind.

Thedra spoke, and I stopped in my steps.

"Mistress, you are Raelle Evamore, the first daughter of King Asher and Queen Yolanda of the Evamore Dynasty. Sole heir to the Kingdom of Garth. Rightful ruler of all four kingdoms. The gods chose you and you bear their mark."

A strange light poured down from the stone ceiling. I looked up for the source of it and found none. It shone all around me. I turned towards my friends, who were standing back, awestruck. There was a rush of sensation that trickled from the top of my head to my toes. I felt my hair come unbound from the tight bun I had placed it in. A curl fell down in my line of sight and I reached up for it. Pulling it straight, I saw that what used to be bright white was now a cobalt blue. I glanced around the room, my eyes landing on Calak. His eyes were nearly bulging out of their sockets. Then a twinge of light pain, nothing hurtful, but something strange ran across my forehead. I reached up, but felt nothing different.

Then I saw them.

My friends, the Unit, on their knees, bowing before me. Raina had helped her mother to her knee as well. They stayed there, heads hung low in respect as the light dissipated.

"Um," I exhaled. "What just happened?"

Calak looked up first, a slight smirk on his face, but his eyes were full of wonder. I'd never seen him look like that before.

"Can you guys stand up? You're making me very uncomfortable."

They all stood, none of them taking their eyes off of me.

"Someone please explain this," I pulled at my blue curls.

"Mistress, you're an Evamore. The last surviving Evamore," Thedra explained.

"How's that possible? All the Evamores were murdered." I was so confused, but the fact that my hair had just turned blue made me think she was telling the truth.

"They were, except for one. My grandmother escaped with you and fled to this cavern with the help of the Sisterhood. Those against your family were led to believe that all of your parents' children had been killed. So no one came looking for you."

I took a breath, slowly shaking my head as I scanned the floor. This was a lot of life-altering, no, kingdom-altering, information to absorb.

"Using the gods' magic, my grandmother put you into a state of sleeping. You rested here, frozen in time, unchanging over the years. When my grandmother died, my mother watched over you, then I did and finally, Raina. For one-hundred and forty years, our family kept you safe and secret from the world."

"Why did I wake up?"

"The magic would only awaken you when the gods believed that your true lovetie existed. When you began stirring ten years ago, we called on Sylvette to help us ferry you to the continent. The influence of Kellar has rotted this land and the hearts of its men. We believed that your best chance of finding a lovetie was away from these shores."

"What have you been doing for the past ten years? Did you not know that I had gone missing? Raina didn't even know that Sylvette had died. I was only nine years old and washed up on the shore, alone. Anyone could have found me."

"We know." Thedra's head hung low. "Shortly after we sent you away, the Raiders attacked. Without you here, the magic that protected this space was gone. Almost all of the Sisterhood were hunted down and murdered. Our resources were depleted. Networks destroyed. We prayed that Sylvette would be able to secure a safe home for you so that one day, you'd return to restore the kingdoms."

"That's...a lot." I was annoyed and overwhelmed.

"Kellar has been poisoning the souls of men and women for decades. The cries of innocent people are the anthem of his followers. Only when you are lovetied will the influence of Kellar break and peace be restored to Garth," Thedra continued.

"Wait, what?"

"You must be lovetied, immediately, Raelle." Raina pleaded.

"Um, I don't think I'm there just yet."

"What do you mean?" Thedra asked.

"Well, to be honest, I'm not even sure what a lovetie is. I mean, Calak," I pointed towards him, "tried to explain it to me back at Castle Mount, but he didn't really do a great job explaining it."

He rolled his eyes at me.

"Mistress, the influence of Kellar will continue to rot this world until you become lovetied. That's the promise the gods made with your ancestors." Raina was getting very passionate.

"I understand what you're saying. It just puts a lot of pressure on me."

Sloan laughed out loud, and Thedra's eyebrows furrowed. I wasn't trying to be funny. This was ridiculous. The fate of the world rested on me finding my true love. I had just turned nineteen and was kissed for the first time a week ago. Why would the gods ever put this kind of demand on someone?

"Mistress, I understand this is a lot of information for you and it's unfortunate that the accident has stolen your memories, especially of your parents and your family's history, but you were born to this. You can do this."

Thedra's speech was an attempt to comfort me, but I still had questions.

"The problem is that I'm not in love," I admitted.

"But I thought, you and Calak..." Raina spoke up.

"What? Why would you think that?" I asked.

"I saw you two together in the forest. The connection, it was there."

"No," Calak spoke up, a little too assuredly.

"Definitely not," I dug back at him.

"That would be awful for everyone," He added.

"Especially me," I snuck in.

The Unit barely contained their laughter; I didn't think Thedra would tolerate another round of comedy from my friends.

"There must be someone you love, someone you are close to. Someone who cares for you?" Raina asked.

"The King?" Sloan suggested.

"King Veras?" Thedra repeated.

"Well, yes, technically. I just call him Veras, but we haven't told each other that we love each other or anything. It's new. We've just kissed and touched each other a little bit, oh gods..."

I needed to stop talking right away.

"You need to find Veras immediately. If he's your lovetie, it's the only thing that can stop Kellar. The fate of all the kingdoms rests on you. There cannot be any more delays. We're running out of time."

Thedra's words were final. There was no more room for discussion.

We needed to find a way back to Veras.

CHAPTER THIRTY-SIX

I SPLASHED COLD WATER against my face, welcoming the shock. Placing both of my arms against the countertop in the bathing chamber, I slowly raised my head to look into the clouded mirror one more time. Across my forehead was the shimmer of a tattoo. Calak had explained this to me. It was a gift from the gods. Only the ruling Evamores bore the cobalt hair and silver markings. I rubbed at the tattoo, curious if it would come off. It just shined brighter.

Unbelievable.

Raina had explained that when I awoke ten years ago, they used magic to conceal my physical appearance, thus protecting my identity. There were many agents of Kellar in Garth who would relish the idea of murdering the last surviving Evamore.

There was much for me to process. I was the rightful ruler of all four kingdoms. I think amongst all the revelations today, that was the one that made me most afraid. There was no desire inside of me to rule anyone. The gods should have chosen someone else. Perhaps it wasn't too late. Maybe they could be petitioned to choose another, a person with experience in leadership and the right connections to unite people. A person like Veras.

Veras. I closed my eyes and allowed myself to remember the feel of his lips on mine. The way that his hands glided across my skin. The taste of his tongue. Gods, I'd give anything to be in his arms again. Laying in his bed, listening to his snoring and feeling his heartbeat as I rested my head on his naked chest.

It's possible that if I could get to Veras, then he'd be able to help me rule. Maybe it was the gods that brought us to each other when Estra ransomed me away. Could I picture myself ruling beside Veras? Being his queen? There were moments during my stay at Castle Mount, because of our ruse, that I allowed myself to envision what a life there with him could be. Sharing a bedchamber. Having quiet dinners together. He was kind and the people loved him. Perhaps Veras was my lovetie. The revelation of my identity would be a shock to him, but with Veras by my side, it's possible this could work.

I exited the bathing chamber and headed towards our living space. Guided by the scent of stew, I floated towards the table. Sitting down, I then realized that my friends weren't seated with me. They stood by the fire, watching me.

"Stop doing this. I know I look different, but it's still just me. Gods, I should have convinced those women to change my appearance back before we left."

Rig walked towards me and extended his hand. Confused, I took it as he led me towards the Unit. Leaving me standing in the middle of the room, the four of them circled around me until one was at each of my sides, in front of me and behind me. Four points. They lowered to a knee, withdrew their swords and held them towards me as an offering.

I was facing Rig, so he spoke first.

"I vow to protect you with my life. You have my sword and my fealty, from this day until I am no longer on this Earth. The East is yours, Queen Raelle Evamore."

Then Yuri spoke, and I turned to him.

"I vow to protect you with my life. You have my sword and my fealty, from this day until I am no longer on this earth. The South is yours, Queen Raelle Evamore."

I moved, so I was facing Sloan.

"I vow to protect you with my life. You have my sword and my fealty, from this day until I am no longer on this earth. The West is yours, Queen Raelle Evamore."

She smirked and gave me a wink.

The last one was Calak. He lifted his eyes to look at me and a flash of memories flooded my mind; when I fell out of the carriage because I refused to take his hand, the way he held me after our fight in my chamber, the sound of his roar when I threatened his son's life, and the wetness of his tears that stained my shoulder as we said goodbye to Bree.

"I vow to protect you with my life. You have my sword and my fealty, from this day until I am no longer on this earth. The North is yours, Queen Raelle Evamore."

My eyes stung as I felt the significance of this moment. I took a deep breath.

"Thank you." I looked at each one of them. "But that's the last strange thing you can do. This is odd enough without the four of you treating me like this."

They chuckled as they rose to their feet and joined me back at the table.

***

"So, how long will it take us to get back to Castle Mount?" I asked between bites of my stew.

"Through the tunnels, it's two days on foot. However, we won't be traveling that way again," Rig answered me.

"Why not?"

"The risk is too high. Without knowledge of who is in command of Castle Mount, it's safer for us to stay hidden in the forests. There's a better chance of survival if a fight were to occur."

That made sense to me.

"So how far is it if we travel outside of the tunnels?"

Yuri turned to me. We were seated next to each other at the table.

"If we can find horses, then it's a week's ride."

"Without horses?"

"Then I'd say ten days, maybe eleven."

Damn. That was a long time, but we had no choice. Finding Veras was my best chance to become lovetied and stop the influence of Kellar. I had to assume that the Raiders, Sutton, and Estra were all under his influence, being used by him. If I could help bring an end to all the pain they'd caused, I had to try.

"When do we leave?"

"In the morning. We'll gather provisions tonight and pray to the gods that we find horses along our way." Rig spoke like he was still in charge. With Calak somewhat back to himself, I wondered if that dynamic would shift.

After we cleaned up our meal, I bundled myself up. I needed to clear my head, and I thought a brisk walk would help. Stepping out onto the porch. The air was cooler than I expected, making me thankful I had worn my cloak this time.

"Going somewhere, your Majesty?" Calak was leaning back in one chair along the veranda.

"Don't call me that."

"It's what you are, though."

"Maybe."

"Raelle, your hair is blue. I watched it change myself. You're going to have to get used to people treating you differently from now on."

"People, maybe, but not you. I need to be just regular Raelle for a little bit longer."

Calak studied me and then stood up.

"Where are you going?"

"I need to walk and clear my head."

"Then I'm going with you."

"I'm not going far. I'll stay close to the outpost."

"It's non-negotiable. I made a pledge." His eyebrows popped up, and he smiled when he saw how annoyed I was.

"Fine." I stomped down the few stairs and onto the grass.

We walked for the better part of an hour. I stayed silent and Calak quietly followed me, scanning the trees for potential threats. There was too much on my mind to effectively sort through it all. The most pressing thought was whether Veras would accept me as a lovetie, but it was then that I realized I didn't even know how that worked.

"How do you know if someone is your lovetie?" I figured Sylvette would have told her children everything she knew about my family and our history. Calak would be a reliable source of information.

We stopped at the bank of a small stream. I found a rock to sit on and Calak sat on the ground next to me.

"My mother used to say that a lovetie was formed when two souls recognized they couldn't exist without the other."

"So it's not like an arranged marriage?"

"No, not like that. Both parties have to agree. Once the souls acknowledge each other as their lovetie, then the bond is formed."

"And what's so special about the bond?"

"Some have said that lovetied Evamores could feel what the other one felt, or know their thoughts. I know that the connection is so strong that one will not rule without the other. Almost like they're not complete if they are apart. There have been no loveties for over one-hundred and fifty years. Since your parents, actually. So it's mostly just fables at this point. You don't have any memories from your parents' relationship?"

"Not yet. That would probably help me understand it all better." I looked down at the stream, watching leaves get caught up in the small current and be pulled away from us. "So could an Evamore be lovetied before they were King or Queen?"

"I believe so. The souls would still connect, but until it was their turn to rule, they wouldn't take on the appearance of the gods."

Calak reached over and lightly brushed the side of my hair.

"Why does it have to be so complicated? So many details to remember?" I picked up a rock and threw it into the water.

"When my mother died, Bree and I spent weeks writing out all the stories she told us. Veras helped. After we had a list, I had these images and words tattooed on my arms, so I'd never forget what she taught us."

Calak rolled up his sleeves, revealing the intricate tattoos I'd seen many times. Without asking permission, I grabbed his arm and pulled it closer to me. Slowly rotating it to take in all of the details.

"That's beautiful."

"It was a way of keeping her close. To make sure I never forgot her."

I nodded my head. "I wish I could remember my parents. Even more so now that I know who they were. I'm sad that they aren't on the earth right now, looking for me. In my dreams, I'd imagine walking into my childhood home and surprising them. Being embraced and cried over. A party thrown to celebrate me coming home filled with family and friends."

Finding out the truth about who I was had erased any possibility of reuniting with my loved ones. My family was dead. Karissa was gone. I had no home to go back to.

We sat there for a while. Eventually the sun got lower, and we headed back towards the outpost.

"We'll need to find horses. I think Yuri is off by his calculations. The journey on foot could take over two weeks. There are no direct paths from here through the mountains."

Calak was walking beside me now.

"Then we'll need horses."

A rustle in the trees startled us. Calak drew his sword as five horses trotted into the clearing we stood in. They were saddled, with reins already in place and no riders to be seen.

CHAPTER THIRTY-SEVEN

WE RODE FOR SIX DAYS.

My horseback skills had not improved from our first journey together, so once again I was left to ride with Calak. Unlike the first time we did this, I was much more familiar with his touch. Although that didn't remove the awkwardness. Whenever I would relax and fall into his hold, I'd jerk myself straight up. Each time earning a chuckle from Calak.

"You know, I won't tell anyone if you like the feeling of my body against yours," he whispered in my ear. All that earned was sneer from me, but an hour later, I was laying against him again.

When the horses first appeared to Calak and I in the clearing, we tied them up and went searching for their owners. We brought the animals back to the outpost after being satisfied that no one was looking for them.

Yuri said it was a sign from the gods; finding the horses exactly when we needed them. I wasn't so sure. Why would the gods pay attention to me now? Where were they when that storm swept our ship away? Or when Estra would torment me as a child? Or when she kidnapped me on my birthday and sent me North?

It would take a lot more than five horses to convince me that the gods were interested in my well-being.

Our journey across the Northern Kingdom was uneventful and quiet. We passed many abandoned military encampments, assuming the soldiers had left to answer Bree's call. The few villages we did visit were pleasant. I had insisted on wearing a white strip of cloth across my forehead, tied at the base of my neck, to cover the tattoo, and I kept the hood of my brown cloak up to conceal my hair.

The Unit had become very protective of me, Rig most of all. I tried not to be frustrated with them. I forbade them from calling me "Queen." I wasn't ready for that yet.

At night, we would discuss the different scenarios we might encounter when we arrived at Castle Mount. If the Northern army was victorious in the battle, then our only hurdle was getting to Veras and explaining the situation. If the Raiders and the East had won, then we'd need to find out where they were keeping Veras and rescue him. All of the Unit's plans had me sitting safely out of harm's way. We'd see about that.

One evening, I asked them if their pledges of loyalty to me conflicted with any promises they had made to Veras or the Northern Kingdom. Calak explained that when the North was formed, all those loyal to the Evamores sought refuge here. I knew this already. What I didn't know was that they considered their kings or queens as stewards, holding court in place of the Evamores. That meant that I superseded Veras under the laws of the Northern Kingdom.

If that was supposed to comfort me, it did the opposite. Would Veras love me if I stole his crown? Taking his place as the leader of his people? It didn't matter, anyway. I couldn't lead without him. Gods, I hoped he understood all of this and accepted it.

At the end of our sixth day of travel, Yuri rode ahead to scout out a safe place to camp for the night. We had stopped to relieve ourselves when he came riding quickly towards us. Instinctively, we all drew our weapons in case he was being followed.

"Yuri, what is it?" Rig asked, glancing behind the horse to see if other riders were following.

"It's the North. They're here. Just over the ridge there."

"What do you mean?"

"Just come. You need to see for yourselves." Yuri motioned for us to follow him. Mounting our horses, we rode out together.

Coming over the ridge, I could hear the faint sounds of conversation and see the gray smoke of cooking fires. When the view cleared through the tree line, there was an encampment settled down by the river. Men, women and children were out playing, carrying supplies and sitting by fires. There were many soldiers among them.

As we approached a group of Northerners came out to meet us. They all recognized my friends, greeting them and celebrating their return. Some soldiers were wary of Calak, no doubt aware of his time in the castle cells, but no one made a move to apprehend him. Dismounting our horses, we walked further into the encampment until we saw him.

Slowly walking towards us, his arm still wrapped in a sling, Bowan appeared through the crowd. Sloan broke free from us first, wrapping her arms around him. He winced when she pressed against his arm. Rig planted a hand on Bowan's good shoulder. They smiled at each other. Yuri approached, seeming more interested in the wrappings around Bowan than the man himself, but he offered him a hug and greeting.

That left Calak and I standing there. Bowan straightened himself, narrowing his eyes at the man who had been like his son. I just stood there, looking back and forth between them both.

"You've got some explaining to do, kid."

"It's good to see you, old man."

Bowan's stern face cracked a bit as he lifted his head towards Calak. A nod of greeting. These two had a lot to discuss. I stepped forward tentatively. Not being as close to Bowan as the rest of them, but still deeply respecting that man, I truly was glad to see him here, safe.

"I'm glad to see you're well, Bowan."

"You too, Princess."

Sloan snorted, and I glared at her. I had made them promise not to reveal my identity. We all agreed that the more people that knew the truth about me, the greater the risk to my life. However, Bowan was part of this Unit. We'd find the right time to tell him, but not out in the open like this.

"What happened?"

I wanted to ask if he knew where Veras was, but I found myself too afraid of the answer. Until this moment I had held onto the hope that he was alive, but seeing these people here, instead of in the castle, made me worried that the battle was worse than we thought. It didn't look like the North had won.

"Why don't we head to my tent? We'll catch up there."

Bowan turned, leading us. Some stable hands came and retrieved our horses after untying our bags. A few howls sounded from behind a tent, as three large dogs came running at us. I recognized these types of animals from my first day at Castle Mount. Dogs that resembled the wolves from Kolt's stories. They yipped and jumped at my feet. Crouching down, deciding they were friendly enough, I thoroughly pet each one of them. Their tongues hung out of their mouths and tails wagged as I scratched behind their ears. A young boy came running up to us apologizing for the inconvenience. I assured him that it was fine, but he herded the dogs back the way they'd come from.

Bowan's tent was modest and felt tiny with the six of us inside of it. Bowan sat on his bed with Sloan and Yuri. Calak and Rig took spots on the ground, as Rig insisted I take the only chair in the space.

"So, what the hell happened to the lot of you?" Bowan asked.

"Veras ordered us to get Calak and Raelle out of the castle if a fight were to break out. After they took down," Sloan paused, "Bree, we made our way into the tunnels. We've been at one of the western outposts."

"I heard about Bree." Bowan's head was down. Everyone paused in silence for a moment.

"What happened? Why are you all here and not in the castle?" I was closer to asking the question I really wanted to ask.

"After the initial fight in the grand hall, Veras sent for our troops in the mountain passes. As far as I understand, Sutton and Leon escaped and rallied with the Eastern army. Veras sent a quarter of our army to get those of us in the shelters out. There's mixed reports about what happened in the battle, but I know Sutton has control of Castle Mount."

"What of the King?" Calak asked.

"Alive."

I let out the breath I hadn't realized I'd been holding. Veras was alive. A single tear of relief slipped out of the corner of my eye. I wiped it away quickly.

"We need to get to King Veras," Calak explained.

"The castle is too well guarded. Many of our soldiers have attempted to rescue him, but never returned."

"We have to get him out," I repeated Calak's words.

Bowan turned his attention to me. "Listen, Princess, it's not possible. He's lost to us in there. Besides, securing the safety of the people needs to be a priority. We haven't spotted the Raiders since the battle. I worry they may attack if they discover how fragile our defenses are here."

"We get the King first." I insisted.

"Gods, child, I know you're a stubborn one, but this is not your place."

"Actually..."

I glared at Sloan as she spoke, but she was right. Bowan needed to understand what was at stake if he was going to agree to our plan. Not that we needed his permission, but he was one of the most senior members of court left in the North. His influence would go a long way with the soldiers and Northerners.

Taking a deep breath, I lifted my hands to my hood and pushed it back off my head, revealing my cobalt hair. Then I untied the wrapping around my forehead, letting the silver tattoo show. As expected, Bowan looked equally awed and confused.

"I don't understand," he said.

"She is Raelle Evamore, first daughter of Asher and Yolanda Evamore. Rightful Queen of the United Kingdom of Garth and ruler of the four kingdoms." Rig spoke with such pride.

"How? It's not possible."

"A group of women called the Sisterhood rescued me after the attack on my family. Using magic, they lulled me to sleep and I was awoken ten years ago. The rest is a long story and you know most of it, anyway."

"So you're..."

"One-hundred and fifty-nine years old. Yes, it appears that I am."

"Gods."

"I need to find the King. If he's my lovetie, then when our souls bond, we'll bind the influence of Kellar and his agents. It's our best shot at saving not only the North, but all of Garth. And after I find him, I'll kill all those who've wronged us, starting with Estra."

"Queen Estra?" Bowan asked.

"Yes, her. Why?"

"She's here. In our encampment. One soldier took her prisoner during the battle."

"The bitch Queen is here?" Sloan stood to her feet.

"Yes."

"She killed Bree," Sloan explained.

Bowan huffed out breaths that sounded angry as he shook his head, staring at the ground. It didn't seem like he knew this bit of information.

"She's heavily guarded."

I stood up.

"I want to see her."

CHAPTER THIRTY-EIGHT

"CALAK, DEAR GODS, is that ye?" Clara's voice cut in from across the path. There she was, standing by a giant black pot hanging over a dying fire.

"Clara!" Calak sauntered over to the cook and wrapped her in a hug. She reached up to squeeze his cheeks and then slapped him hard.

"What was that for?"

"I don't know what ye did, but I know ye've been in those cells."

Calak rubbed his cheek. "A misunderstanding."

"Hm." Clara eyed him. She was not convinced. "Well, don't stand there looking dumb, help me drop these vegetables into dis pot."

She got busy putting Calak to work in her makeshift

kitchen. There was something incredibly comforting about seeing her again. Rig and Bowan were in a discussion, standing behind me. Sloan and Yuri had gone to arrange our accommodations for the night. That left me standing here, watching the two cooks work in unison.

"Princess, if ye not too good for some labor, then grab more logs and add them to the fire."

I jumped to do as I was told. Clara had a way about her. Her requests were commands I suspect even Veras would obey. After I added more fuel to the fire and Calak had finished with the vegetables, Clara dismissed us with strict instructions to come back later for some supper.

We walked back to join the others. As we arrived, Rig set off toward a large tent, which I assumed was reserved for military leadership.

"Rig explained everything." Bowan's voice was hushed. "About why you did it, but Calak, that wasn't the answer."

"I couldn't see another way."

"Your eyes are too young to see everything. Next time, you come to me and we'll find a way."

Calak nodded.

"I sent word to his family. Nial's family." Bowan's voice was barely audible. Calak stared at the old man. "All's well. They're safe, for now. I've instructed them to send word if they need help."

"Thank you."

"Calak, Fulton is in charge of the camp. I think it's best if you keep your distance from him."

"Who's Fulton?" I asked.

"Fulton is a bastard who thinks he's better than everyone else," Calak answered.

Bowan scowled, "Fulton is a commander and the

highest-ranking military officer at this camp. You'd do well to stay out of sight and keep your nose clean."

"If Veras were here-"

"But the King's not here, kid. Which means you don't have his covering right now. I'm telling you, it's not worth the fight. Stay away from Fulton."

"Is Fulton a dangerous man?" I was curious why someone Calak clearly hated so much would be in charge of so many people.

"No, he's not a dangerous man. Calak just did him wrong years ago, and he's never forgiven him."

"And I'm guessing we need his permission to speak with Estra?" I already knew the answer.

"Yes. That's where Rig's gone. He'll petition Fulton for access, but I don't see what good seeing her will do. You can't kill her, not here. She's a prisoner of war and protected under our laws."

"I'm not going to kill her, yet."

"Then what do you want with her?"

"I want her to see me."

Calak grabbed my arm, "You can't reveal who you are to her."

I pulled out of his hold. "I'll do as I wish, but that's not what I meant. The woman tormented me as a child and she killed Bree. I believe that she has connections to Kellar and that I can get information out of her."

"It's too risky," Calak insisted.

"She can't do anything to me. I'm assuming she's bound and well-guarded."

"She is," Bowan confirmed.

"Then I'll be fine."

***

Sloan and Yuri had found us a big tent to share. We

pitched it close to Bowan's. Our sleeping mats would have to do, as there was no more straw available to make beds. I didn't care. My mind was too focused on what I was going to say to Estra if Fulton gave his permission.

I devoured Clara's supper. I'm not sure how that woman could make such a feast over a simple fire, but she did. Once I finished eating, I gathered my things to go wash myself in the river.

"Where's Sloan?" I asked Calak, who was still inside of the tent, laying out his sleeping mat.

"I think she's visiting an old friend, if you know what I mean."

Of course I knew what he meant. Damn. Well, if Sloan wasn't available to take me to the river to bathe, then Rig was my next best option.

"Okay then, what about Rig?"

"I believe Rig and Yuri are over in the south-end of the encampment, currently losing their money in a high stakes dice game."

So much for their pledges of protection and loyalty. The Unit had all but abandoned me. Calak eyed the items I had gathered and smiled. What a bastard.

"I'll take you down to the river."

I sighed. Desperate to say no, I knew I smelled terrible, and I refused to be face-to-face with Estra in this state. It would just give her ammunition against me.

"Fine, but don't look at me."

"I'm offended that you'd even have to say that, your Majesty." He faked a bow.

"You're a pig, you know that."

"I actually knew that."

Calak followed me out of the tent and down to the riverside. We walked far enough away from the encampment so there'd be no onlookers. I dropped my things by the bank and took off my cloak. I glanced around quickly to make sure that no one saw my hair.

"You're clear. There's no one here." Calak assured me.

The river's current was slow, so I wouldn't have to worry about being swept away. If I had to be rescued from the water, naked, I think I'd rather just die. I untied my cape, placed it down, then kicked off my boots. The ground was cold under my bare feet. The snowfall that Bree was so excited about had mostly melted. My chest ached thinking that we'd never get to go tobogganing together.

I untied my pants, but before I took them off, I turned to make sure Calak wasn't looking.

"Don't look. You promised."

"I won't, but I have to keep an eye out for surveillance."

He was right, of course. It would be unwise for him to completely turn away from half of the river. We didn't know where the Raiders were and there could be all kinds of threats out there, especially now when the sun was almost set.

Slipping my pants off, I pushed them over towards my boots. The cool air started to pimple my skin. The water would not feel good. If the air was this cold, I could only imagine how cold the water was, but I needed a thorough bath tonight. Pulling up the bottom hem of my tunic, I slowly lifted it up over my head. I didn't dare look to see if Calak had kept his promise. My entire naked body was covered in goose pimples now. Making quick work of it, I stepped into the water until I was deep enough to lower myself down into it. Once my shoulders were covered, I turned. Calak was staring right at me.

"You said you wouldn't look."

"I didn't."

"You're looking at me right now."

"You're underwater."

"But I wasn't underwater a second ago."

"I wasn't looking a second ago."

I exhaled. This was a pointless conversation. Reaching up to the ribbon holding my hair in a tight bun, I pulled on it and let the curls fall. There was a small bar of soap that I had brought with me and I ran it all over my body, washing away the days of travel since we left the outpost. Once my body was clean, I lowered my head down into the river, letting my curls become completely soaked. Slowly coming up out of the water, my hair falling straight back behind me. This was the only time I had straight hair. I shook out the water, squeezing it, and already the curls were returning. Satisfied that I was clean enough, I made my way back to the riverbank.

"Don't look, I'm coming out."

"Yes ma'am."

I stepped up onto the grass, but my foot caught on a loose rock and slipped. My arms went out to break my fall, but then Calak's hands were wrapped around my waist, holding me in place. I froze.

"Uh, thank you."

"Uh huh."

Calak helped me up onto the shore and handed me my tunic. I looked to see his eyes averted towards the grass. Grabbing the shirt, I pulled it over my head.

"All clear to look." I joked. Trying to ease the tension of the fact that Calak had just touched my naked body. Something that no one had ever done before, not even Veras.

"Here," Calak handed me my pants. I slipped them back on.

"The water was colder than I thought it'd be."

"Yeah."

I put on my cape and cloak. Not bothering to secure my bun, I just pulled the hood up over my head, letting my wet hair fall and stay loose.

"Are you done?" Calak's mood had shifted. He was being playful before, and now he seemed angry.

"What's wrong with you?"

"Nothing." He turned to walk. I stayed where I was. When he noticed I hadn't followed him, he turned around. "Let's go."

"No. Not until you tell me what happened. What changed?"

"Nothing."

"Nothing? You were making jokes a moment ago and now you're being..." I raised my hands and let them hit my sides, "you're being you."

"Me?"

"Yes, you."

"I don't have time for this." He walked again.

"Seriously, Calak. What's wrong?"

"What's wrong?" He turned and came back towards me. "You want to know what's wrong with me?" We were close now.

"Yes." I whispered it because I wasn't sure where this conversation was going. He seemed upset about something, but we had barely talked. I couldn't imagine what I'd done to bother him so much.

He huffed. It was a cross between a sigh and a laugh.

"Gods, Raelle. You want to know what's wrong with me?"

"Yes, Calak. What's your issue?"

"You!"

I said nothing.

"You're my issue. The fact that you exist is my issue, Raelle."

I just stared at him.

"Fuck." He turned away from me, but didn't walk.

"What does that even mean?"

Calak looked at me again.

"It means that since you fell out of that damn carriage into the snow, I haven't been able to stop thinking about you."

"What?"

He scoffed. "This is- let's just go back to the tent, okay?"

"No. No. Not okay, Calak."

"Damn it, Raelle."

"What do you mean, you haven't been able to stop thinking about me?"

"I mean, you occupy every damn thought that I have. Even when I hated you, and gods, I have hated you, there you were. And you know what, I'm glad you love Veras. And the two of you could've been happy and lovetied forever with my congratulations, but then you go and..." He pointed at the river.

I was so confused. It sounded like he was saying he had feelings for me, but he was yelling at me.

"I go and what? Have a bath?"

He sighed. "Just forget it, okay? We've got a lot to focus on. Let's not get distracted."

"It sounds like you are already distracted."

"Yeah, well. I'll get over it."

He was trying to end the conversation, but my mind was racing with thoughts. One in particular jumped to the surface.

"Wait. You were the one who was going to trade

me to the Raiders." I was yelling now. Not caring if we drew attention.

"I've already explained that to you."

"And I understood why you would do that, for Nial, but how can you claim that your thoughts are consumed by me and yet be willing to sell me off to the highest bidder?"

He just glared at me. His chest was heaving. Of course he didn't have an answer to that, because it made no sense.

"That's what I thought." I pushed past him, allowing my shoulder to hit his arm. Calak yanked me back towards him, his grip on my biceps was tight. Pulling me into himself, our faces no further than inches apart.

"That's right. I was going to give you over to them. To save him. To save all of them, but don't think for one damn minute that I wouldn't have spent the rest of my life coming after you. I would've tracked them to the ends of the Earth to get you back." He paused. "But it doesn't matter now." He let go of my arm. "Things are different. You're different. I'll get you to Veras and then this will all be over."

Calak walked away. The conversation was done. I slowly followed behind him and we didn't speak again for the rest of the night.

CHAPTER THIRTY-NINE

LIGHT FROM THE SUN'S RAYS was pushing through my closed eyelids, coaxing me to wake up and join the world. My body was completely relaxed, stretched out in the most comfortable bed I'd ever slept in. I lifted my arms into a morning stretch as a small yawn escaped my lips. Arching my back, I rolled to my left side and opened my eyes. Veras was laying there, perfectly still, a small, adorable snore coming from his partly opened mouth. I moved up his body, turning his head towards me, and planted a kiss on his lips. My eyes were closed again, but I felt him shift as he awoke. His hand came up to rest behind my neck, pulling me deeper into the kiss. My lips opened for him, desperate to taste him deeper and more fully. Like I'd been starved and this was the only thing I'd ever get to satisfy my hunger. Only once my lips had thoroughly gone numb did I pull back to look into his eyes.

"Good morning," I purred.

"Hm. Good morning, your Majesty."

His other hand came up and twisted one of my cobalt curls around a finger, pulling it straight and then releasing it. I smiled. Reaching up, I ran my fingers through his matching blue hair, moving down to trace the silver tattoo across his forehead.

"Good dreams?" He asked.

"Excellent dreams." I sat up and straddled his torso, slowly rocking myself back and forth. Veras flashed me a provocative smile as his hands landed on either side of my hips.

"I missed you." He confessed.

"I missed you, too."

I leaned down and kissed him again. Slowly, I moved to his cheeks, then his jawline. When my lips met his neck, I sucked in the skin, lightly biting down in the same place. The proof of his arousal pushed into me. A moment later, he flipped me over, holding my hands above my head. He laid himself between my spread legs.

"You'll never leave me again."

His lips accented his playful command, lightly brushing against the skin on my chest. The sensation of his breath against my bare skin sent a shiver up my body.

"Never again," I promised.

He lifted his head so we were looking at each other. I couldn't imagine myself ever being as happy as I was at that moment.

"I love you." I confessed.

"I love you."

Veras smiled as his hands wrapped around my throat, cutting off my source of air. I was gasping, clawing at his hands to release me. He kept smiling at me and declaring his love. Tears were streaming down my cheeks as I thrashed in the bed, trying to get him off of me. I felt my chest tighten. There was no more air left in my body. My head was feeling light. My eyes pleaded with him to let go, but he just smiled at me.

I blinked. Darkness was closing in on me. When I opened my eyes again, Veras was gone, but Estra was above me, her hands right where his used to be.

"It's over, Raelle," Estra cooed. "I won."

I shook my head. Trying to scream, trying to do anything. But the darkness was growing. I blinked again and again, then everything went dark.

I sat up, gasping for air. My hands immediately went to my throat. Nothing was there. I looked around. The Unit was asleep all around me. That wasn't a memory. It was a nightmare. Still not able to lie back down, I decided I needed some fresh air. I eased the door flap open so as not to wake any of them. I grabbed my cloak and pulled it over myself, lifting the hood up and stepping outside.

The moonlight shone down around the encampment. Only a few fires were left burning and the odd soldier out patrolling. I sat at the entrance of our tent breathing in the night air. That was one hell of a dream.

After a few minutes, the door of the tent opened and Yuri stepped out.

"Bad dream?" He asked.

"Terrible." I shuddered, either at the dream, the chilly night, or both.

"I used to have awful dreams after Calak found me. The man who I was indebted to would get drunk and then beat me for pleasure."

"I'm sorry." I'd never heard Yuri talk about his life

before the Unit, except for that first time when he explained Calak had paid off his indenture.

"The welts would barely heal before he'd start at it again. That's where I learned most of my medical skills. Taking care of my own injuries and other beaten laborers."

"How did the dreams stop?"

"I woke up."

"Just like that?" I smiled.

"A dream is just a dream. It cannot hold you. The world is changing for you, Raelle. Things will never be the same. Now more than ever, you need to trust what's real."

He made it sound so easy, but how can you trust what is real when truth and reality keep shifting? When I first arrived in the North. I believed that the Evamores were a tyrannical dynasty, rightfully cast down by the people of Garth. I believed that magic was only something from fairytales and that my father had done everything he could to restore my memories.

"Do you want to talk about the dream?" Yuri offered.

"It was Estra. Well, at first it was the King and I, together in his bed." I lifted my eyebrows. Yuri smirked in understanding of what I left unsaid. "But then he was trying to kill me. When I blinked, he became Estra. She was choking the life out of me. She said that she won, and that it was over."

"Well, considering she's our prisoner, I don't see how she's won."

"True."

"Perhaps you should reconsider speaking with her right now." I thought about that for a moment. Yuri could be right. Facing Estra could stir up lots of emotions for me, but I didn't care. I would look her in the eye and prove she had lost. That I was strong and still standing. Then, when the time is right, I will kill her for what she did to Bree.

"I'll think about it," I lied to Yuri.

"Come. I have an oil that will help ease you back to sleep if you'd like."

"That sounds good." I followed him back into the tent.

***

"Fulton has granted your request, Raelle." Rig announced after breakfast. "He has some conditions."

"I expected so."

"He wants to be present. He insists on being the only one present."

That was curious and not what I was expecting, but if it meant that I could speak with Estra, then I'd take it.

"When?" I asked Rig.

"This afternoon."

"Okay. Thank you for arranging it."

Rig nodded and went to get more food from Clara. We had sat ourselves on a log by Clara's kitchen to eat our oatmeal. I was still surprised how she could make the simplest thing taste good.

Calak hadn't spoken to me since our encounter by the river last night. I honestly didn't even know what to think of it. At first I thought he may have been trying to tell me how he felt, but he was so upset. I knew little about love, but I assumed it didn't sound like that. Besides, nothing else mattered except finding a way to Veras and establishing our lovetie. Well, that and confronting Estra.

"So, how do we get to the King?" I asked the group.

"We've been going over the castle's entrances, trying to remember any forgotten weaknesses," Sloan answered.

"There are some lower tunnels that haven't been used in years. It's possible that the Eastern soldiers wouldn't know to look for them." Bowan added.

"Okay. How do we find out for sure?"

"Someone will have to go explore." Sloan didn't exactly sound like she was volunteering for the position.

"I'll go." Calak stood up, not leaving any room for disagreement, and walked towards Clara.

"By himself?" I asked the others.

"Calak's the best one to send. He grew up here. He'll know exactly where the tunnels lead and have the best chance of escape if things go badly." If Yuri had disagreed with my decision to see Estra, he wasn't letting on. I appreciated that.

I nodded. The idea of Calak going into the castle alone didn't feel right, but the idea of any of them going alone felt wrong. Our options were limited and time was of the essence. The longer I was here, the more likely my true identity could be discovered.

The sound of wings flapping caught my attention. I twisted towards the trees behind us and saw a snow owl land on a low-lying branch.

"No way."

I placed my bowl on the ground and slowly stood up. Could it be the same owl? I assumed most owls looked similar, but the way her head cocked towards me made me very curious. Approaching her, I pulled off the glove that was over my hand.

"Is it really you, my friend?"

The owl didn't move as I got closer to her.

Confirming my suspicions that she had come back to see me. What a strange experience to have with a bird. Meeting me at my window made sense. She would likely perch there from time to time, but to be out in the woods exactly where I was, so far from the castle, was oddly miraculous.

I lifted my hand and ran my fingers gently down her back feathers. Pausing, I looked behind me, feeling someone's presence.

"What in the gods?" Bowan was with me.

"She used to visit my window at the castle. I can't believe she found me out here. Veras met her. She even let him stroke her feathers. He was afraid though." I laughed.

"He's always had a thing about birds."

"She's magnificent, isn't she?"

"Yes, she is."

"Would you like to…?"

"No. No, I'm much too old for new experiences."

I side-eyed him. Bowan was definitely not someone who shied away from new things. The owl seemed to disagree with him as well and flapped her wings in protest. She didn't fly away, but settled back again on the branch, her face turned towards him now.

"Seems like she disagrees with you," I added.

He laughed. "Would seem that way. Alight, just a quick touch then." Lifting his finger, Bowan slid it down the owl's head to her back. He moved his hand up and the owl flew off into the morning sky.

The sight of her reminded me of a children's book that Kolt used to read to me. It was about spirits and animals. There was a man who died and his spirit left his body and found a home inside of a wolf. He roamed the world, searching for those he loved, but in his wolf form, people would run from him when he approached, so he never got to find his family again.

I wondered if a spirit lived in this owl and what's why she kept finding me.

"Who are you?" I quietly asked, as I watched her soar away towards the mountains.

CHAPTER FORTY

NO ONE IN THE UNIT liked the idea of me going alone to confront Estra, so Sloan took special care to conceal two knives on my body.

"If they search you, they'll usually stop after they find the first hidden one." Sloan winked at me as she secured one around my ankle. The knives were precautionary. If the Unit truly believed I was in danger, then I would've been locked inside of our tent.

"We'll be waiting outside the entire time," Rig assured me.

Calak had already left to scout out the tunnels we

discussed at breakfast. Yuri was tending to a wounded kitchen maid and would join the group later.

"Don't reveal yourself to her or Fulton," Bowan insisted.

"I won't." Even though I still hadn't decided what I was going to say to Estra, I didn't trust her enough with my secret.

The walk through the encampment felt long and ceremonial. We must have looked like we were on a mission, since several bystanders stopped to watch us pass. The same dogs from yesterday trailed us. I thought I caught a glimpse of Nichelle exiting a tent. Making a note to seek her out later, I kept my focus on what was in front of me.

Estra was being held in a cave inside of a small mountain ridge that ran along a line of soldiers' tents. They posted two guards outside. There was no sign of Fulton. I assumed he was already waiting for me.

"We must search you first, Princess."

To everyone else in the encampment, I was still King Veras' betrothed. Just the adopted daughter of the Western King. I stepped forward, lifting my arms as the guard made quick work of checking for weapons. As suspected, he found the knife hidden by my ankle. Sloan turned as a slight smirk lifted the corner of her mouth. We had safely secured the second knife on my inner thigh, undiscovered by the guard.

"Commander Fulton is waiting inside for you."

He motioned towards the opening of the cavern. I hesitated before taking a step further. Why had I insisted upon this? Was it so important for me to see this woman again that I'd leave the safety of the Unit and walk into a hole in the side of a rocky wall, alone?

My body language gave me away as Rig spoke up. "If you'd like, we can return to the tent, your Highness."

No. I wanted to do this. When Estra sent me away all those weeks ago, I was a girl content to stay in the only home she remembered. Now I was a Queen who had faced uncertainty and death. I may never get the homecoming that I dreamed of, see Karissa again, or be able to speak with my mother and father, but I was not afraid of Estra from the East.

"I'll be fine." I walked into the cave and left the Unit outside.

The path was dim, but the flicker of torchlight ahead helped me find my way. Turning into the cold, dark space, I saw Estra sitting in a chair. They'd bound her hands behind her. She wore a simple purple dress that had small tears throughout it. The light brown hair that usually was worn in a plait down her back was hanging loose around her face. Her brown eyes lifted towards me as I entered.

A shift to my left caught my attention, and I saw Fulton leaning against the stone wall. He was wearing the traditional white Northern uniform, with a red bandolier across his chest full of throwing knives. His hood covered his head, but I saw sandy blond hair peeking out of it. The bottom half of his face was full with a tidy blond beard.

"Look who came to see me," Estra taunted from her seat.

I flicked my eyes towards her.

"What? No hug for your sweet stepmother."

"You're not any mother of mine."

"No. I'm not."

Her wicked grin reminded me of all the terrible things she did when I was growing up. I struggled to maintain my composure.

"You killed my friend."

"Who?" Estra faked a look of confusion. She knew

exactly who I was speaking of. "Oh. That blue-eyed general. Well, she was being vulgar."

I ground my teeth together, reminding myself that I couldn't kill her here. Not with Fulton standing guard so closely.

"You'll pay for that."

"I don't think so. You've never been a risk taker, Raelle."

"You don't know me anymore."

"Is that so? Did someone grow up while they were humping their way through the Northern Kingdom? Oh, that's right. I know of your dalliances. Supposedly, you have become quite the popular princess."

I just stared at her, refusing to let her get a rise out of me.

"Veras was particularly impressed with you."

Hearing her say his name made my blood boil.

"Do you miss the King? Or has that other one taken his place already, the tracker?"

My eyebrows furrowed.

"Calak? That's his name, right, Fulton?"

"It is, your Highness."

I wiped my head towards Fulton. I knew that voice. It was the man who had been in Veras' chamber with him the night before the Eastern Army attacked. He kept his eyes fixed on the wall ahead of him. What game was he playing and why was Estra so familiar with him?

"So, why did you come to see me?" She asked.

"To prove that you've lost."

Estra laughed. The sound echoed around in the small chamber. I balled my hands so tightly that I'm sure my nails were cutting the skin of my palm.

"No." She shook her head. "I haven't lost. You've

just been playing the wrong game. Unfortunately that misstep will cost you."

"You've always been a bitch."

The words flew out of my mouth before I could stop them, although I didn't care, it was a shock to speak so openly with her after years of keeping it inside.

"Oh, Raelle, what would your father say, hearing you speak like that?"

"Considering it was directed at you, I don't think he'd mind."

"From what I hear, King Wren doesn't mind much these days. He's not quite himself since you left, unable to rule, leaving the Kingdom in the hands of your incompetent brothers. It won't be hard to overtake them when we march our army there next."

I sneered at her. Even though I was angry with my family, her threat against them was too far. And why would the East march into the West? Did King Sutton want to claim all of Garth as his own? He certainly had the wealth and power to accomplish that, but not without a very deadly battle. A fight that could claim the lives of my brothers. She was trying to manipulate my emotions. I needed to keep a cool head.

"We?" I asked. "You're being held prisoner in a cave. I don't think you'll be going anywhere anytime soon."

"We'll see." She smiled. "But if I do get out of here, what do you want me to say to your brothers before I slit their throats?"

Her menacing laugh ripped the last tether holding my self-control back. I reached for the dagger tucked between my thighs and lunged for her. Before I could get close enough, Fulton had me in his hold, dragging me back out of the cave.

"It was nice to see you again, Raelle. We'll do this again, soon," Estra called out after me.

Fulton pushed me out of the entrance to the cave and I staggered back, falling on my butt.

"What the hell?" Sloan yelled out as Rig helped me to my feet.

"She tried to attack the prisoner," Fulton explained, unapologetically.

"Why'd you stop her?" Sloan asked.

Fulton just scowled and walked back the way we'd come out.

"So, how'd it go?" Bowan asked from behind me. I was standing, making sure my hood and wrapping were still secure. Seeing Estra didn't satisfy me like I hoped it would. If anything it made me feel less in control. I hated how she always found a way to belittle me. I'd need to find a way to get the upper hand on her. Calak was right, revealing my identity would be too dangerous. As the ruling Evamore, my survival was paramount to stopping Kellar.

The ruling Evamore.

Nichelle.

Magic.

Veras told me that a ruling Evamore was able to harness and wield the power of the gods without the use of relics. Did that mean that I could use magic? Wouldn't I have noticed already if I had magic? But, I had no idea what it would even look like.

"Oh my gods," I whispered.

"What is it?" Rig asked.

"Um," I looked around to make sure no one was within earshot. "Do you guys think that I'm magical?"

"I mean, you're nice and look good. I'd say you're very pleasant and brave. Not sure if magical is the word that I'd use, but..."

"Rig, I don't think that's what she means." Sloan corrected him.

"No, I mean, do you think I have magic?"

"It's likely. According to our history, all ruling Evamores had it," Bowan answered.

"Damn." Sloan was grinning. "Oh, you're gunna be such a badass."

"But, how, I don't remember my parents having powers yet or anything about magic. I thought I saw Nichelle in the encampment earlier."

"You did. She escaped with us." Bowan was watching me, studying me. "If anyone could answer your questions, it's her."

"Do you think it's safe for me to reveal myself to her?" The three of them looked at each other. It'd be impossible for me to get the answers I needed from Nichelle without telling her who I truly was. That needed to be weighed against the truth that the more people who knew my secret, the more danger it put me in. Which meant the more danger it put my friends in.

"I believe we can trust Nichelle. She was a friend of Sylvette's. If the Sisterhood trusted Sylvette with your secret, then hopefully we can trust Nichelle." Bowan's face didn't reflect the surety of his words.

"I don't like 'hopefullys'," Rig spat.

"I know, but Bowan is right. Besides, Nichelle is the one who was helping me get my memories back. Maybe she already knows more than she was sharing with me."

"Calak is not going to like this," Sloan mumbled.

"Calak can kiss my ass."

CHAPTER FORTY-ONE

"ABSOLUTELY NOT."

Calak returned from his scouting mission just before we ate our supper. Yuri had finished up with the kitchen maid this afternoon, only to be called over to help fix a broken bone, but eventually we all convened inside of Bowan's tent. Unsurprisingly, Calak didn't like my plan of going to Nichelle.

"I wasn't asking permission," I clarified.

"I vowed to guard you with my life," Calak explained. "That becomes harder to do the more people that know who you are. This isn't a secure base and we don't have the resources to properly protect you here."

"I understand that. And I truly appreciate each of

you, but if there's a way that I can tap into any power that may be resting inside of me, then I need to at least try. I'm also now hearing how ridiculous that entire sentence sounded."

"Calak," Bowan spoke up from his seat on the bed. "Your mother trusted Nichelle. She trained her. If there's one person in the encampment outside of this tent that I would trust with Raelle, it's her."

Calak sighed, out of defeat.

I smiled. It was settled.

Dinner was rabbit stew. Not my favorite meal, but Clara could do no wrong. I made quick work of my first bowl and sent Calak up to charm a second bowl out of the cook for me.

"I don't know why you didn't just ask her yourself." Calak passed me the bowl and I began to inhale it.

"She likes you better than me."

"She likes him better than all of us," Yuri corrected.

"I sent word to Nichelle to meet us in the forest tomorrow. It'd be best to do this away from prying eyes," Bowan explained. He was right. If we were going to reveal my identity and practice magic, we'd need to make sure no one saw us.

"What of the tunnels, Calak?" Rig asked.

"There's one that could work. Most of the old tunnels have collapsed or closed off. I found a partial tunnel that could get us into the castle. I'd like to do another scout before we commit to the plan. We also need to decide what we'll do once inside of the castle. It's likely they've got the King and any other valuable prisoners in the cells."

"It's a good thing you're so familiar with them now."

I was being cheeky, but I already had my second

bowl of stew, so I didn't really care. Calak just ignored my comment.

"We'll divide into two groups. If one fails, then the other still has a chance." Rig still sounded like the leader. They all shook their heads in agreement. The plan was still to leave me at the encampment with Bowan, but if my magic lessons with Nichelle proved fruitful, they'd be foolish not to let me come. I went to open my mouth to make another argument for my joining the Unit, but Calak interrupted me.

"No, you're still not coming with us."

I glared at him and Sloan laughed.

***

The next morning we waited in a small clearing in the forest for Rig to return with Nichelle. The Unit was completely armed, ready for any possible intrusions. I kept my bow and quiver on my back and had reattached the knives Sloan gave me on my ankle and outer thigh this time.

"Here they come," Bowan announced.

I turned to see Nichelle clearing the trees with Rig by her side. She looked exactly the same as the last time I saw her. I wondered if she had the magical relic on her now.

"Thank you for coming," I spoke first.

"Not at all, my child. I was relieved to see you in the encampment. I feared the worst, but I see now that you were well protected."

"I was."

"What can I do for you? Why have you called me out to such a secluded spot?"

"You once told me that you couldn't tell me who I

was. That it was something I would have to determine on my own."

"Yes, that's true."

I looked around at the Unit. I was conflicted this morning when I woke up. Every decision that I made put them in danger. Calak was right. They'd vowed to protect me, no matter the cost. I weighed that responsibility against what Nichelle could teach me about myself. I hoped that I was making the right decision.

"I know who I am now."

Her eyes widened in acknowledgement as I lifted my hood off and untied the white band across my forehead.

"I'm..."

"Raelle Evamore," she interrupted me.

"Yes. Daughter of King Asher and Queen Yolanda. You knew?"

"Not for certain. The way that the stone reacted to your touch. It's never done that before. I knew there was magic inside of you, but why and to what degree remained to be seen."

"But King Veras said that only the ruling Evamores had magic, who else could I have been?"

"He's partially correct, but there are tales that some others have possessed the same magic."

"Who?"

"Demigods."

"A demigod? What's that?"

"They're the gods' children, born in the mortal realm from mortal women. The stories say that even Kellar had children."

"Shit." Sloan's voice caught me off guard. I'd forgotten anyone else was in the clearing.

"So you thought I might be a demigod?" I asked Nichelle.

"I was waiting for you to discover that for yourself."

Damn. So, not only was it possible that I could possess magic, but there were children of the gods, demigods, out there who could also have the same powers.

"Are the demigods good? Or evil?"

"They're like a man or a woman. Capable of being either." Not comforting. The idea of evil demigods with magical powers was making my head spin. But that's not why we were here. Although I appreciated the information and history lesson. I needed to learn to harness whatever magic was inside of me.

"Nichelle, do I have the power of the gods?"

"As the ruling Evamore, yes, you do."

"Can you show me how to use it?"

Her eyes narrowed on me. "Your memories have still not returned, then?"

"No. I have some, but nothing about magic or my parents, yet."

"That's unfortunate."

"I'd like to learn how to wield it, so I can help protect people."

Nichelle nodded in understanding.

"You have to understand, child, what I have are stories and limited experiences. Most of your knowledge will have to come from experimenting with your powers, or gods willing, if your memories return."

"I understand."

"Then, let's begin."

***

Nichelle explained to me that the gods' magic was given to manipulate that which already exists. Meaning that I couldn't just conjure up some chocolate cake out of thin air. From the stories that were told, Evamores could use their power to influence the wind, earth, water and fire. There was also a healing component to the magic.

"So no mind control?" I asked, a little disappointed.

"Not that I'm aware." Nichelle smiled, but I thought I heard an exhale of relief come from Calak. Or perhaps that was my imagination. The Unit had been standing watch for quite some time listening to Nichelle teach me the magical history of my people.

"However, there were some Evamores who had a connection with certain animals. I believe your great-grandmother was known to communicate with and subdue bears, or something of that sort."

That was interesting, but not as helpful as her other information.

"How can I make the earth do what I want?"

"It's not as simple as wishing it so. You must connect with the earth in order to bend it to your will."

I closed my eyes.

"Remember how to clear your mind?"

I nodded.

"Let the thoughts come and wash away. Do not hold them. Breathe in and out."

I did as I was instructed and soon I felt more relaxed.

"Now, feel the ground that you stand on. The soil. The trees around you. The rocks and mountains. Picture them all in your mind. Once you have that, bend it to your will."

I focused. Trees. Earth. Rocks. Nothing. I couldn't feel anything to bend. I opened my eyes in defeat.

"Relax, my child. No one expected it would happen on your first attempt. Perhaps we should try something different. Sloan, dear, please take the bow from our Queen."

I handed her my bow and quiver.

"Now, shoot that tree."

"Just shoot the tree?" Sloan questioned.

"Yes."

"How will that help me get magic?" I asked.

"You're going to knock the arrow off course." Nichelle explained.

"How?"

"With wind."

Sloan nocked the arrow and aimed for a tree across the clearing. Under Nichelle's instructions I closed my eyes and tried to focus on the air around me. The arrow released and flew straight into the bark of the tree. I was unsuccessful again.

"Another." Nichelle ordered.

Sloan complied and the second arrow split down the first.

I was failing.

"Sloan," Nichelle spoke softly, stepping up in front of the tree where the arrows were lodged. "Another."

"No way. I'll hit you." Sloan protested as the rest of the Unit closed in.

"Nichelle, this isn't necessary." Bowan was trying to talk the woman out of her foolish idea.

"Another." Nichelle repeated herself.

"Listen, I'm not ready, okay. It's fine. We can try again later. Sloan, do not nock that arrow."

"Wasn't going to." She reassured me.

Just then the wind picked up around us. I looked to see if there was a storm blowing in. The Unit was doing the same. But it was only the trees immediately near us that were moving. The trees in the distance were unaffected. The sky was completely clear. This wasn't a storm.

"Focus, Raelle," Nichelle commanded.

Looking towards the storykeeper, I saw a loose arrow lift from Sloan's quiver, floating through the air.

"What the-" Rig shouted.

Nichelle was doing this. She was manipulating the wind. A demigod? The arrow turned so it was directly aligned with Nichelle's chest.

"Stop! I'm not ready!" I yelled.

"Yes, you are."'

At that, the arrow went flying through the air on course to impale Nichelle. My head was spinning, but I had a split second to do this. Calming the thoughts in my head, I focused on the air around me and willed it to bend to my command. Suddenly, I could see it differently, as if each burst of wind was a tangible thing that I could hold or touch. I pushed towards the projectile, seconds before it landed. Taking a deep breath I surveyed Nichelle, with an arrow jutting out from the tree right beside her head.

"Good gods," Calak exhaled as Yuri made quick work to check the side of Nichelle's face which only suffered a small scratch.

"Why would you do that?" I demanded. "Actually, no, how did you do that? Are you a demigod?"

Nichelle stepped forward and lifted the magical relic which had been concealed in her sleeve. It was glowing brighter than when I first saw it.

"In your presence, the power inside of a relic grows. It recognizes you as if you were a god. I used that magic to bend the air. I've never done that before. I'm glad it worked."

I shook my head. This woman was surprisingly insane.

"My child, you did it." Nichelle was beaming at me. "Now, let's try fire."

CHAPTER FORTY-TWO

AS I EXPECTED, both fire and water were unsuccessful. Nichelle said that in time I'd grow accustomed to how the elements felt around me, which should make it easier to use them. I was just exhausted and happy that I didn't kill the storyteller.

Back at our tent, it wasn't long before everyone retreated into different directions. Sloan went to visit her friend again. I had half a mind to follow her to see who this mystery person was. Apparently, Rig and Yuri had lost quite a bit of money playing dice the other night, so they were back for restitution. Bowan excused himself early to rest. Leaving me alone, again, with Calak.

"Don't worry. I don't need to bathe tonight." I was

trying to kill the silence that was deafening between us. The longer we went without talking, the more annoyed I was getting. “You know, I didn’t ask you to say those things to me the other night. I feel like I’m being punished for them though.”

“You aren’t being punished.”

“Really? Well you barely speak to me, except to argue with me and you avoid being around me. That feels like punishment.”

“I thought you’d prefer it this way.”

“Why would I prefer this?”

He went silent. Sitting on our respective mats, we were on opposite sides of the tent.

“What you did today, that was pretty remarkable. I’ve never seen anything like that in my life.” Calak was extending an olive branch and I was about to grab it.

“It felt incredible and terrifying. That woman is insane.”

I huffed out a short laugh that Calak echoed. This was better.

“So, are you ready to rule the world?”

“Don’t say that.”

“Why not? It’s true. You’re the rightful ruler of all four kingdoms.”

“It’s just...I shouldn’t be.”

Calak bunched his eyebrows together, “Why the hell would you say that?”

“I’m not a ruler. I’m just Raelle.”

“Yes, Raelle Evamore.”

“But I’m not, really. I don’t know who Raelle Evamore is. I only know me, and the me that I know is not the right person to rule all four kingdoms. Besides, how does that even work? It’s not like I have a kingdom already. I’m just going to walk up to all of the Kings and demand their thrones? What would I say? Will there be a war? Who's going to fight for me?"

"I would."

I stared at him. He would. I could see it in his eyes.

"Why?" I asked. Calak looked down as he twisted some thread off of his tunic sleeve.

"Because you're the right-"

"Rightful ruler of all four kingdoms," I finished his sentence more sarcastically than I intended. "Doesn't make me the right ruler for all four kingdoms."

"So you'd just walk away?"

"I mean, I thought about it. Thought about just disappearing. Leave the kingdoms to figure themselves out. I doubt a nineteen-year-old-"

"One-hundred and fifty-nine year old," Calak corrected me.

"Right. I doubt that I can make much of a difference in it all."

"You can with the lovetie."

I took a deep breath. "That's the only reason I'm still here. If we can get to Veras and if the lovetie works, then he'll know what to do. He can lead."

Calak's eyes were burning a hole through me.

"So that's your plan then? You think Veras is your lovetie because he'll know how to lead?"

"Well, yes, I guess."

"The lovetie isn't an act of convenience, Raelle. It's when two souls acknowledge that they can't live without the other one."

"I know that. And that could be Veras and I. You don't know."

Calak snorted and shook his head. "You're right. I don't know, but I do know that you were Raelle Evamore the day you showed up in the North. So, if there was going to be a lovetie between you and Veras, wouldn't it have snapped into place by now?"

I refused to listen to him. This entire plan, my ability to get through any of this, centered around finding Veras and establishing a lovetie.

"Why are you saying this? You don't think this'll work?"

"I'm just saying, your soul had a lot of time in the castle to recognize Veras'."

Damnit. The doubt was starting to settle. I needed to stay focused.

"You're wrong."

"Maybe."

"I need some air." I jumped up from my sleeping mat, grabbed my cloak, raised the hood and left the tent with Calak on my heels.

"Where are you going?" He demanded.

"For a walk."

"At night? Alone?"

"No, I knew you'd follow." We walked in silence until we were outside of the encampment. Following a path that led up to a tall ridge, I stopped at the top to take in the view. From here I could see the river I'd bathed in and how it flowed down towards and around the mountains. Valleys of trees were illuminated by the moon and stars. The auroras were faintly dancing for us tonight.

The sounds of owls and night birds echoed from tree to tree. From below you could hear the water as it rushed down, splashing against rocks and fallen branches. Pine and the smell of wet earth filled my nose.

I pushed my back against the rock wall behind me and rested for a moment, taking in the beauty of this night. Turning my head, I saw Calak standing beside me, watching the sky. Under the faint light of the night he was stunning. The moonlight bounced off of every perfect angle of his face.

Despite everything we'd been through, that thing that existed between us was still there. Was I the only one who felt it? No, I'd seen the way he'd looked at me, the way he'd touched me. Maybe it was the Western wine that Sloan had grabbed from one of the supply carts that we drank with dinner tonight, or maybe it was being here under the stars with Calak again, but I made a confession.

"Veras once asked if I had feelings for you."

"Of course he did."

"Why'd you say that?"

"Because Veras is a smart man, but a better friend. He wouldn't want to step in if there was anything here." He motioned between the two of us.

"Right."

"I'm assuming you told him no."

"No, actually, I told him that I thought I might."

Calak, who had been mindlessly kicking small stones on the path, stopped moving and slowly lifted his head to look at me. I was staring straight into the sky.

"Why did you say that I was nothing to you? That night we skinned the rabbit?"

"Raelle."

The way he said my name was so tender, it made me angry. "You piss me off, Calak." He was quiet. It was still my turn to talk. "Some days I couldn't decide if I wanted to hurt you or hold you." I took a deep breath. This could be a huge mistake. "I wasn't lying in the cells." Feeling a small tear form in my eye, I remembered that day, the day I tried to seduce this man and then, when that didn't work, I threatened to murder his son. "I did wait for you to come to me, after Zane. There was no one else that I wanted to see or talk to, and I didn't understand that or what it meant."

I reached over to scratch my left arm, but I felt Calak's hand hold me still.

"Why do you do that?" He asked.

"Do what?"

"Scratch yourself. I've seen you do it before."

"I do it when I'm nervous."

"Why are you nervous now?"

My pulse picked up. Why was I nervous?

Calak spoke next. "I couldn't come up that day, after Zane. Things moved so quickly and Veras said he would go check on you. I couldn't very well argue with him or insist that I be the one to go to you. So we left and then I saw you two together, in the window."

Calak was still holding my hand. We were inches apart.

"And then you planned to kidnap me." I stated the fact, taking a small step forward.

"Yeah, I did." He was looking down at me now. "Did you mean the other thing you said to me in the cells that day?" I looked at him, knowing exactly what I said to him. "That you wanted me?"

I was breathing so heavily now. No space was left between us. There was a rush of something running through my body as I bit my bottom lip.

"You aren't nothing to me." Calak swallowed his eyes fixed on my mouth. "You are everything, and that's the problem."

I felt the wind pick up around us. The breeze pushed me forward and then my lips were on his. Calak reached down and wrapped his arms around me, pulling me tighter against him as we backed up against the rock I'd been leaning on. I ran my hands up his back and through his hair, claiming every inch of his mouth with my own. He opened, pulling at my bottom lip with his teeth and I wanted more. His mouth moved from my lips down my neck. He paused. Pulling back to survey the scar. His fingers ran down my neck.

"I should've killed him." His eyes filled with that same look of disgust I'd seen before, but not disgust; it was regret, sadness. I placed my hands on both sides of his head, forcing him to look me in the eye.

"No, I get to kill him." I claimed his mouth again. Then his lips were on my neck, careful to avoid the scar, sucking and biting as he went down to my collar bone. My body felt like it was on fire, but I welcomed it. I threw my head back, watching the auroras as Calak's mouth worshiped my body. Then he made his way back to my lips.

"Calak." I breathed into him; my need grew. The desire to have him consumed me and I was quickly losing control of myself. Our bodies ground against one another as our tongues met. The wind that had been swirling around us died down and I heard the sound of stones crushing under a boot.

I pushed Calak away and he backed up as Bowan walked around the corner of the path we were on. He'd seen everything.

"Calak." His voice was stern. Like a father getting his son in trouble. I'd heard my father speak to my brothers this way plenty of times. "Rig came looking for you. Said they needed your help with something. Someone at the camp thought they saw you two walking this way. It's probably a good thing that I came looking for you and no one else did."

Bowan was looking at both of us. I felt ashamed,

like I was caught in the act of something terrible. And maybe I was. I was technically engaged to their King and we were actively trying to rescue Veras so that I could establish a lovetie with him and save the four kingdoms. But here I was getting hot and heavy with Calak in the middle of the night under the stars.

"I'll bring Raelle back to the tent," Bowan offered, but it wasn't a choice. Our little dalliance was done for the night and would likely never happen again. I shouldn't have let it happen this time.

I pulled my hood back up over my head, wiped my lips and without looking at Calak, I walked towards Bowan and back to our tent.

***

"Raelle, I'm sorry, but what are you thinking?"

Bowan wasn't exactly yelling at me, but he wasn't happy either. We'd been inside of our tent for ten minutes together and I hadn't been able to look him in the eyes.

"It just happened."

"If anyone else had seen you." He sighed. "You're engaged to our King."

"I know."

"Who's currently imprisoned in his own castle."

"I know."

"Are you in love with Calak?"

"What? No."

"Then, why in the gods names would you risk so much?"

I just shook my head. Why had I done that? What came over me?

"I don't know what to say," I confessed.

"Well don't say anything. Just leave it. Don't even

tell the rest of the Unit. If this gets out, it'll make everything more complicated. Do you still believe that Veras is your lovetie? Even after this?"

"He has to be." Not quite the romantic answer I'd hoped to give him, but I was frazzled and needed to collect myself.

"I'll be outside, Yuri is on his way to stand guard."

"Okay." Bowan left and I got myself ready to sleep. By the time Yuri entered the tent, I was tucked under blankets on my sleeping mat, facing away from the door so no one could see the evidence of my silent tears slowly streaming down my face.

Had I just ruined everything?

CHAPTER FORTY-THREE

THE NEXT DAY we met Nichelle out in the clearing again. This time, Bowan and Calak were noticeably absent from my training. I could only imagine the conversation they were having. Calak didn't sleep in our tent last night; I'd assumed that was Bowan's doing.

I had a long, restless night to consider my life choices. Veras was a good man, who, if Calak was to be believed, loved me. I repaid that by making out with his best friend under the moonlight. But it was more than that. Since the time we ate together in Clara's kitchen my first night at Castle Mount, Calak has infiltrated my dreams and thoughts. When he left with Zane, I started to see what a life with Veras could look like. I found myself lost in the safety and comfort of the King. I should be with Veras. He should be my lovetie. He would be my lovetie. Everyone expected me to find the King and fix everything.

I just don't think I was ready to admit to myself, or anyone else, how I really felt.

***

Since I'd had luck with commanding the wind yesterday, we continued with that. By the end of the first hour I had lifted leaves and flown them around Rig's body. I wasn't sure how that would help me in a battle, but it was a start.

I was getting discouraged by my lackluster ability to summon the magic of the gods. If I could remember how my parents wielded it, then maybe that would ignite something inside me. The Unit had become restless and so I was about to call it a day for magic training, when Nichelle's face exploded with sometime akin to revelation.

"I wonder…" she mumbled to herself, pulling the relic out from her sleeve. I was sure that it rarely left her sight. Something of that magnitude and importance should always be protected.

"What is it?" I asked, moving closer to her.

"Hold out your hand, child."

I did as I was told. Nichelle placed the relic in the palm of my hand, and everything erupted. The ground shook, the trees bent in a roar of wind, water materialized, rising from the ground in droplets, and an ignition of flame burst up from my exposed hand, as if the relic itself was on fire. I felt a surge of power running through my veins, radiating from the source in my palm. Instead of being terrified, which would make complete sense right now, I felt a sense of familiarity. As if the magic moving around me was an old friend who I hadn't seen in a very long time.

Unsure of what to do next. I closed my fist around the relic. The flame extinguished, wind ceased, earth relaxed, and water retreated into the soil.

"Oh. My. Gods." I whispered.

"Badass." Sloan's voice drifted towards me, but my attention was still on my hand. What had I just done?

"The power of the gods is inside of you, but the relic is alive and recognizes you as if you are its source. Your proximity to it acts as a conduit, essentially amplifying your ability."

Nichelle tried to explain, but I was barely hearing anything.

"So, with the relic, will my power work?" I asked.

"It responds strongly to you."

"Can we try again?" I was appropriately cautious, but I'd never felt so confident in my entire life as I had just then. It was a high. With these abilities, there was unlimited potential for how I could protect those I cared about.

"I don't know how long the relic can sustain that level of power. They were only meant to be tiny siphons for magic, to be wielded by those who were not ruling Evamores or demigods. We can proceed, but with great caution."

Nichelle stepped further away from me. What she was saying made sense. I didn't want to ruin the integrity of the stone because I was impatient with my natural abilities. However, I definitely wanted to try using it again.

"Fire is destructive and consuming. It knows no boundaries and spares nothing. In the right hands, fire can devour your enemies, but if the wind shifts, you risk your friends."

I understood what Nichelle was saying. There was an inherent danger in wielding these powers. Wisdom would need to be paramount. I'd have to keep my emotions in line.

Focusing on just the palm of my hand, I slowly lifted each of my fingers away from the relic. A warming sensation radiated from the stone. A small flame sprouted from the center of my hand, resting above the rock. I somehow willed it to grow higher and higher until the flames were licking the air above my head. It reminded me of the pyre we had lit for Bree.

Suddenly, the flame exploded and a ball of firc shot away from me, landing against a tree. Within moments, the bark was a flame. I was going to cause a forest fire. I closed my hand and panicked. Searching the Unit for someone to tell me what to do.

"What cancels out the fire, my child?" Nichelle did not panic. She was calm.

Water.

I needed to summon the water from the ground, but how? The flames were jumping higher up the tree, already spreading to the smaller trees around it. It was catching, and fast.

"We either need to move now, or you need to do something," Rig commanded.

"Calm your mind." Nichelle instructed me. I took a deep breath, and then another. Squeezing my hand around the relic, I focused on the water that was held within the earth. As if there was a magnetic force pulling them forward, small beads slowly released from the grip of the soil beneath our feet. Tiny drops like frozen rain rested in the air around us. The flames were growing. We needed more water. Closing my eyes, I concentrated on the clouds above my head. I knew clouds carried water from place to place. In a similar way, I called down the water towards us. Pushing my hand out towards the fire that had now consumed dozens of trees, all the water droplets raged forward. The wood sizzled on impact. Smoke billowed up towards the sky as rain forced itself down upon us.

The fires were extinguished, and I let out a laugh of relief and unexpected thrill. We all just stood in the clearing, transfixed by what just happened. Even Nichelle seemed speechless at the moment.

"So, how many of those rock things do we have?" Sloan asked.

"There are few relics left in this world. But this is a showcase of what your powers can do once you control them, my child." Nichelle was looking at me now. "You cannot depend on the stone for your abilities. You must pull that magic out of yourself."

I nodded, even though I had no clue how to do that.

"What were you thinking of when the fire exploded from you?" The storyteller had moved closer to me now.

"I was thinking of the pyre we built for Bree."

She nodded. "Your emotions affect your ability to use magic. Finding inner peace will be the gateway to unlocking your powers."

Nichelle extended her hand for the rock, and I gladly parted with it. Even though it felt amazing to use it, I didn't trust myself right now with that kind of destructive force. I liked it way too much.

Lifting her hands towards the charred trees around us, Nichelle spoke quietly as the black ashes transformed back into sturdy branches. Leaves popped back into place and, as if nothing ever happened, the forest was restored to its original state.

"You can do that?" Yuri asked.

"In the presence of the Queen, the relic has much more to offer us. The magic of the gods seeks to restore balance."

The sound of yelps and barks alerted us, and I grabbed my hood, pulling it up to cover my hair and markings. Some of the boys from the encampment showed up along the path we'd followed, their dogs racing on ahead to greet me first. As I had before, I bent down and absorbed their excited licks and tail wagging.

"They don't do that to many, miss, you must smell like good meat." I glanced up at the one young boy as his friend punched him.

"That's the King's girl, you fool. She ain't no miss and you can't tell her she smells of meat."

I smiled.

"It's alright. After the breakfast I ate this morning, it's likely I smell of something delicious."

The dogs continued to shower me with their affection, but when the boys tried to get them to follow, they wouldn't listen. Not until I intervened, jokingly pleading with the animals to listen to their owners. As the dogs and boys disappeared out of the clearing, Nichelle looked squarely at me.

"How long have you been able to influence animals?"

"What?"

"You told those dogs to go and they went," she explained.

"I was joking. They weren't listening to me."

"She summoned five horses out of nowhere over

a week ago." I turned and glared at Yuri, who was beaming with excitement.

"Horses too?" Nichelle's interest peaked.

"No. Horses don't like me. I could never ride one properly back home."

"Raelle, my child, don't dismiss this. Your ancestors had a history of communicating and commanding different forms of wildlife. It's possible that you have this gift."

I considered the possibility of what she was saying. Talking to animals seemed like a stretch. Although, fire did just shoot out of my hand. I wondered for a moment what it would be like to communicate with an animal. For them to know what I'm saying and for me understand their questions or needs. My eyes widened. The day in the forest when I hear someone calling my name. We never found a woman in need of help, just the bear and the deer. A deer that he just been mauled...oh my. It couldn't be. Running through the memory of that day, my mind also set on another question.

"Does it apply to birds as well? Like owls?" I asked.

"It could. Why do you ask?"

"There's this one snow owl that keeps appearing to me. It even followed me here to the encampment. She let King Veras and Bowan both pet her."

"A wild snow owl? She let you touch her?" Nichelle asked.

"Yes. Multiple times. Could that be this animal thing that you're talking about?"

"It's possible."

I was secretly hoping the owl was someone I knew reincarnated to watch over me in the form of an owl, but being able to possibly summon and influence different types of animals was a great consolation prize.

Back at the encampment, sitting on our usual log having lunch, Bowan and Calak rejoined us.

"You missed an exciting morning," Sloan announced to them, standing up to whisper in between them, so no one around could hear. "Raelle can speak with animals."

Both of the men threw their eyebrows up in surprise.

"Not confirmed," I clarified.

"But very likely," Yuri corrected.

"And she lit the forest on fire, then put it out with water that she called up from the ground and sky." Sloan was elated.

"Seriously?" The surprise and doubt in Calak's voice annoyed me. This was the first time he'd spoken to me directly since we'd had our hands and lips all over each other last night. I let that thought drift away as I lifted my chin.

I shrugged my shoulders, as if to brush off the magnitude of what I'd accomplished today.

"RAIDERS!"

A voice yelled from the far side of the camp.

"RAIDERS ARE COMING!"

People broke out, running in different directions. At first it looked like chaos, but upon closer inspection I saw the preparedness of the group. Soldiers were preparing weapons and shields. Those unable to fight were gathering the children and bringing them to the tents at the center of the encampment. Fires were doused with water, sending small gray smoke lines floating up from around the camp. The Unit took all of three seconds to determine that Rig would be staying behind with me while the other three went off to fight.

"No." The confidence of my voice caught me off guard.

"What do you mean, no?" Calak asked.

"I can fight, you know that I can. And now, I have some abilities that could be useful, I'm going to help."

They all exchanged looks, then Rig spoke up.

"We stay at the back of the group. We'll find some high ground and you can use your bow or whatever skills you want. You will not be in the direct fight, that's not negotiable."

"I can live with that." I smiled, then we were off racing after a group of soldiers already heading into the forest.

CHAPTER FORTY-FOUR

BREAKING OFF FROM THE primary group, Rig led me to a spot that would give us a good vantage point, but still close enough to inflict some damage. I wondered if it would bother him to not be down fighting with his friends.

The forest grew quiet, and we waited. I could see Calak, Sloan, and Yuri amongst the other soldiers. Bowan, begrudgingly, stayed back at the camp.

From far off in the distance, I could hear galloping horses approaching us. I shifted on the ledge, trying to get a better view of the size of the host coming. Squinting, I saw the glint of the sun off of what I assumed was a drawn sword. Then they broke through the tree line. Dozens of Raiders on horseback barreling towards my friends.

I reached for my bow, frustrated that I couldn't do more than shoot one arrow at a time.

Unless.

The idea was outrageous, but if it worked, it would give our soldiers the advantage of surprise. I'd done nothing like this before and it was only just suggested by Nichelle that I may have this ability. Taking a deep breath and clearing my mind, I looked down at the impending clash of the two armies. I focused on the horses. Their massive bodies pushed forward as their riders whipped them. Not entirely sure what I was doing, I simply said, "Stop."

Immediately, every horse racing towards my friends stopped moving. Shouts of anger and frustration grew from the Raiders. I winced as I saw whips ricochet off of the beasts. The enemy was so focused on their horses that our army seized the moment of confusion, racing towards them. The Raiders jumped off with no choice but to engage in the fight. I'd evened the playing field, at least for the moment.

"Go home," I breathed, and every single horse turned to retreat the way they came from.

My jaw was locked open in shock. I couldn't believe that worked.

Turning to look at Rig, he had the biggest smile on his face. I'm not sure I'd ever even seen all of his teeth before.

"That was...damn. I don't even know. You're a goddess."

I definitely wasn't that, but what just happened was very badass. And for a second, I thought of how I couldn't wait to tell Holden about it. I allowed my heart two seconds to grieve for missing my brother, before I nocked an arrow and sent it flying into the chest of a Raider.

The battle was gruesome.

Rig was anxious, pacing the ridge while I unloaded arrow after arrow into the crowd below us. It was getting harder to get a clean shot as bodies of Raiders and Northerners collided.

I'd lost sight of our friends in the mess of tangled bodies. Too many white uniforms were laying on the ground, mixed with Raider corpses. Were we winning or losing?

My head spun as I heard a fresh war cry. More Raiders were pouring out of the tree line — fresh troops to finish slaughtering us. They'd strategically withheld the second half of their army until the battle was almost done. Then I saw Yuri, a blur of spins and swords, as he cut his way through the enemy, leaving a trail of blood-soaked bodies in his wake. It wouldn't be enough. We needed to get down there. They needed Rig, and I knew I could do something, even if I didn't have all my magic.

I turned to Rig, my eyes pleading. He knew what I wanted to do because it was all he wanted to do too. We had to help. Our friends were going to get killed. He clenched his jaw and huffed, racing down the ridge towards the chaos. I was right on his tail, throwing my bow over my shoulder and unsheathing a short sword.

Please have magic. Please have magic. Please have magic.

I pleaded with myself.

Now would be a great time for my inner powers to burst to the surface. Although, how would I use them without drawing attention to myself? The predicament was still running through my head when a Raider charged towards me. I twisted out of his way, bringing my sword down across his back. A guttural cry poured out of my mouth. Instinct took over, and I ran forward into my next opponent.

I had taken down four Raiders before I allowed myself space to absorb what was happening. With a break in the onslaught, I scanned the surrounding faces, looking for any of them. My friends.

A blur of red grabbed my attention, and I saw Sloan facing down three Raiders on her own. Her skin and clothes were covered in blood. Gods, I hoped it wasn't hers, but the way she moved told me she wasn't seriously injured. One of her attackers had already fallen, but then I saw five more racing towards her.

Damnit.

I was too far away to help her, but I had to do something. I pulled out an arrow and was preparing to nock it when a breeze flitted across my cheek. Again, without really thinking about it, I closed my eyes and cleared my thoughts. Looking around to make sure no one was watching me, I lifted the arrow up into the air and commanded the wind to take it. As if the air itself wrapped a hand around my arrow, it was pulled from my grip and soared through the sky towards my friend. Focusing on the Raiders approaching her rear, I willed the arrow through the heart of two of them, before launching it into the eye socket of the third.

Okay, maybe I had a thing for eye sockets.

The arrow remained plunged in the skull of the fallen, but Sloan still needed my help. Before I could reach for another arrow, I saw the end of a spear protruding from a dead soldier. I raced forward and in one movement I yanked it from its place and tossed it into the air. Knowing my strength alone wouldn't carry it, I pushed the wind ahead, and it grabbed a hold of the weapon. As if ordained by the gods themselves, three of the Raiders faced off with my friend and aligned themselves in a row, swords drawn, ready to attack. It took just a second before my spear barreled through each of their sides. They fell simultaneously and Sloan reared her head in shock.

She met my eyes, and I thought I saw her mouth the word "badass" before she jetted off towards another awaiting Raider.

The fight was slowing.

With my sword still in hand, I maneuvered across dead bodies, searching for the rest of the Unit. Turning around a giant oak tree, I found myself face to face with Zane.

The hood of my cloak was still secure as I backed up. All of the courage and adrenaline from what I just did for Sloan diminished. My back hit the bottom of the ridge I'd been standing on with Rig not too long ago. I was trapped in front of Zane, whose eyes were feral with lust and violence.

"Well, well."

He moved closer to me. I lifted my sword. This would not end up like the last time. I would protect myself against him.

"The things I'm going to do to you, Princess."

He bit his bottom lip as he adjusted himself under his belt.

"Where are your men? Why would they leave you so unprotected?"

He was mocking me.

"I don't need their protection."

I lunged forward, striking at him. He blocked my sword with his own. We sparred, back and forth, neither allowing the other one a deadly hit. I could feel my muscles burning, but I pushed through. He would not beat me today.

But my foot caught on an exposed root, and I stumbled backwards. Damnit. Zane used the moment to disarm me. My sword falling to the ground, out of my reach. I glowered at him as he approached me.

I needed help, but I couldn't see a soul from where we'd moved to. Our position in the forest shielded us from where most of the fight still rang. Refusing to yell or scream for help, I tried to will my magic, but my mind was racing. I could not calm it. The scar on my neck was tingling as the memory of the last time I faced off against this man flashed through my brain.

Focus, Raelle, I scolded myself.

Zane jumped forward, using his boot to kick me squarely in the stomach. I collapsed backwards on the ground as he took his position above me. Lowering his sword to my neck, he gently traced the blade across the mark he'd left me with.

Knowing my options were limited, I did the only thing I could think of. I reared my leg back and shoved it between his legs. Zane's face burned red in both pain and anger. I rolled away from him as he slammed the sword down where I used to lie on the ground. But I was still trapped, and now I'd pissed him off.

Gathering himself, he roared as he charged towards me. I lifted my chin as three wolves attacked Zane, ripping at his skin and clothes. He tried to fight them off, but it was no use. Their fangs dug into him. These wolves were ruthless. But not wolves, dogs. These were the three dogs from the camp. Had I summoned them without realizing it?

Unable to watch them maul him, I ran back up the ridge where I'd seen the fight begin. I was panting when I reached the top. Looking down, I braced myself for whatever I might see.

To my surprise, there were white uniforms still standing. Had we won? Unable to focus on anything else, I collapsed down on the grass. Laying on my back, I let my body recover from everything that just happened.

***

Sitting up on the ledge, stretching out my aching muscles, I heard Calak's voice.

"So, the horses? That was you?"

I looked up and gave him a half smile.

"Seems that way."

"That's an incredible amount of power."

"I don't understand how it happened. I just told them what I wanted them to do, and they did it."

Calak shook his head in astonishment. Rig, who has been taking a piss in a tree, walked towards us. He'd found me shortly after I returned to the ridge. The Unit was intact. Thank the gods.

"Oh good, Cal, stay here. I'm going down to help them lift the bodies for the fire."

Before either of us could protest, Rig was gone.

I was just starting to recover from everything that happened.

"You didn't stay on the ridge." Calak sounded like he was getting me in trouble and I didn't have the patience for it.

"And because of it, I saved Sloan's life and killed Zane."

"What?" Calak's posture shifted. I knew he wasn't asking about Sloan. It was Zane.

"He was here," I explained. "Cornered me down

there, at the bottom of the ridge. Somehow, the dogs from the camp came. They tore him apart."

"Gods damnit, Raelle." Calak was quiet for a moment. "Are you alright?"

"Yes."

I was okay. The day had proven that I was much more powerful than I ever thought possible.

Calak came to sit next to me on the ground. Something about the closeness of his body eased me at that moment.

"So, what did Bowan say to you?" I wanted to dive right into the awkward topic we'd likely spend the next few minutes avoiding.

"You don't want to know."

"That bad?"

"Worse."

We both smiled.

What did I really want to say to Calak?

I had so many conversations race through my head the night I fell asleep quietly crying in the tent. Did I want to apologize? Or confess my love for him?

But I couldn't love him. I had to love Veras. I needed to get back to Veras.

Then how come the only thing I could think about was how Calak's mouth felt like on my neck and the feel of his body pressed against me?

Maybe we just needed some time to talk and sort this through, whatever this was. It wasn't impossible that things could work between Calak and I.

"We're going to get Veras out tomorrow."

Stunned, I just stared at Calak.

"It's better this way. You were right, Raelle, he'll know how to lead. He's always been that man. With Veras by your side, you'll be able to do what needs to be done."

"Calak." His name was but a whisper on my lips.

"I'm just a tracker, Raelle."

He was staring at me and I could see into his soul. Behind the layers of his need to protect and fear of losing, he was just a man who wanted a place to belong. Somewhere to be safe with those he loved. I wanted that too. But he wouldn't stop talking.

"I wasn't meant to rule or lead people. I'm the guy who says the wrong thing at the wrong time to the wrong people."

"Calak."

He ignored me.

"This is too big. You're too important to waste on me."

My heart broke in half when he said that.

"So, we'll get the King free and you two can save the world together."

Calak stood then, keeping his back to me as he looked out over the ridge.

I refused to let my tears fall.

He was saying everything that I had said to him before. Veras was the right one to rule. I couldn't be a queen without him, but what if I didn't want to be a queen?

What if I just wanted to be the girl who was in love with a tracker?

CHAPTER FORTY-FIVE

THE FOLLOWING DAY was filled with final preparations for the rescue attempt, as well as assisting the army with injured soldiers from the battle and restocking supplies.

Once the sun had set, the Unit prepared to leave for the tunnel that Calak had scouted. I still refused to cry over what Calak had said to me. He wasn't wrong. My hair was blue and I had the power of the gods inside of me. I couldn't just do whatever I wanted. I needed to find the right match for the lovetie, and that was Veras.

Veras was a kind and loving man. When I was with him I felt safe. He knew how to lead and make people feel relaxed in his presence. There couldn't be a better person to unite the four kingdoms than him. At least, that's what I kept rehearsing in my mind over and over when it wanted to think about Calak.

The plan was that I would stay behind with Bowan, who was currently at a meeting of elders within the encampment. So, Sloan had hand-selected two soldiers to stand post at the tent while they were gone. I wondered if one of them was the mystery friend she'd been spending time with. Without much ado, the Unit was gone and I was alone with my thoughts.

They'd be quick. Veras would be in the cells. Once he was rescued, then they'd take the same tunnels back out. Everyone would be fine. No one would get hurt.

I should have gone. How does it make any sense to break into a castle full of enemy soldiers and not bring the one person who has magic? Albeit my magic isn't that reliable yet, but it could come in handy. They were just being extra cautious, but was this really their decision to make?

According to them, I was their queen. They'd each pledge their fealty to me. From my experiences, kings and queens did as they pleased. They didn't sit back when their guards told them to.

Why was I still inside of this tent?

I got to my feet and filled a bag with a few supplies still left in the tent. My arrow, quiver and daggers were here. I quickly attached them to myself and threw my cloak on, lifting the hood. Damn. I forgot about the soldiers outside. Looking around, I tried to quickly come up with a solution.

My idea was a little obvious and would piss everyone off, but if I didn't leave soon, then I wouldn't be able to catch up with the Unit.

Using one of the knives, I slowly cut a hole in the

back of the tent, just large enough for me to squeeze through. Glancing around to make sure that no one saw me, I darted for the tree line and disappeared.

It didn't take me long to catch up to their trail. I had a pretty good idea of the direction they'd be heading after the many conversations I'd listened to over the past three days.

Staying back, I kept following them. If they discovered me too soon, then Rig would've been likely to carry me back to the tent himself. I'd have to wait to show myself until it only made sense for me to continue forward with them.

They traveled in silence, as always. So I had to keep my eye on them, as their voices would give me no indication of their whereabouts. After an aggressive trek through the trees, we finally arrived at the base of one of the mountains. Satisfied that they wouldn't likely turn back now, I stepped forward.

Before I could get close enough, Yuri was behind me with a blade to my throat.

"Ow, Yuri, damnit, it's just me."

He released me and I took off my hood.

"Shit," Calak swore, not under his breath.

"What the hell are you doing here?" Rig demanded.

"First of all, I'm the Queen. That's what you all said when you took the knee back at the outpost. So I made this decision. Plus, I'm the only one with any magic. Right? That's got to count for something."

"Well, I was fine with you coming all along," Sloan admitted with a wink.

The three men clearly did not share her feelings on the matter.

"It's too far now to take me back and there's no point in wasting one of you out here babysitting me, so we'll all go in and we'll all come out with Veras."

With huffs of annoyance from everyone except Sloan, we moved forward into the opening at the base of the mountain. As I remembered, the tunnels were damp and extremely dark. Rig had lit a torch and led the way. We all had our weapons drawn. I was sandwiched between Yuri and Sloan, with Calak taking up the rear of our entourage. A small part of me felt bad that I had pushed myself into their plans, but I couldn't have waited back at the encampment. I needed to be here.

It only took us just over an hour to reach the first sign of the castle. Faint sounds of carts being wheeled and feet walking down stone corridors carried down the tunnel. Rig extinguished his torch once we stumbled upon a manmade barrier, likely put in place hundreds of years ago and forgotten about. We slowly lifted pieces of the barrier off, placing them silently on the ground behind us. Once there was enough room for our bodies to climb through, we were back on our way. There was a soft glow of light now coming from somewhere ahead of us. Just as we were reaching the end of the tunnel, I saw that it was gated shut. Did Calak know this already? Were we on a fool's errand?

Moving up the line, Calak stepped in front of Rig and led us down a second tunnel to our left that I didn't see before. This one was very narrow; at some points, Rig had to turn sideways. I wasn't sure he was going to make it. How would we be able to quickly escape this way if the need arose?

We stopped walking and I heard the handle of a door turn. I held my breath. Pushing the door slowly open, Calak led us into what looked like an abandoned storeroom.

"Okay, change of plans. I'll take Raelle down the

alternate route, and you three head straight for the cells. Remember, if you're spotted, we retreat and live to try another day."

They all agreed.

Yuri, Rig, and Sloan slipped out of the room first. Calak waited at least ten minutes before taking us out the same way. We stayed close to the walls, hidden in the shadows. Wherever we were in the castle, it didn't seem to be a well-used place. As we turned a corner, Calak pushed me against the wall and covered me with his body. I heard the sound of soldiers marching down a corridor to our right.

When the sound carried off, Calak was still pressed against me. Our chest rising and falling together. I felt his breath on my forehead. I told myself I wasn't going to look up at him, but of course I did. His eyes were fixed on me. I cleared my throat and he stepped back.

"This way," He motioned and I followed him further into the castle.

We weaved our way in and out of rooms and halls, completely undetected by the Eastern soldiers. I wondered if the others had success. It was likely that Veras was being held in the cells. How would we know if they'd found him or not? And where exactly were we going to look? These were questions I wouldn't be asking, as even when I breathed too loudly, Calak was shushing me with his finger on his lips.

Turning the next corner, my breath caught in my throat as Veras was standing in front of us. Alone and unbound. He looked like he'd seen a ghost. Without thinking, I ran towards him. Wrapping my arms around his neck he pulled me into his hold.

"How?" He asked, looking up at Calak.

"Long story, but we need to get out of here. Yuri,

Sloan, and Rig are looking in the cells for you. We can rendezvous with them and get the hell out of here."

"Okay," Veras swallowed, looking down at me. "I can't believe you're here." He smiled and my heart melted. I had missed him. As he pressed a gentle kiss to my cheek, I closed my eyes. "Calak, you go and get the others. I'll take Raelle and we'll meet you where you came in. Raelle, do you remember?"

"Yes," I nodded at him.

"Okay. Be safe, my friend." Veras stepped forward and wrapped Calak in a hug. Over Veras' shoulder, Calak was staring straight at me. Nodding my head, we held each other's gaze until Veras broke the hug.

Then Calak was gone.

"This way," Veras grabbed my hand and led me quickly down a corridor and up a stairwell. Things were beginning to feel familiar. But how was Veras allowed to roam so freely through the castle? As a prisoner, I would have expected him to be more confined.

The pressure of Veras' hand wrapped around mine caused a surge of emotions to run through my body; comfort, desire, and confusion. I'd forgotten just how tall this man was and how secure it felt to be with him. He led me through corridors, somehow unnoticed by any lingering soldiers. My eyes adjusted as Veras pulled me into a darkened alcove. Pushed back against the side wall, no one could see us between the shadows and the heavy curtain that fell down beside me.

My chest was heaving from the thrill of finding him and our race through the castle. Veras' eyes were locked on mine. His hands, one resting on my waist, the other tracing lines down my face before resting on my lips.

"Gods, I missed you."

He took one more breath, waiting for any sign of hesitancy, before his soft lips touched my mouth. This kiss was full of desperation and want. I relaxed into his hold, opening myself up for him. He tasted so good. I'd almost forgotten what this felt like. With my eyes closed, I relinquished all worry or doubt as I roamed my hands up his body, around his neck, and through his hair.

His hair.

I pulled back, breaking the kiss to examine it. The blond waves still rested there. Why wasn't it blue yet?

Our attention shifted to the passageway, effectively putting my questions about the lovetie on hold. Muffled conversation between Eastern soldiers forced us deeper into the shadows. I held my breath until they passed.

"Come."

He led me back into the corridor. We successfully evaded our enemy and before I knew it, we were standing in front of his bedchamber doors. He opened them quickly and ushered me inside.

"Why did we come here?" I asked, confused.

"This is the safest place for you right now."

"I thought we were going to meet the others."

"No."

No? Now I was confused. Veras walked over to this drink cart and poured us both a glass of ale.

"Veras, what's going on?"

"I've missed you so much." He placed our glasses on the table and pulled me towards him again. The feel of his hands running down my arms and back sent a wave of goose pimples over my skin. But then I realized, my cloak was still on. My hair was still concealed. I stepped away from him and turned around.

"Veras, I need to tell you something."

"Okay." His voice was calm.

"It's big. It's going to change a lot of things."

"Are you alright?"

"Yes, I'm fine. It's just that..." Deciding to get it over with, I lifted off my hood and turned to take Veras' reaction. There was a flash of surprise and then his features settled into instant acceptance. That was quick.

"I can explain," I said, lifting my hands up to pull at one of my cobalt blue curls.

"You're beautiful," he confessed, closing the space between us again. "Raelle, I'm not sure I'm worthy of you." Before I could process his words, his lips were on mine. I hesitated for a moment. He should be more surprised by the magnitude of what I just revealed. I broke the kiss.

"Veras, do you understand what this means? My name is Raelle Evamore. I'm the oldest daughter of King Asher and Queen Yolanda. Rightful ruler of the four kingdoms and sole heir to the Evamore Dynasty. I'm one-hundred and fifty-nine years old."

"Raelle, I don't care who you are, or where your family is from. I just want you. My body has ached not being able to see you every day, to touch you."

His arms were wrapped around me now. Completely at a loss for words, I just submitted to his desires. It thrilled part of me he didn't have an adverse reaction to my news, but he was too sure of it. Before another question could pop into my brain, we were kissing again.

Something happened when his mouth was on mine. I forgot about everything else. With the onslaught of revelations and changes that have happened in the past month, I welcomed the reprieve that came from his touch.

Slowly, he backed us towards his bed.

Somehow over the next hour I forgot about everything else except how his body felt against mine. My clothes still stayed on, but Veras effectively aroused every inch of me. I was lost in his passion and it felt good. It wasn't until we lay in each other's arms, staring at the ceiling that all of my doubts came flooding back to me.

"Why are you in your room and not a cell?"

"They allowed me to maintain some level of comfort while I was here."

Okay. That made sense, but something else was wrong. I pushed myself up, so I was resting on my elbows. This wasn't right. We shouldn't be here. The Unit. Gods. They were waiting for us. I jumped to my feet.

"Veras, we need to go now. Calak, the others, they'll be in the forest now."

"We can't leave the castle, Raelle."

CHAPTER FORTY-SIX

"WHAT THE HELL are you talking about, Veras?"

"It was the only way to make peace."

I was keeping my distance from him. Staying on the far side of the room.

"I don't understand. How did you make peace?"

"By making a deal with Sutton."

"You negotiated with Sutton? He had your father killed. His daughter killed Bree!" I was screaming at him now.

"I know." Veras hung his head. "That wasn't supposed to happen, and I'll never forgive myself for it."

"Wasn't supposed to happen? What exactly was supposed to happen?"

"Raelle, please, I'm begging you. You have to trust me."

"Trust you." The words came out like a laugh. "Veras, I don't even know what to say to you. What could Sutton possibly offer you that was worth betraying everyone?"

"Peace." He yelled it. It was all he'd ever wanted. He told me so himself. This man would sell his soul to find peace for his kingdom. The problem was that the devil who owned him couldn't be trusted. No one who shared blood with Estra would hold true to their word.

Before we could say anymore the door to his chamber opened and in walked Estra, right into his room, like she owned the place. Veras was still sitting on the edge of the bed. I had backed myself up against the window.

"Raelle, you finally joined us," Estra cooed.

Veras immediately stood, coming to stand defensively in front of me. He had no weapons on him. I realized that I still had my bow. I nocked an arrow before anyone could speak and aimed it at Estra's head.

"I wouldn't do that," she chimed.

"Why not?" I asked.

"Because if you kill me, then they'll send our army to wipe out that little encampment of Northerners." My heart dropped as I lowered the bow. How was she even here? Just then Fulton entered the room.

"You?" I sneered at the commander. "You're a traitor."

Fulton ignored me.

"Traitors betray their kingdoms. These men have worked hard to save their kingdom and they've been well rewarded for it," Estra explained.

Wait. Well rewarded? I stepped in front of Veras, pushing his shoulder back so that he had to look me in the eye.

"What does she mean, Veras? What was your reward?"

"I told you, Raelle." His eyes were soft and broken. "I want peace. This was the only way."

"That's right," Estra continued. "The handsome King made a deal with my father and me. He'd align himself with the East, win over your little heart, and we'd protect the North and rid them of the Raiders."

"What?" I was only looking at Veras now.

"Oh, he hadn't told you yet? Damn, I feel like I'm overstepping." She laughed at herself. "You were always the game, Raelle."

Unable to hold in the emotions, a tear fell out of the corner of my eye. Veras was holding my gaze, his eyes threatening tears as well.

"When that storyteller brought you to the Raider camp all those years ago, we had a spy in place. It didn't take long for him to inform father that the last remaining Evamore was in the North. We lost track of you for a while, but when you washed up on the shores of the West, I discovered what you were. My father forbade me from killing you. Apparently, Kellar has a plan, and sweet, little Raelle is a key player in it."

I whipped my head over to Estra.

"Kellar?"

"That's right, child, but in order for the plan to work you needed to be lovetied. And who better to pair you with than a handsome young King who swoops in to save a young girl from her evil stepmother? It was a tad cliché, but I knew you'd fall for it. We offered Veras peace and security. In return, he got you."

"Got me?"

I couldn't decide who to look at. My head was moving from Veras to Estra and back again.

"But then Veras went and actually fell for you. Men and their cocks." She rolled her eyes.

"Veras?" My voice was a whisper. unable to hold in his own tears, one streaked down his cheeks as he looked at me.

"I'm sorry."

"When we arrived, he sent you off with those trackers, but he's been punished for that, haven't you, Veras?"

Estra was moving closer to me now. I knew I had my knives still on me. Could I kill her and escape before anyone got me? Fulton was right here, but maybe Veras would take him. Although I didn't even know where Veras' allegiance lay anymore.

"But all that matters is that you're back now. But, oh no, I can see the bond hasn't been established. Tsk. Tsk. I was hoping to avoid this, but Raelle, you only have yourself to blame." She turned to Fulton. "Kill the tracker."

"NO!" I screamed at her, but Fulton was already gone.

"Estra. This is enough. Calak was not part of the deal."

Veras' posture told me that he wanted to fight. However, I knew that nothing, not even Calak, meant more to the King than peace. Estra walked towards me, picked up a strand of my hair and pulled it.

"I thought it'd be prettier, huh."

"Don't touch me," I gritted out of my teeth.

Her attention shifted to Veras.

"The lovetie cannot be established because our little princess loves someone else." Neither Veras nor I looked at each other. I wanted to deny it, but the evidence was right there, in the form of sandy blond hair. In a moment I had both condemned Calak and betrayed Veras. "Once we eliminate your competition, then her heart will be free to fall for you. Once again, Veras, you'll owe me."

I was facing her now. My hands flexed away the urge to bury my knife into her throat, but there were too many innocent lives at stake for me to act out so rashly and my mind was too chaotic to summon any kind of magic. She was going to kill Calak.

"Now, I'll leave you two lovers to sort this out. Seems like you have a lot to talk about."

I hated her.

The main door to his chamber slammed shut behind her and I heard the click of a lock from the other room.

I couldn't look at Veras. Whether it was the pain of his betrayal or the pain of mine, the room was full of quiet, palpable tension.

"You love Calak?"

"Don't," I shook my head. "You don't get to question my choices right now."

I turned to look out the window, opening it for some fresh air, as I felt him walk away from me. The door to the room I was in closed. He was back in the sitting area, likely grabbing another drink.

Moments ago I was lost in selfish, ignorant bliss. Part of me wanted to go back there. To shut the world out and just get wrapped up in Veras' touch. As distorted as that was, but it was like a drug that I knew could take away the pain.

They were going to kill Calak. I couldn't let that happen. I wouldn't let that happen. But I couldn't see any way to stop it. Walking back towards the bed, the blankets still ruffled from Veras and I, I laid down on my back and the darkness overcame me.

***

"Asher," my Mama's voice was coming from their bedchamber. Still dragging my small blanket behind me I continued down the corridor towards her. She sounded upset.

"Yolanda, I just don't understand why you wouldn't discuss this with me first."

My Papa was back from his trip. He sounded upset too.

"There wasn't time. Besides, I assumed that being Queen meant the ability to make decisions without having to run them through a man."

Papa chuckled.

"That's not what this is about. Nice try."

"I think it's about the fact that I made the choice and you didn't like it."

"That's exactly what this is about."

"Right. Okay. Well, it's done. I can't change it back now, so you can be angry or you can accept it. I'll let you decide."

I pushed open the slightly ajar door and peeked my little five-year-old head through.

"Mama? Papa?"

"Look who's awake."

My Papa got to me first. He scooped me up into his arms and planted kisses all over my face. I giggled and squirmed as his rough beard tickled me.

"Hello, my little Rae of sun. I missed you."

Wrapping my tiny arms around his neck, I squeezed him as hard as I could.

"You were gone a long time, Papa."

"I know. Too long. Never again."

With a kiss to my forehead he passed me off to my Mama.

She wrapped me up in her arms while she reclined on the settee. I was curled around her swollen belly. Another baby was on the way. I lifted my hand and played with the long strand of her straight, blue hair.

"Why are you awake, little bug?" She asked.

"I heard you fighting with Papa."

"Oh, no." My Papa leaned down. "That wasn't fighting. That was your Mama setting me straight again." He pushed in to kiss Mama first, then me, then the belly. "Without her, I'm lost at sea."

They kissed each other then, deeply, as they often did. It made me smile. Then their attention landed on me. The creases in their foreheads, folding the shimmering tattoos, told me that something else was wrong.

"You're in a difficult situation, aren't you, little one?" Mama asked me.

I furrowed my little brows and looked at her confused. She returned with a smile, the warmest smile in the world. My Mama was beautiful.

"You need to send the owl. She'll bring a message to your friends."

Papa spoke now and I looked at him. Still unsure what they were talking about. As if a switch was flipped, they instantly went from worried and consoling, to carefree.

"Okay. Well, it's time for bed, little princess."

Mama handed me to Papa, who carried me back down the corridor to my bedchamber.

***

I sat up, still in Veras' bed, alone. Thank the gods.

Was that a memory? Or a dream?

My parents. That was them. I knew in my heart that it was them. It was definitely a memory, but their words, it was as if they were speaking to me now. How was that possible? But they were right. I needed to get a message to the Unit. They'd be waiting for Veras and I to come out of that tunnel. How long would they wait before they went back to the encampment, or worse, came back inside looking for us?

Looking around Veras' room I found paper and a quill. My hands trembled as I quickly wrote out my message.

Veras betrayed us. They are coming. Get to safety.

I'll find a way out.

Would my friends get this in time or was it already too late?

Rolling it up tightly, I looked around for some string or ribbon. Not finding anything, I ripped a piece of my tunic off. After securing the letter, I shoved it into my sleeve as his footsteps approached the closed door.

I held my breath.

My lips were still red from earlier. He'd never kissed me like that before. There was a desperation to the way he touched me, as if I was going to disappear and he'd never see me again. Now that made all too much sense.

Not that long ago his touch sparked such desire through me, but now I wasn't entirely sure how I felt. Although part of me still longed for him.

Damnit, Raelle.

All that mattered was that this note got to them before it was too late. Calak's life was in danger and it was clear that escaping to warn him myself was not going to be an option.

The footsteps retreated. I ran towards the window, still open from earlicr.

Where was she?

"Where are you, my friend?" I whispered, looking around, I couldn't see any sign of her. As I turned to walk away, the flapping of giant wings of the snow owl pulled me back as she landed on the windowsill.

"I need your help, lovely. Can you bring this to Bowan? The old man I was with at the camp?" I tied the rolled message as tightly as I could to her leg. And she jumped off the window and soared through the air.

"What was that?" Startled, I turned to see Veras standing in the doorway.

"Nothing." He couldn't be trusted with my secrets, not anymore.

"Raelle. I don't want to lose you."

"I think it's too late for that." Seeing him standing there my heart was so conflicted. Was he still the same man who cared for me and comforted me? Was any of it real? He did send me away with the Unit, so perhaps Estra's claim that he'd fallen in love with me was true. But did that matter anymore? Could I still love him knowing he knew who I truly was the entire time?

"Have I ruined everything?" he asked me. I didn't know how to respond. The most important thing right now was endurance. I needed to stay alive and healthy. Perhaps there'd be an opportunity for me to escape, but for now, I needed to gather information and survive.

"Veras, everything has changed. From the moment you met me, you've been lying to me." His head fell again. "Because of you, Bree is dead and soon, maybe Calak..." My voice cracked and he looked at me. "I don't plan on dying here." I was digging into whatever strength was left inside of me. "You may be willing to trade your soul for peace, but I'm not."

"Raelle, there's nothing we can do. You don't understand the powers that are at work here. It's not just the East. There's so much more that you don't know." Was he talking about demigods? I wish I had more time with Nichelle. Maybe if I had trained more, I wouldn't be stuck in this situation. In the absence of my magical mentor, Veras would have to do.

"Well," I took a deep breath. "Then you're going to explain it to me. And when the time is right, I will get myself out of here and kill Estra. And if you get in my way, then the gods help you."

"I won't get in your way, but they aren't going to let you out of here. You're more valuable to them than I realized. We need to work together, Raelle. I need you to trust me." Shaking my head, I scoffed, but he stepped closer to me. "We need to give the appearance that we're working to establish the lovetie. It's the best way to buy time. Right now, it's their greatest desire. I don't know why yet, but I'm going to find out."

"Are you suggesting another ruse?"

Somehow he managed a half smile. "I suppose I am."

My mind flashed back to the first time I met Veras and we agreed to pretend to be engaged in order to protect my life. And here we were again. There were no other options before me.

"Fine." I agreed. "But no touching this time."

I glared at him. He sighed a breath of relief, and nodded. He lifted his hand and rustled it through his sandy blond hair, not cobalt blue.

No, because it wasn't him. Veras wasn't my lovetie.

And he never would be.

CHAPTER FORTY-SEVEN

The Western Kingdom

"Danier, get your feet off the table. I've already had to replace these maps because of your filth and I'd rather not do it again." Kolt was sitting, flipping through various reports from their scouts throughout the kingdoms. With the recent moves by the East, the brothers have been carefully tracking the situation, desperate for news of their sister.

The training room had been transformed into a makeshift office for Kolt, after he assumed much of his father's diplomatic duties. Ever since Raelle had been taken to the North, King Wren hadn't been the same. When the news of her knowledge of their betrayal came, he was so distraught that he didn't eat for four days.

"I'm tired of papers and maps. Let me go to the North myself. I'll find out where she is and if she's safe. These reports take too damn long."

Danier was standing now, pacing the training circle he'd spent hours in. Picking up a set of throwing knives, he launched them one at a time into a hay-filled target resting against the far wall, all the knives hitting their intended marks.

"I cannot sanction sending one of our princes into another kingdom without going through the proper channels."

"Kolt, look at what's happening. There are no proper channels anymore. King Sutton has marched his entire damn army into the North and we haven't heard from King Veras or our sister."

He slammed the last of the knives down on the table. As a warrior, Danier was not comfortable with the waiting game that statesmen played.

"What'd you say to piss him off this time?"

Holden entered the room carrying a stack of fresh reports from his spies.

"The usual," Kolt replied. "He wants to rush in and I'm exercising caution."

"There's nothing new in these." Holden set the papers onto the table. "The Eastern army has control of Castle Mount. A contingent of the Northern army as well as some civilians have built an encampment, but haven't retaliated as yet. The rest of the Northern army is dead or scattered. The reports are conflicting. One states that King Veras is alive and being held in the castle. No mention of our sister in any of them."

"So, she could be dead," Danier surmised.

The three brothers remained silent as the

possibility that Raelle was lost to them forever set in. The guilt of withholding the truth of their father's deception had already eaten away at them. Now their lack of action against her kidnapping had left them unsure if their sister would even want to see them again.

"Damnit!"

Holden shoved the stack of papers off the table, leaving them scattered all across the floor.

There was a knock at the door.

"Enter," Kolt yelled from his seat, and a soldier entered.

"Pardon the interruption, your highnesses, but there's a man here to see you."

"A man?" Danier asked.

"From the North."

"Who?" Kolt was standing now.

"He says his name is Calak."

"Send him in." Holden turned to his brothers as the soldier left. "What is he doing here?"

Danier walked over and picked up the largest sword on the rack.

"We aren't going to kill him, Danier," Kolt said, lifting a hand to his brother.

"I know, but maybe we can make him piss himself a bit."

The door creaked open again and Calak walked into the room. He was dressed in common clothes, no markings of being a soldier or from the North. His look was very disheveled, like he'd been through a war.

"Calak," Holden greeted him. As spymaster, Holden was very familiar with the Unit and their reputations.

Calak nodded in response.

He'd barely slept in the past few days. After the Unit

had escaped the castle unnoticed, they waited in the forest for hours. When there was no sign of Veras or Raelle, Calak wanted to go back in for them. The Unit disagreed and while they stood there arguing there was a sound of branches cracking under pressure behind them. Drawing their weapons, they turned to see Bowan. He was holding the same slip of paper that Calak held in his hand, ready to show the brothers.

A message of warning from Raelle.

Another sound through the tree, coming from the opposite direction that Bowan had just arrived, drew the Unit's attention. A shout of pain erupted, an arrow protruding from the old man's leg. He collapsed to the ground. Rig lifted him up, determined to carry him to safety as a horde of Eastern soldiers approached. Bowan insisted they leave him behind. Calak refused. For a moment the two men had a standoff.

"You need to get to safety, then find a way to save her," Bowan insisted.

"Not without you." Calak tried to lift him again. The soldiers were getting closer. "Rig, help me get him up."

Bowan was looking at the rest of the Unit. "This is bigger than me. You need to get him out of here. She must be rescued."

Sloan's eyes were red. Yuri's face was drawn down. Rig nodded in agreement. They pulled on Calak, dragging him away from Bowan.

"Don't do this, old man." Calak's voice was raw from the pain of losing too much. They were retreating further away from Bowan now. "I'm going to get you back. Don't die. Don't you dare fucking die."

Bowan nodded and the Unit was gone. Running through the forest as they heard the soldiers catching up to their friend, who leaned against a tree, unable to move his leg.

Calak settled his eyes on Danier and the giant sword. Ignoring the obvious threat, he turned to Kolt.

"I'm here about Raelle."

The brothers all looked at one another.

"What about her?" Danier challenged, taking a step closer to the Northerner.

Calak huffed out a sigh. "There's a situation."

"What kind of situation?" Holden was studying every movement Calak made.

"She came with us on a rescue mission for King Veras. In the castle we came across the King and he instructed me to get my Unit out, and he'd get Raelle out. They never joined us in the forest. A few hours later, we received this note in your sister's handwriting, delivered by an owl."

Calak extended the note and Holden took it. After reading it he passed it along to his brothers.

"How? As the King's betrothed, should she not have been better protected? Why would you needlessly risk her life like this?" Danier took another step closer to him.

A muscle in Calak's jaw ticked as he clenched. "Your sister is not as you remember her." He swallowed. "I believe that she is in grave danger inside of Castle Mount."

"When did you receive this?" Holden asked.

"Five days ago."

"Why have you come here? Is it just to bring us word of our sister's capture?" Kolt's voice had a kingly manner to it.

"No. I came to ask you to join me and my Unit. I'm asking you three to break into the Castle Mount and help me save Raelle."

The End

Raelle will be back in The Evamore Series Book 2.

THANK YOU FOR READING KINGDOMLESS

If you enjoyed this book,
please consider giving it a review.

Don't forget to sign up for Michelle's monthly newsletter for upcoming book releases, special offers and bonus content at:

www.michellegaryfalakis.com

You can also connect with Michelle on her socials:

Twitter: @m_garyfalakis
Facebook: @michellegaryfalakis
Instagram: @michellegaryfalakis
TikTok: @michellegaryfalakis

Acknowledgements for Kingdomless

AH! You read my book. I'm so honored that you took time to dive into this world with me. Part of the fun of writing fiction is talking about it with other people. Please head over to my socials and give me all your thoughts. I want to hear the good, the bad and the ugly. Are you mad at me for killing off a certain someone? Because even I'm still mad that I did that.

This was my debut novel. So basically, I had no idea what I was doing when I sat down and started imagining Raelle's world. It was exhilarating. I need to thank a lot of people. First you, the reader. My desire was to write something that would connect with people. If there was something that stood out to you in this book or helped you, please share that with me. I'd love to hear from you.

I also need to thank my husband, Josh, and our kids (Liam, Alexis, Lacey and Landon) for letting me lock myself in the office day and night to write this story.

I sent each chapter of Kingdomless to my sister-in-law Nicole as I wrote them. Her excitement to see what would happen next kept me motivated and I'm so grateful. I want to thank Ashley, Amanda and Leah for letting me talk nonstop about this book and picking their brains on ideas and concepts. And thank you to Jessica for challenging me to go off script and let myself be surprised by the characters. It opened up my writing and really made the story what it is.

This was my first time ever hearing the words "beta readers" and I'm pretty sure I found the best ones right out of the gate. Special thanks goes to Kat Blackthorne, Emilie Hrabak, Kaycee Racer, Liljana Bokan, and Nadene du Plooy. All of your feedback and encouragement helped amplify Kingdomless to its full potential. I'm truly grateful. A shoutout to my editor, Kyla Stocks and Jocelyn Phillips Branding for my headshots. My amazing cover art was designed by 100Covers.com and the world map by Sekcer on Fiverr.com.

Thank you again for supporting my writing habits and don't forget to hop over to my website to sign up for my monthly newsletter. Then you can stay up-to-date on book releases, special deals, bonus content, and more! www.michellegaryfalakis.com

About the Author

MICHELLE GARYFALAKIS was born and raised throughout Ontario, Canada. She currently lives just outside of Hamilton, Ontario with her husband, four kids and Snowy (their friendly Samoyed-Border Collie). When she isn't obsessively typing out new stories on her computer, you can find her drinking coffee with a friend, snacking on some guacamole or binge watching Outlander (again). Michelle loves finding creative ways to communicate with people, and her passion for storytelling is the newest addition to that list. She would love to connect with you through her social media accounts, which can all be found on her website: www.michellegaryfalakis.com.

Manufactured by Amazon.ca
Bolton, ON